For my
who got me starte
and interrupted me

CW00346279

Author's Note

This paperback includes some needed corrections identified by readers of the eBook's first edition – specifically a handful of typos and a misplaced comma or two. I thank those Elven-eyed readers for their diligence and constructive suggestions.

Two corrections suggested by spell-checking I will never make: You **nock** an arrow before **loosing** it. You do not **knock** an arrow before **losing** it. Although, I suppose you may.

For your convenience, I have 'translated' the speech of the Ancient and Elder Races into the Common Tongue. However, where most appropriate, I retained some formal names in their original languages.

I hope you enjoy the beginning of Chork's story. Yes, he follows a well-trodden literary path; but his destination, when he gets there, may surprise you.

--- John Fedorka

Contents

Lower Brehm

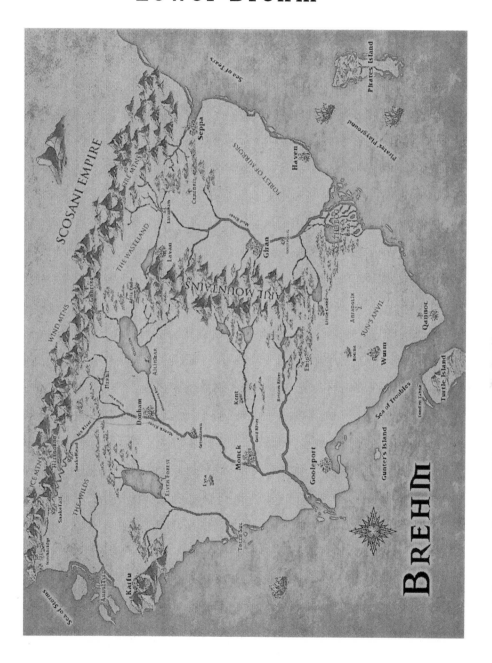

Prologue

A rolling wave of fire surged through the tunnel, its intense heat leaving the rock hissing and smoking.

To avoid the fatal flames, Jolph Rhince slipped into an alcove. He cursed. He had hoped the dragon would not awaken until all the soldiers had reached their positions. However, at the first human footfall, the beast had been aware. Now, of the 5,000 who had entered this massive lair, less than 600 remained.

Another blast of fire rolled through the tunnel. Melting stone hissed as it dripped into puddles on the floor.

"Have you come to steal my treasure?" a guttural voice boomed.

Rhince waved his soldiers to move faster. Reluctantly, they went.

The dragon gave a huge snort. "Men! I smell your fear!"

Rhince closed his eyes. He counted 20 heartbeats. Opening his eyes, he pointed to the herald and said, "Now."

The soldier worked saliva into his mouth and blew one long note on a ram's horn.

A massive roar erupted in the cavern. The bellow came not from the dragon. It sounded from the soldiers who emerged as one from the tunnels and side caves. Dressed in mithril armor, carrying long pikes with mithril tips, they poured into the lair.

"What's this," taunted the dragon, "you come to slay me!" He reared his massive head and sucked air into his gullet. The furnace in his chest thundered, preparing a fire stream strong enough to melt a small mountain.

The soldiers were but a diversion.

Rhince stepped from the tunnel. Lifting his right arm as if it carried a yoke of oxen, he hurled his blizzard spell at the dragon. The enchantment, the largest and most powerful Rhince had ever made, hit the dragon's snout.

Caught by surprise and the utter cold, the dragon choked back his fire.

Rhince fell to his knees behind a mountain of golden goblets. Creating and sustaining the spell while he had wended his way into the dragon's lair had taxed him to his limit. Launching it at the dragon had spent Rhince's last ounce of energy.

The soldiers rushed in, their pike tips twinkling red from the firelight.

Coughing and sputtering, the dragon swatted a hundred men with his left foreleg. He swung his tail and swept away the soldiers on the right.

Then, a deafening rumble arose. It sounded as if hundreds of massive boulders rolled down a mountainside.

The dragon's chest exploded.

The force of the explosion killed all but a handful of the soldiers.

Rhince was lucky. The goblet pile shielded him from the main shock. He lay against the far wall, battered, bruised, and bleeding from a score of wounds.

"Milord?" The herald stepped from the tunnel and stood over Rhince. "Milord are you hurt?"

"Of course, I am, you fool!" Rhince got to his knees. Using the cave wall for support, he stood.

The stench of burning dragon and human almost returned him to his knees.

Rhince looked toward the dragon, writhing in its death throes. The sorcerer took a measured step and then another toward the dragon.

"Milord!" cried the herald. "It's not dead!"

Rhince pointed to the massive hole in the dragon's chest. "It soon will be."

Now opposite the great lizard's head, Rhince marked its eyes. They remain closed. He slowly walked by its large razor-sharp claws. They remained motionless.

Rhince stepped to within an arm's length of the half-exposed, slowly beating heart. He drew his dagger and plunged it into the heart.

One beat ... another ... The cave fell silent. The last dragon died.

As the last beat faded, something awakened.

Rhince heard a whir, a humming so rapid it sounded like bees buzzing.

A flock of hummingbirds swooped toward him.

He wondered from where they came. From behind the dragon? From within? Really? From within the dead beast?

They dove at him, their pointy beaks aimed at his eyes and ears.

Rhince threw his hands up and swatted at the birds.

A ruby-throated male drove its beak into Rhince's cheek. Its tiny tongue licked at the sorcerer's blood.

The sorcerer cried out in pain. He could feel its little tongue tasting his blood. He smacked a second bird from the air and grunted with satisfaction as the bird hit the cave floor, damaging its right wing and tiny right foot.

Before Rhince could squash it with his boot, two other birds swooped in and carried the hurt male to safety.

The stunned sorcerer voiced his amazement, "How is that possible?"

The remaining birds pressed their assault.

Rhince rolled his right hand and conjured a wind spell.

Before he could unleash it, the birds flew up and away. The enraged sorcerer bellowed his anger and loosed the spell at a nearby mound of gold coins.

The sorcerer and the herald dropped to the cave floor to avoid the flying coins.

In the Elven Enclave of Emig, 2,600 miles south, as the last beat of the dragon's heart faded, a different sound pierced the noon sky. The shriek lingered in the air, until all movement in the forest stopped. Then, it ebbed to end with a single sob.

At that moment, each elf felt a pang in his or her heart. Each elf had one thought in mind.

Gisel Hummien'dulin, holding her newborn babe only minutes alive, gave voice to that thought, "The Mother Tree!"

A Mother Tree stands at the center of every Elven Enclave. It connects every elf with a vast spiritual network. This network teaches elves how to co-exist with and support every other living thing. Most importantly, this connection bestows immortality to the ancient race.

They all ran to Her now. They gathered in a circle at the edge of Her boughs.

They watched in silence.

The first leaf to turn yellow was near the top. It faded to brown, then spoiled black. It fell. Another leaf did the same, and another, and another. When the last black leaf touched the ground, each elf felt an agonizing loss. In his and her mind, each elf knew that the last of their race had been born. No more would follow. And, none, not one of them, would ever pass through this world to join The Only One in paradise.

Across Brehm, the scenario repeated itself in the other eight remaining Enclaves. From the Ice Mountains in the far north to Qannoc in the southern desert. From Dalathbar on the west plains to Cenedril in the eastern woods. Each Enclave was silent. Each elf knew that the Last had been born.

In Emig, Gisel looked at her first and now only child, The Last Born Elf. "That's it then. The time has come. You are the one foretold, my son. You shall be called Lye Tella'estela, "Our Last Hope." She smiled and teased his cheek with her little finger.

"A burdensome name for one so small," remarked Erison, her husband. "And much to carry throughout his life." He leaned in and kissed his son on the forehead. "Though your mother has named you, to me, you shall be Chork, after the sound of ..."

A deep vibrating thrum interrupted the elf. The air above seemed to fold, and a hummingbird swooped from the sky, leading a small flock. They flit this way and that. Their antics brought smiles to the couple's faces. The leader, a ruby-throated male, hovered above the baby's head for a moment, chirping. With a bow of its head, its tiny tongued flicked a kiss on the babe's forehead. At a second nod, the ruby-throat led the flock of dancing birds away.

Emig & Environs

Kent
Gruene's
Crossovers
Dale
DALE LAKE
Little Creek
Sun's Anvil
Desert Rubin
Aschaigln
Deslis
Boerne
Emig
BOTTOM MILL
Moon's Quench

1 – Lye Tella'estela

Not only was that name burdensome, it came with a prophecy which carried the added weight of a dying race's hopes and expectations.

Then comes the Last Born,

> *On midsummer's morn, to mend what was torn.*

Near the Fire-Wurm's shade,

> *With words and a blade, their lives they do trade.*

And, lo, the Last Leaf,

> *Overcome with grief, gives birth to belief.*

For 13 years, the young elf carried both, faltering only once, when his father died in the Lizard Wars in the 5th Year of Misery. The loss of his father created a hole in his heart so large that no amount of motherly love and devotion could fill it. Without a father's tutelage and steady hand, the sprout often turned inward to question the reason for his birth and life, growing to despise his name, his title, and his prophecy.

Gisel did what she could. She gave him the freedom to discover who he truly was while gently nudging him into the life of a responsible member of the Enclave. She promised that his 13th birthday and the Test of Bowls would reveal a new path. A path that would lead him to fulfill his true destiny.

Loving his mother and hoping for the best, the young sprout continued to bear his burdens, ever anticipating the midsummer's morn that marked the end of his 13th year.

Yet, fate dealt him another blow. This in the form of his fellow sprouts, all older of course, since he was the last.

It began, as most things do, with his name. His peers shortened it to 'Lye,' or worse, to 'Estela.' Moreover, the repeated sing-song, 'tell-yah ess-stell-yah,' was most embarrassing.

The announcement of his preference for 'Chork,' the nickname bestowed by his dead father, did not help.

"That's not even a real name," laughed Annongwen, his older cousin. "Besides, you don't have a father." Then, she began to sing, "Chork, Chork, the ugly stork, smells as bad as month old pork."

The other sprouts picked up the chant and used it whenever the near-adult blades and elder leaves were not in earshot to admonish the derision and to salve the wounds that felt like knife cuts.

Through the years, the name calling evolved into stone throwing, and then physical attacks. The blades insisted he fight back and showed him how. Yet, when he did and bested an older elf, which of course they all were, the leaves took him to task for his belligerence. "Last Born, learn to work with others." Then, they sent him home for his mother to tend his bruises and cuts.

"My son." Gisel only used his full name when she was disappointed with him. "My son," she explained, "try to understand. They are jealous of you, especially your cousin."

"But, what are they jealous of? They are older, stronger, faster. And the blades and leaves are wiser." His shoulders slumped. "I'm bullied on all sides."

"They are jealous because of what you are and the hope you promise. Your name gives the reason. Our Last Hope." She tugged at his chin with her thumb and forefinger. "Now come and get ready for bed."

He would fall asleep to dreams of the Elven Forest, the largest and most beautiful of the Enclaves, the site of his race's birth. He would be welcomed by the great Prince Zaedron Auvreatear and his wife, Princess Jeardra Sage. In this dream, his name would not be a belittling chant but a song of praise and respect. He would awake from his fantasy, refreshed and full of hope, his only hope.

So it was on his 13th midsummer's morn. A day especially important to all elves, for it marked the day of their maturity, a passage from sprout to shoot, the day every elf took the Test of Bowls and came to I'ere'er, the Only One. A day that promised change. Yet, no one expected the change of such magnitude that this day would bring.

The day started as many others had in the past. The sun crested the treetops. Its warm light streaked through the open window shutters and kissed the sleeping elf's face, waking him to the promise of his special day.

With the joy of expectation only a child knows, Chork bounced out of bed, ready to put his past suffering behind him and to take his rightful place among his fellow elves. His bright, green eyes glistened with excitement. His thin pink lips formed a perfect smile. He ran his long delicate fingers through his shoulder-length, wavy brown hair. He pulled the hair from his temples back in typical elven style and secured the soft curls at the nape with the enameled green leaf hairpin from the night table.

In his mother's small bedroom, a twin image to his, lay two sets of clean clothing on his mother's bed. One, a pair of dark brown pants, a white forearm-sleeved undershirt, and a sleeveless green tunic, was his daily attire. The other were the clothes he would wear for the Test of Bowls, deep olive pants, white full shirt with ties at the collar, and a thigh-length jacket to match the pants.

He ran his hand across the breast of the jacket and smiled in anticipation. Then, he donned his everyday clothes and stepped into the main room.

A plate with two slabs of dark bread and some fruit greeted him from the table. Beside it was a brief note in his mother's delicate Elvish script:

Went for red berries for your birthday pie.

Remember your chores before leaving.

He frowned at the loss of his favorite chore because he always ate twice as many as he picked.

After breakfast, he cleared the table. He washed, dried, and put away the plates and cups. He readied his bed for the night, though he knew he would be too excited to sleep. He prepared the fireplace, so that his mother would only need to light it to bake his red berry pie. He refilled the tinder box and swept the floors of all three rooms. Last, he took two pails to the Enclave's well.

It was there that things began to go wrong.

As he stood in line awaiting his turn at the well, Annongwen cut in line behind him. She poked him in the small of his back once, thrice, and again. "You'd need the whole well to get rid of your smell," she announced in a voice loud enough for all to hear, poking him yet again, this time with her fist.

The other shoots in line laughed.

Spurred on by their response, Annongwen said, "Tonight, you'll finally get to be the first. The first to be rejected because of your stench."

This drew a few hoots of agreement.

"If we had a large enough bucket, we could bathe him in the well," one ventured.

"No, no," countered another. "He'd taint the water."

"Forever," added a third.

They all laughed.

Why? The Last Born asked himself. Why do you all hate me so? What is wrong with me? I didn't choose to be the last born. I-I'm just like ...

Annongwen poked him in the back again. "Quit your daydreaming, Twig! It's your turn!"

He filled his two buckets and hurried home. On the way, he took stock of himself. I look just like them. A little taller than some. A little shorter than others. I wear the same clothes. He sniffed at his underarms. I smell the same. I talk the same. Why am I so different?

His mother's words came to him. "They are jealous, son."

He had asked, "Jealous of what?"

"Jealous of whom you will become. Jealous for the opportunity of what you will do."

"Mother, what will I become? What will I do?"

"Whatever you want, my son. Whatever you want."

Well, tonight, I want to take the Test of Bowls! He smiled, then frowned when he remembered Annongwen's words. *Will I be the first who is rejected? What will happen?* In his mind, he saw everyone laughing, even his mother.

He ran the rest of the way home to an empty house.

Odd, he thought. She should have returned by now. The berry patch is only a short walk along the path out back. He searched about for the baskets they used to collect berries and other items. Only one is gone. It shouldn't take this long to gather berries to fill only one basket. Especially since she doesn't eat as many as she picks.

He set the buckets down and picked up his short bow and quiver. Moments later, he followed the well-worn path through the brush and trees toward the berry patch.

Silence was his first clue that something was not quite right. Trampled grasses and broken branches provided the second. He rounded the turn and stopped.

A body lay on the path before him. It had been hacked to pieces. Its choice bits consumed. Its bones gnawed. Three dead lizardmen surrounded it.

He saw the discarded berry basket and the shredded remains of his mother's favorite green tunic.

At first, Chork did not want to believe it. "This is someone else," he lied to himself.

Yet, his green eyes did not deceive him. The hummingbird hairpin, a present from his father, still clung to her long blonde hair. Chork removed the pin and placed it in his pocket.

Accepting the truth, he fell to his knees and bowed his head. He chastised her, "It should have been me. Picking berries was always my chore." He looked at her remains and sobbed, "Why didn't you send me, as you always did?"

The anger building inside him turned from his mother to The Only One. "First, you took my father and now, now..." The beginnings of his rant trailed into nothingness, because he could not pronounce his mother dead.

Internally, his anger continued to grow, refocused on the three dead lizardmen that lay around his mother. They were but part of a larger rogue band, not unheard of during his brief lifetime, but exceedingly uncommon this far north. He counted their number by their unshod footprints. He would find them. They would die.

Chork stood to his full six feet with a purpose. He would track them all down and hack them to bits and pieces for the carrion birds.

To avoid looking at his dead mother, he cast about for sign. Counting the number of unshod footprints, he slowly realized the futility of avenging his mother. A 13-year-old elf with a short bow and his father's old dagger was no match for a rogue band of 20-plus ravenous lizardmen.

Staring at the sun, his loss struck him. "What will I do? What will happen to me?"

Fear seized his heart.

The Elders could order he live with his uncle and cousin, Hűchon and Annongwen, As the bile filled Chork's throat at this possibility, he shook his head.

More likely, aware of Annongwen's bullying, the Elders would make him a ward of the Enclave. "After all," they would say, "you are the Last Born Elf. We expect much of you." Already, their expectations, often undefined but voiced, were unbearable.

He would be forced from his home. He would live in a large room to eat, sleep, and train with other orphans. He would have no right to privacy, no freedom to pursue his desires, and no family.

With a firm set of his mouth and a nod of his head, he knew what he should do.

He took one last look at the blood smear that was his mother. He fixed her smiling face in his mind and vowed never to replace that vision with any other. This image took its place beside that of his father.

Chork sprinted home.

* * *

Chork entered his small house and slammed the door. Not satisfied with the sound from the wooden door, he picked up a pot and threw it to the floor. Then, another, and another. He overturned the table and the two chairs. He kicked at the chairs, splintering their rungs. He grabbed an apple and hurled it at the lone mirror. The sound of its shattering glass released his tears.

Sobbing, he ran to the battered trunk at the foot of his mother's bed. Rather than delay himself with picking through the memories inside, he upended the trunk and scattered its contents on the floor. Spying his father's large backpack, he snatched it up.

He did the same with the trunk at the foot of his bed. He yanked pants, tunic, shirt, and smallclothes from the pile and stuffed them into the pack. He briefly considered the clothes laid out on his mother's bed and then stuffed those into the pack.

From the larder, he took some dried apples, a loaf of bread, a large slab of yellow cheese, some elven wafers, and as much meat as he found. He wrapped all of this in waxed parchment and dropped them into the pack.

At the fireplace, Chork took flint and steel, a small cast pot, and an iron hook. He stopped and examined the floor. Seeing two unbroken candles, he stuffed them into the pack. From the wall, he retrieved a length of stout, twisted rope. He kicked through the mess on the floor until he found their sharpest table knife which replaced his dull left boot knife.

From under his mother's bed, he gingerly removed a small, intricately carved wooden box. His father had given this to his mother to mark the first year of their marriage.

The Last Born held his breath and opened it.

Magically, a tune began to play while a small hummingbird turned in the center. When he was a tiny sprout, his mother had hummed that same tune to help him sleep at night.

Delicately, he tilted the carved metal bird forward, backward, and forward again. A drawer in the box's base popped open. In the drawer sat one gold coin, three silvers, and nine coppers. He plucked these out and put them into his father's old coin purse, which he tied to his belt. Wrapping the box in a soft scarf, he kissed it and slid it into the pack.

Chork paused and looked around. He eyes lingered over things that tempted him, but he resisted. His concern, now, was weight.

Back at his bed, he folded and began to roll his blanket. Midway, he stopped. He glanced at his mother's bed. Her blanket was slightly larger and thicker. More importantly, it smelled of her. He rolled her blanket and tied it to the bottom of his pack.

Again, he paused, scanning the room. He filled a water skin from the bucket of water he had fetched earlier.

Then, he hefted the pack. It was heavier than he thought. Nevertheless, he squatted, inserted his arms through the shoulder straps, and stood. He grunted with the weight. Pulling on the straps as his father had taught him, he jostled the pack until it sat comfortably high on his shoulders.

He shouldered the water skin and his green cloak.

Beside the door stood his mother's yew bow and quiver. It was nearly as tall as he was. Crafted by Pengon, Emig's master bow maker, it was well-balanced and matched his height. The grip seemed made for his hand. The pull was smooth and required the right amount of effort.

Bow in hand, quiver slung onto his back, he reached for the door handle.

He took one last look around. His bottom lip trembled. Before the tears started, he furrowed his brow and focused his mind's eye on the remembered images of his mother and father.

He slipped out the back door. A quick glance this way and that. A brief pause to confirm the best path. A short nod. He sprinted through the back woods toward the river.

Only once, did he stop and hide. He waited patiently as a group of blades, bows in hand, marched past. They grumbled about losing the lizardmen's trail.

At the river, Chork selected a coracle, a plate-like boat made of deer hide stretched over interwoven willow rods. With its broad-bladed paddle, he could easily maneuver the boat along the shallow stream leading away from Emig.

The Last Born paddled out and let the swift current take the boat downstream, where it would join with the Bottom River. The Bottom emptied into the Monck River. Crossing the Monck, he would travel through the Wilds to the Great Enclave in the Elven Forest, birthplace of his race, and hopefully, toward peace and respect.

2 – Narrow Escapes

All that night and into the next day, the Last Born fled down the river. Though Chork never saw or heard any pursuers, he had to assume they would come after him. The thought of capture drove him to pull the coracle forward with rapid and deep strokes. Aided by the shallow draft of his boat and the swift current, he flew downriver.

Late afternoon, the stream narrowed, and the current grew stronger. It rushed downhill toward its meeting with the Bottom River.

The Bottom received its name for one or all of three reasons. It originated in the Aril Mountains to the east, where the Bottom Door of the Dwarves' Holdfast, Arilgirn, lay. Spanning the distance between the mountains in the east and the Monck River in the west, the Bottom marked the lower or bottom boundary of Monck, a realm of men. Finally, for most of its length, the river ran along the bottom of a deep ravine.

Lulled by the rapid current and lack of whitewater, Chork's sense of urgency gave way to fatigue. With the paddle across his knees, he soon began to doze. He snapped awake when the coracle twisted slightly. He corrected his angle with the paddle. After a short while, he nodded off again.

When the whitewater appeared, the young elf was unprepared. He awoke to a rapidly spinning boat, jostled this way and that. He fought to regain control; but when his paddle snapped in two against a rock, he simply grabbed the ends of the boat and held on.

The coracle rode the rapids until it reached the waterfall. There, it teetered on the edge and then tumbled over, spilling the elf and his belongings into the water below.

* * *

When the young elf regained consciousness, he lay on a slate stone shelf. His legs dangled in the swirling water. Without thought, he pulled himself onto the ledge, rolled over, and stared at the twilight sky.

"Thank you," he said to I'ere'er.

Miraculously, his bow and quiver lay a pace away, next to half of his paddle – the half that had broken off and had rushed away in the whitewater.

A large water oak that had fallen from the cliffs above lay at the far edge of the ledge. One of its broken branches had snared his backpack. The pack's top flap fluttered open, releasing a wrapped bundle whisked away by the water. The flap fluttered again. Another packet swam away.

He crawled over to the oak, intending to slide across it to retrieve his pack. However, when he put his weight on the soaked, decaying trunk, it disintegrated beneath him. He blew out some air and tightened his lips.

With bow stave in hand, he slipped as close as he could to the edge of the shelf. He easily snagged the pack's strap and pulled, breaking the branch. Yet, now he struggled against the weight of the pack and the river's current. Just before the strap slid off the tip, he leaped, frog-like into the water, and secured the heavy pack in his hand, but lost his special shirt and pants to the current.

Gasping for air, he fought his way back onto the ledge; pack in one hand, his bow in the other. Again, he rolled onto his back and thanked the Only One.

His gratitude was short-lived. Chork faced a bigger problem.

How do I get off this ledge? Upriver and down, there was white water and sharp rocks as far as he could see. *I'd never make it. Alive.* He looked across at the waterfall that had dumped him where he now stood. Though it was only five short paces high, he laughed at the idea of swimming up a waterfall.

The Last Born turned to the ravine wall, maybe twice the height of the waterfall. He saw many hand and footholds; but the wall curved from its bottom outward toward the river.

Overhanging the cliff was another water oak. It would soon join its brother on the ledge.

Wondering if the dead tree would support his weight, he removed the rope from his pack. He coiled the length on the ledge, tying one end to his pack. He removed the broken string from his bow and tied that to the other end of the rope. From an inner pocket, he retrieved another bowstring, which had remained dry in a waxed pouch, and restrung his bow.

With the broken string tied to an arrow, he took aim and shot. The arrow flew up over the water oak, reached its peak, and fell to ground beside him, pulling the rope just over the tree. He grabbed both ends and tested the oak's strength. Satisfied, he climbed, hand over hand, and pulled his pack up after him.

By then, night had fallen.

He selected a tree further away from the cliff, but near enough to provide a vantage for him to watch the waterfall. He still worried the Elders pursued him. Using the rope to secure his body in a crook of a large branch, he ate a little cheese and meat, and fell asleep.

* * *

The next day and two days after that, Chork followed the Bottom River westward. On the morning of the fourth day, he saw thin plumes of grey smoke rising above the tree line.

Cook fires, he immediately thought. *Humans!* Though his mother had taught him to speak the Common Tongue, he never had the chance to speak with a man. He preferred not to take that chance now, but he did want to see one.

With his best woodcraft, he crept as close as he dared. From the cover of a leafy maple's branch, he looked down, wide-eyed, into a camp bustling with activity. He counted more than 13 branches of men. Like all elves, he used the leaves and branches of the itchoak as a counting aid. The bush, known to humans as poison oak, has 13 leaves on one shoot, 13 shoots to a branch, 13 branches to a trunk, 13 trunks to a stand, 13 stands to a copse.

Men in forest green tunics with a pinkish-orange circle over the left breast worked at breaking camp. They kicked at fires, collapsed and rolled sections of a large tent, stowed gear onto donkeys, and harnessed oxen to a large wain covered with canvas.

To the elf, the humans looked strange and fascinating.

Whereas elves are of a similar size and shape, the humans varied wildly in height and girth. Generally, they were rounder than elves. Their movements lacked grace. Some jerked like newborn foals. Others waddled as ducks. All walked heel to toe, awkward and slow.

They had hair on their chins! It was curly like a young lamb's coat. Most had hair long as Chork's, but theirs was uncombed and unpinned. Their noses were broader and their lips fatter. They had rounded eyes and ears. Their fingers, rather than long and nimble, were meaty and stubby.

Suddenly, Chork heard two men talking. Alarmed and holding his breath, he watched them pass beneath him, oblivious to what or who was above or around. Their voices lacked the musical lilt so common to elves. Almost guttural they were, like the croaks of lizardmen.

He studied them as they walked toward the camp. They were dirty from head to toe. Their hair oily, their hands and faces smudged with grime, their clothing soiled. Worse, their odor caused the elf to suppress a gag, fearing they would hear him.

When Chork returned his attention to the camp, the men had already started moving off down river. A van of three scouts led them, followed by a third of the troop in an unorganized mob. Then the wagon came, surrounded on all four sides by another third. Men guiding the donkeys were next in line. The rear guard lingered a while, joking and laughing, and then finally followed.

Their abandoned camp was like an open wound on Mother Earth. Their smoldering cook fires, haphazardly strewn under tree limbs and near dry brush, threatened to ignite dry grasses or young saplings. Discarded bits of food and tattered clothing, a broken cook pot here, a soiled bedroll there, dotted the area. Before leaving, some had relieved themselves or squatted against trees, leaving stench and filth unburied.

Bewildered, the Last Born sat in the tree, shaking his head. *Elder Nimtil was right,* he thought. *They will destroy our world.*

He waited until the sun peaked and then descended. He had no desire to follow in the humans' wake of destruction, so he angled northwest through Lustataur, the Empty Forest.

He pushed hard that day, running through brush and bramble to wipe the human's blemish from his mind. When the moon rose, he stopped. Exhausted, he spurned the safety of a tall tree and settled in a tiny hollow next to a little stream. As he dozed, a light drizzle began. He wrapped his cloak tightly around him and fell asleep.

Mid-dream, he awakened to dawn breaking and a sound he had never heard.

'Snick, snick, thiiisssss. Snick, snick, thiiisssss.'

Frightened, he grabbed his bow and nocked an arrow. He frantically searched the foliage for the cause.

The sound came closer. 'Snick, snick, thiiisssss.'

A giant spider, the size of a dog cart, its long jointed legs long covered with stubby spikes, pulled its black, bulbous body through the bushes.

Fear bubbled in Chork's blood. It made him shake and whine.

Without thinking, Chork released an arrow, aiming just above the spider's eyes. He missed his target. The arrow lodged in the spider's carapace directly above and behind its head.

Chork cursed. He had no time to nock another arrow. He ran to the nearest tree and scrambled into its branches. Halfway up, he turned around.

To his chagrin, the shelob followed him up the tree. Its two black bulbous eyes gleamed though no moonlight penetrated through the clouds. Venom dripped from its dagger-like fangs.

Chork screamed and climbed higher. He perched on the highest branch that would hold his weight. Nocking another arrow, he took aim, ensuring no branch or leaf lay between the point of his arrowhead and the shelob's brain.

Then, a strange thing happened. The spider stopped its ascent and shook itself. It shuddered, screeched, and fell from the tree, bouncing off a large branch. It hit the ground with a wet-thud, convulsed, and lay still.

Chork watched the spider for a count of 100 heartbeats. Then another count before he climbed halfway back down the tree. He sat on the limb and counted a third 100-beats of his now slowing heart.

On the ground, the young elf poked at the spider with his bow. When it did not respond, he breathed a sigh of relief.

Puzzled, Chork used his knife to remove the arrow lodged in the rock-hard spider. He examined the missile. Its head was cracked and not re-usable. He spied a red band around the shaft. Curious, he inspected the other arrows in his quiver. Some had the red band, most did not. Those that did had a viscous substance on their heads.

"Basilisk venom," he whispered. He recalled the image of his mother and silently thanked her. He returned the arrows to his quiver, organizing them so he knew where the red-banded arrows stood.

* * *

After a sparse breakfast the next morning, he set off again. It was a day when the sun threatened to bake him, and the tiny biting-insects feasted on his blood.

Crashing through some brush, Chork came upon a boar path. With the opportunity to secure fresh meat, he decided to follow it. For most of the day, he held an un-banded arrow nocked, expecting the bull rush of a large, angry pig.

As the sun touched the tree line, the possibility of roast boar that evening seemed remote to Chork. He returned his arrow to his quiver and searched for a tree in which to spend the night.

Suddenly, on his left and slightly behind him, a doe burst from the trees. When it saw the elf, it stopped long enough for Chork to draw an arrow. As the deer leapt back into the forest, an arrow from the Last Born's bow chased it.

He heard the arrow hit and the doe complain. Yet, he knew it wasn't a killing shot, because the deer continued to run. It would do so until it bled out. He would have to follow.

The sounds of two large animals hurtling through the foliage startled him. Not 10 paces in front of him, two large gray wolves barreled across the boar-path and after the deer.

Chork stood, stunned, as he realized, if not for the doe, those wolves would be chasing him. Shaking himself to activity, he ran in the opposite direction.

Coupled with the shelob encounter, the incident caused Chork to alter his direction. He thought it wise to get out from under the forest's canopy and to put the Bottom River behind him.

A handful of days running northwest brought him to the Gold River. The Gold was a major trade route. Grains, salted meats, fruits, and vegetables from Monck went east to Arilgirn in exchange for precious metals and gems, and mithril armor and weapons.

The young elf turned west, tramping through the low brush just inside the line of trees. He feared an encounter with humans or dwarves on the river. His precaution rewarded him three days later.

The birds of the forest alerted him first. They fell silent.

Chork stopped and listened. At first, he heard only the pounding of his heart. Off in the distance, there was a shout, followed by another. He scrambled up into the nearest tree and waited.

Complaining oxen announced the arrival of two large river barges. With cracking whips and shouts, men drove the straining beasts eastward upriver along the towpaths on the north bank. A small group of armed guards walked alongside the oxen.

Somehow, Chork sensed these men were different from the others. For one, the guards and the drivers appeared to be organized. Each man had a job to do and he was doing it. For another, they were cleaner, even though they worked hard in the heat of the day.

Chork sniffed. The smell of these men was from work on a hot day, not the stench of dirt and garbage like the others. He watched silently as the barges passed.

Men stood atop canvas covered crates and boxes, using long poles to keep the barges in the middle of the river. They called out instructions to the drivers on the towpaths. The men ashore responded by slowing or angling the oxen's direction.

Slowly, the company moved up river and vanished.

The Last Born climbed down from the tree and continued his westward journey.

His next encounter with humans came the following day. His nose caught the smell of burning wood. His ears, the sound of children shouting.

Another camp?

From the safety of a brambleberry, he looked across the river. He saw a small village nestled against the bank.

A few small docks jutted into the river. A small river barge and two small riverboats lay tied to them. More boats, some with single sails, for one or two occupants, sat on the bank. To enable the towropes to clear the docks and the boats, the towpath climbed and descended a slight but steady rise of maybe four or five paces high.

A narrow road separated two neat rows of squat wooden buildings. At each end, a tall stone tower stood like a sentinel. At watch atop each, a man in blue tunic and silver conical helmet, shouldered a bow.

Chork eased backward into the brambleberry.

On the far side of the village, teams of oxen waited in pens. Near there, some children fought over a colored ball with crooked sticks.

Adult humans walked from one building to another.

Maybe Elder Nimtil was not right, he thought. These humans are peaceful and quiet, clean and organized.

With a shrug of his shoulders, the elf eased his way out of the bramble and into the woods. He skirted around the village, staying under the trees. On the far side, he hid behind a tree for one more look.

His only warning was the snap of a twig behind him.

Chork lurched to his right as a war axe the size of his chest sliced into ground beside him. He groaned as the axe split his bow in two. To avoid another strike, he rolled further right, slipped out of this cloak, and dropped his pack. He rolled again as a third blow came.

This one cleaved his pack in two.

Chork could hear an alarm from the town, metal clanging on metal. He got to his feet and spun, pulling the kitchen knife from his boot. His jaw dropped, and his eyes popped wide open. He faced an ogre, three times his size.

The snarling, green beast swung its axe again.

Chork ducked as the iron blade swooshed overhead. He reached behind to his quiver, groping for one of the venom-coated arrows. His fingers grasped at air. The quiver lay on the ground two paces away.

Another swing came.

He ducked again.

This time the ogre followed his right-handed swing with another from his empty left hand. He caught the elf on the shoulder, bowling him over.

Chork heard something inside crack and felt his right arm go limp. His knife slid from his hand. He slammed into the ground, numbing his left arm. Using his legs, he pushed himself along the ground like a worm, barely evading two killing blows.

The next blow, however, would end his life. He had jammed himself against a tree trunk. He had no place to go.

Chork looked up into the ogre's face. Its head was smaller than the elf's. Its pointy ears larger. Its two fire-red eyes gleamed with victory. Its green swollen tongue slavered over its lower lip in anticipation of its meal. Its axe poised overhead to split this meal in half.

Chork closed his eyes.

A guttural war cry, "Kee-yaaagghhh," rent the air followed by a mighty whirr, as if a flock of birds flew by.

Chork felt something hit his chest. He opened his eyes. The ogre's head sat on his stomach. Its eyes still had the victory gleam.

The elf then looked up and saw the ogre's body teeter. Blood spurted rhythmically from its neck. From behind the headless body, he heard, "Aw crap!" The dead ogre teetered and fell onto Chork. The weight drove his breath from his lungs as he fell into darkness.

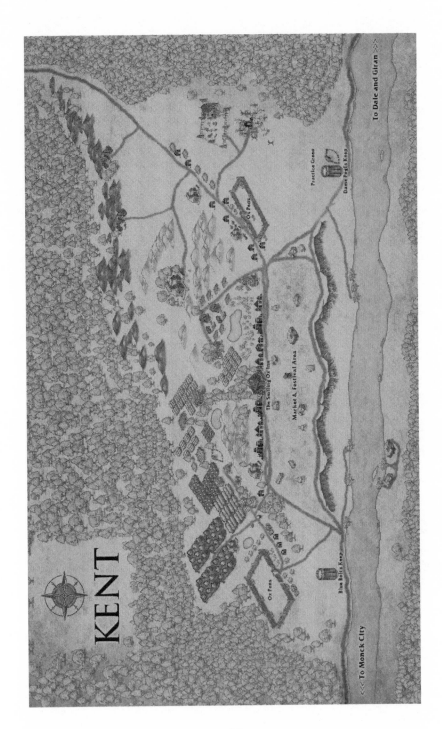

KENT

O Fens

O Fens

The Smiling O Inn

Market & Festival Area

Practice Green

O Fens

Blue Bolt's Keep

Dame Pyglo Keep

<<< To Monck City

To Dale and Giran >>>

3 – Two Tales

He lay in his own bed. His mother sat beside and hummed along with the hummingbird music box. He tried to sit up to embrace her.

"Don't try to get up." The voice, though soft, was not his mother's pleasant lilt.

Now out of the dream, his vision blurred, his mind befuddled, Chork asked, *"Manke ils im?"*

"My Elvish is not that good, especially that dialect." The soft voice replied. "I think you asked where you are. Well, you are safe." He heard an object placed on a table and a splash in a cup. The cup touched his lips. "Drink. Slowly."

Chork sipped and frowned at the taste.

"All of it, Elfling. Merriwin says you must drink all of it if you want to heal."

Chork finished the bitter liquid and forced his eye to focus on the woman who held the cup. *"Ya ier lle?"*

She paused before answering. "Who am I?" At his nod, she replied, "I am Dame Pogi Becker of the Order of the Knights of the Lily. You speak the Common Tongue?"

Chork nodded again and asked, "A knight?"

"Most call us the White Flowers." She smiled, warmly. Her cornflower blue eyes, split by a large nose, glowed with intensity and joy. She had round rosy cheeks. She was broad in the shoulder. Her hands were meaty, thick, and strong. "I'm fond of that name." She had close cropped, soft-red hair. She wore studs in both of her large ears. In the right, a white lily. The left bore something black and unrecognizable in the shadows. She retrieved the music box from the table.

"A beautiful music box," she said, opening its lid. "A beautiful tune." She fingered the hummingbird. "This is beautifully carved and familiar." She turned her head to show the left stud. A black hummingbird in flight. "Carved by the same man as that hairpin in your pocket, I'll wager."

Chork didn't reply.

"A friend of mine." Still no response. "A mage."

"They were gifts from my father to my mother." Chork tried to move his right arm to take the box from her, but found the arm snugly secured to his torso.

"That arm is broken." Dame Pogi set down the box, picked up a spoon and dipped it into a bowl of oats and cow's milk. She stirred it for a second or two and then collected a moderate mouthful. "Now, you just eat and listen. I'll do the talking and answer your questions." She offered the spoonful to Chork, who accepted it with a wince.

"Where to start," she considered. "Two days ago, I heard you in the woods. At first, I thought you were the ogre I was tracking. However, when I saw you, I became curious and followed. Somehow, the ogre got between us. It attacked you. Before I could get there, it broke your arm." She pointed with the spoon. "I think you bruised the left when you fell."

"I am sorry I was not quicker to act." She bowed her head in apology. "I took the ogre's head just as it was about to finish you. When the ogre fell on you, well, uh, it knocked the wind out of you and cracked your skull and ribs."

She continued to feed him. "This is my keep in Kent, a small village and tow station on the Gold River. I have sworn to protect and serve it and its citizens. They are good people, honest and hardworking. We have no mage for healing. Just old Merriwin, the Herbwife. She was afraid to touch you. Didn't want to catch the Elves' Curse." Dame Pogi rolled her eyes. "The Barrens she called it, though she's too old to bear children." The dame shook her head with a chuckle. "I know the sickness is not passed on, but she wouldn't accept my counsel. She prepared a healing salve for your wounds. But, I had to apply it."

Chork yawned. "Thank you for saving my life. I owe you a debt difficult to repay."

"We can discuss that later. Merriwin says you need plenty of sleep and food. So," she set the empty bowl aside, "it's back to sleep with you. When you wake, I have some questions for you."

* * *

When Chork awoke the next day, Pogi was there ready to feed him and to ask questions.

"I know elves mature sooner and age later than humans," she began, "but, aren't you a bit young to be wandering the Monck forests by yourself?"

Chork cast a sheepish look and did not respond.

"You ran away?" she ventured. When Chork remained silent, she inhaled audibly and exhaled with an even louder huff. She narrowed her eyes as she changed her path.

"You need not fear me," the Dame said. "I am sworn to protect the defenseless. I assume you come from Emig." She mispronounced it as ee-mig.

"Em-mick," he corrected in a soft voice. "Will you send me back?"

"Do you want to go back?"

"No."

"Your mother and father..."

"They're dead. I have no family to speak of."

Pogi nodded. "So, you just decided to roam the world?"

"I'm on my way to the Elven Forest."

Pogi nodded again. "Do you have a name?"

"Lye Tella'estela Hummien'dulin, but I prefer Chork."

"That's a mouthful, so Chork it is," smiled the Dame. "Yet, I wonder." She furrowed her brow. "I do not have much Elvish, but, in the Common Tongue, your given name means Last Hope?"

"Near enough."

She nodded again. "Last Hope," she repeated. "Your parents placed a huge burden on you. Does the weight of it trouble you?"

Chork looked at the knight. Her blue eyes held concern and sorrow. The elf knew that if she could remove the weight from his shoulders, she would truly try to do so.

His story tumbled out of him in segments. The name, the prophecy, the expectations, the bullying. His mother's death. His likely plight as an orphan. His decision to leave. His journey to this point in time.

She listened with patience and compassion, placing a hand on his shoulder. When he finished, she sat for a time in thought, her head bowed, and tears in her eyes.

"Well, Chork of Emig," she announced with resolve. "Let's get this young body of yours mended, so you may resume your journey." She handed him a cup. "Drink it all. Sleep and heal."

* * *

Later that day, Chork dozed and watched Pogi polish her armor.

When she saw that he was awake, the knight set aside her breastplate and took her seat next to the bed.

"I was born to my father's second wife," Pogi began. "My father was knight and protector here in Kent. He expected a son to continue his family's service to his liege, Lord Monck." Her blue eyes searched back through the years.

"Instead, my mother gave birth to me. A disappointment to my father. My birth placed a burden on my mother's health. She

26

eventually succumbed. This left none to carry the name of Becker. Another disappointment for my father.

"My father was a good man, a true and just knight. The loss of his wife and the twice failure to produce an heir changed him. He became depressed, and then bitter."

Pogi reached for a bottle of red wine and uncorked it with her large hand. She considered for a moment, and set it aside, recorked.

"I accepted the blame. I had killed my mother and disappointed my father. To make matters worse, I turned out to be the least comely lass in Kent. Another disappointment for my father. Suitors would be few and lowly."

Pogi paused, remembering. Her bottom lip quivered. After a moment, she regained her composure and continued.

"My life was miserable, lonely. I had only one friend, Edmod, a member of the Blue Bolts militia whom Lord Monck had named my grandfather's second. When my father discovered our friendship, he forbade me to see Edmod. I cried a lot in those days. Until I realized it just made things worse."

She sighed. "One day, Helga Hundin called me a 'big-nosed, big-eared donkey.' Something inside me broke." Pogi looked at her large right hand and made a fist.

"I hit her. Knocked her down into the mud. When her three older brothers confronted and threatened me, I knocked them down."

Pogi frowned. "My father flew into a rage. He confined me here." She gestured with a hand and cast her eyes about the room. "He threatened to send me to Lord Monck as a kitchen scullion."

She shook her head. "I refused to spend my life scouring pots in a dank castle kitchen. So I ran."

The Dame stood and walked, aimlessly, about the room, touching this and that.

"Where did you go?" coaxed the elf.

"Gunter's Island."

Chork shook his head.

Pogi returned to her chair. "Sir Gunter Taafe is the Knight Commander of the Order of the Lily," she said. "He makes his home on a small island off the coast of Goole, where he trains knights. My father trained there." She retrieved a map from a shelf and pointed it out to the elf.

"I arrived sick, filthy, and penniless. A cook from Sir Gunter's kitchen took pity on me. I began work the next day, scouring pots.

"One day, thinking I was alone in the kitchen, I pretended a ladle was my sword. I imitated the training forms I had seen on the practice field. In my fantasy, I skewered orcs and bandits. I didn't see my benefactor, the cook, in a nearby larder.

"The following day, I answered Sir Gunter's summons and brought the ladle as instructed.

"Believing he would chastise me, I was mortified," Pogi said. "He ordered me to repeat what I had done with the ladle in the kitchen. Three sword masters stood with him. I was so afraid that I dropped the ladle."

Pogi smiled. "Sir Gervis picked up the ladle and handed it to me, like this." She bent her left arm in front of her and gestured as if she were handing Chork a sword, hilt first, across her forearm. "It was his abrupt nod that convinced me he was not mocking me. So, I took the ladle and did as instructed."

Pogi revealed the white lily tattooed on her right palm. "Six years later, Sir Gunter knighted me. He sent me to serve Lord Monck who gave me the choice to stay at Monck Castle or return."

"You came back?" asked Chork, amazement in his voice.

"It was my duty," she replied. "The people of Kent needed me." She let out a deep breath. "It's my home."

4 – A Tale Finished

A few days later, Pogi entered the room in a knee-length ring-mail shirt and a conical iron cap. She pointed to an older man in uniform and a large brown wolfdog. "Elfling, meet Edmod and Nudge. You'll be in their care today."

"You're leaving?" Chork showed concern.

The knight grabbed a boar spear from the corner. "A mama boar and her piglets got into Neel Tilly's crops and chickens last night. I organized a few men to help run them down. Papa boar is probably roaming around as well."

"Chickens?" Chork frowned.

Pogi gawked at the elf. Then, she laughed. "I forgot elves don't keep livestock. You never saw a chicken?"

The Last Born shook his head.

"Well, well," Pogi mused. "Neel said he'd pay me with a bag of oats. Maybe he will part with a bird or two instead. If so, you're in for a treat." She turned to Nudge. Using a mixture of voice commands and hand signals, she asked the wolfdog to guard Chork.

Then, she addressed Edmod. "Old friend, I leave this young elf in your care until I return. Ensure he doesn't hurt himself or frighten the townsfolk."

"And you," she commanded Chork. "Mind Edmod and Nudge as you would me. It's time you were up and about. The three of you have fun." Her mild laughter sounded like music.

Chork, Edmod, and Nudge watched Pogi depart. Then, they eyed each other suspiciously.

Edmod was the oldest looking human Chork had seen. Wispy grey hair sparsely sprouted from his head and chin. Wrinkles lined his face and the back of his hands. He walked with a limp

29

and slight stoop, as if each year of his life had added weight on his shoulders. Yet, his brown eyes were bright and revealed an agile mind.

Edmod strode forward, his hand extended. "Edmod Pelk, Blue Bolt Bannerman, and Second to Dame Pogi Becker. Good to see you up and around."

In elf fashion, Chork clasped Edmod's forearm. "Chork of Emig. Thank you."

Nudge, who had more wolf than dog in him, padded over and sniffed. All shaggy brown with amber eyes, his head rose above Chork's waist. He likely weighed more than the elf. When Chork went to one knee and extended his palm up for the dog to smell, Nudge obliged. After a good sniff, the dog nudged Chork's hand with his large snout.

Chork scratched behind Nudge's ears and stroked his flank.

"Well met!" exclaimed Edmod, obviously delighted. "Let's take a walk."

The three climbed the inner staircase to the tower roof. They walked to the parapet and looked down into Kent.

Below, children played at the stick and ball game. Men tended the ox pens or readied their fishing boats. Women, holding baskets of clothing or food, tended to their morning errands. The warm morning breeze carried the wonderful smell of baking bread.

The Last Born closed his eyes and enjoyed the warmth and the aroma.

"Come," said Edmod, "I'll show you the town."

Though there was little to see, Edmod's tour lasted the entire day. He possessed an extensive knowledge of Kent history, sharing nearly every detail with the elf. Edmod also greeted everyone they met along the way, engaging them in conversation.

Without fail, the Bannerman manipulated every conversation to include the elf.

At first, Edmod's ploy failed. The townsfolk, wide-eyed with fear, abruptly ended the talk with excuses of chores and errands. However, Edmod persisted, and took to draping his arm about the elf's shoulders as they walked. By noon, the old Blue Bolt had convinced most of the 'Kenters,' as he called them, that the elf would not give them the Barrens.

Toward evening, Edmod led Chork to the other tower. "Hungry?" Edmod asked. "Let's see what Aelmar has made for supper."

The two-story tower that housed the four Blue Bolts stood the same as the one that housed Dame Pogi. A staircase spiraled around the outside and led to the top parapet. A heavy oak door at one end of the roof guarded a similar spiral staircase into the interior. The upper floor was devoted to a kitchen complete with fireplace for roasting and baking, a larder, and two large tables. The lower room was reserved for beds and an armory.

"Just in time," greeted Aelmar Wuerst, a good soldier, but even better cook. "Sausages and fresh bread." Graying at his temples but agile and graceful in his step, Aelmar had deep half-moon creases on either side of his thin lips, which meant his broad welcoming smile was a perpetual feature. Thin, angular, and ruddy, he was taller than Edmod and years younger.

"W-wait!" another voice shouted. "W-what's he doing here?" The voice belonged to Gary Bell, a young Blue Bolt with short, sandy colored hair and blue eyes. "He'll blight us all."

"Settle down, Bell," growled Edmond. "There's no danger."

"Hell you say," replied Bell. "If he eats here, I eat elsewhere." He gestured to the other young Blue Bolt in the room. "C'mon Tim, we'll eat at the inn."

31

Timothy Barclay, taller and darker than Bell, looked from Edmod to Bell.

"I'll buy," urged Bell.

"I don't like sausages," said Barclay. The two young Blue Bolts left without another word.

"Bah," complained Edmod. "Ignorant young clods."

"More for us." Aelmar rubbed his hands together as his smile widened.

* * *

After the meal, Edmod and Chork climbed to the top of the tower. They sat in silence with their legs dangling off the parapet. Edmod packed and lit his pipe. Nudge joined them, lying midway between.

Muted song and laughter gently floated up from the inn. An owl called for its mate. The river softly lapped at its banks. A gentle evening breeze tiptoed through the forest.

"Peaceful," commented Chork.

"Yep, usually is. Us Kenters like it that way." Edmod relit his pipe. "Dame Pogi does a good job."

"She's the reason?"

"Most would say that. If it weren't for her, there'd be no Kent."

Chork tilted his head quizzically.

Edmod began his tale in a voice so soft that Chork had to move closer to hear it.

After Pogi had run away, her father, Sir Pieter, thought his daughter dead and blamed himself. In his despair, he burned his home on the east side of town, moved into the east guard tower by himself, and rarely emerged. As he spiraled downward into depression and madness, Kent followed. Ogres raided the ox pens and outlying farms. Toughs fought nightly at the inn, twice killing Kenters in their brawls. River pirates preyed upon merchants' barges.

"Sir Pieter was really a good man," whispered Edmod. "He just had bad things happen to him." Edmod stood and stretched his legs. He massaged his right knee.

"The worst then happened." Edmod's voice rose an octave, as he continued the story.

Helga Hundin, ever the opportunist and troublemaker, offered herself to the aging knight. Her price was a place in the Blue Bolts for each of her brothers. Sir Pieter, blinded by his hope for an heir, agreed.

That winter, a son was born. Yet, the timing was wrong. Kenters had long whispered rumors of incest among Helga and her brothers, especially the eldest, Gauner. However, the old knight, so eager for a male heir, ignored the obvious.

As the child grew, so did Helga's influence over Sir Pieter. She convinced the knight to make Gauner his second over Edmod and to install their cousins as Blue Bolts. In a short time, this small army of Hundins bullied the townsfolk into submission.

They lashed Reinfred Plancke, the baker, and placed him in the stocks for speaking against them. When Niklas Klaeber packed his family and home into wagons to leave, Gauner hanged Niklas, burned his wagons, and sold his family into slavery.

Sir Pieter could do nothing, falling ill with a strange malady. Confined to a bed in the east tower, he withered and lay at death's door. Merriwin, the herb-wife, stealing a glimpse of the afflicted knight, suspected a slow poison.

"Several of us tried to get word to Lord Monck," said Edmod. "Helga somehow always learned of our attempts." The old bannerman sighed. Holding back a sob, he added, "Some paid with their lives."

Aelmar joined them on the battlement, bringing three mugs of ale. Edmod downed his in one long pull. Chork, disliking the brew for its bitterness, handed his mug to the man. Edmod smiled in gratitude and continued his tale.

The Kent townsfolk attempted to organize a rebellion. Meeting in numbers greater than three was ill advised. Helga's informers were everywhere. For coppers and choice bits of food, hungry children began spying on their parents and older siblings.

Kent was like a sheaf of dried grass awaiting a spark from flint and steel. That spark could come from anyone at any time. Good and bad people would die. Kent would burn.

That spark came on Midsummer's Day 13 years ago in the form of a knight.

"Pogi!" Chork whispered.

Aelmar grinned and nodded.

Edmod frowned at the cook for stealing the bannerman's thunder. He described the knight, ignoring the correct guess and grinning affirmation.

The knight sat atop a black destrier in full barding. A white lily stemmed from a mithril helmet, its visor down. Her white lacquered armor gleamed in the sun. A single-edged black mithril sword without sheath hung to the left. A morningstar holstered on the right. Her gold shield bore a large black ox, the sigil of House Becker, on a field of white lilies.

Edmod rasped, caught up with emotion, "In the middle of Kent, she asked in a loud voice, 'Who serves the Lord Monck in this village?'"

Aelmar interjected, "You were the first to reply."

"Aye," acknowledged Edmod, "and you, the second."

Slowly, and then with increasing ferocity, the Kent townsfolk, who gathered in a semi-circle around the knight, shouted their allegiance. The spark struck, the flame burned.

Gauner and his two brothers pushed through the crowd, yelling for the Kenters to quiet. Helga appeared on the east tower battlement and called for silence.

"My husband, Sir Pieter," she yelled, "stands for Lord Monck here. Who are you, Poser, that you wear the mark of House Becker and challenge the peace of our village?" She grinned as her cousins and mercenaries joined her brothers.

Pogi turned to face Helga and lifted her face guard.

Helga's eyes bulged in horror. Her face went white. "Seize the troublemaker!" she screamed.

However, untrained toughs posing as Monck Blue Bolt militia posed no threat to a Knight of the Order of the White Lily.

With the first blow of her morningstar, Pogi crushed Gauner's head. Spurred by the dame's knees, her destrier lurched forward, crumpling the Hundin brothers to the ground.

Kenters, using whatever they had at hand, belt knives, walking sticks, rocks from the ground, pummeled the brothers to death. Wielding short swords, Edmod and Aelmar dispatched three cousins and a hired thug.

The remaining mercenaries fled, pursued with vengeance by Kenters. Not one escaped the village alive.

Pogi removed her helmet and dismounted, sword in hand.

When they saw her face, the townsfolk gaped in surprise and then cheered. Helga disappeared into the tower.

Pogi started for the tower stairs, removing pieces of armor as she went. Breast and back plates, greaves, paldrons, all fell from her ascending body. Up the stairs and into the tower she went, clad only in mail shirt and small clothes.

"All of us stood around the tower, waiting," said Edmod. "What exactly happened inside? What was said? The Dame never revealed. We can only guess." Edmod fell silent.

Aelmar looked at his comrade. The cook scratched at the hair on his chin a moment and then picked up the tale, "The Dame emerged from the tower, gently weeping. She carried her father in her arms like a baby. Emaciated, grey in pallor, his heart stabbed with Helga's dagger."

"And Helga?" Chork asked breathlessly.

"Dead," replied Edmod. "We think by her own hand. Poison. Some, the more fanciful, say fear. Fear of Dame Pogi's retribution."

"The boy? The son. What became of him?"

Edmod shook his head. "No one really knows. He was not in the tower, nor anywhere in Kent."

5 – An Agreement

The three sat in silence atop the tower, each with their own thoughts in mind. Edmod ruminated on Dame Pogi's tenure as the protector of Kent. Aelmar pondered the disappearance of Helga's son. Chork contemplated his journey since leaving Emig.

The elf retraced his steps, his actions, his fears. He wanted to believe that he survived by skill and wit. Yet, he knew he owed his life to luck. He wondered how long his luck would hold. Would it hold all the way to the Elven Forest? If he got there, what would he be? Just another Leaf on the Branch?

However, he mused, *if I arrive as a Knight of the Order of the White Lily, then ... Sir Chork of Emig.*

No, that did not sound appropriate.

Sir Lye Tella'estela Hummien'dulin, the White Flower of Emig.

That brought a smile to his face.

Nudge jerked upright and barked.

"Dame Pogi has returned," said Edmod. Led by Nudge, they ran down the stairs.

Pogi led six men carrying three pigs on poles. She had three chickens by their feet in her right hand. Her boar spear was resting on her left shoulder. She had a wide grin on her face, her blue eyes sparkling.

Most of Kent turned out to welcome home the boar hunters. A few cheers rang out. Some coins changed hands.

"For breakfast, please." Pogi handed the birds to Aelmar. She called out, "Gerbert! Where is that innkeeper?"

A thin balding man in an apron came through the crowd. "Here I am!"

She handed Gerbert Fass a small bag of coins. "Tomorrow, you'll roast these three pigs with all the trimmings," she hooked a thumb over her shoulder, "and open your cellar for some of that Bog's Beer you been hiding."

She then told Jorryt Klack, the head ox tender, to roast an ox.

With a smile and in a voice loud enough for all to hear, she finally addressed Edmod. "See that everyone in Kent gets an invite to our pig and ox roast tomorrow night."

The crowd cheered and rushed off to tell family and friends.

"Now," the Dame said seriously, "I am in bad need of a bath." She walked off to her tower, humming a lively tune.

* * *

Chork, tired from the long day, walked slowly down the tower stairs to find Pogi reading by candlelight at the table.

Before he could say anything, Pogi asked, "How was your day with Edmod and Aelmar?"

The elf thought a moment and replied, "Tiring, but interesting."

Pogi smiled.

"I have made a decision."

"A decision?" Pogi snapped her book shut. "This sounds important."

"I will be a knight," announced the elf. "How do I get to Gunter's Island?"

Pogi blew air out between her lips.

"Has there ever been a knighted elf?"

"Two. One still lives."

"Then, I wouldn't be the first."

"You could be the last."

Chork hung his head for a moment. "All the better," he finally said. "What better way to remember my life."

"I can think of a few," Pogi murmured to herself. Aloud, she asked, "What led you to this decision?"

38

Chork told her about his earlier thoughts. How he realized that only by luck had he survived the journey from Emig. He voiced his doubts about his ability to get safely to the Elven Forest. If he did make it there, he suspected contrary to his dreams, he would face the same fate as the one he avoided in Emig.

"I have something to show you," he said. He reached into his inner shirt pocket and removed the black hummingbird hairpin. He held it up. "The same design as your ear stud." He withdrew his mother's music box. "The same." He pointed to the tattoo on her left palm. "Again, the same. My family name!" He shook his head. "Do you think this is happenstance?"

"No, I do not." Pogi's bright blue eyes glowed with intensity.

"Nor I," replied the elf. "It means we are somehow connected. Our meeting was destined, perhaps by The Only One." Chork hesitated for a moment and said, "I cannot return to Emig as I am. Untrained and untested. Therefore, I wish to become a knight. As such, I will be loved and respected as you are here in Kent."

The Dame examined the hummingbird items and considered. She shook her head and said, "Elfling, knighthood is not about getting love and respect. It is ..."

Chork interrupted, "So, you will not help me."

"I would finish." Pogi's blue eyes bored into Chork's green eyes as if to touch their very soul. "To be a knight is to serve. To give, not to get. It is I who give the good people of Kent the love and respect they deserve. In return, they give me the responsibility to protect their lives and the lives of their loved ones. A burden so heavy, that many greater than I have fallen under its weight. To be a knight is to accept this burden with humility, gratitude, and courage and to expect nothing in return."

She softened her tone and gave him a look of challenge. "To me, it seems this burden I carry and what you now wish for is the same from which you run."

"It's not the same!" he pleaded. Chork's eyes narrowed in defiance. "This is what I want! Not what they want! You think me foolish!"

"No, young one, I do not," she repeated. "Maybe as you say, there is more here than what you or I want. Maybe … just maybe."

Pogi looked at the lily on her right palm. "Knighthood is not all waving swords and jabbing boar spears. It is…" She paused and looked directly into Chork's eyes. "It is an oath to yourself. One that binds you more tightly than any noose. One that binds you to everything you say and do. To everything you believe or want to believe. Forever. Even with your last breath."

With each of her words, Chork's head dipped a little lower and his pales cheeks tinged a little redder.

Her mind decided, the Dame walked to a bookcase and rummaged through some scrolls on a shelf. She selected one and blew the dust from it. Returning to the table, she took a deep breath

Chork lifted his head, tears in his eyes.

She dropped the scroll on the table. "I am told, the oath I follow as a White Flower," she showed him her right palm, "is like the bond between elf and Mother Tree. My oath defines how I relate to every living thing." She closed her palm and added with a chuckle, "With more waving swords and jabbing boar spears."

She unfurled the scroll and laid it on the table. "There are 10 virtues we hold most dear."

Pogi extended the thumb of her right hand. "First and foremost, humility, the foundation of our pledge."

Her blue eyes, now ablaze with fervor, held Chork's green eyes. "Then, those four Sir Gunter calls our cardinal virtues. Prudence, justice, temperance, and courage." For each, she raised a finger.

"Our four contracts with society," she numbered them with the fingers of her left hand. "Integrity, gratitude, a positive attitude, and love."

Again, she paused. "Last, but just as important as the first," she extended her left thumb, "hard work."

The Dame held her pose. "Aspire to these 10 virtues daily, without fail," she closed her fingers into fists, "and you will attain the knight's strength and value."

Chork nodded eagerly. "I am not discouraged. As you say, in the Enclave, many of these qualities are taught from birth."

"My intent is not to lighten your burden, Elfling, but to impress upon you that knighthood is a lifelong pursuit, not a whimsical dance at a harvest ball forgotten with the first snow of winter. Many set feet upon the path, but few remain there."

"You think I can't do it!" Chork rose to his feet, nearly toppling the table.

The Dame smiled at the defiance in the elf's voice.

"You think I am too young!"

"No, Elfling," Pogi calmly said. "Most start their training when they are younger than you."

"Then, I am too old?"

"No, no. Listen, I have a proposition for you. Hear me out."

Chork nodded.

"I propose this." She again looked at the black hummingbird. "Become my squire. I will train you, as Sir Gunter trained me."

"I accept!" Chork declared without hesitation.

Pogi spit onto her right palm and presented it to Chork. When he looked questioningly at her, she indicated he do the same. They shook and sealed their bargain.

"When and where do we start?" asked the elf.

"Tomorrow. Training is hard work and being a knight is hard work. That is where you will begin." She held up her left thumb. "With hard work. And," she held up her right thumb, "humility."

6 – Hard Work

Hard work began every day at sunrise and lasted well into the night.

Duties and chores came first and filled the morning. He dumped dirty water and fetched clean – chopped firewood and carried it into the tower – fed and combed Blaze and Wink, Pogi's destrier and palfrey – mucked their stables – repaired, cleaned, and polished armor and weapons – ran errands and delivered messages – ordered the tower.

Pogi assigned many of these tasks to increase Chork's stamina and strength, greatly needed for the afternoon's routines. "It's said elves can run for an entire day before tiring," Pogi said. "You will be able to run for two!"

Immediately after the midday meal combat training began, both afoot and on horse.

First, Chork practiced grappling, which Pogi claimed was the key to winning many fights even those with weapons. "Fighting, no matter the weapon, is about leverage and balance," Pogi declared.

Sword training was next, at first with wooden blades, left-handed until the other arm healed. The elf learned and practiced closing, trapping, deflecting, pommeling, and disarming methods. Graduating to the use of real blades, he repeated these techniques and added thrusting, cutting, slicing, and stabbing skills. His foes were posts and tree trunks.

Chork repeated these lessons with every weapon in the tower's arsenal, blades of all sizes and shapes, pole arms, and blunt or cleaving weapons. The long sword and dagger, Pogi's weapons of choice, received extra and more detailed sessions.

Every day, a changing group of young and old Kenters and at least one Blue Bolt participated. Edmod, Aelmar, and, occasionally, Barclay offered advice and encouragement or demonstrated proper technique.

Bell, however, kept his distance until sparring sessions began. During these, he not only tried to win, but also to inflict as much pain as possible. When successful at either, he celebrated with enthusiasm.

Sparring with these weapons proved dangerous and exhausting. Hits from blunted blades and padded bludgeons bruised Chork from head to toe. One strike from Bell's halberd blurred the vision in Chork's left eye for two days. Yet, training continued.

"Your foe will not relent because you have a bruise, Elfling," roared Pogi, as she whacked his left arm with a long pole. "Learn to overcome your injury! Use your brain and your training!" Her pole flicked out and jabbed his thigh. "Fighting, no matter the weapon, is about perseverance," Pogi declared.

"But, I thought balance..."

She whacked his left ear. "Don't think, react!" And she whacked his right ear.

Once, when practicing traps and takedowns, Chork blocked an overhead sword strike with the edge of his own sword. Pogi saw the error and swung the long pole in a wide arc, sweeping the elf's feet from beneath him. Chork landed heavily on his rear. His jaws snapped shut so quickly he nearly bit off the tip of his tongue.

"Are you daft, Elfling?" yelled Pogi. Another pole swing and Chork's long sword flew across the practice ground. "What right do you have to damage my long swords?"

"I-I'm sorry," Chork apologized.

"Sorry!" A third swing caught the elf's side, doubling him over. "We parry! We deflect! We catch! We avoid!" With each statement, she demonstrated the technique. "I have taught you these! Have you not yet learned them?"

Chork, fighting for his breath, croaked, "Y-yes, Dame."

"Bah! Today's training is over! You will repair and sharpen each blade in the arsenal before retiring for the night!" Pogi dropped the pole in Chork's lap and strode off.

Each day before twilight, Chork and Aelmar practiced with bow and sling. Aelmar, noted as the best bowshot in Kent, also made bows. One day, he presented Chork with a new one.

"I copied the design of your riven bow," he said, indicating the ox tendon sandwiched between two pieces of yew. "I couldn't match the craftwork but came as close as my skill allowed. The next one will be better."

Chork, overcome with emotion, received the bow with two hands and bowed his head. "Thank you, Aelmar. Pengon, the master bow maker of Emig, would be delighted with this."

Aelmar smiled broadly. "Let's go try it!"

Even bathing became an opportunity for training. Daily, before supper, Chork jumped into the Gold River and swam twice the length of Kent to remove the day's dirt and odor.

Aelmar usually served supper in the Blue Bolt's tower. Pogi, Chork, Edmod, Aelmar, and sometimes, Barclay and the Robins brothers, Mark and Martin, the other two Bolts, sat at the long table and relived the day's events. Bell, still refusing to eat with the elf, would take his turn at guard duty.

A leisurely stroll through Kent always followed supper. Pogi and Chork took this opportunity to talk to the townsfolk, collecting news and resolving issues.

Pogi set aside the evenings for social and intellectual education. Basic good manners, proper attire for knights in and out of court, and appropriate forms of address for nobles, merchants, and fellow knights soon gave way to discussions on military strategy, philosophy and simple economics. Occasionally, Edmod and Aelmar would join them.

Late one night, Pogi unrolled a large scroll. "The artisan who crafted the maps in Monck Castle also drew this." Anchoring the corners with whatever was at hand, she said, "This is Brehm."

Chork looked with wonder. The map seemed to be alive and he said so.

"Yes, it has some magic," said Pogi.

Unlike other maps Chork had seen, this map was in color. Moreover, the colors seemed to move and dance. The blue rivers flowed from their headwaters to their mouths. The light green forests danced with growth. The yellow sands swirled in the wind. Seas lapped at shores.

"Here is Kent." Pogi pointed to a small glimmering dot just west of the map's center.

As Chork focused on the spot, it came alive. He could see the two towers, the ox pens, the squat wooden buildings lining the Gold River. People! Kenters hurried about their day, Startled, the elf flinched.

"Yes." Pogi grinned. "Amazing, isn't it." Her finger traced the Gold River west, stopping at larger radiant point. "Here is Monck City."

Chork saw a massive, black stone castle nestled against the banks of two rivers. A large, bustling city with stone-paved streets and tall stone buildings spread eastward from the castle.

Her finger moving west, Pogi said, "The Monck River, the Wilds, Firefield, home to the Lyrani. And here," she stopped at a pulsing emerald green blotch, "the Elven Forest."

Staring at the mark, Chork frowned. "I don't see..."

"No, you won't. Same as here." She pointed southeast of Kent to Emig. "Or here." Her finger moved to the Dwarves' Holdfast in the Aril Mountains. "I believe the magic only works with human cities and villages."

"What does this say?" Chork pointed to a label beside a glowing point south of Kent. He saw a large city with docks and people dressed in red.

"That's Gooleport." Pogi jerked upright. "You can't read?"

"Not the Common Tongue."

From that time on, Chork's evenings included lessons on reading and writing. He spent hours studying Gunter's Codex on the Knightly Arts and Tactics of Combat.

After 11 days of regimented training, the two-day weekend was considered a time of rest and recreation. Though for Chork, many of the activities available applied or enhanced what he had learned and practiced. Bow hunting with Aelmar sharpened his archery and woodcraft skills. Shinning (the stick and ball game) with the Kent youth reinforced teamwork and increased stamina. Playing any game with pasteboards taught strategy, tactics, and patience.

The days marched by quickly. New moons came and went. Summer gave way to autumn, autumn to winter to spring, and summer returned. Midsummer's morn and the Last Born's 14th birthday passed with a clap on the back and red raspberry tort baked by Aelmar.

Chork thrived under the strict routine of Pogi's tutelage. She said that the boy was becoming a man. Chork frowned at this. He preferred the elf version. The shoot was growing into a blade.

He felt for the first time in his short life, he had direction. His ambition to become a knight had transformed the vague expectations of his early years into a goal. Moreover, he felt he made progress, sometimes slow, sometimes fast, toward achieving that goal.

I have a place in this world, he thought. It's not the place my kindred expected; but, it is the place I choose.

7 – Humility

"Stand. Nock. Draw. Fix. Aim. Release. Hold." As he recited them, Chork demonstrated the six steps in shooting an arrow to his students. He repeated the sequence twice and said, "Fix the arrow. Let it sit flat as you draw. Otherwise, your arrow will fly high." And, "Hold steady at your cheek after releasing the arrow. If you drop too soon, you will miss your target."

He went through the sequence again, this time slowly and deliberately so he could correct the flaws made by the eight Kenters as they performed the steps. Chork used his bow, not a long pole, to move their arms and legs into the correct positions. He did not leave bruises or welts.

Eight arrows hit the swinging, round wooden shield suspended by rope from a post.

"Again." Another eight arrows flew. "Again."

Marigold struck center all three times.

Pogi had planned for Aelmar to train a small contingent of townsfolk as archers. However, the Blue Bolt's duties had often interfered. Therefore, Pogi decided to give the job to Chork. She also intended it to provide him with a taste of command, a critical skill a knight must learn and master. "After all," she told him, "today marks one years since you became my squire."

The Kent Archers had been practicing for 11 straight days, from Katyr're to Joril're.

"Marigold," Chork instructed, "walk them through another three arrows. Make sure Alvy holds after the shot."

The Last Born strutted, his chest puffed, to where Aelmar stood watching.

"They are doing well," the Blue Bolt complimented.

"The Kent Archers will be the best in Monck," said Chork. "I'd even wager that Marigold will challenge you as best shot."

Aelmar blew out air and shook his head with a grunt.

Dame Pogi, sitting atop Blaze nearby, had heard. She had been practicing. Fully armored, her shield hand on Blaze's reins, she had charged across the field, slashing at melons on post tops.

"Proud of them, are you?" Pogi asked.

"They could barely hold a bow when we started. Now, you must admit I have done wonders." Chork beamed and winked his right eye. "Hard work."

The Dame signaled Edmod to her. She instructed him to retrieve her coin purse and the blunted practice arrows from her tower.

Pogi then turned to Chork and said, "Place your troop on this side of the Butts, facing the Yard." She pointed with her sword. "Tell them that whoever hits my shield shall receive a purse of gold coins." She reined Blaze in a tight turn and raced back down the field.

Edmod returned with the arrows, tipped with blunted iron to give them weight. Yet, when they struck a rock or shield, the rough-forged iron would crack and crumble, and the shaft would shatter. Edmod looked at Chork and chuckled. Then, he signaled to Pogi.

Chork relayed Pogi's challenge to the would-be archers. "Do not waste your arrows! Remain calm!"

At the far end of the Yard, Pogi kicked Blaze into a trot and then a gallop. Halfway to the line of archers, she drew her black-mithril sword and leaned forward to whisper one word into the horse's ear. "Arrows."

The black destrier tore across the remaining distance. His hoof beats sounded like booming thunder. His nostrils flared and snorted. At a full clip, he swerved in smooth shallow arcs toward his target.

"Nock and draw!" screamed Chork.

"Strike!" bellowed Pogi. She whipped her sword to the right extending it behind her, outward and low. She, somehow, made her body smaller, so that it hid behind her shield. Only the top of her helmet from the eye slits up was visible.

To Chork's disbelief, Blaze seemed to double his speed. "Loose now! Now!"

Alvy dropped his bow and ran.

Within a heartbeat, Blaze passed between Rainhard and Herman, knocking the boys to the ground. Pogi swung her sword, first to the right, then the left, over the archers' heads.

Marigold shot one arrow, directly upward. The other Kenters fell to ground, Aldrik breaking his bow in two.

Pogi turned Blaze on a barrelhead, pointed her blade at Marigold, and demanded, "Yield!"

The girl dropped her bow and quivered in fear.

Pogi slid from saddle and sheathed her sword, leaving her shield hanging from the pommel. She removed her helmet and gauntlets. "Is anyone hurt?" She looked at each in turn. She watched Rainhard get to his feet. "No? Good." With Edmod's help, she removed her breast and back plates.

"You did nothing to shame yourselves," she told them. "I have seen grown men, tested in battle, turn and run from a destrier's charge. For each of us," she spoke slowly so they heard her admission, "fear is the real foe in battle. Now that you have tasted it, you will learn how to overcome it."

Pogi faced Chork. "Edmod," she said, holding Chork's eyes with her steely blue ones, "distribute the coin in my purse evenly among the Kent Archers. Let them know I expect them on the

Butts first thing Katyr're morning. Oh, and have Aelmar find a suitable bow for Aldrik."

Chork opened his mouth to say something, but Pogi shook her head. She held his gaze while everyone slowly left the field. When only they remained, she asked in a calm voice, "What did you learn?"

"That a knight on horse ..."

Pogi shook her head.

"That archers ..."

Again, the Dame shook her head.

Chork took a deep breath. He tried to puzzle what lesson Pogi sought from him. He shook his head rapidly back and forth, "Maybe, if I ordered them to ..."

"Pride."

The one word hung in the air between them.

"I was proud of them."

"Now, you're not? No, you were proud of yourself. Your pride clouded your judgment. Admit it, Elfling!"

Chork lowered his head and nodded.

"Vanity."

That word hung heavier.

"If you are lucky, pride and vanity kill only you. More often, they kill those whom you swore to protect, or worse, those whom you hold dear."

Chork shuffled his feet.

"Humility teaches us that pride is both a vice and a virtue, like two sides of the same coin." Pogi reached for the elf's chin and raised his head so that her eyes held his. "A vice, when you strut like a peacock for no good reason. A virtue, when temperance and truthfulness are applied."

She released Chork's chin. "Sir Gunter's <u>The Pride and Humility of a True Knight</u> will be helpful. You'll find it among the

52

scrolls on the third shelf. I suggest you find a comfortable spot up river tomorrow. While you read and consider the Knight Commander's thoughts, watch for a small boat or raft. My friend sends something that will help with your training."

"Yes, Dame Pogi," Chork said, obediently. His voice also carried a tone of anticipation.

"Hard work, Elfling. Hard work. Here." She pointed to her head. "As well as here." She spread her arms out, indicating her body.

* * *

Rather than go for the usual swim, the Last Born walked through Kent looking for Aldrik. When he found him, Chork handed his bow to the young man. "I am sorry I caused you to break your bow, Aldrik. Please take this one."

"B-but that's yours. You need it."

"I will find or make another. You will need this next week. We have much to learn. Come early and tell the others."

Aldrik ran off with a wide grin. Chork wandered over toward the Smiling Ox Inn.

Had it been a real charge, they would have died. I failed them. In doing so, I failed her. Pride. Vice and virtue. How do I know when it is one or the other?

He frowned. I did strut like a peacock. Boasted like a drunken lumper. Insulted Aelmar's ability with a bow. I must apologize to him.

Then, I claimed their progress as my own. I raised myself above them, as though I was solely responsible for what they had achieved. The elf shook his head in fury. Foolish. Vain.

"You'll never be a knight."

Chork snapped his head around. It was Bell.

"You don't have it in ya." The Blue Bolt cackled. Leaning on the inn's porch railing, he held up a mug of beer. "No elves do."

"I will," Chork declared.

"Rot and dung," Bell replied. He grimaced and shook his head. "All talk an' a w-waste of time. Play at yer games, ya pointy-eared d-dolt."

"Why do you dislike me? I have done you no harm."

"Dislike!" Bell bellowed. "I hate ya! All ya earth pixies! N-nuttin' but a d-dyin' race. Think yer better than us. B-blighted 'n' oh so snooty. W-we'll see who runs this w-world. This is w-what I think of yer Mama Earth." He pulled his manhood from his pants and relieved himself onto the ground. Then, he cackled again and went back inside.

Chork was proud of his elven heritage and the respect it taught for Mother Earth. He sighed. *Is that a vice or a virtue?*

8 – New Friends

Chork skipped a stone out into the river. The stone bounced seven times and disappeared beneath the water. His best had been a flat stone half the size of his hand. It had skipped 13 times before sinking.

Sitting under a willow tree, he had read and re-read Sir Gunter's treatise, until his head pounded, and his eyes burned. When the words had lost all meaning, he began skipping stones across the Gold River.

Searching the ground for smoother flatter stones, Chork thought of something his father had once told him.

"No matter how good you become with a bow," his father had said, "there is always someone better. If not today, then tomorrow."

"What about the day after that?" Chork had asked, thinking to trick his father.

"That's why you practice every day," his father had replied. "For the day after tomorrow."

The Last Born bent over and picked up a flat grey pebble. He flung it sidearm, snapping his wrist. "... ten, eleven, twelve, thirteen, fourteen ..." he counted. He smiled.

This is good pride, he thought. The satisfaction of beating my best throw with a better one. This is humility. Trying to better that throw. He looked for another pebble, selected one, and threw. Eleven.

"Good throw!"

Chork looked up.

A boy, a year or two older than the elf, poled a small raft along shore. He had long unruly black hair, bright black eyes, and a large grin with perfect white teeth. He was barefoot, and his black pants sagged, as if they were too big for his body. He carried a long, black-bladed dagger, tucked into a wide black belt. A black vest covered a dirty white shirt, its laces missing.

"My best is 16!" said the boy. He beached the raft. A lone, partially, covered crate sat on the front. A small, makeshift tent stood on the back.

Chork laughed and inwardly acknowledged his father. "Fourteen is my best."

The boy extended his hand, smiling. "My friends call me Fat Nat the Water Rat."

The elf took the boy's hand. "Chork." He looked quizzically at Fat Nat, who was as thin and wiry as a young sapling.

"Yeah," Fat Nat said, "it's just a nickname because it sings." He grinned. "Never shook hands with an elf. Feels no different." He pointed downriver. "You from Kent?"

Chork nodded.

"Thought so. You said your best is 14?" He bent over, picked up a stone, and flicked it into the water. The stone skipped nine times.

The two took turns skimming stones while discussing ideal size, weight, and shape of the stone, the perfect angle of throw, and the proper flick of the wrist.

Fat Nat revealed he came from Gruene's Crossovers, a tiny hamlet near Dale Lake. Most people there, he said, were shepherds or wolf hunters. He confessed a lack of desire to follow either occupation. Therefore, he said, he delivered things for a small fee to towns and hamlets up and down the Gold River. "As far west as Monck City. As far east as the dwarves' stronghold." This, he stated, kept him away from sheep and wolves and provided him the opportunity to travel and meet interesting people.

"For instance," Fat Nat said, "meeting you is interesting. You are my first elf. Up close that is. I've seen elves from a distance before."

"So you find me interesting?" Chork asked, deadpanned.

"Mildly. You do anything other than skip stones?"

"I am training with Dame Pogi Becker to be a knight."

"That is very interesting. Tell me about it while you help me pole into Kent."

As they slowly poled the raft down river, Chork described his life in Kent.

* * *

Young Frank Pandl first saw the raft approaching. He ran through Kent screaming, "Fat Nat! Fat Nat!" His screams drew an excited crowd, who gathered quickly next to a low dock. As the raft swung into view, they cheered and repeated young Pandl's shouts.

Fat Nat was the first off and tied the raft to a stone cleat. He turned to the crowd and exclaimed, "Hide your cat and doff your hat!" The crowd joined in for the next line, "It's Fat Nat the Water Rat!"

A huge cheer rang out.

Fat Nat bowed low and greeted many by name. He dashed back onto the raft and, from under the tent, grabbed several small parcels and a bundle of letters. These, he handed out to their intended recipients.

As the crowd thinned, Pogi stepped forward. "Welcome to Kent, Young Nat. Can you stay the night for news and Aelmar's supper?"

"Dame Pogi," greeted Fat Nat, bowing low again. "For a supper by the best cook this side of Monck Castle, I can. How is Aelmar? And Edmod?"

"Truly well, both." Pogi raised an eyebrow and asked, "Do you have something for me?"

"I do, Ma'am. From Master Timo." He produced a letter from within his vest and handed it to her.

Chork noticed the letter's seal. It was the black hummingbird in flight and matched Pogi's earring and palm tattoo and his hairpin and music box.

"Thank you," Pogi said, opening the letter. As she read, she first frowned and then laughed. She pointed to a partially covered crate on the raft. "Is that also for me?"

Fat Nat held up a hand. "Uh, beggin' your pardon, ma'am, yes and no." He smiled. "Yes, it is from Master Timo." He looked at Chork. "But, he was quite insistent that only the dogs' master may touch the cage. Once the elf opens the cage, I give him this." He withdrew another letter from his vest.

Pogi frowned at Fat Nat. She turned to Chork and said, "Well, go ahead. I got them for you. They are meant to mark your first year as my squire. A bit late," she raised her eyebrows in a mock admonishment at Fat Nat. "Go on. Open the cage."

"Dogs!" Chork cried.

He raced to the raft and knelt before the cage. Two male dogs, about a year old, slept peacefully in the cage.

His hand shaking with excitement, he reached for the pin that locked the cage door. The moment he touched it, a thrumming filled the air. He felt a mild jolt.

He opened the cage.

Another shock hit him, and the thrum increased in pitch and volume. The enchantment, somehow, someway, connected him to the dogs.

The dogs leapt from the cage at Chork. Their impact drove the elf off balance. He teetered on the edge of the raft. Grasping, he caught the dogs as they jumped into his arms and the three rolled into the water with a shout and yips.

Pogi and Fat Nat laughed.

Chork climbed onto the dock, a dog on either side of him. They shook to dry themselves, spraying Chork with river water.

Pogi and Fat Nat hooted.

Sniggering to fight back the guffaws, Fat Nat approached Chork and handed him Master Timo's letter.

Careful not to let his damp hands ruin the ink, Chork read the short note:

> *Since I can't be there, the minor spell*
> *of bonding will have to do.*
> *Gimlet and Slick will be good friends*
> *if you treat them well.*
> *If you don't, they will return to me.*
> *From Fat Nat and Pogi,*
> *you can learn to communicate*
> *with your new friends properly.*
> *Visit when you can.*
>
> *– Timo Koira*
>
> *PS: Ask the dogs who is who.*

Chork looked down at the dogs and asked, "Which of you is Gimlet?" The dog on the left pawed at the elf. Chork then turned to the other dog. "You must be Slick." Slick wagged his tail.

Gimlet was the taller by a knuckle and the wider by a hand. He was dark grey with a white fore chest and white socks. The tips of his ears and tail were black as night. Slick had amber eyes and tan fur with cream undertones beneath. The tip of his tail was a dark brown, matching the tips of his ears.

Each had a black hummingbird tattooed inside their ear – Gimlet's on the left and Slick's on the right.

* * *

Fat Nat followed Pogi and Chork into the Blue Bolts' tower for supper. When Fat Nat watched Bell walk out, Fat Nat whispered to Chork, "That one is just not socialble." He shook his head. "Mean too."

During the meal, Fat Nat regaled his hosts with stories about his travels up and down the Gold River. Most of the tales drew huge laughs. Some were not so funny and caused Pogi to frown. She questioned Fat Nat when he said that Harley's Peaches, a fierce band of mercenaries, had been seen further up river.

The Peaches traced their beginning to the Goole Orchard Wars, a series of savage and costly battles among fruit orchard owners. To protect his peach trees and distilleries, Greyson Harley reinforced his pickers with a generous complement of sell-swords. This merciless group of thugs slashed and burned their way into Goole history and would have won Harley sole proprietorship of the realm's fruit trade if not for a mule. The beast accidently kicked the drunken Harley to death.

Harley's heirs began their own internal battles and the Orchard Wars dissipated into a few minor squabbles resolved by exchanges of coin. The Peaches, without benefactor, disbanded, except for a core of die-hards. Keeping the name and uniforms, forest-green tunics emblazoned with an embroidered peach, they turned to banditry, kidnapping, murder, and arson.

Chork realized they were discussing the men he had seen on the Bottom River a yer ago. He told Pogi, who grew quiet and thoughtful when the elf said the troop had moved down river.

After supper, Fat Nat demonstrated the hand signals used by Master Timo to communicate with Gimlet and Slick. With the dogs sleeping at their feet, Fat Nat and Chork spent the night on the parapet. They talked about the things young friends usually discuss: family, friends, favorites, and fate. Pogi arrived with the dawn and chased them off to bed.

By noon, it was time for Fat Nat to leave Kent and continue down river. He accepted letters and small packages from the townsfolk to relatives and friends in Monck. Then, Pogi announced she would accompany Fat Nat as far as the western-most farms and return the next day.

Chork was sad to see the young lad leave. In the short time they had spent together, a bond of friendship, without the help of magic, had formed.

Fat Nat promised to return by winter's end. He clapped Chork's shoulder and said, "Watch this, Elf-friend." Just before the river current caught his raft, he took a stone from his pocket and flicked it into the river. The stone skipped 17 times. "Beat that!" he cried and was gone.

* * *

Chork's bond to the dogs was unique, something he had never felt. It gave him an affinity for the dogs, and they for him. He no longer felt alone. Curiously, the bond also affected his feelings about Dame Pogi, Edmod, Aelmar and the other Kenters. He now felt part of something larger. It was like the kinship experienced when he lived in Emig, but more so. More like being a member of a large loving family.

The elf puzzled on it as he walked through Kent with his new friends, Gimlet on his left and Slick on his right. Chork passed the east tower and made for the spot he met Fat Nat. He intended to solve this riddle and to best Nat's last throw while he did so. However, the dogs had other ideas. They demanded attention by constantly nudging and shouldering the elf.

Chork eventually relented. For the rest of that day, he and his new companions practiced the verbal and voice commands Fat Nat and Pogi had taught him.

9 – New Family

The next day, Pogi returned to Kent and found Chork and the Kent Archers on the butts. They worked at hitting moving targets pulled back and forth by Gimlet and Slick on Chork's commands.

With a grin on her face, her bright blue eyes shining, the Dame watched. She nodded to Edmod when he joined her. The Blue Bolt raised his eyebrows and cocked his head toward the Archers. Pogi smiled broadly and slapped Edmod on his back.

In between shots, Marigold caught sight of and drew Chork's attention to Pogi. Chork called for a break in training and walked over to face the Dame.

"Not only did they return," Pogi gestured toward the Archers, "but their number has increased."

"Thanks to Aldrik and Marigold," Chork offered. "They did the recruiting. I did the apologizing."

Pogi looked at the elf with a critical eye. "Show me what they have learned."

"What *we* have learned," corrected Chork.

"Maturity and humility?" Pogi smiled.

* * *

After supper that evening, Pogi presented Chork with a Blue Bolt uniform, saying, "You've earned this." The uniform's color and cut demanded attention to and compliance with its wearer's orders. The bright royal blue coat was purposely broad in the shoulders, tapered tightly at the waist, and flared widely at the knees. Though bulky looking, a snap release of its broad silver belt and a quick shrug dropped the coat to the ground to reveal a snow-white tunic and matching stirrup pants. These form fitting garments enabled quick movements for Bolts adept with either blade or pole.

Edmod and Aelmar nodded and cheered. Barclay made a wry face and grudgingly congratulated the elf.

Chork beamed, thanked Pogi profusely, and promised he would uphold the honor of the Monck Blue Bolts. He asked, "Am I the first elf to become a Blue Bolt?"

"No, there is a thief-catcher in Monck," replied Pogi. "You are probably the last to be named."

With a frown, Chork tried on the uniform. It fit perfectly, and he said so.

"Excellent," said Pogi, "now go relieve Bell so he can eat his supper."

The Last Born, astonished, gaped at Pogi.

"Go on," she insisted. "Barclay will relieve you."

As Chork went up the spiral staircase with his dogs, Aelmar called out, "Stay awake." Edmod chuckled.

Up top, Bell stood watch at the west parapet. Hearing a noise from the stairs, he turned and asked, "Is that Aelmar's roast?" At the sight of Chork, Bell snapped his mouth shut. Then, he scowled. "W-what are you dressed for?"

"I'm here to relieve you."

Bell glared and spat. "She made you a Blue Bolt, eh? W-who's next? Those mangy curs at your feet? Bah! Try not to fall off, Elf!" Scoffing and mumbling, Bell left the tower roof.

Chork watched the surly Blue Bolt descend. The elf wondered why Bell treated him so. No one else in Kent behaved like this. Most were friendly, though Barclay occasionally joined Bell in disparaging the elf. The Robins brothers barely acknowledged he existed.

When Chork had asked Edmod about it, the old Blue Bolt simply pursed his lips and shrugged. "He hates everyone. Including himself." Then, he added, "Has the wrong disposition for a Bolt. 'Belligerent' is what Merriwin calls 'im. 'Too quick with the blade and pole,' Aelmar says. I say he hurts others because he likes it so much."

As a member of the Blue Bolts, the Last Born's days were so busy that he rarely had time to think. Chork took his turn standing guard atop the towers and at the ox pens. He kept order at the inn when barge crews passed through Kent. He responded to calls for help from the few farms and homes surrounding Kent. He still had to do his morning and evening chores; and, he continued to train in the afternoons, as well as practice with the Kent Archers. During all of this, Gimlet and Slick were constantly at his side. They helped when possible, especially with drunken bargemen, crop-eating deer, the occasional wandering ox, and late night guard duty.

When he did have a few moments to think, he realized he was as happy and content as when he lived with his parents in Emig. In truth, more. He did miss his mother and father, but Pogi, Edmod, Aelmar, Gimlet, and Slick were his new family. And, the Kenters, his new cousins, uncles and aunts, helped create his new Enclave.

Moreover, he now had a goal – knighthood. Most importantly, he now had purpose – protecting his new family.

10 – The Bell Incident

On the Last True Day of Winter, Fat Nat arrived, as he had promised. He lingered in Kent for three days. He spent them with Chork, Gimlet, and Slick, skipping stones, fishing the river, and hunting the Wilds. He left with Chork's promise to visit Gruene's Crossovers at spring's end.

On a bright spring morning a week later, word of an overnight fire on a barge train came from downriver. Several bargemen had been seriously burned. Others had suffered from breathing smoke as they put out the fire. Two men had died. The survivors had struggled to salvage a sunken barge and to defend their oxen against raiding wolves and feral cats.

Pogi quickly gathered Aelmar, Merriwin, and two handfuls of Kenters. She rushed off, leaving Edmod in charge.

The day passed in Kent without incident, but the next saw a dwarf barge train from Arilgirn. Dwarves were very good at two things – mining the precious ores in their mountain home and negotiating. They attempted to negotiate the price of everything, from dock and ox fees to the price of the next mug of beer.

Disputes pulled Edmod in many directions.

Around noon, Frank Pandl ran into the village, shouting and waving his hat. He ran right up to Edmod and Chork, who stood in front of the inn, and screamed, "You got to hurry! They took my Maizie! They will skin and roast her!"

"Calm down, Master Pandl," said Edmod. "Who took her and when?"

Pandl said two men, armed with swords and pikes, came to his front door. They offered to buy Maizie. When Pandl declined to sell his only dairy cow, the men became angry. One threw a silver coin in the dirt. The other grabbed Maizie's tether and led her away. When Pandl tried to stop him, the first man stuck his pike against the farmer's belly.

"I ran here as fast as I could." He sobbed. "They'll kill and eat her."

"Which way did they go?" asked Edmod.

"Up river." Pandl pointed.

Just then, an argument erupted between Gerbert Fass and a dwarf about the freshness of Fass' beer. They were near blows. The old Blue Bolt let out a long breath. Too much at one time, he thought.

As Edmod rushed to step between them, he called over his shoulder, "Chork, find Barclay and Bell and three others. Follow Pandl and get his Maizie back."

Chork pointed to three Kent ox tenders nearby. Two had long daggers at their sides, one a cudgel. All three had staves. "Let's go!" He signaled Gimlet and Slick to follow.

They found Bell and Barclay lounging by the east pens. Chork said to them, "Edmod said we should help Master Pandl recover his cow."

Bell looked at the elf and spat. "He did, did he?" Bell stood and picked up his halberd. "P-put you in charge, d-did he?"

Barclay, worried about a clash between the two in front of so many witnesses, grabbed Bell's shoulder and voiced his thought in a quieter tone. "We're not farmers or cowherds or ox tenders. We're Blue Bolts. And..."

"And Blue Bolts should help me get my Maizie back!" shouted Pandl. "Two armed men stole her and threatened my family!" He pointed first at Barclay and Bell. "It's your job, and your job too," he pointed at Chork, "to get her back and to protect us from thieves and ruffians."

Bell's curiosity was piqued. "Two armed men?"

"With pikes and swords," Pandl nodded his head.

"Lead the way, Master Pandl." With a mocking grin, Bell gave a slight bow and waved his arm in a courteous manner.

Within a short time, the small troop arrived at Pandl's farm. They quickly located the thieves' trail and gave chase. Following the river, they heard Maizie complaining before they saw the two men. The dairy cow stood on the rocky bank tied to the end of a fallen tree. On the other end, one of the thieves sat with his pike across his knees. The other stood looking upriver.

Before anyone could do or say anything, Chork approached the men, who now turned their attention to the party. One whispered something to the other who nodded. Chork signaled Gimlet and Slick to sit and do nothing. He said, "We are Blue Bolts from the village of Kent. That cow belongs to Master Pandl here. We'd like you return it to him."

The Last Born eyed the men. They looked to be thrice his age. One sported a full shaggy beard. The other a long mustache that grew down the sides of his mouth onto and under his chin. As Pogi had taught, the elf looked at their eyes.

The bearded man had brown eyes sparkling with amusement. His eyes flitted back and forth, taking in every man facing him. Mustache man's eyes were grey and oozed menace. He focused solely on Chork.

The elf judged the bearded man more dangerous and the leader and addressed him. "We want no trouble. Just return the beast and we can all be about our business." He scanned the surrounding trees, looking for signs of more men.

"But I paid for the cow," refuted the bearded man. "I don't have a bill of sale. Yet, I would wager that the farmer there has a Wurmi piece of silver in his pocket."

Chork held his hand out to receive the coin from Master Pandl. "He told you he didn't want to sell. That cow provides his babies with milk and his wife with cheese." The elf tossed the coin in the dirt at the man's feet.

"He's a baby elf," said Mustache Man. "With a bunch of ox tenders. And two uniformed farmers."

"We are Monck Blue Bolts, in the service of Dame Pogi Becker, who speaks for Lord Monck, the liege lord of this land. You have your coin back. Return the cow."

The bearded man replied, "I am Randal Tibbet. This is Mattin Illorryl, cousin to Ramie" He opened his cloak to reveal an embroidered peach on his tunic. "Do you know what this means?"

Barclay whispered, "The Peach. They're Harley's Peaches!" The ox tenders groaned and took a step back. Bell edged forward, his halberd within easy striking distance of Illorryl.

"No emblem gives you the right to steal," said Chork. The elf could see knuckles tighten on pikes. He had to find a way to ease the tension. "If you require food, that silver coin will feed you for a week in Kent."

Tibbet cocked his head and looked at the elf. He considered that the elf may be right. There would be no gain in killing these villagers. On the other hand, visiting this Kent would pit him and Mattin against more foes.

Meanwhile, Illorryl grew angrier by the second. He sensed that Randal was considering the elf's words. No baby elf and a gaggle of ox tenders could stand up to two Peaches. Bloody hell, they were already quivering in fear.

"Well, Elf, maybe you are right," said Tibbet softly, "and maybe you..."

It all happened so swiftly.

Illorryl spun to argue with Tibbet. As he did, he swung his pike.

Bell, mistaking the swing as an attack, lunged with his halberd. Illorryl collapsed, skewered by the halberd blade.

Tibbet's eyes went wide open. Rage covered his face. He brought his pike to bear, a grim look on his face. He lunged, aiming for Chork's heart.

Sensing his dog's reactions, Chork yelled, "No!" However, Gimlet lurched forward, tripping the attacker.

As Tibbet fell to the ground, his pike tore through the elf's coat.

Barclay rotated his halberd blade and, with the strength of panic, chopped down.

Tibbet's head rolled a pace away from its body.

Pandl vomited. The ox tenders dropped their staves and ran. Gimlet and Slick looked to Chork.

Chork fell to his knees. In the dirt, he saw the silver coin. "No," he cried. "No!"

Gimlet nuzzled Chork, seeking to console him. Slick sniffed at the dead bodies.

Chork took a deep breath and stood. He glared at Barclay. He told him to fetch a wagon for the bodies. As the Blue Bolt ran off, Chork turned his attention to Bell.

Bell had bent over Illorryl's body and was now rifling through pockets. He giggled when he found the man's coin purse full of gold and silver.

Chork walked to him, raised his foot, and half-pushed, half-kicked the Blue Bolt to the ground. "Leave it," he commanded, his voice cracking. He placed the tip of his now-drawn sword against Bell' neck.

"There was no need," said the elf, kicking the man.

"He swung his p-pike at you," shouted Bell. "I saved your life, you ungrateful ..."

"There was no need," Chork repeated. "Leave the dead man's possessions. Go! Leave!"

Bell reached for his halberd.

Chork stepped on the pole.

"B–but, t–there might be others! I would be defenseless!"

"And Kent?" snapped Chork. "You may have placed the entire town in jeopardy."

The Last Born watched Bell scuttle away, then sat on his haunches and worried. If the stories were just half–true, Harley's Peaches could level the town in a matter of hours.

In his mind, he saw Pogi's face when she returned to find Kent a smoking ruin. *What would Pogi do?*

The Last Born tried to calm himself. Yet, with every sound, he jumped up expecting to see an army of pike men charging him.

"One thing at a time," he said aloud.

"Who you talking to?" asked Edmod.

"Myself," replied Chork, relieved to see the old soldier. Edmod led a mule pulling a dog cart. Behind him, the elf saw six Kent men, armed with bows and swords.

"Barclay told me what happened," Edmod said climbing off the dray. "Half proud when he told me, the fool." The old man looked at the headless corpse. "Curse Bell for a bigger fool."

"Edmod," Chork interrupted. "We need to learn if they had companions."

Edmod nodded. "I sent Tyon and Mikel up the road. Told them to go as far as the Big Bend and report back."

The men loaded the bodies on the cart and set off for town. Edmod led the wagon with Maizie tied to the back. Chork plodded alongside, each step adding to his fear and worry.

Late that night, the scouts returned. They had seen nothing.

Chork breathed a little easier, until Edmod mused, "They could be across the river."

Kent boiled with fear and anger. Fear of an attack by Harley's Peaches. Anger with the actions of Bell and Barclay, which could cause that attack. Pandl and the ox tenders, who witnessed the killings, ensured that everyone in Kent knew that the two Blue Bolts had precipitated the current predicament.

Edmod convinced the townsfolk to adopt his simple plan until Pogi's return.

Women and children from the surrounding farms and orchards came to stay in town. No man could leave the town alone. Groups of four to six men went to each farm and orchard in turn and tended to chores. Scouts watched the east and west roads, and up and down river. Young lads stood watch atop the towers night and day.

Bell and Barclay remained in the west tower for their own safety.

The first day passed without event. However, on the second day, anger boiled over.

A little before sunset, Bell said he refused to be caged like a criminal. Defying anyone to stop him, he left the tower to take supper at the inn. He got there to find the inn teeming with women and children. Since he and Fass were the only two men, they gravitated toward each other.

Bell ate his supper, listening to Fass complain of crying children and screaming women. Pushing his empty plate away, he said, "Get me a beer, Gerbert."

"That's not a good idea," replied Fass. "Maybe you should ..."

"W-what else do I have to do?" growled Bell. "Surely, a m-man can have a beer, even a s-sour beer."

"My beer isn't sour!' complained Fass. "I'll prove it." He brought Bell a tankard.

"Tastes perfect to me," smiled Bell. As Bell finished his beer and began another, he scowled at the women and children.

The woman returned his grimaces with glares. The more they glared, the more Bell drank.

Finally, one, Hildie Strumpf, stomped over to his table. "It's because of you I won't sleep in my own bed tonight!"

"Your husband w-will thank me in the morning," Bell countered, and snickered at his own quip.

"Well, I never!" whined Hildie.

"It's plain to see you never w-will." Again, Bell snorted. Anger took the better of him. "Bah!" he growled and stood up, a little unsteadily. "Listen, you righteous p-peahens, I didn't start the fight. The c-cursed elf did. He threatened those two. I saved the elf's life and Pandl's milk c-cow. And, this," he waved his hand around, "is the thanks I get for d-doing my job."

Edmod and a small group of men entered the common room. They had just finished their tour of the farms. They were tired, hungry, and thirsty.

Bell glanced at Edmod, and continued, "But you good folk of Kent do not side with one of your own." He slammed his tankard onto the table. "No, you side with an outsider. Not even a m-man! But, an elf!" He reached for the tankard but knocked it to the floor.

Edmod breathed out heavily and stepped toward Bell.

"Tim and me," shouted Bell, "saved some of your husbands that day! The elf w-would a' got 'em killed!" He tried to focus on Edmod, but his eyes whirled with drink and anger.

"You!" he pointed. "You know w-what's happening! That she-knight chose a cursed baby elf to train rather than a man like me."

"Enough!" bellowed Edmod. He drove the shaft of his halberd into Bell's mouth. Shards of teeth exploded from Bell's mouth. Edmod's second blow dropped Bell to the floor.

Gesturing to two men, Edmod ordered, "Take this drunken lout to the tower. Put him in his bed. We'll treat with him tomorrow!"

11 – A Death in the Family

That night, asleep in his bed, Chork turned and squirmed. In his nightmare, he sat on a throne in the center of Kent, half a bow in his left hand, a wooden sword in his right. Around him, bright red flames ate at every building. Headless bodies lay at his feet. Only Maizie the dairy cow was alive. For every step closer she took, she said, "Elfling." Step. "Elfling." Step.

"Elfling," said Gerbert. "Wake up, Elfling." Gerbert jostled Chork.

With the flames fading and the bodies dissipating, Chork clawed to wakefulness.

"Chork, please, Chork, wake up," implored Gerbert.

"What is it, Gerbert?" asked the Last Born. Irritated he snapped, "Stop pushing me!"

"Sorry. You wouldn't wake. It's Edmod."

Chork stood. There were no dead bodies at his feet. There were no flames. Most calming, Maizie was nowhere in sight.

"Edmod?"

"Yes, please hurry." Gerbert turned and ran up the stairs.

Chork chased the innkeeper through the town.

The sun had been up for hours. Many of the townsfolk as well. They sensed the urgency of Gerbert and Chork. They fell in behind the elf.

Amazingly, given his age and his girth, Gerbert took the high steps two at time and disappeared through the door above.

Chork gestured for the crowd to remain below.

At the top, the lad on watch started to follow.

The elf said quietly, "Stay your post, Roderick. If we need you, we'll call you." He entered the tower.

Edmod, in a white nightshirt, spotted reddish-brown, sat at the table in the kitchen. His right hand lay on the table, his index finger pointing to something. His head, with eyes closed, bowed in sleep.

"I found him like this," informed Gerbert.

Chork blinked.

Edmod was dead. The spots on his shirt were blood from his slit throat.

Tears flooded Chork's eyes. *This cannot be,* he told himself. *This cannot happen again. To lose another who means so much to me. How? Why? Who?* Chork looked at the table where Edmod pointed. The old soldier had used his own blood to write three letters, b-e-l, and the beginnings of a fourth letter that was just a squiggle.

"Where's Bell?"

"Don't know." Gerbert ran down the stairs. After a few seconds, his voice floated up from the bedchamber. "All his stuff is gone. So's Barclay's. And the Robins's as well." Returning to the kitchen, Gerbert, seeing Chork's tears, also cried. Through his sniffles and throat clears, he told Chork about Bell's appearance at the inn the night before. When he mentioned Edmod slamming his halberd's grip into Bell's smart-alecky mouth, Gerbert had a little jealousy in his voice. His tears flowed again as he blamed himself for Edmod's death.

Just then, Roderick sounded the alarm. "Hoy, hoy, hoy!"

Chork looked to the heavens. *No, not now,* he protested.

"Hoy, hoy, hoy!"

The Last Born dashed up the steps. Gerbert, his excitement spent, labored up behind him.

The young lad stood at the parapet, pointing. "Hoy, hoy, hoy!" he hollered again. When Chork drew alongside of him, the lookout shouted, "There, on the west road, a troop!"

With his elven eyesight, Chork easily detected the approaching troop. "Men and oxen," he said. He turned to Gerbert with a huge grin on his face. "One knight, on horse."

"Dame Pogi?"

"Let everyone below know," Chork instructed, nodding.

* * *

As Pogi led her small group into Kent, she was surrounded by nearly every man, woman, and child. Many attempted to gain her ear, shouting over others as they did so. There were pleas, demands, and requests.

Chork remained on the tower stairs, watching the scene. The second Pogi glanced in his direction, he signaled her. "Urgent," the gesture said. "Follow me."

Pogi quieted the crowd with her own gesture. "Yes, yes," she said. "I will hear everyone's story in due time." She dismounted and followed Chork into the tower.

The Last Born said nothing as Pogi descended into the kitchen. He merely pointed.

Pogi let out a soft 'Oh.' Then she began to weep, her soft blue eyes tearing. When she read what Edmod had written, those eyes turned to ice. "Tell me," she demanded.

Chork told her everything.

"Edmod's death is not at your feet," Pogi said, "nor at Gerbert's. Though his pride clouded his better judgment." The Dame let out a heavy sigh. "Bell has long been a problem. His selection as a member of the Bolts was my mistake. I told him I had made that mistake. I hoped it would change his disposition. He thought you were being trained to take his place." She just shook her head. Then, resolved, she changed the course of her thoughts.

"Who leads the dwarves?" Pogi asked Gerbert.

76

"Threfrac Minemantle."

"Bring him here. Tell him I have a bargain to discuss."

Pogi placed a hand on Edmod's shoulder and muttered a few silent words. Finished, she said to the elf, "Take your dogs and find their trail. Do not chase after them," she cautioned.

Outside on the steps of the tower, Pogi addressed the crowd.

First, she told them that Aelmar would arrive soon with the survivors of the barge fire. She asked the Kenters to provide care and assistance to these unfortunates.

Next, the Dame revealed that Bell had likely murdered Edmod. When the angry shouts died down at her insistence, she said that Chork currently sought the suspects' trail. She commanded anyone with knowledge of Bell's overnight activities come forth and be heard. No one did.

Last, she addressed the possibility of retribution by Harley's Peaches. The last word on the Peaches' location, she said, put them on the Bottom River, near the city of Secondbridge. So, the two dead men in Peaches uniform were likely deserters or rogues. Maybe even frauds. However, since Edmod's plan was a good one, she would follow it for at least three more days. This drew groans, mostly from the women and children.

Her meeting with Threfrac was brief. She convinced him to delay his journey downriver for three days. The price was free food and lodging and the prospect of a fight with Harley's Peaches.

Chork returned with news that Bell and Barclay had stolen a boat. He had tracked a left boot (Bell's or Barclay's he could not yet say) with a missing a knuckle-sized wedge on the heel. The unique boot print led from the Bolts' Tower to the docks.

"Downriver makes more sense," Pogi mused, rubbing her chin, "it's faster. But, they knew I and Aelmar were downriver." The Dame called for Kent's best hunters. She split them into four groups and sent them up and down both sides of the river. "Find where they left the river and return."

Later that day, the hunters from the north downriver side returned with word that the four fleeing Blue Bolts had apparently beached and hid their boat after a short distance. After Aelmar and the salvaged barge passed, Bell and the others continued their escape downriver.

Pogi had to make a difficult decision. Sending men after the murderers could cripple the town's defenses should the Peaches attack. Moreover, there was no guarantee that the troop would catch the two fleeing felons, who had nearly a day's head start. Yet, the idea of allowing them to escape was loathsome to her.

She decided her best course was to inform Lord Monck. By bird, she sent a brief narrative of the crimes, descriptions of Bell, Barclay, the Robins's, and a request for a small company of Blue Bolts to replace her losses and to help defend Kent against a possible attack.

As for the Kenters themselves, Edmod's death made them, old and young, face their own mortality. They did so with a solemnity and reservation that caused Chork to reconsider his opinion of men. *They do understand their place in nature,* he thought. He expressed his new found respect by joining them in their celebration of Edmod's life and contributions to their community. These commemorations included hoisting a mug or two at the Smiling Ox in Edmod's honor or a reverent pause in the street with a bowed head and a few teary words. Most often, they took the form of repeatedly embellished tales that soon stretched the limits of belief. These exaggerations bemused Chork since he had witnessed some of the feats as they had really happened. Nevertheless, he joined in.

As for laying Edmod to rest, Pogi insisted they build a cairn on her family burial grounds at the foot of her father's mausoleum.

78

Kenters spent an entire day piling the rock and stone, creating a 10-foot high memorial at which they lay flowers and items Edmod would need to continue his journey. This confused Chork.

First, elves did not cover their dead loved ones with rock or dirt as this would prevent their return to The Only One. They preferred sky burials wherein the deceased was placed high on a hill or even in a tree. Or, they simply left the corpse upon the ground, sometimes covered with a shroud or the deceased's green cloak. In either case, nature's creatures could feed and complete the cycle of life and the deceased's soul could freely complete its journey.

Therein arose Chork's second confusion. He was unsure of what journey humans believed their deceased would make, if any. When he asked, he received varying answers ranging from hands waving off into the skies to thumbs turning down into the ground, and from a description of a lush paradise where all mortal wishes were fulfilled to a terrifying netherworld constantly aflame featuring a demon who delighted in torturing the recently departed.

Nevertheless, after completion of Edmod's interment under the stone and rock, Chork joined the Kenters at the Smiling Ox for a meal feasting Edmod's life. This pleased Chork, who believed such an event honored Edmod and brought closure for him and the town.

12 – The Hunters

Threfrac and his company left Kent four days later. The Kenters, who felt safer with the dwarves' presence, were sorry to see them go and said so. To his credit, Threfrac promised to return from Monck with as many of his companions as he could spare as quickly as possible. The barges, he said, could follow.

That day and for the next four days, Kent held its collective breath. So worried were they, the Kenters even whispered to each other in broad daylight in the middle of the town. Tensions were high and tempers short.

Chork tried to lighten their mood by entertaining the townsfolk with Gimlet and Slick, and the tricks he had taught them. One afternoon, with sticks tied to the dogs' tails, he challenged the Kent children to a game of shinning. Within a short time, Kenters gathered to watch. Cheers and howls of laughter rang out, as the dogs continually outwitted and outran the children, scoring almost at will.

Every night after supper, Chork sat on the steps of the Smiling Ox and spun out tales told by his mother and father. He spoke of Elm and her Blessed Helm, which protected her as she traveled the world and named all The Only One's creations. He regaled them with the story of Katyr and his pet deer. He brought them to tears when he related the love story of Vesstan and Vulen. Their favorite, Mnementh's daily attempts to paint all the trees on Brehm green, caused gales of laughter.

The Last Born had never felt so accepted and so content. He greeted every Kenter with a smile and they returned it eagerly and sincerely. He had made a place in their hearts, and they in his.

When another four days passed, and then a fifth and sixth, Kent returned to normal. Pandl and the other farmers returned to their plows and livestock. Merchants scurried about arguing prices and quality. Ox tenders, after a muckraking day in the pens, sang ribald songs in the Smiling Ox over mugsful of beer. Children played stickball in the road. Men fished the river.

Yet, Pogi, Aelmar, and Chork remained alert.

* * *

Crack! Marigold's foot snapped a twig in two.

The doe jerked her head up from the small stream and bounded off into the brush.

"Shall we chase it?" asked Aldrik.

Chork frowned and shook his head. He looked down at Gimlet and Slick, who waited for Chork to signal the chase. He motioned for them to stay.

"I'm sorry," said Marigold, her cheeks red.

Chork smiled. "Remember," he whispered, "go slow and watch where you place each step."

Marigold Boer, dark-haired with green eyes, had pressed the Last Born to teach the Kent Archers to hunt. After all, she told him with a bright smile, arrows are not just for killing knights on horseback. They could provide meat. Besides, if she brought home dinner now and again, her parents would not complain about the time she spent practicing archery.

Aldrik Fass, a year younger than the elf, hated working at his grandfather's inn and wished to spend the least amount of time possible collecting dirty plates and mugs. Since he joined the Kent Archers, he had lost weight and his pale color. Steady improvement with bow and arrow had helped him find an inner strength and confidence. The loss of both parents in a fire created a special bond between the young man and the elf.

The five companions crept through the trees and brush as quietly as Marigold and Aldrik would allow. When Aldrik kicked a loose stone into a tree trunk for the third time, Chork lowered his head to hide his grimace. Catching a glimpse of Slick's reaction, the elf would swear that the dog had winced.

Suddenly, Gimlet stopped, his ears turning this way and that. Less than an eye blink later, Slick also stopped with his muzzle furrowed and tail tucked.

Chork held up his hand and placed a finger to his lips. Off to the left, he saw a bramble patch with broken shoots. On the ground, leaves no longer lay flat and evenly. The Last Born took a slow, quiet step forward and saw a large unshod, ogre footprint pressed deeply into soft soil.

The elf held out his hand, palm down. The signal spoke to both the dogs and humans. He examined the area around them with care. His eyes penetrated through the tree limbs and brush. Satisfied that the ogre was not near, he let out a breath and looked at his dogs.

Gimlet and Slick sat on the ground, their mouths closed, their tails lowered.

Chork bid Marigold and Aldrik to approach quietly. He pointed to the footprint. "Ogre," he whispered.

Their eyes opened wide in fear. Marigold reached for an arrow

Chork shook his head. He breathed, "The path heads that way." He pointed southwest. "Eventually, the ogre will catch scent of the oxen and turn south." He then pointed southeast. "That way lies the stream where we saw the doe."

Marigold and Aldrik nodded.

"I want you to go that way quietly. No talking. No running." He gave them a serious look. "When you reach the stream, follow it, running as fast as you can. Together. Hear me! Together!"

They nodded again.

"Tell Dame Pogi what we found, and that the ogre is headed toward the pens." He looked into their eyes. "Repeat my commands!"

Satisfied they understood his orders, he waved his hand in a shooing motion. "Go."

With Gimlet and Slick, Chork set out along the ogre's trail. He judged it less than an hour old, and indicated, indeed, that the ogre headed toward the ox pens.

Soon, they entered a denser part of the Wilds. Thick underbrush covered the floor, hiding fallen trees and ruts waiting to trip an elf or dog. The canopy of branches allowed thin shafts of bright sunlight that further impeded vision. Brambles with knuckle-long thorns threatened to shred clothing and skin. In truth, this part of the forest was so inhospitable, that all manner of creatures avoided it.

Chork and his pups followed the trail blazed by the ogre. By now, their noses full of the beast's scent, Gimlet and Slick led the chase. They quickened their pace. Their ears turned forward to catch the slightest sound of their prey. They made themselves look small, crouching as they padded along quietly.

Slick pulled up first. He stopped, his ears turning front to side and back again. He lifted his nose, taking short, silent sniffs. After another step, Gimlet did the same.

Chork stepped beside them. He could hear the ogre, crashing through the vegetation ahead. The elf unshouldered his bow and nocked an arrow. Looking at the pups, he nodded. The three moved forward.

The Last Born realized he had to get close for his bow to be effective. Attempting a shot from a distance, through the brush and branches, though safest, would likely miss its intended target. He shouldered his bow and drew his sword with utmost care. It meant a dangerous close encounter, But, by getting close, he gambled the ogre would focus solely on him, and not notice Gimlet and Slick circling to attack from the flanks.

They followed quietly for a time, Chork wishing for a clearing, no matter how small, in the forest growth. He looked up through the trees and frowned. Twilight began its descent, blurring small branches and casting black patches of shadow. There would be no moon tonight. He decided the time had to be now.

He gestured to the pups. Gimlet crouched low and, without a sound, crept off to the left. Slick slid silently through the brush to the right.

Chork counted to 20 and ran forward. He shouted, "Turn and fight," even though the ogre had no language.

However, the ogre did recognize the challenge in the tone. It turned, spotted the elf, and charged Chork. The massive, two-handed sword in its left hand was nothing more than a dagger to the ogre. It swung the blade, slicing through saplings and brush to clear its path.

Chork countered with a blade swing of his own. It bit into the ogre's right shoulder. Chork stabbed and impaled the creature's right hand. His sword imbedded in the ogre's right fist, Chork turned and ran, and unlimbered his bow. Counting his steps to 10, he nocked an arrow, and turned, ready to shoot.

Gimlet bounded in from the left to distract the ogre, while Slick darted in from the right. As the ogre swung its sword at Gimlet, Slick sank his fangs into the ogre's upper thigh, ripping out a mouthful of green flesh.

The beast bellowed.

The dogs circled.

Chork let his arrow fly. This one took the ogre in the throat and caused it to drop its massive weapon. It gurgled in pain, clutching at the arrow with its now free hand.

Gimlet clamped onto the beast's right forearm and violently shook his head.

Chork's sword, shaken loose by Gimlet's vicious attack, dropped to the ground.

Slick darted in again and savaged the thigh he had bitten.

The ogre fell to one knee, crying out in terror and agony.

In a blur of motion, Chork shouldered his bow, raced toward the ogre, and retrieved his sword. In the next blur, the elf leapt into the air and swung. His blade cleaved the ogre's head from its body.

Gimlet howled in victory while Slick made a meal of the ogre's entrails.

Chork sat on the ground, his pride burning in him. He watched the dogs feed for a short while, and then retrieved the ogre head.

13 − All Is Lost

Now that there was no ogre trail to follow, moving through the forest toward Kent became more difficult. Burdened with the green, hairless head, Chork slashed his way through the underbrush with his sword. It was slow work.

Through the earliest of morning hours, he hacked his way south. Gimlet and Slick followed in his wake.

Suddenly, above and through the trees, he noted an orange glow in the night sky.

"They've set watch fires," he told the dogs. "We are getting close."

A short while later, through the branches and brambles, Chork caught glimpses of the ox pens. A grey haze rolled toward him, bringing the smell of burning wood and something else.

"Just a little further," he said. Gimlet responded with a growl. Slick howled. "What is it?" the elf asked.

He quickly pushed through the last few bushes, tearing his cloak and pants. When he reached the pens, he gasped. All the oxen were dead. He raced around onto the road.

Kent was a burning ruin. The dead lay everywhere.

Dropping the ogre head, Chork ran toward the Blue Bolts' Tower. The voice he heard was his own screaming, "NO!" Over and again.

Aelmar's crumpled body lay at the foot of the stairs, his broken bow nearby. At his side, his quiver was empty. He had used those arrows to kill the men who also lay nearby. They wore dark green tunics with the sigil of Harley's Peaches.

With tears in his eyes, Chork ran across Kent, avoiding the dead and carnage, heading for Pogi's Tower.

The main building fires, which Chork had mistaken for watch fires, had nearly burnt out. They left blackened, smoldering nubs of wood and stone, standing as markers for the dead. Here and there, the heat ignited some fuel and tongues of orange flames leaped into the air with a hiss.

The bodies of his friends lay scorched and charred, hacked and dismembered, bloody and broken. Some, he recognized. Many he could not.

"Elf!"

Chork stopped and turned.

Merriwin led a gaggle of old women and young children out of The Smiling Ox. Black soot covered their faces and clothes. Their wide eyes were full of fear. Several women wept. The children made no sound, but the fear on their faces revealed their thoughts.

Chork ran to them, circling a knee-high wall of dead Peaches. On the other side of that wall, he saw a horror that stopped him cold, as if he had slammed into an invisible barrier. He fell to knees and wailed.

Pogi and the Kent Archers, what remained of them, smeared the ground between the Peaches and The Smiling Ox.

Pogi's bright blue eyes, now dull and lifeless, stared at something Chork could not see. A pale orange-tasseled pike lodged in her armpit. Her white lacquered armor, dented and spattered with blood, sprouted arrows. Her right arm was gone. A war axe had cleaved the helmet from her head.

Chork reached to remove the white lily earring from her ear, in remembrance. However, it was gone, lost when her murderers hacked off her right ear. He took the black hummingbird earring from her other ear and held it tightly in his fist.

Marigold's ravaged body sprawled on the right, her face a red pulp. Aldrik's corpse curled on its side. When Chork rolled it over, it revealed Pogi's right arm, her hand still clutching her black-mithril sword. The elf pried the blade from her fist and slid it into his belt. Between racking sobs, he vowed to use that sword to avenge her death. Everyone's death.

Meanwhile, Merriwin had directed some of the women to find water and blankets. She also dispatched two others to locate a safe place for the children, away from fire and death.

The herb-woman knelt beside Chork. They wept together.

One word leaked out between Chork's moans, "How?"

Merriwin described what happened. Everything, she said, happened at once.

A disturbance broke out at the ox pens. Men were shouting and the oxen complaining. As people began to drift toward the pens, word came of a raft from upriver. Men on the raft called for help. So, some Kenters headed toward the docks.

Then, Marigold and Aldrik ran into town, screaming about an ogre. This drew Pogi's attention. She asked about the elf. Before she got an answer, a flight of fire arrows sprang from across the river. Within seconds, the inn, the docks, and the tanner's building were aflame.

Suddenly, Harley's Peaches were everywhere. At the pens, on the docks, at the edge of the Wilds. Behind Kent. On both ends of the road. On and across the river.

Pogi shouted for the Kenters to run for the towers.

However, the Peaches had already blocked the road. They cut down everyone and anyone, man, woman, and child. They set fire to every building, to every stick of wood they passed.

Aelmar appeared on top of the Blue Bolts' Tower. Every arrow he shot felled a Peach. But, they stormed the stairs, protected by shields, and threw him to the ground.

Gerbert's wife, Eva, gathered as many elderly and children as she could. She led them into The Smiling Ox to hide in Gerbert's secret beer cellar.

Pogi, who had donned full armor for her morning's practice, took a position with some men in front of the inn. Marigold and Aldrik organized the Kent Archers and joined them to set a defensive line.

They held for a while. Yet, outnumbered and surrounded, they fell one by one. Pogi was the last. She took many with her.

Then, the looting began. The Peaches ransacked the towers and the burning buildings. They killed all but a handful of oxen, driving a few upriver. Two squads marched brazenly through the town, questioning and killing the wounded and bewildered.

She, Merriwin, barely made it into the secret cellar. She waited a good amount of time after the last sounds of death and pillaging stopped.

"That's when we came out and saw you," Merriwin said.

Chork looked around, shaking his head. He felt sick that he wasn't here to help. Icy fingers clutched his heart. A hot poker seared his mind. He shook violently and vomited.

Wiping his mouth on his sleeve, he whispered, "I should, I should have been here."

"More Peaches would have died, yes," responded Merriwin. "In the end, though, you would not have made the difference." She placed a hand on his chest. "It was you they wanted. They shouted to one another to find you. I heard them ask several of our," he voice trembled, "our friends before killing them."

"Me?" Chork was stunned. "Why me? What did I do to them?" An idea took hold. "Merriwin, do you think Bell is somehow involved in this?"

The herbalist narrowed her dark brown eyes and pursed her thin lips. She nodded. "Old Marie said she saw Bell in Peaches' green, not his Bolt blue."

* * *

They sheltered the survivors in Pogi's Tower. A few blankets, some fresh water, a small cooked meal of slaughtered ox, and a warming fire were enough to quiet the children and calm the grandmothers who began to think of their dead.

Chork stood watch above. If the Peaches returned, he had no hope of preventing another slaughter, but stand watch he did.

He watched the last few fires die out. He watched the hot embers cool. He watched the smoke and ash drift away.

Mostly, he watched his dead friends just lay there. With his eyes, he saw their mangled, slashed, and burnt bodies. With his mind, he saw those special moments of happiness with each. These images, he placed next to those of his mother and father.

Soon, the tears came again. Not the racking sobs of horror and denial at what had happened. These were the soft, slow tears of loss and pain. Through the night, those tears found and nourished the seed of revenge. By morning, that seed had taken strong root.

* * *

The dawn brought the sun from the east and a company of Blue Bolts from the west. The sun, occasionally hiding its face behind grey clouds, brought no warmth to the elf. The Blue Bolts, who had orders to pursue and destroy the Peaches, helped bury the dead and the town of Kent.

With the aid of a few Bolts, Chork built Pogi's barrow, marked with her cleaved helmet, to the left of her father's. On Edmod's left, the elf placed Aelmar. That night, he slept on the ground facing the gravesites.

Six days. It took six days to bury the Kent dead. Six days and nights of shoveling earth under the waxing Planters' Moon. Sowing not seeds, but bodies.

Who will harvest this crop? asked Chork. He had already decided who would avenge them.

The Last Born rose that morning with a grim purpose. To mark his final farewell, he snapped three arrows in two, and placed one on each barrow to mark his pledge of vengeance. He gathered what few salvageable items he needed for travel, called his dogs to his sides, and took one last look at Kent.

Attempting to conjure an image of the town alive and flourishing to place alongside his other cherished memories, he could only see death and destruction. It was now the grave of the new life he had hoped to lead. To mark its passing, he left what remained of his broken heart.

14 – The Chase Begins

Locating and following the trail of Harley's Peaches was easy. For one, it was a large troop with two laden wagons and stolen oxen. Carving its path through the Wilds would require enormous amounts of effort and time. Therefore, they took the road of least resistance, the towpath up river. For another, the Peaches did not bury their offal and garbage. Bits of food, discarded tatters, and ox dung marked their route as sure as any signpost.

Not waiting for the company of Blue Bolts to begin their pursuit, Chork followed up the towpath with Gimlet and Slick at his sides. Although his first instinct was to run after them since the Peaches were a half week ahead, he walked at a leisurely pace, considering his alternatives. Patience and planning, Pogi had once told him, bring success.

If he overtook and confronted the Peaches, well, that would be folly indeed. The best way, he thought, would be to force a battle between the company of the soon-pursuing Blue Bolts and the Peaches. But how?

He could slow the Peaches' march, not by blocking the path ahead, but by harrowing them at every opportunity. He could attempt to pick them off, one or two, maybe three, at a time. Alternate between the rear guards and the scouts in front. He would have to be clever and quick and plan every move. Most of all, his luck must hold.

He had no guarantee that the Bolts would win the battle. Yet, maybe they would reduce the number of Peaches to a more manageable number for a patient and focused avenger.

Chork quickened his pace, thinking he would overtake the Peaches' rear guard sometime the next evening. However, two hours later, he found a puzzling turn of events.

A wagon sat in the middle of the path. Carrion birds picked at something in the wagon bed. More of the vile creatures also helped themselves to the slaughtered remains of the stolen oxen, scattered around the wagon.

Chork sent Gimlet and Slick to chase away the birds. He approached the wagon and looked inside. Four eyeless, lipless Peaches sat waiting for the vultures to return and finish their feast. The mercenaries' slit throats and bellies spilled soft bits that also pleased the birds.

The elf shook his head. Why kill your own? An argument, obviously.

He slowly examined the ground around the wagon, looking for anything that would tell him more. Using his dagger, he pushed aside the bloody tatter of a cloak and found a boot print missing a knuckle-sized wedge on the left heel.

Excited, Chork got down on all fours and looked for a second print. Failing, he rose and cast a wider net, making wider and wider circles. He found one that might be, but the overlay of another print caused doubt.

Nevertheless, the Last Born believed the one print was enough to place Bell, Barclay, and the Robbins brothers with the Peaches. He became anxious, wanting to overtake the Peaches as quickly as he could. He sprinted up the path, slowed to a trot, and then stopped.

Running into their rear guard would not be a good idea. He calmed himself. I have the beginnings of a plan, he thought. Best stick to it. He refined that plan as he continued up the towpath.

Toward evening, dark clouds dropped a light sprinkle that soon became what the farmers called 'a good dousing.'

Chork smiled. Mud would slow the remaining wagon. He found an abandoned bear cave, sat dry and comfortably between the dogs, and slept.

"If you hadn't chased that ogre," said Pogi, "I would still have my arm."

"And me, my head," said Gerbert Fass.

"And us, our lives," chimed Aldrik and Marigold, in unison.

"And us," intoned the people of Kent.

Chork jerked awake. The nightmare still clenched his heart. It left him gasping for breath, chilled to the bone, sopping with perspiration, and numb of mind.

He cried himself back to sleep.

* * *

"Today will be the day," Chork said to Gimlet and Slick, as dawn broke. The dogs perceived the elf's anticipation and expressed their own with their heads laid low, rumps held high, and tails wagging like tree branches in a violent spring storm.

The rain had stopped during the night, but not before it turned the towpath into a quagmire as Chork had hoped. However, the mud slowed the elf as well as the men he pursued. Twice, he slipped and almost fell. Twice, he slipped and did fall. The second time, he sat in the mud and laughed. The laughter didn't mean he was amused. Rather, it came unexpectedly to relieve some of his nervous energy.

The sun burned as hot as a midsummer's day. Through the morning, steam rose from leaf and twig. By noon, the mud had caked and dried.

Suddenly, there, in the middle of path, sat the second wagon, its wheels trapped by the clay-like muck.

This time, there were no vultures, no dead Peaches, no slaughtered oxen. Just plenty of clean boot prints. They led in two directions.

The larger set, more than five itchoaks, 65 men, went south across the Gold River. The other group continued east. Only seven men made up this band. One owned the left boot with the missing wedge.

The Last Born called to his dogs to follow and raced up the path at full speed.

Hours later, breathing heavily, Chork stopped to rest. When Slick startled him by alerting to something upriver, the elf slid further into the tree line. Nocking an arrow, he waited and watched.

Shortly, two men appeared, trudging along the path. Then, a brace of oxen, followed by another drover and more oxen, plodded along.

Chork relaxed, returned the arrow to his quiver, and shouldered his bow. He recognized several of the men and they him.

"Ho, Elf," greeted Syward Kempers, the lead drover. "Long way from Kent." He raised his hand and waved it forward, indicating the others should continue their march down the path.

Some of the men, whom Chork did not know, quickly moved from the elf's side of the column to the river's side. They did not look again at Chork.

Syward shook his head and spat. "Just ignorant, some are."

Chork pursed his thin lips and raised his eyebrows. "Did you come across seven men walking east?"

"You lookin' for 'em?"

Chork nodded, his excitement barely contained.

Syward shook his head. "Naw, saw no one or nothin', except the backsides of these ..." Syward trailed off, as he pointed to the oxen and the other men.

Disappointed, Chork frowned.

"How's Kent?" Syward asked.

Unsure of what to say, Chork looked squarely at the man. The elf's bottom lip quivered slightly. He licked his lips and said, "I have to go." He ran off up the path, without looking back.

Syward watched the elf go. His brows furrowed. "He can't give me the Barrens," he announced to his comrades loudly, "but most times, he does give me the creeps."

Chork ran because he must. To stop and remember would render him useless. He blamed his young age, his inexperience, his incomplete training. If he were older, more seasoned, and a real knight, he would be able to bury his misery deep inside. He would have told Syward what had happened without flinching. Then, he would have recited his pledge of vengeance and, perhaps, recruited some of the drovers to assist him.

This day, he thought, I cannot add years to my age. This day and the next, I cannot gain the experience needed to avenge my friends with swift and sure coldness. This day and the remaining days of my life, I will not earn the title of knight.

So, he ran from his loss. He ran to focus on what he must now become – a weapon. As cold and as hard as steel. Harder. As hard as Pogi's black mithril sword now hanging at his side.

At first, with each stride, he felt the emptiness within. So, he ran faster and harder. Soon the strides began to fill that hole. Each containing a shovelful of hate and revenge.

As his mood blackened, his eyes regained their focus. He clearly read the prints and clues on the towpath.

The seven men had left the path to avoid the drovers and their oxen. Then, they returned to the path and continued their escape east. They headed toward Gruene's Crossovers, the home of Fat Nat. They were unaware that vengeance followed.

15 – A Respite

Three chilly and starry nights, followed by crisp and sunny days, proved uneventful. The Gold River lazily bent southeast and sharply returned northeast. Locals called this stretch the Elbow where the path split in two. The upriver path, of course, followed the river. According to Pogi's maps, the downriver path provided a shortcut for returning oxen. This track directly connected the wrist to the shoulder.

The Seven, as Chork had begun to think of them, followed the towpath. They were unaware of the alternate path.

Chork faced a minor conflict. If he took the shortcut, he could gain on them, fall further behind, or lose their trail, depending on what the Seven did.

The opportunity to gain ground won Chork over. Taking the shortcut proved right. Where the two paths re-met, the trail of the Seven reappeared. Less than a half-day ahead lay Gruene's Crossovers, Fat Nat's home and, hopefully, allies.

His approach to this small town took him past a large garden of neatly arranged plants he could not identify. On the far end of plot, the Last Born saw a blonde-haired woman, hanging laundry to dry near a small cottage. He decided to ask her if she had seen the Seven pass.

As he approached, the woman turned. She had twinkling green eyes and a pleasant smile. Her shoulder-length hair formed a halo about her head, and not a strand was out of place. Sturdily built, she wore a white ankle-long dress with a bright green bib apron.

"Good day to you, Master Elf," she greeted. In one glance running from his head to his toe, she assessed him and gave a slight nod. Then, did the same to the dogs. "And you too," she said to them. She made a gesture of welcome, which brought them to her side. She scratched each behind their ears.

A little surprised at the dogs' behavior, Chork stuttered his greeting. "G-g-good day."

"Is there anything I can do for you?"

"Maybe," answered Chork, collecting his wits. "I am a Monck Blue Bolt. I track seven criminals who passed this way. Have you seen them?"

"Seven criminals, you say? Hmmm." The woman placed her long-fingered, delicate hand on her cheek.

"Two of the men are wanted for murdering Kent's banner man."

"Edmod's dead?"

Chork nodded.

Yet, before he could remark further, she continued. "Dame Pogi sent you alone, a young elf, to track down seven killers. How old are you, 14?"

"Dame Pogi is dead."

A look of horror crossed the woman's face. "There is more to your story that I would hear, Elfling."

"I don't have time," the Last Born said. "Did they pass this way?"

"Please," she said. "I am Gildona Lingan, friend to Dame Pogi and Bolt Edmod." She removed her left hand from her cheek and revealed the black tattoo of a hummingbird in flight on her palm.

* * *

Chork sat at the small table in Gildona's cottage, a plate of stew and a mug of cider in front of him. Despite his desire to leave and continue the chase, he realized his mouth watered and belly ached. Without apology, he shoveled the stew down and washed its savory taste from his palate with the tangy cider.

98

The food and drink must have contained magic, because he couldn't stop talking. He had begun with his flight from Emig to Kent. He spoke of his recovery, aided by Pogi and Merriwin's care. After a quick sip of the cider, he launched into the details of his training, and followed that with the death of the Peaches at the hands of Bell and provided the details of Edmod's death.

A brief pause, a heartbeat, only noticeable to a learned ear, marked the loss he felt. He drained the mug of cider, wiped his mouth on his sleeve, and pushed on with his narrative.

A short introduction of the Kent Archers preceded his account of his hunt for the ogre that pulled him away from Kent on that fatal day. His detailed description of the lifeless bodies of his family and friends, and Kent's destruction, brought tears to Gildona's eyes.

He picked up the empty mug and turned it round and round in his hands. With each turn, his voice gained intensity as he related the chase up the Gold River, his plan to harry the Peaches, and the divergent trails.

He had talked through the late afternoon and into the evening. Though exhausted from the telling, he had a fire in his eyes. His mouth, set in a grimace, quivered with purpose. He squeezed the mug, trying to squelch the life it didn't have.

Gildona reached across the table with her tattooed hand. "Peace," she said softly. Her hand touched Chork's and she whispered a few words.

The elf let go of the mug. His eyelids got heavy. "B–but," was all he could say before sleep took him.

16 – Two Paths

Something wet and cold nudged Chork's hand. He pushed it away, but it nudged again. Something else pulled at his pants' leg. He kicked it away, but it pulled again.

Irritated, he opened his eyes. He lay on his bedroll, next to the hearth.

Gimlet and Slick yapped their approval.

"I asked them to wake you for breakfast," said Gildona.

"Breakfast?" Chork stood up. "I slept all night? I must leave." He looked about for his gear and weapons. "You cast a sleep spell on me!" he accused.

Gildona smiled. She placed a bowl of porridge on the table. "Eat this while it's hot," she advised. "You can leave after you change your clothes."

Chork looked down at his Blue Bolts uniform. He brushed at its wrinkles and travel stains. "What's wrong with my clothes?"

"Gruene's Crossovers is one of the few free towns on Brehm. Lord Gidric Monck does not rule here. Nor does Queen Terilyn Rose of Giran. Here, your uniform will do you more harm than good."

She walked over to a wooden chest and pulled a bundle from within. "You can wear these. They're Ollie's, from when he was younger and slimmer. You look like you will fit them." She dropped them on the table and sat.

Chork saw a metal brooch pinned to the jacket's breast. It was a black hummingbird in flight.

Without a word, he removed Pogi's earring stud from his pocket and placed it on the table. He withdrew his mother's hairpin from his inside pocket and laid that beside the earring.

Then, he reached into his pack and pulled out and opened the music box.

"Just answer one question," he demanded from Gildona. "Do these hummingbirds mean something more than just my family name?"

Gildona regarded the elf for a moment. She shifted uneasily in her chair. To Chork, she appeared to argue with herself. Having settled the argument, she said, "Sit. Eat. I would tell you of a prophecy."

Her bright green eyes focused on something distant and Gildona said, "On the day the Great Mages opened the first level of the Tower of Learning, Jhodon Rafke, the Council's original First, fell into a stupor while climbing the stairs. Upon revival, he demanded a pen and paper. Never a poet of any skill, nonetheless, he wrote these lines:

> *Then comes the Last Born,*
> > *On midsummer's morn, to mend what was torn.*
> *Near the Fire-Wurm's shade,*
> > *With words and a blade, their lives they do trade.*
> *And, lo, the Last Leaf,*
> > *Overcome with grief, gives birth to belief.*

"I know the prophecy too well," Chork said, an acid in his voice.

Gildona nodded, "Yes, but do you know what it means?"

Chork adjusted his seat and asked, "You do?"

"Maybe," Gildona confessed. "And maybe not. As with most prophecies, the meanings depend on the interpretations. Sometimes, even the prophet doesn't know."

Chork shook his head. *More reason to ignore it,* he thought.

"For this one, there are two dangerous interpretations."

"Dangerous for whom?"

"You," Gildona went to the fireplace and retrieved the pot of oats that cooked there. She filled Chork's bowl, though it was near full. She sat down and set the pot on the table between them on a ceramic inlay.

"The first is the belief that you will avenge the great wrong done to your race, thereby returning to balance the good and evil intended by the Creator. Those who claim this seek to drive you to that end," Gildona leaned forward over the table, "no matter the cost to them and you."

"And the second?" Having lost his appetite, Chork pushed the bowl to the side.

"Those who hope you will restore your race to its former glory. As well, returning the balance."

Chork grunted. "Which do you believe?"

"I believe that choice, or another, is yours," she pushed the bowl back to Chork and gave him a stern motherly look.

Dutifully, Chork began to eat. "You haven't answered my question," he said. "What do the birds mean?"

"The birds mean that you can trust whoever wears them." Gildona picked up the pot and took it to her sideboard. She remained there, staring out the window.

Chork swallowed another spoonful. *She's not telling me everything. What does she hide? Why?* In Emig, he had heard both interpretations. Some professed both. *This is just more of the same.* He snorted.

Gildona spun around. "You have already seen the proof, Elfling." She walked over to Gimlet and Slick and gently pulled backed their ears to reveal their tattoos. "Remember Pogi's earring and tattoo. Your mother's music box and hairpin." She then showed her tattoo. "This means you have those who believe in you, no matter what other beliefs they may hold."

"What if I choose to follow a path other than the prophecy?"

The motherly stare returned to Gildona's face.

"As I said, young one," Gildona smiled, "your path is yours to choose."

Chork finished his oats and walked the bowl to the sideboard.

"I would suggest," said Gildona, "you take the Test of Bowls. Without elven elemental magic, you are but half prepared to walk upon whatever path you take."

Chork's embarrassment turned his cheeks red. At the time he ran from Emig, it seemed the right thing to do. Now, after a year of tutelage under Dame Pogi, he felt ashamed. *A knight would not have run. A knight would have faced the obstacles and overcome them.* But, he wasn't a knight back then. He was a sprout, alone and frightened. He would have been forced to choose a path, both of which this woman said were dangerous to him.

Gildona sighed. "I do not suggest you abandon your chase but deviate from it for a short time. Return to Emig and complete the ritual."

Chork refused to consider her suggestion. He would lose their trail, which was fresh and easy to follow. *How long would I be in Emig? What if they don't let me go after the Test? Do I run away again?* He knew he would. They would force him to choose what they wanted. *My life would be miserable.*

"I thank you for your suggestion," he said.

Gildona frowned. "Your path is yours to choose, Elfling. Do as you will."

She pointed to the bundle of Ollie's clothes. "Now change. Emig lies south through town as do those you chase."

17 – The Only One's Finger

Dressed in browns and grey, with his long hair and pointy ears stuffed under Ollie's old, broad brimmed hat, the Last Born entered Gruene's Crossovers. It was not much bigger than Kent, but it had ambitious plans.

At this point, the Gold River split in two, creating the North and South Forks, both stemming from small lakes, less than half a day away. Three towpath crossovers, built by Cornelius Gruene, gave the town its name.

Two large ox pens with room for 100 oxen sat on either side of the Gold, just before it split into the forks. Next to the pens were two fenced dray fields, areas for securing laden wagons.

The town nestled in the triangle created by the Forks. A black stone inn, the size of The Smiling Ox in Kent, rose from the point. From a few carts and shops, men and dwarves hawked their wares, more successfully to each other rather than to the few townsfolk.

Chork stood in the center of the town, which aspired to be a large market square someday. He scraped his leather boot across the road surface. The crushed stone and sand was packed tightly. In the distance, he saw a black stone keep sitting between the two lakes.

At least five itchoaks of men worked on building a wall around the keep. They used black stones about the size of a small wagon. A portcullis was already set in position and lowered.

Chork estimated the human population to be the same as Kent. He figured the number of dwarves to be half that. Most seemed to be merchants, traders, and lumpers waiting for work. Most wore garb like his. However, in such a small community, it was easy to identify a stranger.

The elf drew more attention than he wished. He declined numerous offers for a variety of items from the hawkers. The lumpers glared at him, thinking he was competition for the next available job.

Chork wanted to find Fat Nat, who lived in a small hut near the South Fork Crossover. Yet, when the elf started toward the lumpers, their glares grew more intense and a few weapons were drawn.

He hurried through the town toward the South Fork Crossover. There, he stopped at a cart worked by an elderly woman selling meat pies. He bought one for two coppers and took a bite. It was so delicious; he wolfed it down and considered buying a second.

"Not from these parts," the woman stated.

"No, good woman," Chork replied, wiping his mouth with his sleeve. "I'm looking for Fat Nat. He's supposed to have a small hut near here."

She pointed to a wooden hut 100 paces up the Fork.

"Thank you."

"Not there."

"You know where I can find him? I'm a friend of his from Kent."

The woman looked Chork over. Her right eye was so milky white that the Last Born doubted she could see with it. Her left was dark brown and worked very well.

Chork looked the woman in the eye. She would answer for a price. He wanted the answer, but he also wanted another pie. He withdrew a silver coin from his purse and held it flat in the palm of his hand.

The woman snatched the coin and placed a pie on his palm. She turned and pointed to a small cemetery across the South Fork. "There. Fresh dug's the one."

"Fat Nat is dead?" Chork was stunned. The dogs, sensing his shock, mewled. "When? How? What happened?"

"Two day ago. A gaggle of hooligans came. Odd way of dressing. All had the same shirts and pants." She reached out to pet Gimlet, who let her.

"Dark green?"

The woman nodded. "Lumpers gave 'em what for, just because they looked funny. Them hooligans didn't take kindly to bein' the butt of jokes. So's, they lit into the lumpers. Beat Brown Jakob and Long Dil bad."

"Afore the townsfolk could get straight, the hooligans lit out. Came this way. Wanted my pies for half what I normal get." She shook her head. "The big one pushed me into my cart." She pointed to a recently repaired wheel.

She paused while she tried to remove the lump in her throat. "Fat Nat, he tol' 'em to leave me be. Fat Nat recognized one-a' 'um. The one that stuck his dagger in Fat Nat."

"A man with broken teeth?"

The woman nodded. "After that, the big one panicked. They ran across and kept runnin'. The town chased 'em a short way. Gave up when they took a few arrows for their trouble."

Chork no longer had an appetite for the second pie. He returned it to the woman and told her to keep the coin.

The woman glanced at his bow and sword. "Gonna kill 'em, eh."

Chork stared into the woman's eyes.

"There's some that deserve killin'," she said. Then, she turned her back to the elf and shuffled her pies.

"Thank you," said Chork, softly. He hurried onto the crossover, his dogs in tow.

Chork easily located the Seven's trail on the other side of the South Fork. He no longer needed to see the wedge shape to identify their trail; he had come to know the other six prints.

The Last Born had no room in his heart for more grief. It was filled with anger and a thirst for blood. He and the dogs jogged along the entire day, stopping once to eat from a small package that Gildona had given him. Meat pies. They were even tastier then the cart woman's.

Toward dusk, Chork stopped. The road ended. It didn't even dwindle off into several smaller paths. It just ... ended. In the waning light, he could see trampled grass and kicked up stone. So, he followed for a while.

When the sun vanished, he decided to rest for the night. He didn't want to lose their trail and need to back track. Rather than start a fire, he just unrolled his blanket and lay down. Gimlet and Slick joined him.

Rolling onto his side, his hand touched a stone. It was smooth and flat. A very good stone worth 15-16 bounces. Chork cried himself to sleep.

The next morning, Chork was up with the sun. He drank a little water and ate some crusts of brown bread, also given to him by Gildona.

Gesturing, he told Gimlet and Slick to go hunt. They raced off. Knowing the dogs would find him no matter how far he went, Chork set out on the trail, which now bent due south.

A couple of hours later, two sounds caused Chork to halt. The first was the return of his dogs. Gimlet still licked at the blood on his snout. Slick's belly seemed to bulge.

The second sound was a crack and a rumble.

Chork turned and glanced at the northern sky.

Massive, black puffy clouds rolled and tumbled toward him. They loosed long bolts of lightning and complained loudly with thunder. The winds picked up, bending brush and branch in their path. Large droplets of water began to fall.

As Chork bent over to scratch Gimlet's ear, something hit the elf between his shoulder blades. It felt like a stone. After several more hits, he became irritated. He looked around and saw white pellets hitting the ground.

Hail! The pebbles soon doubled in size, then again doubled.

The elf dashed for the woods, as hail, now the size of his fist, broke branches and made the dogs whimper. He just reached the safety of the canopy when the hail stopped.

Silence enveloped the forest. The birds stopped complaining. The insects stopped chirruping. Everything stilled.

A massive roar pierced the air, growing in intensity and volume. The dogs howled in fear. Chork screamed from the pain in his ears.

The elf watched, stunned, as a thin finger of cloud poked down from the sky about 200 paces away. His eyes wide, his mouth agape, he felt terror in his heart as never before. He had heard tales about the Fingers of I'ere'er but had never seen one.

The cloud spun, faster and faster, pulling up dirt, grass, shrubs, and, finally, trees. Now the width of Pogi's tower, it bounced, once, twice, toward the elf, then rapidly away.

Mesmerized by horror and wonder, the Last Born stood petrified, unable to divine a course of action.

The whirling funnel lurched west into a field and then twisted violently into the forest. It pulled aged trees and half buried boulders into its vortex and spun them out hundreds of paces away. A tree the girth of Chork's torso landed not three paces away.

The Last Born cowered on the ground, pulling his dogs to him. He prayed to the Only One, yelling until his throat grew raw with the effort. His ears heard none of his plea, only the roar of wind, and the brutal screams of tree and rock.

Then as quickly as the cloud came, it was gone, sucked back up into black clouds overhead. Those clouds rolled south, dropping rain in buckets.

Above him, the sky was clear, as blue as a sapphire.

Chork wandered about the area, still stunned by the experience. The dogs stayed close to his sides, fearful and quiet.

Slowly, the elf regained his sense of purpose. He examined the destruction left by the funnel cloud. Whole sections of the forest were simply gone. Piles of debris lay strewn in every direction.

Chork spent the rest of the day searching for the Seven's trail, unsuccessfully. The following day, he examined a wider arc, beyond the path cut by the spinning cloud. He found nothing. On the third day, he marched south along for a day and turned east in an arc until he arrived back at the site of the storm's destruction. Nothing. He repeated this, turning west. Again, nothing.

The Last Born sat on a tree log, his head in his hands. Admitting he had lost the trail, he became angry. He railed against the Only One, shaking his fist skyward. He cursed Her Finger that came from the north and took the trail from him. Frustrated, he pulled the hummingbird brooch from his chest.

"Where are you now?" he screamed. "I need you now! Where are you?"

His screams went unanswered. No old woman with a tattoo happened by. No tattooed knight on destrier charged to his aid.

Chork sat on the log and laughed – not a laugh of amusement, or a laugh of joy, but a laugh of disbelief, a laugh of hopelessness.

"You know," he said to Gimlet, whose ears twitched, "it appears as if the Only One agrees with Mistress Gildona." He turned to Slick and said, "Maybe a quick visit to Emig is the right path for now."

Slick stared back, his tongue out, his nose sampling the air, waiting.

When the Mother Trees lived, every elf, no matter where he or she stood, no matter the distance, could point directly at the Mother. Since the Mothers had died, few elves retained this ability.

Chork slid from the log. He faced due south. With narrowed eyes, he concentrated. A few heartbeats later, he turned his head slightly, a smidge, to the west. "Emig is there," he pointed. "Let's go."

18 – Emig

Five days later, Chork stood on the north bank of the Bottom River. He had never run so far so fast. He had plowed through fields of tufted grasses and waves of wildflowers, had scrambled through brush and bramble under wooded canopies, and had skirted around giant boulders and brackish ponds.

Although the river was not particularly wide or the current especially quick, he decided not to swim across. He could make it, pushing the bundle wrapped around his bow, quiver, and sword. However, he wasn't sure Gimlet and Slick could. They enjoyed playing in water and often showed the ability to swim short distances. He just felt the risk too great. Besides, the jump from the bank into the water measured at least 10 paces.

He turned upriver and soon found a ford. Once across, he turned back downriver toward the falls where he had lost the coracle during his flight from Emig. The tree that enabled his escape from the ledge was gone. Allowing his curiosity to get the better of him, he walked over to the cliff and looked down on the falls.

The rotting shards of the tree lay scattered on the rock ledge. Yet, now nearly two years later, the tattered remains of a shirt still clung to a withering tree branch. The weight of water pulling at the cloth slowly bent the branch. The shirt and limb fluttered in the white water, as if debating which would succumb first. Both whisked away. As the bit of cloth disappeared downriver, a chill ran up the Last Born's spine. That this happened now, while he watched, left him with a sense of defeat.

Is this an omen? What will they say when they see me? Will they admonish and punish me? Will they make me live with the orphans? Will they deny my right to the Test of Bowls?

He trembled as dread captured his heart.

Violently, he took hold of himself. From his inner pocket, he removed his mother's music box. He opened it and listened to its tune, growing calm, and gaining courage and strength.

Steeled now in his intent, he put Pogi's earring in this left ear. In Elven fashion, he pulled the long hair from his temples back and secured it with his mother's hairpin. Though he mimicked her special weave to hold the pin in place, he also felt the biting clasp of the pin's magic. Gildona's brooch nestled on Ollie's shirt, directly over his heart.

Armored so, he raced down the stream the elves called Aisira. "I am the Last Born," he said to Gimlet and Slick. "I will mend what was torn."

Halfway from the falls to the Enclave, he expected a hunter or scout to shout at him. Halfway again, he wondered why no scout or guard had challenged him. After that, he grew anxious with each stride. When Emig lay just around the next bend, Chork slowed to a walk, apprehension pounding in his chest. He had thought he would burst in, running full tilt through the Enclave, announcing his return. However, he sensed that what lay ahead was not the home he knew. He braced himself for another scene like Kent.

Fortunately, those fears did not prove true. There were no bodies scattered about the Enclave. There were no dismembered limbs, no fires, no destruction.

Simply put, Emig was empty.

Chork splashed across the Aisira, ran past the small boats tied at the bank, and sprinted to the foot of the now dead Mother.

"I have returned!" he yelled. "Come out!" When none answered or showed, he raced to the far end and shouted, "It's me, Chork, the Last Born! Show yourselves!"

From the trees, a redbird warbled, a few sparrows chirped.

Panicked, he ran through the Enclave, checking homes, shops, carved into hill and set in trees. He found no one.

A quick thought stabbed his reeling mind. He tore up the road to his home.

Slamming through the door, he found it as he had left it. The overturned table and splintered chairs greeted him. The scattered contents of his mother's trunk said hello.

He fell to his knees. Despair clutched his heart. Misery choked his throat. Anguish filled his mind.

He collapsed.

It was Gimlet's insistence that revived him hours later. Slick's persistence returned his senses shortly thereafter. Sitting on the floor, Chork placed an arm around each and hugged them. He felt their bond deepen and that brought a gentle smile to his face.

"Well," he said to them, "it looks like it's just the three of us."

Gimlet and Slick responded with licks and nuzzles.

"Let's see what we can find."

Chork used the rest of the day to examine the homes and shops of Emig. After the first few, he realized that his brethren had merely abandoned the Enclave. He recalled the rumors from his younger days about how the smaller Enclaves forsook their dead Mothers and sought to join other, larger Enclaves. Just days before he fled from Emig, he'd heard that of the 13 original Enclaves, only four others survived – the Elven Forest in the west, Ailinmar to the north, and Cenedril and Bria to the east. When asked if Emig would also be abandoned, the Elders simply hung their heads and replied, "Maybe."

It seemed that 'maybe' had now come and gone. They had taken what they needed to travel and little else. Where they went, he could only guess.

The Last Born gleaned a few useful things from the deserted dwellings. Some spare flints, an extra belt knife, a few forgotten coins, a leather bracer, a sturdier water skin, and some clothes that fit.

Two finds at opposite ends of the Enclave made him think that the Only One finally smiled upon him.

The first was in Tanulia's shop. In a back room, hanging on a peg, he found a newly finished cloak. Though a little large for his stature, the green wrap would provide him warmth and cover against winter weather. When he put it on, he discovered that Tanulia had woven threads of magic into its design. Although not capable of complete invisibility, the enchanted cloak would render itself and its wearer difficult to see in forest and field.

His second valuable discovery came at Pengon's workshop. While searching for arrowheads and more of the basilisk venom, he came across a short bow wrapped in a soft cloth. He admired the beauty of its artisanship, intended for hunting game and close quarters combat. He took it, as well as a quiver of arrows with red bands on their shafts, a carefully wrapped vial of venom, and a small drawknife used when making arrows.

That night, he tried to sleep in his own bed and failed. At every instant, he expected his mother to walk through the door and sing to him, as she often did when he was a sprout. Finally, sleep overtook him. A fitful sleep with nightmares of deserted and burning buildings, screaming winds and people. The lines of the old Prophecy wove through all.

19 – A New Old Home

Leaving Emig, the Last Born traveled eastward, because as he said to the dogs, "Going north feels like going backwards. Heading south leads to the Sun's Anvil, and you two wouldn't like the heat. West? Well, I tried that once." Therefore, east he went, but not in a straight line. Terrain, weather, and game runs forced the trio's path to mimic the flight of a drunken midge fly. Once, he even circled, winding up in the exact same spot, scratched his head, laughed, and set off in a different direction.

As spring ended, he realized he had made a circle, east, north, and back around. Mid-morning on the Last True Day of Spring, he recognized the same trees, the same rocks, the same path. On that path, he would swear to all that his footprints from half a moon ago still were visible.

Chork plopped onto a half-buried boulder and huffed, "What magic is this?" He raised his head to the cloudless sky and screamed, "What are you doing to me? Why?"

An anger grew within him. "You have no right! I choose my own path!" With that, he jumped up and took four purposeful strides eastward. "This is MY choice! Leave me to it!"

Off he went, with each step daring The Only One to block or divert him.

This time, Sajura's Moon waxed and waned. In 26 days, he had made a larger circle, east, north and around again, and found himself back at the same spot. In fury, he threw his bow and gear to the ground. He seethed with anger.

In his mind, he lashed out at The Only One. How can this be? Has The Only One reordered the sun, stars, and moon? Am I going mad? Is this my path? To wander in circle until... He didn't want to continue that thought.

Gimlet and Slick lay at his feet, their heads on their paws. Gimlet stood and turned his now full grown body west. Slick copied him.

"Maybe you're right! West it is! Back to Emig and out of this god-made trap!"

On Midsummer's Morn, his birthday, Chork stood in front of Emig's dead Mother Tree.

Nothing had changed except the surrounding foliage. It was greener and fuller. Otherwise, the same bits and remnants of abandonment loitered the ground.

Chork sat and studied the Tree. Once a vibrant brown bark shielded the trunk. Now, a silver, dusty powder of aged death threatened to flake away in the slightest breeze. Once, an explosion of living green leaves glinted in the sunlight. Now, lifeless brittle branches poked this way and that, jagged, gnarled without grace or stature.

Except...

Chork stood and stepped to the left. He craned his neck befitting the bird named for the movement. Another step left. Too far. A half step back. There!

Snug against the trunk about an elf's height off the ground projected the knuckle-long node of a newly sprouted limb. Attached to that tiny bump was a black and curled leaf the size of Chork's little fingernail.

Chork stepped closer and extended his left forefinger to touch the brittle sprout. When he came within a hair's breadth of it, he stopped, worried that his touch would break the leaf. He couldn't bear the sight of it crumbling and falling to the ground to join the decayed leaf pile surrounding the base of the trunk.

If I break it and it falls, will I die? What if it's not me, but another? Maybe there are others.

He carefully examined the Tree, as best he could, given the Tree's height and the light. He began an effort to climb the tree to look at the higher limbs but stopped. He worried that even jostling the tree would detach the dead leaf he had found.

Dead leaf. The words repeated in his mind. Dead leaf. Am I that dead leaf? Am I dead? Oh no, I still live in body. But am I dead to The Only One? Are we all dead to The Only One?

Why his next thought popped into his mind Chork could never understand, but it did. He remembered something his mother had done when a deer had trampled her favorite buttercup, the large one that grew appeared year after year on their doorstep. In fact, he had noticed it flowering as he passed it by when approaching the Mother Tree.

Disregarding the Elders and herb wives who told her it couldn't be done, Gisel had placed the broken flower in a shallow bowl full of dirt. Every day, she had watered it and sung to it. The song was that tune in her music box.

To everyone's surprise, the flower took root and prospered. Gisel returned the flower to its rightful place outside their door, where it still stood this day.

Chork secured a small bowl from the nearest abandoned home. He scooped it full of earth from the base of the Mother Tree and set the bowl aside. He withdrew his belt knife and tested its edge. Finding it dull, he sharpened it on a small whetstone from his pack.

He hesitated for a second. *Will I die?* He dismissed the thought Courage is a knightly virtue.

With care and a smooth stroke, he cut into the Tree. Rather than just slice the nub off, he made sure to cut a shallow crescent-shaped piece of wood from the trunk, all the while pleading for the leaf not to break and fall. He planted his prize in the center of the bowl, giving it some water from his waterskin.

Last, he retrieved his music box, placed it next to the bowl, and opened the lid. The tune played through its length as Chork sang along in a whispering lilt trying to match his mother's melody.

Smiling, Chork carried the blackened leaf to the front door of his home and set it next to the buttercup.

"Our new old home!" he announced to Gimlet and Slick, as he opened the door.

20 – Sick and Lost

The weeks of summer brought routine to Chork's life. He rose at dawn, watered the dead leaf, and sang his mother's tune accompanied by the music box. After a quick breakfast, he hunted and trapped, and observed and learned the ways of tiny and large creatures. At night after a quick meal, he again watered and serenaded the leaf before retiring to his bed.

Gimlet chose to sleep on a blanket just inside the front door. Slick nestled on an old cloak at the foot of Chork's bed.

Summer faded, and autumn's colors exploded all around. Yet, the leaf remained black and showed no signs of growth. Still, Chork did not despair.

"Good things take time," his mother often said while they waited for a raspberry pie to bake. Chork would then go out back to watch the birds sing and the plants follow the sun. The waiting, almost unbearable, would always be rewarded with a savory delight.

As fall marched on, Chork noted the signs of a bad winter to come. Caterpillars were fat and fuzzy with orange bands around their middle. The woodpeckers out back shared a tree. Raccoons sported thick tails. The geese left before Kubarith's full moon. Gimlet and Slick worked non-stop to prevent mice from eating into their home.

Only three times during his 13 years in Emig did the snow come. Twice it fell in the early morning and melted away by noon. Once, it piled itself as high as Chork's 7-year-old knees and remained for two days.

When this winter's snow fell, it brought bitter cold and lingered for days, only to be reinforced by another storm with icy winds. Chork worried about his toes, nose, pointy ears, and long delicate fingers. Mostly, he worried about the last leaf. Its pot now stood on the sideboard, far away from the window's cold but still within sight of the winter sun. Its appearance was the same as the first day he saw it.

Gradually, Chork toyed with the appeal of life-long solitude. He reasoned that since everyone he came to love died a violent death, he should not embrace another soul with his heart. Since his close relationships always ended badly, why bother making friends or acquaintances? Indeed, he asked, why run the risk by meeting another human or elf?

This led him down a slippery slope.

Soon, the Last Born began to withdraw into himself. He shunned what little human contact became available. Twice, circling north to fish along the Aisira, Chork saw men. One, dressed like an ox tender, was hunting a small deer herd. The elf guessed he had wandered down from the Bottom River, watched the man for a short while, and then quietly stole away. The next encounter was briefer. A man similarly dressed was collecting firewood when Chork saw him. This time, the elf noiselessly crept into the trees without as much as a second glance.

As the uncommon freeze of winter lingered, hunting and fishing became difficult and often required he spend the entire day away from the warmth and comfort of his hearth.

One day, under the quarter moon of Cesoren, he ventured too far afield to return safely before night fell. Toward evening, he happened upon a bear's cave and found it occupied. A few well-placed stones drew out the resident. Gimlet and Slick distracted the animal by darting in from the sides. Chork brought the bear down with two venom-free arrows.

With its entrance facing away from the wintry winds, the cave was a warm place to spend the night rather than risking the long dark trek home. The cave's width was roomy enough to sleep the three companions. Its natural flue helped clear smoke and pull in heat from the fire Chork built at its entrance to cook three large bear steaks. After a satisfying supper, the three settled in for a snug night.

Chork awoke the next morning to Gimlet's and Slick's complaints. It was bitter cold, and the wind howled. The three huddled together for a few hours, trembling inside the bear's carcass. After a few hours, the cold relented and the snow came.

Chork struggled through a wall of blown snow to find some wood suitable to burn. With a small fire, another meal of half-cooked bear meat in their bellies, and the bear skin, the three spent the day and another night watching the snow pile threateningly around the cave's entrance.

The following morning dawned sunny and crisp.

Chork felt dark and soggy. His clothes were damp. His stomach rumbled. His head ached. The thought of another day of bear meat in the cave caused him to retch. He emerged from the cave on unsteady legs.

Gimlet and Slick jumped around, playing in the deep, dry snow, ready for whatever their friend desired. Gimlet burrowed into a waist high drift, disappeared for a second, and burst upward with a playful growl and bark. Slick balanced his weight as he tried to dance atop the snow, yipping each time a foot broke through the white crust with a crunch.

Chork mustered a smile and said, "Let's go home."

The elf marked a tree in the distance and picked out a straight line toward it. As he wallowed along, his chin, at first upright, fell to rest on his breast, his eyes half-closed, his breathing labored, his head fogged. At a short bark from Gimlet, Chork raised his head and saw that he was abreast of the marked tree, but 20 paces north of it.

Shaking his head, he pointed to boulder half buried in the snow. "There!" Off he went, his head held high, his watery eyes trying to focus on his mark. This time a yip from Slick alerted the Last Born. He had again missed his mark.

His head muddled, his balance first listing left and then right, Chork continued through the morning, zig-zagging his way toward where he thought his home was. Perspiration had drenched his clothing, even leaving wet spots on his cloak. He trembled. His stomach gave up its last meal. His eyes watered. His head felt heavier than a rock 10-times its size.

"It's the half-cooked bear meat," he said to the dogs.

But Gimlet and Slick were not listening. They had grown quiet, their ears and noses upright in the air, their tails straight out. They lowered their frames and crept forward.

Gathering himself to face the danger ahead, Chork followed and joined his friends who had stopped atop a hillock covered with the tips of tall grasses poking through the snow.

Below, two young children talked and played in snow.

Chork watched as the obvious brother and sister worked to build what human children called a snowman. They rolled a large ball of snow for the base. Then, a smaller sphere for the middle, which required all their strength and height to place above the first. However, the last orb, already adorned with stones for eyes and a mouth and a short stubby stick for nose, thwarted their capabilities.

Chork took a tentative step from behind his vantage. He bit his lip. A tear formed in his right eye. Another followed. Then, one more from his left. Back moved his foot. His head bowed, a frown on his face. The tears came quicker. Turning away from the children and their half-built snowman, the Last Born ran heedless of the noise he made.

Gimlet and Slick gave chase, thinking this was the beginning of a new game or hunt. Their ears and tails revealed their confusion and disappointment when the dogs saw Chork's signals for them to remain behind and not follow.

The elf continued to run, his head pounding, his chest laboring to gulp air. Tears mingled with the beads of perspiration rolling down his cheeks. He began to wonder if he ran away from or toward something. That thought caused him to stop. Crouching to regain his wind, his heavy gasps filled the air around him.

His breathing slowed, but his mind continued to race. Conflicting thoughts pelted his consciousness. They came so quickly and so hard that he felt like a newly planted, single leaf sprout battered by a spring deluge, its merciless raindrops threatening to beat the new growth back into the mud and end its hopes to be a tree.

He felt bowed, ready to break.

Then, three of the biggest, heaviest raindrops hit the budding leaf in rapid succession.

"To be a knight is to serve." It was Pogi's stern voice.

"To give, not to get."

And finally. "An oath you give to yourself."

He had chosen not to help. No matter they were children building a snowman. He had the ability to help. But, he had forsaken his oath to himself when he ran.

Why? To protect me from harm? I help them. We become friends. They die. And I ... I am left with less than I have now. Memories of loss and sorrow. More images to place in my already too full head. Another hole in my aching heart.

Mud sucked at the leaf, pulling it deeper, holding it tighter.

No more images! No more holes! No more tears! No more pangs of sorrow!

The shoot groaned as it bent, stretching its fibers to their tensile point.

Gimlet and Slick, sensing their friend's struggle, had disobeyed Chork's signal to stay and had followed their friend. Gimlet nuzzled at Chork's left pant leg. Slick licked the back of the elf's empty right hand.

To what horrible death do I lead you two? It would be best to end it now. "Leave!" Chork screamed. "Run!" He waved his arms frantically.

The dogs simply sat back on their haunches and stared at him. Their eyes bore into his, saying, "You know we will not leave you. Our bond is eternal. We are as one. As you suffer, so do we."

Chork fell to his knees, an arm around each of their necks. Heavy sobs racked the Last Born's chest. He wailed and cursed The Only One and all the human gods he knew. The weight of his sorrow and misery, the burden of his desires, the yoke of his foretold obligation, all threatened to crush him right then and there. It was more than he could bear. His hand slowly crawled toward the handle of his dagger.

Yes, best to end it now.

Suddenly, pain gripped his hand. Slick's teeth drew blood as they slowly pulled fingers away from the blade. Gimlet, his green eyes admonishing the elf, raised his head to clip Chork's chin. The blow was so heavy and unexpected that the elf bit his tongue and cried out in pain. The elf rolled over onto his back in the wet snow and tried to collect his senses.

Gimlet sat on Chork's stomach. The dog's paws held the elf's shoulders to the ground. Slick's head loomed over Chork's. Slick's amber eyes drilled into Chork's green.

In those dog's eyes, Chork saw something more than sorrow, grief, and despair. He saw love, unconditional love. He saw the bond that held Slick to him in a grip so tight that even death would not break it. The same bond held Gimlet. Chork realized, the same bond held him to them as well.

Its battle won, the sprout jerked upright, daring the rain to attack again.

"I understand," Chork said to the dogs. "I am sorry. Truly sorry."

Gimlet stepped off Chork and lay down beside the elf, muzzle buried deep into Chork's left side. Slick did the same on the other side.

"I'm sick and lost," Chork whispered, struggling to stand. "Lead us home. We have work to do."

21 – An Arrow in the Eye

An early thaw changed the weather. So too, did Chork change.

He abandoned his old routines. By the end of the week, he had recovered from the food sickness. Now, he arose each morning and practiced his sword and bow before breaking his fast. He worked with the dogs as he had on the butts of Kent. To return his stamina, he swam in the Aisira instead of fishing in it.

On the First True Day of Spring, he moved the dead leaf pot back outside and placed it next to the sprouting buttercup. "You are not the path I choose," he said. "Whichever you choose, is now yours alone."

With that, he picked up his gear, turned to the dogs, and said, "Let's go! South to the coast, a boat, and Gunter's Island!"

Their departure from Emig felt like freedom.

Four days brought him alongside a tall ridge, its western slope protected by a dense wall of brambles. The impenetrable wall forced Chork southeast. Several times during the next few days, the landscape thwarted his attempts to turn west, throwing up similar bramble walls, un-crossable ravines, or sheer-face cliffs.

Chork wondered, not for the first time nor the last, if magic forced his march southeast. If he continued along this line, he would likely arrive on the edge of the Sun's Anvil. He said so to the dogs.

Gimlet and Slick had no complaint. They ran and capered. They teased him to follow.

He did.

Two days later, Chork abruptly left the canopy of live oaks, cedar elms, and sycamores. One heartbeat, he was under the leaves. The next, he stood on a strip of ankle-high grass about five paces wide. Beyond the grassy strip, he saw a vast, desolate ocean of sand and hardscrabble, tortured by an unrelenting sun.

"The Sun's Anvil," he said to the dogs. Though he did not intend to set foot on the sand, he felt an urge to check his water skin. Relieved that it was full, he nodded.

The Anvil was home to basilisks, giant scorpions, and the lizardmen, which brought the image of his mother to mind. South across this hostile land, many leagues distant, sat the human city of Wurm, and beyond that, the human city and the abandoned underground Elven Enclave of Qannoc. The Emig Elders said that no elf had crossed the length or breadth of the Anvil, though a few had attempted it.

At first, Chork fancied the idea of being the first. The congratulatory shout of "The Last Born, first to Cross the Anvil!" echoed in him mind. A grunt and laugh ended the thought.

He stepped forward, the toes of his boots coming to rest on the last blades of grass before the countless grains of sand marching into the distance. He turned to the right and left. As far as he could see, the forest trees stood like a fence, marking the boundary between two distinct owners. The grass sward, never varying in width no matter the curve of that fence, served as a warning to prevent either property owner from trespass.

Once more looking out onto the Anvil, with hands shading his eyes, Chork spotted a tower. A broken tower. No, he counted four broken towers, just on the horizon. He stepped out onto the sand. Squinting with his eyes against the fiery, morning sun, he saw other smaller structures, west of the four towers.

His curiosity piqued, he said, "That's not far. We can look and be back here before noon."

Halfway toward noon, Chork shook his head. Gauging distance across the sand was very deceiving. He seemed closer to the towers than when he started; however, he judged he was only half way there. He did have a slightly better view of the smaller structures. Their distance from the larger structures now seemed questionably shorter, given their original relative distance.

Chork stopped and wiped the sweat from his eyes with his shirt sleeve. He focused. Was this a visual deception caused by the heat and sands of the Anvil? Shrugging, he pushed on with the dogs in tow.

Just as the sun reached its zenith, Chork arrived at the edge of a deep slope. Sidestepping down the face of the dune, he lost sight of the structures on the other side. Halfway down, he lost his balance and rolled to the bottom. The floor before him stretched about 100 paces before it rose again in an almost vertical wall of sand. In the center, he passed several oval–shaped rocks, partially covered in mixture of sand and a green sap.

Gimlet and Slick sniffed at the oval rocks and immediately backed away. Chork gave the stones a curious look but thought nothing more about them.

Tiring, Chork crawled on all fours up the opposite face for what seemed an interminably long time. Nearing the top, he heard shouts and paused. Looking up, he saw the very tops of the four broken guard towers. Then, a huge shower of loose sand cascaded over the rim and pushed him backward the length of his body. He scrambled back up and pushed his head over the dune's brim.

He saw a frightening scene.

A massive green lizard swung its long black-and-green-striped tail at a wagon, smashing it and its cargo to kindling. Mules broke their leads and harnesses and galloped this way and that. The beast's long, stiletto tongue flicked out, encircled a mule, and pulled it whole into a maw with saw-like teeth. The other animals, struggling against the loose sand, disappeared over the next dune.

To Chork's left, five men and four mule teams ran toward the nearest tower and, hopefully, safety.

A bare-chested and tattooed man shouted and poked the lizard with a trident. He was crushed for his effort. Another man, in a chain mail shirt, tried to whack the beast's tail with a large war axe. A flick of that tail sent him into the air to land 20 paces away broken and lifeless.

The basilisk, for that was what it had to be, was olive green in color, as long and thick as the damaged wagon and the eight mules that had been pulling it. Slightly above and between its protruding, revolving eyes, it had a large dirty-white spike. High fin-like crests ran down its back. Its skinny fore legs were shorter than its thick hind legs, which sported large feet with flaps of skin between its toes. Its red tongue was long as its tail. A kiss from the tip of that tongue injected venom that was always fatal.

Chork, nearly frozen with fear, watching in horror, began to reach for his bow.

Two archers, with arrows nocked, tried to work their way around the lizard, possibly to shoot at its eyes. However, when the basilisk faced them, they turned to run. Two strides were all they took, before sharp teeth bit them in half.

From the lip of the dune, Chork pulled his bow from the protection of his bedroll and strung it. From his quiver, he pulled two orange-banded arrows, the ones with shelob venom. He nocked one and paused.

He wondered aloud to Gimlet and Slick, who crouched to either side, "Will venom from a spider kill it?" When the dogs returned a blank stare, Chork shrugged and said, "Now is a good time to find out!"

As the elf rose above the edge of the dune, he saw a man confront the basilisk. The man wielded a rusty two-handed sword. He wore breast and back plates strapped together over his shoulders and at his sides.

As the basilisk's tongue shot toward him, the man sidestepped and swung his sword.

He missed!

The force of his swing turned the man's back toward the beast. Its tongue slammed into the back plate, not penetrating, but sending the man face first into the sand.

As the lizard bent to devour this morsel, Chork, his heart pounding, loosed his arrow and nocked the second. The arrow pierced the basilisk's right eye dead center, nearly driving its entire length into the soft tissue. Only the fletching remained visible.

The beast reared up on its massive hind legs and opened it mouth wide in a mock scream, uttering no sound. Its front legs unsuccessfully tried to paw at the eye. Its head thrashed back and forth.

Chork, his bow drawn, looked for an opportunity to shoot again. He didn't need to let the second arrow fly.

With a death rattle, the basilisk collapsed, sending a massive cloud of sand into the air.

Faint cheers erupted from the direction of the nearest tower.

As the cloud of sand settled, the man who had swung the sword coughed. He fought to get his legs under him, but only kicked up more sand which caused him to cough and choke.

Chork grabbed the back plate's edge at the man's nape and, with an audible effort, lifted the man a hand's width upward. It was just enough to allow the man to get his hands and arms underneath to push himself erect.

"Thank you, sir, thank you, indeed," the man said. "You are definitely ..." The man recognized Chork's elven features. "An elf!" he finished. He quickly withdrew his hand from Chork's grasp.

"Yes, I am," Chork flatly replied. "The elf who saved your life."

22 – The Trail Recovered

The man was Sa'Mael 'al Jusur, a Fili merchant and owner of the caravan. He had three noticeable characteristics – watery blue eyes, a red bulbous nose, and an enormous round belly. As he continually apologized for his initial insensitivity and thanked Chork for "saving my worthless life," Sa'Mael's eyes watered more, his nose grew redder, and his belly threatened to burst the straps holding the armor plates.

Despite his huge belly, Sa'Mael ran to his drivers, who emerged from the safety of the towers. The large merchant appeared genuinely more concerned for his surviving drivers than for his goods. He clapped brothers Rafa and Jafa on their backs, gave Little Herve a massive hug, punched Bear as hard as possible in the arm, and scolded Bowlegged Bob for taking so long to run to safety. Then, Sa'Mael introduced his drivers to the elf, who greeted each and patiently accepted their pats, claps, handshakes, and promises of lifelong devotion.

While the drivers examined the dead basilisk, Sa'Mael took Chork by his arm and pulled him aside. He explained that five of the wagons (only four still stood intact) in his caravan carried rough-cut, cherry wood planks from Giran. In Wurm, the planks were worth more than everything Sa'Mael had before traded in his lifetime. This deal would have made him a very wealthy man, not that he wasn't already.

The sixth wagon had carried food supplies and water barrels. The smell of water aroused the basilisk from its slumber and lured the beast from the same arroyo whence the elf appeared.

Sa'Mael said the basilisk attacked so quickly and so violently, he and his crew had no time to react. The beast went straight for the supply wagon and demolished it, immediately killing the driver, poor Lemmy. The basilisk briefly turned its attention to the six frightened mules, freed by the wagon's destruction; but the caravan guards gathered their courage and attacked the beast. The mules escaped by running off as a team into the desert.

"I was about to end the beast's rampage, when you appeared," Sa'Mael said, sheepishly. "And, well, thank you again."

Chork smiled and walked over to the wagons. They sat on a hard scrabble mixture of stones, sand, and some other white material like that in Gruene's Crossovers. The Last Born scooped a handful of the substance and examined it. To his horror, the scrabble contained crushed bones! He showed it to the merchant.

Sa'Mael did not know who had built this road or when. He had learned of it only a month before from a trader in Giran. The woman claimed it was built a 1,000 years ago by the Wurmi army to supply and reinforce the four guard towers. Why the towers were there, the woman couldn't or wouldn't say. Sa'Mael had decided to use the road, rather than his usual route, because it would reduce his travel time by two days. He vowed he would never use it again.

"Listen," said Sa'Mael, tapping the road with the sole of his boot. "This road leads to a small town, Boerne by name, just a day's march from here. There," he pointed west. "I have a modest residence. "We'll never recover the mules and," he lowered his head and made a sad face, "well, there are only two guards to bury. Neither with families."

"Did any of your guards have broken teeth?" Chork interrupted, thinking it was worth the chance.

Sa'Mael furrowed his brow. "No, why?"

Chork shook his head.

Sa'Mael shrugged and continued, "Look, we're not fighting men. We could use one such as you, a Slayer of Basilisks. I can pay you handsomely to escort us safely to Boerne." The merchant withdrew a hefty purse from the belt hiding under his belly. "I'll pay you all of the wages due my former guards."

The Last Born's immediate thought was to decline Sa'Mael's offer. He felt he had done enough and should not get further involved with these humans. Yet, they were headed in the same direction as he – south.

Chork's gaze ran across the weapons the drivers carried. A belt knife with a nicked blade and cracked handle. Two smaller cudgels best used for rapping the heads of older children who tried to cut your purse strings. A short dagger with bent blade and curled tip used to pry open a locket or small chest. A club with a rusty nail through its head had seen the most use and was the most useful of the lot. But not against basilisks nor scorpions. Especially not against lizardmen wielding pikes, shields, and scimitars.

Left alone, these six would be nothing more than belly food for the first desert denizen to find them. It would be kinder to end their lives here.

Chork closed his eyes as Pogi's words came to him. "Knighthood is not all waving swords and jabbing boar spears. It is a way of life. A map one must follow without diversion. Set one foot off the path and you could be lost forever."

'Lost forever ... forever ... ever' echoed through the Last Born's mind. I don't want to be lost forever.

* * *

Though Chork agreed that following the road may provide the most direct path to Boerne, he believed it wasn't the best or fastest route to safety. To avoid the risks of another basilisk and scorpions, he insisted they take a direct route westward toward the nearest tree line. Once they left the desert, they could turn south and recover the shortcut or the usual road to Boerne.

When Sa'Mael agreed, Chork directed the drivers to secure the dead guards' weapons and as much water from the wagons as they could carry. When they asked about food, the Last Born permitted them to gather enough for one meal.

While the men complied with the elf's suggestions, Rafa and Jafa located one of the stray mules, which trebled the group's load capacity and doubled its speed. The mule's scent worried Chork. It could attract another basilisk.

After some lengthy hand signals from Chork, Gimlet and Slick, who had noses for water and for plants storing water, left the road and set off for the nearest edge of the desert. One elf, six humans, and one mule followed in their wake.

Their trek across the hot sands did attract a giant scorpion, a young one about the size of the mule. But, while the dogs provided distraction, Chork's arrows dispatched the creature.

The encounter prodded them to double their speed and by sunset, the small group reached the edge of the Sun's Anvil. There, they stopped briefly for food and rest. Hours later, they saw Boerne's dim glow on the horizon.

As they neared the town, Sa'Mael stepped into the lead. He led them through a guarded gate in a chest-high wall, across a small courtyard, and into a building slightly larger than Gerbert's Smiling Ox.

* * *

Chork, tired from the long day, found himself in a large room with a large bed, a dining area for three, a comfortable sitting area, and a work table stained from repeated use. Gimlet and Slick lay on the floor with huge mutton joints trapped by their front paws.

A short, bald man in livery bowed and said, "Rabb Sa'Mael begs your indulgence and hopes this room is sufficient for your needs."

When Chork realized the man awaited his reply, the Last Born nodded.

"Most excellent, Rabb Elf." The man bowed again and then waved his arm. Two stout fellows dressed in the same livery entered carrying a large metal tub, followed by a line of lads toting buckets of hot steamy water. "Rabb Sa'Mael prays you will enjoy your bath, followed by a light dinner, and a pleasant night's sleep. He begs your company at breakfast at first light."

With that, the man bowed for the last time and departed. The stout fellows gently placed the tub in the middle of the floor, bowed and left. The lads filled the tub with water, bowed, and left. Lastly, two young maids placed a flagon of wine and platters of meat, bread, and fruit on the dining table. They bowed and left, leaving Chork with his mouth agape in the center of the room.

* * *

The Last Born awoke clean, fed, and rested the next morning to the sound of his gear hitting a wooden table top. Gimlet and Slick, each gnawing on a large bone of venison, ignored the noise and the man who made it.

The bald man apologized, "Pardon, Rabb Elf, I am clumsy this morning. Everything is cleaned and repaired, Rabb Elf. Rabb Sa'Mael bid we burn your old clothes and provide you with these." The servant bowed.

"What does 'Rabb' mean?" asked Chork. "In the Common Tongue."

The man in livery creased his brows and pursed his lips. His eyes and mouth opened wide in horror. "Oh no, Rabb!" He dropped to a knee and said, "A term of deep respect, Rabb. Please, I mean no insult."

Chork touched the man's shoulder and urged him to stand. "It is I who should apologize for frightening you. Thank you for cleaning my clothes and repairing my gear."

Still flustered, the man nodded.

Dressing, Chork said, "Master Gerbert could have learned a thing or two about running the Ox Inn from you."

Again, the man nodded. He waved his arm toward the door. "Rabb Sa'Mael awaits your pleasure in his private breakfast nook. I am to escort you when you are ready."

Chork forsook his morning practice, dressed quickly and followed the man through the building to another wing. He watched as men and women in the same livery tended to morning chores, polishing, sweeping, organizing, and carrying various trays and gear. With so much activity, the elf surmised the inn was full. He entered a small room with an enormous eastern facing window. The sun, a fiery red ball, had just crested a balcony railing.

Sa'Mael, sitting at a table for two, looked up from a scattering of papers and said, "Ah, finally, the Slayer of Basilisks who saved my life!" He gathered the papers into a neat stack and handed them to a man at his elbow. "We'll finish this later, thank you." He gestured to Chork. "Come, let's eat and discuss today's plan." He turned to the bald man, "Mahdi, you may serve us now."

The Last Born took the seat opposite Sa'Mael. He was startled when a young lass placed a square of white cloth on his lap, followed by a gaggle of young boys who deposited plates of bacon, bread, and orange and green fruit on the table.

"Dig in!" exclaimed Sa'Mael laughing. "We'll talk as we eat." Whereupon, he loaded his plate with a full rasher of bacon. "What do you think of my modest residence?"

Chork nearly choked, which drew a chuckle from Sa'Mael. The elf jumped to his feet and bowed his head. "I had no idea, my lord."

"No, no, no! Not a lord! Just a moderately successful merchant. Sit down! Break your fast while I make my proposal." Sa'Mael reached into his voluminous green robe, extracted a small sack, and dropped it on the table with a loud clunk. "What I promised for escorting me home."

"You needn't ..."

"Tut, tut. I promised, and you earned it. You can earn twice as much again should you accept my offer." He picked up a huge slice of the orange fruit. Around a healthy bite, he said, "Melons from the Moon's Quench. They just arrived this morning. Try some."

Chork bit into a small piece of the orange pulpy fruit, enjoyed what he tasted, and gobbled it and another piece.

"I want you to help me recover my cherry wood. You may choose as many men and mules as you think you will need from my household, lead them to the site of the basilisk's attack, secure the wagons, and bring them back. For this, I will pay you twice that," he pointed to the sack of coins on the table. "And," he paused for effect. "When you return every plank, I will offer you the position as my chief caravan guard, the former now residing in the basilisk's stomach. As such, you will be due a modest portion of the profits from each van you lead. I have been looking for someone with your capabilities for a long time."

With a full mouthful of the green melon, its juice dripping down his chin, Chork was dumbfounded. He chewed and swallowed. "Sa'Mael, you ... I ... it ..." Then, he slowly shook his head. "Let me explain who and what I am."

The Last Born spun out his tale from when he first left Emig to his brief training as a knight, from his hunt for Bell to right now.

He reminded Sa'Mael of his young age and his inexperience. Most importantly, he spoke of his desire to reach Gunter's Island.

Sa'Mael was not one to be so easily diverted or discouraged. "Twice as much again for all," he insisted. When Chork shook his head, Sa'Mael countered, "We'll hire one of these White Lilies to help you complete your training. It's a wise investment." The merchant leaned in closer. "I know this, uh, soldier. Trained at the Onesill Medraza in Qannoc. He has a knack for finding the one sought, though he doesn't come cheap. As well, I would hire him to find this Bell for you."

Chork smiled and politely refused. "Sa'Mael, no. I must move on. I truly thank you ..."

The offers and denials continued as the sun climbed into the sky, tiring Chork and frustrating Sa'Mael. Finally, Chork, near mental exhaustion, agreed to lead an expedition to recover Sa'Mael's cherry wood planks. "However," the Last Born disclaimed, "once I recover the wagons, I'll move on."

Sa'Mael, hoping he could later persuade the elf to take the job, agreed to Chork's offer. "Then rest today. Enjoy my hospitality. I need time to organize such a large party of men and mules."

Chork spent the remainder of the day with the basilisk attack survivors. He let them show him the benefits and comforts of Sa'Mael's employ but did not succumb to such an obvious tactic. When Little Herve (who wasn't little and named for his father) invited Chork to join the guards for dinner, the elf readily accepted, thinking that it would be more enjoyable than listening to Sa'Mael's continued proposals of employment.

Rather than sup in their mess at the manse, the guards took Chork to a tavern called The Dodging Drayman. The food and clientele were exotic to Chork. He enjoyed roast lamb, chickpeas, spicy olives and red peppers, flavored goat cheese, and a flaky pastry drizzled with day-old honey. His mouth agape, the elf watched dancers in sheer veils shake themselves while performing wondrous feats of contortion.

As the evening ended, Bowlegged Bob asked Chork, "Did I hear you ask Rabb Sa'Mael about a man with broken teeth?"

Chork, startled, gathered his composure and replied, "Yes. Did you see him?"

Bob picked up a frayed stick from the table and cleaned his teeth before answering. "Maybe. In a small town on the way down from Giran. Bear! What was the name of that sheep town?"

Bear drained his mug and sat it down in front of him. "Which one? There were four."

"The one with the wide fields, in a bowl."

Little Herve snickered. "Which one. There were three!"

The guards laughed and ordered one last round of drinks.

"What did the town look like?" pressed Chork.

"Like a sheep town!" deadpanned Bob. This drew hoots and guffaws.

"Where? Can you tell me how to get to it?" Chork grabbed Bob's arm.

"Careful, Chork, that's my drinking arm."

"Don't touch the other either," advised Little Herve, "you don't want to know what he does with that one!"

This jest made Bear spray his mouthful of wine across the table. The others erupted in laughter.

"No need for a bath tonight!" announced Jafa, who had taken the worst of it.

The jests and jibes continued until the guards got up to leave.

On the way out of The Dodging Drayman, Chork said, "Please, Bob, I need to know where you saw this man."

"You recall that road in the desert?" When Chork nodded, Bob continued, "Well, you follow that north across the Anvil's Top.

That's the road that sits along the edge of the Anvil just inside the woods."

He stopped to think for a moment and shook his head. "There's four, maybe five or six small sheep villages. He was in one of those. I remember him arguing with an old shepherd about crossing the road in front of him. Looked like he, the man with broken teeth that is, was ready to hit the old man. I was thinking about stepping in, but Sa'Mael was shouting orders about moving on."

* * *

The next day at mid-morn, Chork led a large caravan of 50 men and 50 mules onto the Sun's Anvil. They arrived the next day at the site without incident and found the wagons of cherry wood untouched. The supply wagon had been destroyed. Of the basilisk, only the bones remained, already picked clean by vultures and scorpions.

The elf, full of curiosity, stepped to the edge of the dune he had climbed and looked down expecting to see the strange rocks at the bottom. They had been replaced with what looked like broken shards of large vases.

"Eggs," said Rafa, standing by his side. "Basilisk eggs. She was a female protecting her young. I doubt they survived without her."

Chork merely grunted, but inside, a pang of sorrow touched his heart.

Bowlegged Bob, Bear, Little Herve, and Jafa joined the two at the dune's edge.

"You're going to look for that man with broken teeth, right?" asked Bear.

"I must," answered Chork. "I gave my word."

"Sa'Mael said you would," said Bob.

"You told him?"

"Yeah, I'm sorry if it was the wrong thing to do."

Chork pursed his lips. "No, I should have told him."

"He said to give you this." Herve handed Chork an oversized coin.

Chork hefted the coin and examined it. On its face was the likeness of a man with a large nose – obviously Sa'Mael. A bridge joining an anvil and a bucket was on the reverse. The anvil represented the Himari, nomads from the Sun's Anvil. The bucket symbolized the Fili, farmers from the Moon's Quench. The bridge embodied their alliance to form the city-state of Wurm.

Showing this coin, Herve said, to any Himari or Fili merchant anywhere on Brehm would introduce Chork as a trusted friend and obligate the merchant to assist the elf with any matter. Though not currency of any realm, Herve cautioned, the coin's value was priceless and should be used sparingly and wisely. "These are not freely given," Herve said. "Sa'Mael must have a special place in his heart for you."

"As we all do," said Rafa. The others voiced their agreement.

"And I, you," Chork said, touching his breast.

"So," Chork added after a moment, tucking the coin in his pants pocket. "Herve, I guess he told you to take charge?"

Herve nodded.

"Then Sa'Mael has found his new chief guard." He clapped the man on the shoulder. "Listen well to your new leader."

23 – New Boots & an Old Foe

Chork shaded himself from the autumn sun in a copse of acacia, oak, and eucalyptus trees. He contemplated the odd-looking coin that Little Herve had given him 18 days ago. He wondered about where and when he would use it. What would happen if he presented it to Sir Gunter Taafe? Would the Knight Commander take Chork under his wing and train him?

Reacting to a pain in his left foot, Chork scowled. "Maybe I should use it get a new pair of boots!" he said to Gimlet and Slick, who stood in the shade of an acacia, their tongues rolling out and in to cope with the heat.

Chork returned the coin to his inner pocket to hold it safe and secure. With a grunt, he removed his left boot and examined the sole of his foot. He gingerly poked at a rough red callus that had grown larger each day from the widening hole in the boot's sole. Each touch sent a spike of pain up his leg.

Eighteen days! The first six, he ran from dawn to dusk and saw no town or village. The middle six, he took at a jog and came across two clusters of four buildings each, hardly deserving of the title of hamlet, let alone town or village. The last six days, he had walked and then limped through three towns. Each had been a sheep town, but not one had a cobbler or a man with broken teeth. For the former, they suggested he continue north. For the latter, they shrugged.

With a blow of air and a shaking head, Chork wrapped a dirty white cloth around the foot and replaced his boot. He said to the dogs, "If only I had sturdy pads like you. Alas, I must be shod."

Chork stood, "I fancy brown leather, not cord wain. A knee-high pair with waxed-flax double stitching. As well as a thicker sole. For that, you need a cobbler of some skill. I'm told that the one in Little Creek below is one of the best."

The dogs yipped and wagged their tails in eagerness to run down the hill into town.

Little Creek rested where its namesake stream met Shepherd's Lake in the foothills of the Aril Mountains. Its inhabitants had two main interests, sheep and wolves. To protect the former, Little Creek inhabitants paid a handsome bounty for pelts of the latter.

The elf studied the town's layout. He immediately had the impression of looking down into a bowl from its rim. Vast meadows dotted with shepherds' huts and flocks gently sloped toward the town. In the bowl's bottom, small wood and stone structures stood along both sides of the creek which flowed toward a hodgepodge of wooden docks providing access to the lake. Nestled in the crooks of the 'L-shapes' formed by the buildings and the docks, large corrals held flocks of straw-colored sheep, waiting their sheering or slaughter.

Occasionally, a dog barked, ordering a stray to return to its fold. Once, off to the left, a snarling, growling dog dashed up toward the bowl's rim, presumably driving off a curious wolf. In the town, two women strolled from one building to another. On the docks, a handful of men lounged, dangling unshod feet in the water.

Rubbing the pain from his injured foot, Chork sighed. "Just down the hill and into the town," he said aloud to Gimlet and Slick. They sensed the pain in his voice. Gimlet whimpered in sympathy. Slick wagged his tail and started down the hill. Chork limped in pursuit. Gimlet followed beside him.

The Last Born stopped in front of small wood building. He read a neatly lettered sign nailed to the wall, 'Bounty – 1 silver for 1 wolf pelt.' Hastily scrawled underneath was 'by order of Master Avery Kobs, Mayor.'

This puzzled Chork, remembering that, since its civil war, Giran had been ruled by queens. According to Pogi, this concept of matriarchal power extended down into every fief, town, and hamlet. No man could hold title or wield the power of office. Certainly, Little Creek sat in the influence of the Rose Crown.

Two men, sitting on the building's wooden porch, stared blankly at Chork for a moment. Then, the one in brown rose and sauntered over to the door, opened it, and said something to someone inside.

A short, thin, balding man emerged from the building, eating an apple. He looked at Chork, burped, and tossed his apple core aside. "You have business here, Elf?" He examined Chork from head to toe and spat.

"The cobbler," answered Chork. He raised his damaged boot to show the man. "You the mayor?"

"Aye, he is," growled the man in brown. "Not that it matters to you,"

"Oh, but it does, Rollo," said Kobs. "Those look like wolves to you?"

"They're dogs," Chork quickly interjected. "A present from Dame Pogi Becker of Kent."

"A present or stolen," snapped Kobs, "get your boots and get out a town. We don't need your kind lollygagging here abouts. Get my drift?" He pointed down the street. "Cobbler's there. Be quick about it."

Chork had faced this attitude once or twice in the previous towns. He knew he had no choice but to do as the man said. Anything other would result in a fight and no new boots. He smiled and nodded, "Yes, Mayor Kobs. Right away, sir."

The two men, now standing to each side of the mayor, their hands on cudgels, chuckled.

Chork quickly walked down the street and found the cobbler. In the front window, he saw his new boots.

"Wait here," he told Gimlet and Slick, extending his hand palm out and pointing to the ground.

To Chork's delight, the boots fit near enough. They would need a few days to learn his feet and would punish the elf for having to do so. Yet, in the end, they would submit. Their lessons began immediately.

Newly shod, a gold and silver coin lighter, Chork emerged from the shop, admiring the boots. Gimlet's low growl caused him to stop short and frown.

Another man had joined the two from Kobs' place. They teased the dogs by feigning lunges at them. When the dogs flinched, the men laughed. A few townsfolk had gathered to watch the sport.

Chork didn't want any trouble. He called Gimlet and Slick to him.

"Seems to me, stranger" spat the man in brown, "there's a lotta' wolf in those dogs."

"What say we collect the bounty," suggested the other. "Two silver coins would buy a night of drink and fun at Fleece's Tavern."

The third man pulled a rusty short sword from his belt. The three took a tentative step toward Chork, watching to see if he would draw his sword.

"Five g-gold 'queenies' for the elf's s-skin," said a new voice. This stopped the men short. They turned toward the man who had spoken.

Chork recognized that voice. His hand immediately went to his sword. His low growl was deeper than Slick's, and more menacing.

It was Bell!

On the other side of the road, the murderer stood with Kobs, Tim Barclay, and two others.

Bell shouted, "That's the b-blighted elf that killed K-Kent!"

The gathering crowd gasped. A woman shrieked and fainted.

Chork started to object but thought better of it. A quick glance made him realize that arguing and fighting would be a lost cause.

"Get him!" cried Kobs. He and the two toughs rushed forward. Bell and Barclay delayed, allowing the others to take the lead.

The three men, who had teased the dogs, brandished their weapons and charged.

Not waiting for Chork's command, Gimlet launched his heavier body into the one man's belly, driving the man to the ground. He savaged the man's privates; shredding cloth then flesh with his sharp fangs.

Like a silver blur, with ears laid back and teeth bared, Slick darted toward the man in brown. He hamstrung the man's right leg. The man fell to the ground with a yelp. Slick turned, his finger-long, razor-like teeth poised to strike at the man's throat.

Yet, that strike never came.

The third man swung his rusty short blade in a shallow arc. Its tip caught Slick just behind his shoulder. With a whimper, Slick collapsed, blood squirting from the wound.

Chork, at first surprised by his dogs' attacks, started forward.

Ignoring the elf, Kobs and the two toughs surrounded Slick and kicked the dog to the ground.

Chork charged toward them but pulled up short when a rock hit him in the chest.

The crowd roared with anger. They wielded whatever they had at hand – rocks, stones, belt knives, hand shears, and even sheep dung from the road. They surged toward the elf.

Chork turned and ran.

24 – Vengeance

Reaching the crest of the bowl, Chork crashed into the copse from where he had earlier studied Little Creek. He slid behind an acacia tree as thick as his torso and drove his back against its trunk. Taking in huge gulps of air, he fought to rein in his panic.

As his breathing slowed, he regained a sense of control and quickly peeked around the tree. He expected to see villagers, charging up the hill after him, waving weapons, and screaming for his death.

However, no one had followed.

Chork looked down into the village. What he saw puzzled him.

The villagers stood in a circle around the remains of Gimlet and Slick, obviously arguing, their words heated and loud, but unrecognizable. A scuffle started. Men pushed and yelled. Kobs ended it by knocking down a man.

With his sword hovering over the prone villager, Kobs spoke to the crowd. Whatever he said, it quieted the crowd. Then, he sheathed his sword and helped the man to his feet.

Chork unsuccessfully tried to find Bell and Barclay in the crowd. By the time he returned to focus on Kobs, the mayor had formed two groups of villagers and was now urging them up the hill. One group approached Chork's hiding spot from the left and the other from the right.

The young elf turned away from the villagers and quickly assessed his options. He could try for the woods to his right, but the villagers would crest the hill and spot him before he disappeared under the trees. His best chance for escape would be in the rocks and boulders to his left. He ran to them as fast as he could.

For the remainder of the morning and all through the afternoon, Chork played 'hawk and rabbit' with the villagers. As the rabbit, he darted from hole to trees to rocks and back again.

As dusk approached, the 'hawks' tired of their search and returned to the village.

Chork returned to the copse of brush and trees and waited for the town of Little Creek to fall asleep.

#

Now that he was not pre-occupied with avoiding the search parties, Chork had time to think. Those thoughts brought pain and that pain led to tears. With his face cupped in his hands, he silently wept for the loss of his two friends. Their death coupled first with the memories of Kent and Emig, and then again with the deaths of his parents, threatened to overwhelm him. He saw himself clinging to the edge of a deep black hole, which had no bottom and offered no escape. Part of him struggled to climb out. Yet, another part wanted to let go and fall endlessly into the darkness. Shutting his eyes so tightly they hurt, he let one hand slide off the edge. A worm of madness slithered up his free arm, across his back, and began to inch its way toward his remaining hand. From the darkness below, he heard the whispers of a bawdy song and a guttural laugh.

When other peals of laughter chimed in, Chork opened his eyes and gasped. He no longer clung to the edge of the hole. He sat with his back to the acacia. The song and laughter he heard came not from the imagined pit, but from Little Creek's inn.

That laughter saved Chork's sanity, though what he then decided to do was not totally devoid of madness.

As the half-moon ascended, Chork crept down into Little Creek. He easily avoided the two town guards, one who walked the docks and another who walked the main road. He made straight for an empty shearing barn. In a corner shielded from outside eyes and the night's cool breeze, he struck a small fire of dried grasses and sticks. Chork would soon have the distraction he needed.

To get to the building where Kobs and his henchmen slept, Chork had to cross the road. He decided to use the creek bed to do this. As for the guard on the docks, a man who had kicked Slick to death, the elf used an orange-banded arrow. The spider venom killed quickly and silently.

In near total darkness, Chork crept toward the mayor's building. He spotted the other guard at the end of the road, 100 paces away, staring up into the hills or the sky. Chork nocked another red banded arrow, but hesitated. This was the man Kobs knocked down. Pursing his lips, Chork shook his head. He focused on Kobs' building.

After a short while, the elf smelled smoke. A moment later, he could see a faint red glow emanating from the direction of the shearing barn. He waited for the alarm to sound.

With no guard on the docks, the fire grew and spread to adjacent buildings, threatening all Little Creek. Finally, an alarm was given, and townsfolk poured into the streets.

Kobs, pulling on his pants, appeared in the doorway. Chork's arrow took him in mid-shout through the throat.

Risking discovery, Chork dashed across the road and into the building. With bow drawn, he met the man with the rusty sword, emerging from a back room.

"What's happen..." the man started to say. He looked down in wonderment at the arrow in his chest before collapsing on the floor.

Chork cautiously walked into the backroom and found the man that Slick had hamstrung. The injured thug struggled to get out of bed.

Chork drew his dagger. The man's eyes bulged with fear.

"You're lucky," said the elf. He slammed his blade into the man's heart. "That was a lot less painful than Slick savaging your entrails."

Chork quickly searched the rest of Kobs' house and discovered no one. At the back door, he found stacked wolf pelts. He used them to climb onto the roof.

The people of Little Creek fought desperately to save their town. They had formed bucket lines to douse the smoldering wood of buildings around the fire. Others worked to pull down already burning planks, smothering the boards with dirt to prevent flying sparks. Small children sat at a safe distance, crying and screaming for their mothers. Everyone who could heft a bucket of water or an axe had been pressed into the battle against the fire.

Chork studied their soot-covered faces, one by one, looking for Bell, Barclay, and the Robins brothers. Unsuccessful, he emitted a low growl and rapidly scanned the road, the docks, and the alleys.

Then, a woman shouted, "Where's the mayor?" Others took up the call. Two women and an old man set off toward Kobs' house to find out.

Chork slid off the roof and dashed up the hill, opposite his original vantage point. He found some rocks, settled in, and watched the people of Little Creek fight the spreading fire. The flames and smoke brought images of Kent to mind. With tears running down his cheeks, exhaustion overcame him. He fell asleep.

* * *

Next morning, the elf awoke to loud and angry voices. Fearing he had been discovered, he nocked an arrow and peeked over the rim of his rocky hide-out.

Below, Little Creek seethed with activity. The inhabitants had saved their town only losing only the barn, two adjacent buildings, and the docks. They now gathered outside Kobs' house around the bodies of Kobs and his two dead henchmen. Around them, men and women wielded spears, swords, and a variety of tools. A group of soot-covered men armed with crossbows and pikes ushered six others through the crowd to stand before the bodies.

Chork recognized Bell, Barclay and the Robbins brothers as four of the six. He fought back the urge to stand up, take aim, and let fly.

An old woman wearing a long red cloak with white fringe stepped forward. She addressed the crowd, pointing to the dead bodies and to the six men.

Chork couldn't hear what she said, but he watched in fascination as she raised and shook her fists in anger. Then, she abruptly dropped her hands to her sides.

A young girl appeared from Kobs' house. She carried a shepherd's crook in both hands. As the crowd urged her on, the lass offered the staff to the old woman.

The woman raised a finger and quickly turned a circle, pointing to the residents of Little Creek. In response to her finger, they each nodded. She gently took the crook with both hands and raised it above her head. The crowd roared their approval.

The woman in red nodded reverently. She spun around to face the six. The crowd hushed. She stepped forward and looked each of the six in the eye. She uttered a word and slammed the butt end of the crook onto the ground. Again, the crowd roared with approval.

Puzzled, Chork watched the crowd break into three groups. One escorted Bell and Barclay into Kobs' house. Another walked the remaining four into the stone inn. The third disappeared into a shearing barn opposite the one that had burned.

A short while later, the three groups rejoined on the east road leading to Dale and Giran. Chanting one word over and over, they lined the road for a short distance. They shouted with angry gestures as Bell, Barclay, and the four others led two mules laden with food and water out of town.

Baffled, Chork looked on. It came to him. The six had been banished! He had to follow; but, the lake, the creek, and the town lay between him and his prey.

25 – The Breeder

To overtake Bell and Barclay, the Last Born had two choices. The first was to head west, circle around Little Creek, giving the town a wide berth, and then turn north to meet the Dale Road. He would fall at least a day behind, maybe more. Or, a safer and probably faster route would be north along the lakeshore. He could slip right past Little Lake and pick up the Dale Road, which eventually turned north. But, should Bell leave the Dale road ...

Chork turned his back toward Little Creek and ran northwest to the lake. Within an hour, he was jogging along an ill-defined path that skirted the shoreline.

A short time after noon, a fence appeared on his left. Its posts slanted this way and that, some still supporting cross rails, others just serving as boundary markers. Even if in good repair, the fence would not prevent sheep from wandering away.

Since the fence seemed out of place and useless, Chork gave it no thought until he came to a gate. Its posts bore the mark of the black hummingbird.

The mark of someone I can trust!

The Last Born approached the rickety gate and extended his hand to push it open. He received a shock that rode up his arm and knocked him to his rump on the ground.

On the other side, wolves slowly emerged from the trees to stand before the gate. Their number, 11 total, was alarming. Their size, at least half outweighed the elf, was intimidating. Their silence was frightening. As one, they sat and stared at him, as if they assessed their impending lunch.

Chork slowly got to his feet. The wolves stood. He took a step to the left. The wolves did the same. He stepped back to stand before the gate. The wolves followed.

Chork scratched his head. He considered running; but, his quick glances up and down the broken fence line made him abandon the idea. He did the only thing he could think to do. He sat down.

Directly opposite Chork sat a dark grey male with a head the size of two hand-spans. A dark brown stripe ran from his nose, between his bright green eyes, up over his head, along his spine to the tip of his tail. He had short socks the same color, which also tipped his ears. His pink tongue was as wide as Chork's hand, and almost as thick. He pushed his massive snout through the gate and sniffed Chork.

"Who are you, big one?" Chork asked. The wolf tilted its head. "What's your name?" The animal turned its head the other way.

"The whelp's name is Maul." The voice came from behind the elf.

"He's a puppy?" Chork spun around. "Hey, how did you sneak up on me?"

"Maul is not yet full grown. I didn't sneak. I walked up along the same path you did." The man sat down beside Chork. "For an elf, you possess a less than adequate sense of awareness."

"I was preoccupied." Chork pointed to the wolves.

"For the path you must walk, preoccupation is death. So too are excuses."

Chork gave the man an angry look. "Who are you?" he demanded.

"Some call me mage," the man replied. "Some, sorcerer. Many calls me crazy, because I sit on this mountainside and crossbreed wolves with dogs." He showed Chork the hummingbird tattoos on the palms of his hands. "You may call me Timo Koira."

"You provided the dogs Pogi gave me!" Chork exclaimed. At the thought his dead friends, he frowned and held back a sob. "They're dead."

Timo stood and placed his right hand on his heart and his left on the elf's shoulder. He then gestured to the wolves. All but Maul padded away.

"Hmmm," hummed Timo, pleased. "I do think a formal introduction is required."

Timo pushed Chork's hand palm up in front of the large wolf. "Maul," he said, "this is Chork, a preoccupied elf."

Maul first sniffed Chork's hand and then began to lick it.

"Chork," said Timo, "this is Maul, a wolf with a taste for preoccupied elves."

Chork laughed and scratched Maul's throat.

What happened next happened so quickly that both Chork and Maul were stunned.

With his belt knife, Timo nicked Maul's left ear, then sliced Chork's left palm. With his other hand holding a talisman of cold metal, the breeder pressed the two cuts together, mingling the bloods of elf and wolf. A thrum wafted on the wind.

In Chork's mind, a new awareness surfaced. He sensed Maul's presence, felt the wolf's anxiety at what had just occurred. In some mystical way, Chork knew Maul felt the same. "What did you do?" Chork asked, awe in his voice.

Timo wiped his bloodstained hand on Chork's cloak. "I sensed the bond beginning when I sat down. I just hurried it along. Come," he said as he opened the gate.

"I have no time. I will lose my," he hesitated, "friends, if I delay too long."

Timo gave him a stern look. "We have much to discuss," he pointed to Maul, "and the price of a wolf to haggle over."

Chork had no choice but to follow Timo. Maul had no choice but to follow Chork.

* * *

Chork and Timo sipped cider from wooden bowls. They sat on wooden fan back chairs on an uneven wooden porch attached to a ramshackle, cockeyed wooden cottage. Chork absent mindedly scratched Maul's head.

"You carve this?" Chork held up the bowl, admiring it.

"A friend. He has a talent for shaping wood."

"These comfortable chairs as well?"

Timo shook his head. "Payment from a Dale house noble for a brace of hunting hounds. I expect his heirs to try to take them back. Maybe tonight." Timo looked around and cocked his head as if hearing something Chork did not. "Yeah, tonight."

"Why would they take them back?"

"The noble beat the dogs. They turned on him. An unpleasant sight, I hear." He shook his head and took a pull from his bowl. "Tell me about Pogi and Kent. Everything until you arrived here."

"It's a long story."

Timo again raised an ear. "We have time."

Chork took a large pull on his bowl of cider. He began his tale with the day Pogi left Kent, leaving Edmod in charge.

When Chork described the destruction of Kent, Timo sighed, "Sometimes, the Gods require too great a sacrifice."

Chork told him of Fat Nat's murder. Timo became angry and slammed his cider bowl onto the wooden porch. "Curs and mongrels," he growled.

Chork's voice grew hoarse as he spoke of the tornado and abandoned Emig. His voice cracked and, sobbing, he described the incident at Little Creek.

"So, Last Born, vengeance is your game, eh? Will you kill them all? The Harley's Peaches? Will you return to deliver vengeance to the good people of Little Creek? Know that I have friends in Little Creek. Should you harm them, would I then have reason to visit my vengeance upon you?"

"No, I," Chork's face grew red with embarrassment. "Well, I, just the men who killed ... That is, just Bell, Barclay, the Robins brothers and, maybe, the other two if I must. I have not thought about returning to Little Creek."

A warning howl came from off in the distance. Maul awoke from his slumber and stood up. He nudged Chork, as if to urge him to stand as well.

"They're here!" announced Timo. He took a deep breath and replied to the howl with one of his own. "Follow," he commanded, "and stay close." Off he went at a lope.

Chork and Maul raced to keep up.

Timo led them down the hillside. They could hear growls and barks. They also heard men's shouts and cries. They burst into a small clearing.

A growing pack of wolves and dogs circled an itchoak, 13, of men. The men formed their own tight circle.

One of the dogs feigned a rush into the men. A man knocked the dog aside with a small shield and raised his sword for a killing blow.

Chork, on the run, nocked an arrow to his short bow.

Timo yelled, "No, do not kill anyone!" He shouldered Chork, sending him tumbling.

Chork crashed into a tree and lay stunned.

Timo raised his right hand in the air. He yelled a single word of warning to the wolves and dogs and followed it with another word.

A deep thrum sounded. A brilliant white light flooded the area, blinding everyone but the wolves and dogs, forewarned by Timo's alert.

Timo walked up to the man who had raised his sword. "I take it, Young Neff, you have come to avenge your father's death. Does your mother, the Lady Dorah, approve?"

From his knees, the man nodded. He had dropped his shield and sword to rub at his eyes, hoping to restore their vision.

"I did not kill your father. His dogs did."

"You trained them!"

"To hunt, not to kill their master. Your father taught them that." Timo glanced at the other men. "Perhaps you should consult with your father's huntsman."

The older man next to Neff spoke up, "The dogs were weak! Lord Neff had to whip them!"

"Ah," sighed Timo, "the huntsman speaks. Did you also advise Young Neff to come here with an armed troop?" When the huntsman didn't answer, and Neff hung his head, Timo continued, "I guess that is a yes."

Timo picked up Neff's sword. "This was your grandfather's," he said, inspecting it. "Though I knew him for only a short time, I quickly learned that he was a just man. He believed as I do that vengeance breeds more vengeance." Timo placed the blade in Neff's hand. "In memory of your grandfather, I will help you do the just thing." He drew Neff to his feet.

Still blinded by Timo's spell, Young Neff was confused. The man he had come to kill had just given him the means to do so. Yet, now, Neff was not sure the breeder's death would be the just thing.

"I offer you a trade," said Timo. "Leave your huntsman with me until the first day of winter. In exchange, I will provide you with a brace of hounds trained to defend you even unto their own death." He paused. "And, I will return your huntsman suitably trained to care for your new pets."

The huntsman began to object. "L-lord Neff, please, I only meant to ..."

"Silence, Varden!" commanded Neff. He then bowed in the direction he presumed Timo to be and said, "I humbly apologize for my intrusion this night, Mage Koira. I gratefully accept your offer."

Timo put an arm around Neff. "You know, you look and sound a lot like your grandfather. I will have my friends escort you down the hill. Your sight will return by then." Timo made a series of hand gestures, as a thrumming filled the air.

The dogs and wolves took jacket and cloak sleeves in their jaws, tugging the men along. Two wolves escorted Varden away in a similar manner but in a different direction.

Timo walked over to where Maul licked Chork's face. "Are you unhurt?"

"Except for my eyes, and the wolf slobber, I'm fine."

"Well, stand up!" Chork did so. Timo knocked him back down. "Never take a life unless you have no other choice."

Chork got back to his feet. "I didn't have any other choice. I am not a mage who can fling light spells about on a battlefield. I have a bow, a sword, and a dagger. Those are my choices."

"You have no magic?" Timo sounded incredulous.

Chork shook his head, "None that I know of."

"Bah," Timo waved his hand at the elf. "Come, let's finish our haggling."

"But, I can't see!"

"You have Maul's eye, do you not?"

Chork grunted with concentration, striving to see through the dog's eyes.

"Not like that, you fool!" laughed Timo. "You're no beast master. Let him lead you!"

26 – Apple Seeds

The bright morning sun forced Chork to open his eyes. They felt gritty and sore, but they could see. His body ached from spending the night in the chair on Timo's porch. His head pounded from too much cider and his left palm throbbed.

Timo snored in the chair beside him, an upside down bowl in the center of a drying wet stain on his chest. An alert Maul sat upright between them.

A pang stabbed Chork's palm. He grimaced, shook it, and felt a second, stronger stab. Suspecting the diagonal cut from little finger to thumb had opened, he looked. Shocked, he saw a second cut crossed the first. He immediately turned to Timo, now considering the empty bowl with a frown.

Just as Chork opened his mouth to ask the breeder what had happened, a cold, wet nose touched his right hand. Startled, the elf leapt out of his chair and confronted another wolf.

This one had fur so light gray that he appeared silver. Half the size of Maul, he stood nearly as tall, his slim body obviously built for speed. His eyes were a bright amber. Long white socks matched the tip of his tail and the twitching tips of his ears.

"That's Dirk," mumbled Timo. "He disobeyed my command to accompany Young Neff's party last night and followed you back here." The empty cider bowl clattered to the floor as Timo rose and approached Chork. "Let me see that hand." The breeder placed his palm over Chork's and uttered a soft chant.

The Last Born heard a low thrum and felt a tingle. The pain in his palm vanished. The cuts had healed. Only a faint scar in the shape of an 'X' remained.

"When? Why?" Chork muttered. Through the fog of cider, he brought last night to mind. Maul had led him back to Timo's porch. The elf remembered accepting another bowlful of cider and listening to the breeder describe the various traits, characteristics, and personalities of wolves and dogs. As Timo droned on, Chork had grown sleepy. At that point, just before he fell asleep, Chork recalled Timo hovering over him with belt knife and talisman in hand.

Timo disappeared into the wooden shack and returned with another bowl of liquid. "Drink this," he commanded.

"No more," said Chork, running his sleeve across his eyes. The faint smell of cider almost made him gag.

"Hair of the dog that bit you," replied Timo, "plus something to clear the head." He pushed the bowl into Chork's hand. "Drink it all down in one gulp."

Chork did as instructed. He scrunched his face at the taste. "Ergh," he muttered. Yet, immediately, his head cleared. His body no longer ached with sore muscles from the chair. His eyes regained their clarity.

He also felt Dirk's presence, as different from Maul's as their appearances differed. Maul projected a sense of strength and serenity, whereas Dirk exuded curiosity and anticipation.

"Let's discuss payment over breakfast," suggested Timo, as he entered his home.

Chork followed and saw a man dressed in the Neff livery placing a large loaf of crusty brown bread on a table covered with plates full of meat and fruit. The elf surmised this was Varden, the huntsman. His guess was proven when Timo thanked the man by name and invited him to join in the meal.

Chork took his place at the table. He selected some cuts of venison, a yellow apple, and a slab of the brown bread. Before taking his first bite, he placed his coin purse on the table and asked, "How much?"

Timo took a bite from the slice of meat he had skewered with a short dagger. Scowling through a chew, he looked at the elf, the coin purse, and back at the elf. "Kindly remove that from my breakfast table."

Chork furrowed his brow and complied.

"Thank you." Timo took another bite. He then gestured toward the elf's plate. "Dig in."

The three ate in silence. Chork and Varden found this uncomfortable but made no attempts to relieve their uneasiness.

Eating his fill, Timo selected a green apple and eased back into his chair. "You both seek revenge for the taking of a life by taking another life." The mage looked at the apple and polished the fruit on his sleeve until it gleamed. "Ah, the sweet promise of vengeance!" He bit into the apple. Making a sour face, he complained, "How bitter it tastes! How its pulp when swallowed will sicken the stomach!" He spat the mouthful onto the floor. Then, he flung the apple out a back window. "No doubt its seeds will dry and wither as the flesh that protects them. With luck they will not produce more bitter green apples."

"In the other hand," he said, selecting a bright red apple from the platter of fruit, "justice!" He took a bite and smiled. "Ah, much better. This true sweetness when swallowed will nourish not only the body but the soul as well." He took another bite and another until only the core remained. "Yes, true nourishment for body and soul."

Both Chork and Varden squirmed in their chairs.

"I see my arrow has hit its target," said Timo. He took a deep purposeful breath and leveled his gaze first at the elf and then at the huntsman. "Justice demands we respect the rights of all living things. The first and most important of which is the right to life. Will vengeance restore this basic right to the dear one who have died? No! Will their honor be restored? No! Is justice served?" He paused, considering the apple core. "Perhaps."

Timo stood. "Varden, take this core and plant it next to the porch so it may take root and produce more of its kind. Return and clean the cottage."

The huntsman rose, nodded, took the core, and left.

Timo turned to Chork. "My price for your new friends is threefold. First, you will find the green apple core and destroy its seeds so that they cannot take root. Do you agree?"

"Of course," snapped the Last Born.

"Second, your pursuit will eventually lead you to Giran City. Or, at least, in that direction." The breeder reached inside his tunic and withdrew a small block of wood. "Deliver this to Mage Paul Keyes at the Starling's Song."

Chork accepted the wooden cube. A slight tingle teased his hand. "What is it?"

Timo smirked. "A small block of wood. Do you agree?"

Again, Chork readily agreed. "And third?" he asked.

"If you do not meet the first two payments in full," Timo's eyes drilled into Chork's, "then Maul and Dirk will exact the same justice that befell Lord Neff. Do you agree? Think before you reply, Elf."

Chork was puzzled. *Why would the nonfulfillment of two simple tasks warrant death? Was there more here than met the eye? The wooden block perhaps? Did it have hidden value? Destroying the apple core was a mere matter of walking outside, locating it, and crushing the seeds with a large stone. Or was it? Did Timo provide me a riddle I must solve? An allegory that I must learn from?*

The Last Born considered this notion so strongly that he asked the mage, "Does the first payment mean I have to destroy my own desire for vengeance?"

"A little late to be asking since you have already agreed to make the payment." Timo deadpanned. "That is not what I intended, but if you wish to take it so, I will accept that."

"No, no." Chork shook his head and his hands. "I ... well ... the third payment seems out of proportion to the first two."

"Too steep a price to pay?" Timo rose from the table. "Then, I will remove the bonds and you can be on your way."

Chork objected. "No, don't. I accept the costs."

"Then, we are agreed as to price." A thrum filled the air. Chork felt a chill settle over him.

"You cast a spell on me."

"No, Young Elf, you cast the spell."

"But I don't have magic ability."

"So you have told me." Timo shrugged. "I would add a suggestion. Take the Elven Test of Bowls as soon as possible. Normally, you would do this before the elders in your Enclave. Since Emig is no more, you may do so in Bria or Cenedril."

"The Elven Forest?"

"You could," replied Timo, "but your path leads east not west." With that, he started for the door. "I have chores and you have an apple core to find. We will meet again later today for cider on the porch." Before Chork could protest, the mage walked out.

The Last Born ran to the cottage door. He expected to find Timo crossing the porch, but the old man had vanished. In his place sat Maul and Dirk.

Chork laughed. "Well, you two won't help. Not unless I was looking for a piece of meat." As he rounded the house toward the back window, his cheerful mood collapsed.

The cottage sat on the bank of a steep cliff full of rocks, boulders, and scrubby bushes. The core could be in any of a thousand nooks or crannies.

"By the bow!" the elf exclaimed.

* * *

As twilight faded into darkness, the exhausted and tattered Chork decided to end his day-long search. He had worked his way about half-way down the hill, crawling like a bug over stones and around boulders, prying apart thorny stems and unyielding stalks. Just as he turned to scramble back up the incline, his hand fell upon the now-shriveled apple.

"The luck of Elm Himself!" he shouted. The Last Born slid the once-bitten apple into an inner pocket and felt about for a flat stone and round rock. These he placed into his pants pocket. A few stumbles and slips brought him back to the edge of the hill and to Timo's porch.

There, the mage lounged, a huge bowl of cider at his lips. "Oh-ho, thirsty?" Timo pointed to the chair beside him. On it sat a matching bowl of cider.

Chork knelt at Timo's feet. He pulled the flat stone and round rock from his pocket and placed them on the floor boards. With his dagger, he extricated each seed from the apple and placed them on the stone. Then he mashed them to a watery pulp.

"My first payment is made!"

Timo snickered. "I agree."

For the rest of that night, Chork and Timo once again sat on the porch, sipping cider. Their conversation ranged from Chork's day long search to breeding, of which Timo could talk for days. From the quality of apple needed for a tasty and potent cider to the meaning of the search for the green apple.

"Your quest for vengeance is like your search for the apple. You waste a whole day in the hot sun, tattering your clothing, scraping and bruising your body, risking a fatal fall to the jagged rocks below. For what? Do you really think the apple's seeds would have taken root on that hill?"

Chork was flummoxed. "But, it was the price you demanded for the wolves!"

"Was the price the search or the lesson it taught?"

Timo said, "I won't be here when you wake. So, I'll say, farewell Chork the Last Born." He stood and grasped Chork's hand. The breeder's hand held a buckle, which he passed to the elf. "This will help you with more than your pants."

Chork looked down at the silver-colored metal buckle. Its face bore a carved black hummingbird in flight, matching exactly the others he possessed. When he looked up to thank the breeder and ask which interpretation the mage believed, Timo was gone.

From nearby, a howl split the night air. Others, in the distance, replied.

* * *

The next morning, Chork woke to something wet and raspy rubbing his cheek. It was Maul's huge tongue. Chork scratched the wolf behind its ears and entered the cottage.

A breakfast of meat, fruit, and bread lay waiting for him on the table. A slip of paper sat next to a pitcher of cold water. The message was in a hasty scrawl and signed with the black hummingbird.

Tell the girl's mother that a suitable friend will arrive on the summer's last full moon.

"Tell who?" Chork asked Maul and Dirk. Maul yawned, and Dirk twitched his ears.

With a shrug, Chork stuffed the note into his pocket. He ate his fill, sharing the meat with the wolves. Finished, the elf gathered his gear and set out.

He found the gate open. Passing through it, he heard a distant howl. As he closed the gate, Maul and Dirk replied.

27 – An Explanation

Realizing he was at least two days behind his quarry, Chork raced along the lakeshore with Maul on his left and Dirk on his right. Turning along the north shore, he slowed to a trot. In the distance, a barge poled by men and dwarves came toward him.

The barge was heavily laden and rode in the water, which Chork reasoned was why it held close to shore. If an accident occurred, or a storm hit, and the barge sank, recovery of the goods would be much easier.

Sure that he had not yet been seen, Chork turned north into the foothills of the Aril Mountains. Wary of any alarms the people of Little Creek may have spread, he wanted to avoid contact.

Later that day, his luck betrayed him. As the three companions topped a hill, they heard a flock of sheep on the other side. Chork worried that the wolves would attempt to make a meal of one or two. However, Maul and Dirk remained at his side. They did growl and bark, warning the sheep to get out of the way. As the sheep scattered, Maul seemed to chuckle. Dirk's ears twitched.

Rounding a large boulder, Chork came face to face with a shepherd, holding a crook.

The man saw the elf, recognition blooming. The shepherd ran.

Without thinking, Chork waved to Dirk, pointed at the man, and made a grabbing gesture with his left hand.

Dirk bolted after the man. He used a mound to launch himself onto the shepherd, knocking the man and the crook to the ground. As the man reached for his dagger, Dirk bared teeth and growled.

The man left his dagger in its sheath and made no sound as Dirk dragged him along the ground toward an approaching Chork.

Chork looked at the quivering man. "We won't hurt you." He asked the wolves to sit.

The man shook and licked his lips. His eyes darted from Chork to Dirk to Maul. When he looked at Maul, his eyes grew wider with fear. "Youse gots to unnerstan'!" he cried. "T-t-the town threw 'em out. Him an' his fren's."

Maul sniffed at the man's legs.

The man squirmed and mewled. "We gots t'gether. 'lected a new mayor. Daisy Wilmer."

The man slid his legs away from Maul's huge snout. "S-she made t-the troublemakers leave. We meant no harm to you."

"Where did they go?"

"I dunno. M-Mitch, my brudder, was with 'em t-that walked 'em out. H-he said they t-talked about G-Giran."

Chork looked at the man. He noticed the wet stain spreading at the man's crotch. Disgust quickly gave way to pity. He pulled the man to his feet.

"W-w-whatcha gonna do with m-me?"

"Nothing." Chork looked into the man's eyes. He saw fear, confusion, and then guarded relief.

"L-look, they's g-good people. The others, Kobs an' 'em, jes' took over. Frightened us. H-hurt a few. M-maybe you b-been there? Y'know?"

"Yes, I know," Chork said.

"C-can I go?" the shepherd asked.

Chork nodded and said, "Tell your new mayor we have no more quarrel."

"T-thanks!" The man took off at a dead run, forgetting his crook. He ran down the hill and disappeared around the next.

Maul and Dirk looked at the shepherd, at the sheep, and then at Chork. Chork smiled and pointed. He also had a taste for lamb for supper.

170

28 – Through Dale

Dale was much larger than Little Creek and boasted two minor nobles, always at odds, and a full company of the Brigade of Thorns, the all-female militia and constabulary of Giran.

Most of Dale's inhabitants earned their living by fishing the lake, trading with the dwarves, and herding sheep and goats. The remainder ran the two inns and various shops that sat in two straight lines along each side of the town's docks. A bridge across the North Fork of the Dale River sat south of this line.

With his hat pulled down over his ears, Chork entered Dale. Walking down the street, he was pleased no one gave him a second glance. He entered the first inn he saw and strode up to the bar. He withdrew a silver coin from his purse and slapped it on the counter. "A mug of beer."

In the corner on a small stage, a long-haired bard played a stringed instrument. He smiled and nodded to Chork, who a bit startled, smiled and nodded back.

The heavyset man behind the bar took the coin, set a mug of warm beer in front of Chork, and returned a few coppers. He barely looked at the elf and gave the wolves an equally indifferent glance.

Chork sniffed at the mug and took a sip. He grimaced at the taste and hoped the barkeep had not noticed. "I'm looking for some friends."

"Well, ya' won't find any here," replied the barkeep.

"One has broken teeth."

"That dullard!" The large man turned to Chork. "If he's yer friend, then finish that mug and get out!"

"Ah, he's not exactly a friend," Chork confessed.

The man examined Chork's eyes. Somehow, the man recognized Chork's true intent. "Yeah, not exactly, eh? What did he do to you?"

Chork shrugged. "What he did is my business." He sipped the beer and grimaced. "I take it he was here."

"Yeah, he was here." The barkeep spat on the floor. "Started a fight but didn't stick around to finish it. Got a table an' chair busted up. Broke my best barmaid's arm. Ran off 'cross the bridge afore the Thorns got here."

"How long ago?"

"Two days." The man poured Chork another beer. "You gonna catch 'im?"

Chork nodded. He sipped from the second mug. It was no better than the first.

"You give that bastard something from me," the man growled. From beneath the counter, he pulled a rusty dagger and slammed it point first into the wood.

Chork looked at the man and nodded. He left the coppers on the counter and walked out.

"Now, we wait for nightfall," Chork announced, as a soft rain began.

* * *

Chork waited until the early hours of the morning, when night would be its darkest. Quietly, he and the wolves circled around Dale to the bridge's north end. Hiding behind decorative hedges, he studied the bridge and its approach.

A guard slouched against a tree stump, her halberd on the ground beside her. Rain rolled off her helmet.

Sneaking past this one would be easy. Before Chork left the safety of the hedges, he craned his neck to look to the other side

172

of the bridge. Though he couldn't see them, he could hear two guards laughing and talking.

Chork decided his only course of action was to sneak past this guard, creep across the bridge staying to shadows, and then make a run across when the two guards challenged him. With luck, he would find some brush and trees that would hide him and his wolves.

He crept halfway cross the bridge when he saw six guards. One, an officer saw Chork at the same moment.

"Hoy there!" called the officer, her hand on her sword pommel. Two of her contingent aimed crossbows at the elf.

Chork stopped and gestured for Maul and Dirk to do the same.

"Where are you headed, traveler?" asked the officer.

"To Giran," replied Chork, looking for an opening into which he could sprint.

"What's your business in Giran?"

Chork gave the woman the answer that popped into his head. "I have a gift for Mage Paul Keyes of Giran from Mage Timo Koira of the Aril Mountains."

"That explains them two big dogs," said one of the Thorns, pointing with her crossbow.

"Then come across to complete your business, elf." The officer turned and walked to a small wooden shed, muttering about rain, mold, and sickness.

Chork reached the south side of the bridge.

"Big dogs," said a Thorn, trying to get a better look.

Chork chuckled. "Breeder Koira does like them big." To his astonishment, he continued off the bridge, past the shed, and down the road without another word or challenge.

Reaching a bend in the road, he turned to look back. No one followed. He dashed off into the brush, his wolves running beside him.

He spent an hour, in the rain, looking for the right place to sleep. He found it in a stand of needle trees. Although with a roof of pine needles, two wolves to keep him warm, and the soft sounds of the night to lull him, Chork slept uneasily. He did not understand why the officer let him pass. It never occurred to him that the Thorns had no reason not to let him pass.

29 – Along the Road

Chork woke from his fitful sleep to see two plump dead quail on the ground beside him. Sitting up, he looked at the wolves. Maul, his huge tongue and teeth working methodically, groomed Dirk. Dirk's ears twitched in satisfaction.

"So, you two have already broken your night's fast," he said. "Thank you for my morning meal." The elf scratched the wolves' rumps just above their tails. When they rolled over onto their backs, he scratched their bellies.

With roast quail in his belly, Chork set out. Not 200 paces up the road, he found the remains of a campsite. He decided to examine the area, hoping he would find something to tell him more about the men he chased.

Dirk, who had been circling the camp, helped him. The wolf stood beside a fallen tree and whined. He poked at something with his nose.

"What did you find?" Chork asked. He walked over to the dead tree. Behind it, lay man's body, half buried under stones and dead branches. When he pulled the corpse out, he realized he had found the right camp.

The body, with two dagger wounds in his stomach, belonged to one of Kobs' toughs.

Chasing the wolves away, Chork examined it. He found nothing of interest. He briefly considered burying the body, but decided against it, because of the time and amount of work involved. Rather, he meticulously examined the ground around the sloppy cairn.

He uncovered two other sets of footprints. One was new and was immediately memorized. The other, however, brought a smile to his face. The left boot was missing a knuckle-sized wedge on the heel.

He spent a few moments recovering the body, adding some larger rocks and dirt.

Back on the road, Chork located the tell-tale boot print. It and the others tromped off east He looked up at the blackening sky and quietly asked The Only One not to weep.

Near nightfall, he found a second camp. So engrossed with his search of this one, he did not pay heed to Dirk's soft yip of warning.

When Maul nudged him, Chork looked up just as two men smiled and walked toward him.

"Ho! Well-met!" the important looking one said. His pants looked to be gold thread with scarlet brocade at the seams. He wore a snow-white tunic, embroidered with red tulips. He flourished a red satin cape and matching hat. As the man neared, he extended his hand to Chork.

Chork stared wide-eyed at the man, ignoring the hand. He then looked at the man's companion. This man was taller and wider, but since he was dressed in all browns and greys, he was nondescript next to his extravagant colleague.

"Well-met, says I," insisted the man, pushing his hand closer to Chork. The elf took a step back and fingered his sword hilts.

"Oh, no, dear me!" cried the dandy. "We mean you no harm!" The man dropped his hand to his side, but only for a moment, because he used it while he talked. "We thought to use this space to camp for the night. But, alas, if you are here first, we shall have to seek our refuge further down the road."

"No," said Chork. "I'm done here. I'll be on my way."

"Pray dear elf," the man said, "stay and share our meager supper." He waved his arm toward the road. Several wagons rounded the bend. Brightly painted, they varied in shape and size. The first was lettered:

Donald Dafoe's Dance and Drama – Delighting Dozens Daily

"I am Dafoe," the man announced, "and this rather tall and stout..." Dafoe's eyes opened wider than Chork thought possible. "Wolves!"

"They won't harm you," Chork said. He gave Maul a hand signal. "Maul, say hello to Dafoe." Maul howled. He gave a different signal to Dirk. "Dirk, greet Dafoe." Dirk yawned.

"My word, such intelligent beasts!" Dafoe beamed a smile at Chork. "And your name?"

"Chork." The elf saw the tall man tug at Dafoe's sleeve. He bent down and whispered something in Dafoe's ear.

Chork distinctly heard the word "Barrens." He pursed his lips and shook his head. He looked pointedly at the tall man for a heartbeat or two, and then asked. "Tell me, did you happen to pass a man with broken teeth in the company of four others on the road?"

"Alas, Master Chork," breathed Dafoe, "we did. Are they friends of yours?"

"No. How long ago?"

"Thank all of the gods above and below!" Dafoe wrung his hands. "We met them on the Giran Road two days past. Invited them to dine with us. They proved to be unpleasant creatures. They teased and hooted at our women, using profane language and gestures. They stole from us and departed in the middle of the night." Dafoe's hands flapped and rolled.

The tall man finally spoke out loud, "Ya shudda lemme go affer'm and break mora his tees."

"Now, now, Albert, we must handle these things with civility." He turned back to Chork. "I hope your business with them," he paused for effect as he flipped his hand from palm up to palm down, "does not bring you harm."

"My business," Chork said pointedly, "is my business." Chork also noted that Dafoe's hands bore no tattoos.

Dafoe chuckled. "Yes, sir, it is. Forgive me for asking." He rolled his forearms one over the other. "However, I do have another question. One that will require an answer."

Chork put his right hand on his sword and readied his left to signal the wolves to attack.

"Oh, you won't require violence," Dafoe giggled. "Would you join us for our evening meal?" Dafoe made a low bow. "It would be a treat to converse with you. And, may I humbly add, it would be a treat for you to meet our modest troop."

"Thanks for the information," Chork said, "and for your kind offer. But, I'm in a hurry." To the wolves, he gestured and ordered, "Let's go."

In defiance, Maul yawned and lay down. Dirk twitched his ears and sat.

Dafoe and Albert broke out in guffaws.

Chork shrugged and said, "I guess we accept your offer."

"Most excellent," cheered Dafoe, waving his hands about his head. "Pray, give us a few moments to set up camp and set the cook fires aflame."

Chork offered to help but received smiles and headshakes. He watched the troop work.

Everyone had necessary tasks to perform, except Dafoe. With arms flailing, he un-necessarily gave directions, which no one appeared to mind or heed.

Chork enjoyed the meal. His trencher of day old dark bread contained boneless, roasted chunks of fowl with spiced dumplings in thick, heavily spiced, lard gravy. His mug held heavy, fruity ale, also spiced.

Dafoe told Chork that most of the members used mealtime to practice and refine their acts. Dancers, tumblers, and jugglers moved through the camp to the applause and shouts of their comrades. To end the revue, a bard with long stringy hair stood on a rock and recited an ode.

When Chork complimented the troupe, Dafoe took a bow, as if he himself had performed. "Now, the ale," informed Dafoe, "is Albert's own. See those two wagons?" He pointed to two large red box wagons set off from the circle. In bright yellow letters on the side, read, "Albert's Amazing Ale. Alluring Appetizing Ambrosia."

Chork laughed and shook his head. "He brews it in the wagons?"

"Haw!" spat Albert. "Innna wagons! Yah, Elflet," Albert joked, "I burn da' wagons ta cook da barl'. I rebuild 'em ever' nigh'. I didna know the Barrens make ya stupid!"

A dark cloud came over Chork's face. He set down his mug and stood.

Dafoe jumped up to stand between Chork and Albert. He flourished his red cape and said, "Now, Chork, Albert means no disrespect. Do you, Albert?"

Albert stood with his feet wide apart and his fists balled. "Nah, no disrepec'. Was silly ta thin' I brew it in the wagon. Cum, I show you."

"Actually," informed Dafoe, "he brews it when we stop to perform. He sets up his kettles and whatnot. Sometimes, we must wait for Albert to finish before moving on. But, it is always worth the wait."

"Yeah, when we stop." Albert sat back down. "Tell me about the Barrens, Chor'. Is it catchin' like sum sez?" Albert added, "Always thought Barrens soun' a lot better an' Scourge or Curse. Is it catchy?"

"No." Chork sat as well. "The Barrens describes it accurately. Though to elves, it is a curse."

"You shame of it?" asked Albert. His large features showed concern. "Dere's no shame, Chor. It's not sumthin' you did. Like me. I born too big. Kill my mam comin' out. Den I grows bigger. Have dis bi' tong'." He stuck out his tongue. "Makes me tal' funny."

Albert took a pull on his ale. "Peoples ma-make fun uh me. Make jokes. Laugh." He shook his head. "Thin' I'm stupid." He drained his mug. "Bu', I makes the bes' ale in Brehm. An' I more stron' than two men."

He walked over to a wagon, grabbed the side, and tilted it off the ground. A scream came from inside the wagon. Albert set it down and yelled an unintelligible apology.

Sheepishly, he sat back down at the fire. "Wha' I am makes no d-diff."

"Difference," helped Dafoe.

"Yeah, tha'," smiled Albert, "it make no tha', no d-diff, ta who I am."

"You're Albert," said Dafoe. "The strongest man in Brehm. The best maker of ale ever born."

"I am the Last Elf Born," Chork announced.

Dafoe's eyes lit up.

"Fer real?" asked Albert.

Chork nodded. "The last of my kind born to the world. That's who I am."

Albert shook his head. "No, Chor'. Thass a lie. Tha' wha' you are, no who you are."

Chork looked at Albert, considering what the man said. He narrowed his eyes and turned inward.

"Albert's right, Chork," interrupted Dafoe, "and it would be an interesting discussion. But it's late. I need to sleep." He turned to address the troop. "We all need to sleep."

The troop slowly wandered off to wagons and bedrolls. Some glanced at Chork before they walked away. Others looked at Dafoe and nodded.

"While you're falling asleep," whispered Dafoe to the elf, "consider this. Chork's Cunning Canines – Charming, Captivating, Comical." He looked at Chork. "People would pay handsomely to see 'The Last Elf Born'." He punctuated this with his hand, as if reading it on the side of a wagon.

"We could have the wagon ready tomorrow," he added. "Join us. I can offer you an equal share, less expenses, of course. Think on it."

Chork sat and watched Dafoe's Dance and Drama troop retire for the night. Within a short time, he was the only one staring into the fire. Maul dozed at his left foot; Dirk slept at his right.

Chork did think on it.

Dafoe asks that I join his carnival. A carnival of freaks! Is that what I am? A freak. Come see the Last Born Elf for a copper!

He recalled the words of his cousin and the others in Emig. They certainly treated me like a freak. Is that why they considered me different? Because I am a freak?

His mother's words argued differently. "They're jealous."

Jealous of what, mother?

"Jealous of whom you will become. Jealous for the opportunity of what you will do."

Mother, what will I become? What will I do?

"Whatever you want, my son. Whatever you want."

I want to be a knight. But, he had never said that to his mother. He said it to Dame Pogi. And she took me seriously. She didn't think I was a freak!

Freak. What a horrible word that is. What a horrible thing to call someone! Anyone! Just because they look different or act different. Just because they were born first or last. What matters most is what they do! That's what makes a knight!

Albert's right! The Last Born is what I am, but not WHO I am! There is a difference!

Night crept into morning, close to dawn, and still, the debate swirled in his head.

Finally, in the darkest part of the night, he asked himself, "What am I?" To which he answered, "Lye Tella'estela Hummien'dulin – The Last Born Elf." Then, he asked, "Who am I?" and answered, "Chork – squire and keeper of oaths."

His words woke the wolves. Maul stood up and slowly looked around the camp. Dirk walked around the fire pit, twitching his ears.

Chork turned to Maul, "I know who I don't want to be." He nodded his head emphatically. "I do not want to be a member of Dafoe's Dance and Drama. Do you, my friend."

Maul seemed to understand. He cocked his head to the left and then to the right. He waited a moment and then shook himself as if he were throwing water from his fur.

"Maybe others think we belong in a circus." Chork gathered his gear and weapons. "We do not."

The elf considered waking Dafoe and Albert to thank them. He looked to their wagons and somehow sensed they were watching. He made an ostentatious bow of thanks, one that Dafoe would envy.

Turning to the wolves, Chork asked, "Are you ready to leave?"

Maul and Dirk bolted down the road into the darkness.

Chork followed.

* * *

To clear his mind and to gain on his quarry, Chork jogged the entire next day. He stopped only to eat his brief mid-day meal and to verify that the boot prints still followed the road.

As night approached, so did exhaustion. The rain, which threatened all day, finally came. Fortunately, a crowd of boulders along the roadside offered meager shelter.

Too tired and too depressed to open his pack for some dried apples and meat, he sat and stared into a puddle. Large raindrops sent concentric circles across the surface of the puddle, mesmerizing him. He dozed fitfully, and eventually slept badly.

The morning greeted him with a moist fog. Damp clothes, a hungry belly, a muddled head, and a sore body also bid him welcome to the new day.

The wolves were gone. He hoped they would not return with breakfast. Everything was too wet to start and sustain a cook fire.

Chork took the dried apples and meat from his pack and silenced his stomach. To relieve the soreness in his body, he walked in a circle to locate the direction the wolves' hunt had taken. To clear his mind, he calculated the distances between where he stood, the probable location of his quarry, and Giran.

He could do nothing about his damp clothing, except suffer it.

Maul and Dirk appeared, their legs covered in mud, their snouts, in blood. Thankfully, they brought him nothing.

On the road, Chork zigzagged to avoid the puddles of rainwater and mud, while Maul and Dirk did their best to walk through each one.

At the South Fork Bridge, Chork planned to use the same half-lie he told to cross the North Fork Bridge. If it worked once, he reasoned, it should work again.

When a slight stab of guilt poked him, he rationalized. *It's not really a lie. Timo told me to deliver the block to Mage Keyes.*

Yet, the guilt poked him.

"Listen," he said aloud, "I can't say to them, 'The man I need to kill is on the other side of the bridge. Let me pass.'"

Before his conscience could reply, he rounded a bend and saw the bridge. This time, two guards stood on this end of the bridge, not sleeping, but talking and laughing.

Chork approached. His damp clothes made him self-conscious and irritable.

The guard facing the elf shot a glance to Chork and nodded once, as if to say hello. Her eyes gaped at the sight of the wolves. She elbowed her companion, mumbled a word, and pointed. The second guard had been focused on the wolves the whole time, his jaw agape, his eyes wide with fear and wonder. She swallowed the lump in her throat, nodded her head as fast as a gnat's wings, and urged the three travelers across with a wave of her free hand.

Chork stepped onto the bridge and walked across with Maul and Dirk at his sides. As he reached the other side, another guard waved to him and, without waiting for an acknowledgement, resumed sharpening the blade of her halberd.

Walking down the road with his back to the bridge, Chork was amazed. *I just sauntered across. No one said a word!* Again, he didn't realize that the guards had no reason not to let him pass.

From here, the road meandered eastward until it joined the southern trade route at a town called Three Points. From this large town, the road went due north to Giran City.

Chork set out at a run and kept his pace until evening fell. Half of him wanted to continue running through the night. The other half cried for food and sleep. *Which half wants which?* He wondered. Still running, he debated with himself. Soon, he realized that he avoided a decision because he feared he would make the wrong one.

In the end, Maul and Dirk decided for him.

Maul stopped and raised his nose high into the air. He had obviously caught the scent of prey. Dirk also stopped and turned his ears so that he could hear what Maul smelled. They both turned to Chork.

Chork signaled, "Go on." He added, "Bring me back something to eat." The wolves tore into the brush at a lope.

If I sleep well tonight with a full belly, Chork thought, I can run all the faster tomorrow.

They spent the night in a small clearing about 50 paces from the road. They ate and slept well.

30 – Gratitude

Two days later, Chork arrived on the outskirts of Three Points. The size of the town surprised him. There were scores of buildings and hundreds, no thousands, of people. Finding Bell and Barclay, if they were still in Three Points, would not be easy.

The town was divided into three sections by the horizontal 'T' where Dale Road ended at Giran Road. South of Dale Road sat the Low Quarter, home to the town's working class in houses of wood and thatch. North lay the High Quarter, populated by Three Points' wealthiest citizens in keeps, mansions, and estates. Giran Road split these neighborhoods from the East Half, where merchants, traders, and city officials lived and worked.

Boldly, Chork walked down the middle of Dale Road with Maul and Dirk in tow. To his right, he saw men, women, and children dressed in browns, greys, and greens. They were simple folk, tending to chores and each other. They reminded him of his friends in Kent. On his left, he noticed guards in livery at every door and gate. They reminded him of Sa'Mael and Boerne.

Maul and Dirk grabbed everyone's attention. Many pointed in silent awe. Some put a hand on their companions' shoulders to stop their progress along the road. Mothers held their young close. Fathers slid their hands to weapons. All ceded a wide berth.

Ignoring the disruption, Chork continued down the road, favoring its southern side, and wondered where to begin his search for Bell. Ahead, he saw a small group of people laughing and dancing to a tune that sounded vaguely familiar. As he worked his way through the crowd, he realized it was a variation on the tune from his music box.

At the center of the group, an old man with one leg and one arm sat in a chair in front of a small wooden shack. He began a lively ditty on a silver flute. He played rather well despite his handicap, using a metal harness to hold the flute in place.

Some of the crowd clapped in time with the music. A few others began to dance a jig. A charwoman grabbed Chork's elbow and tried to spin him around in time with the music.

Chork resisted.

"What's wrong, Elflet?" cackled the woman. "Am I too much woman for you?" She rolled her hips to the beat of the flautist's tune.

Men and woman whooped with laughter. One man pushed Chork aside, saying, "Lemme shows ya how a man turns a woman."

Chork almost lost his footing, falling up against a large man in a leather vest, who pushed the elf into a woman, clapping to the music. To keep from falling, she grabbed Chork's forearm.

Maul growled, baring his teeth and raising his hackles.

"Settle that mutt down!" ordered the man next to the woman. He pulled his wife away from Chork, placed his big meaty hand squarely on Chork's chest, and shoved.

Chork stumbled backwards into a line of people, who pushed him to the side into others.

A scuffle broke out. Men and women pushed and shoved each other.

Chork, remembering Little Creek, had the presence of mind to emphatically gesture toward Maul to sit and be quiet. He looked around for Dirk and found him sitting away from the crowd, twitching his ears.

Shouts of "Stand down!" split the air. Three Thorns waded into the tussle, using their glaives to break up the crowd. "Go on about your business," ordered one, directing part of the group down the road.

Soon, Chork and the flautist were the only two people who remained.

"Well, Elfling" said the old man, "you sure know how to kill a good time!" He reached down to pick up an intricately carved wooden bowl. Sifting through the coins it contained, he added, "Cost me half my usual take."

"Sorry," Chork muttered. He called Maul and Dirk to his side with a simple gesture.

"Mathieu Wye." The old man offered his hand.

Before taking the hand, Chork noticed a black hummingbird tattooed on the palm. "Chork."

"Lye Tella'estela Hummien'dulin, the Last Born. I know." Mathieu reached into an inner pocket and produced a long wooden pipe. He lit it and sat back.

"That tune you were playing when I walked up," Chork began, "how..."

"I wrote it years ago," Mathieu interrupted.

Chork withdrew the music box from his pack. "Then ..."

"That's one of mine. Sold it to your father. If you look closely, you will see two etched diamond shapes. An 'M" and a 'W' connected, bottom to top."

"You knew my father?"

"Nope." Mathieu pointed to a rickety chair against the shack. "Grab that and take a seat. It hurts my neck to look up at someone while talking."

Chork did as he was asked. Maul and Dirk settled in at his feet. They laid their heads between their front paws and watched Mathieu.

"You didn't know my father, but you sold him this."

"Yep, one Rose. Coin of the realm. But that's not what brings you here."

"A man with broken teeth. Have you seen him?" Chork asked.

"Not only did I see him," Mathieu removed the pipe from his mouth and grinned, "I had the pleasure of his generosity."

"He gave you coin?" Chork voiced his amazement.

"No, he laughed at me, called me an old cripple, and kicked my bowl over."

"I'm sorry. How long ago did he do this?"

"Last night." When Chork rose from the chair, Mathieu added, "He is no longer here. He and four others took the Giran Road first thing this morning." Mathieu pointed northward.

Chork turned to go.

Mathieu used his pipe stem to point at the chair, "Stay a moment longer. You will catch your prey soon enough."

Chork, still standing, showed his frustration. "I have a question."

"Just one?' Mathieu smirked.

Chork ignored the sarcasm and blurted out, "Which do you believe? Vengeance or glory? And, why do you all delay my pursuit? First Gildona, then Timo, now you. I mean, if you are here to help me, why can't you just point me in whatever you believe is the right direction and let me go?"

"You ungrateful Twig!" roared Mathieu.

Chork's posture stiffened with anger at the slight. Yet, he stood perfectly still. Though Mathieu was but half a man in body, Chork had no doubts he faced a mage who could crush him with a single word. The elf's anger quickly dissipated, only to be replaced with shame. His face grew red and hot.

"Let you go?" Mathieu calmed. He thought a moment and shrugged. "Maybe we should. Maybe Jhodon was mad, or his prophecy false."

Mathieu no longer spoke to Chork. He talked to himself. "Maybe," he whispered. "But if not, what then? Will fate see it

189

through?" He closed his eyes and lowered his head. The internal debate consumed him, while Chork sat quietly and waited.

Finally, Mathieu nodded, opened his eyes, and said, "It is your decision, Last Born. If you no longer require our help, we will honor your wish." The white bearded, white haired mage leaned forward. His black eyes caught and held Chork's green ones. "Decide," he commanded.

The young elf held Mathieu's penetrating gaze for several heartbeats. Then, Chork's defiance shattered. He plopped back into the chair, hung his head, and blew a long breath through his frowning lips. "I ... I need your help."

"Yes, you do." Mathieu eased back into his chair, relieved by the Last Born's decision. "But, not with seeking revenge on a petty thug. You have larger ..." Mathieu stopped talking and looked over Chork's right shoulder.

A brown-haired girl, not yet seven years old, timidly approached. She curtsied, barely maintaining her balance, and placed a copper coin in the mage's bowl.

Mathieu extended his hand to the girl, and asked, "Dear Julie, whatever is that for?"

Julie took the mage's hand and replied, "I just wanted to thank you for making mama happy for a little while. Since da got the grips and can't work, mama's been sad. Today, she listened to you play and came home singing and hugged me. It made da smile."

The little girl looked at Maul and Dirk with big eyes. "Those are big dogs, mister. Da said I could save up to buy a puppy." She turned back to Mathieu. "That's where I got the coin, from under my pillow."

"Well, young lady," smiled Mathieu, "your gratitude is accepted and well-timed."

"What is g-gratie ..."

"Gra-ti-tood," Mathieu pronounced it slowly. "Gratitude is the secret of a happy life." He threw a glance at Chork, as if to say, "Pay attention."

"Gratitude is the greatest of virtues. It sires the other knightly virtues. It grows friendships. It holds communities together. It makes our lives better. It helps us to think good thoughts.

"Grateful people sleep better than resentful people. They wake up more refreshed with a positive outlook. Grateful people control their purpose in life."

Mathieu would have continued in this vein, but he happened to glance at Julie, who frowned. He tousled her long curly hair

"Think of it this way," Mathieu chuckled. "When someone gives you something, or helps you to do something, you say thank you. Sometimes, it makes you want to do something for them."

Julie nodded her head. "Da says I should always say thank you."

"Your father is a smart man." This made Julie beam with pride. "Did your father also tell you to always count your blessings?"

"No," corrected Julie, 'but mama does. When I go to sleep at night, I think of all the good things that happened that day."

Mathieu smiled. "You are wiser and more grateful than someone who is twice your age." He shot another glance at Chork.

"Now," he said to Julie, "I wish to express my gratitude to you for helping me." He reached inside his jacket and withdrew a tiny clay bottle. He held it to his mouth and whispered a few words. A low thrum caused the wolves' ears to stand up.

"Pour all of this into your father's cup of tea. Make sure he drinks the entire cup. Down to the last drop." Mathieu wagged his finger at the girl. "When he wakes, he will feel better."

Julie accepted the bottle, curtsied a little steadier, shouted, "Thank you!" and ran off.

As the little girl scampered away, Mathieu emptied his pipe, then fumbled in his pockets for more tobacco. When his hand came out empty, he frowned.

Chork reached deep into his pack and withdrew a wax-wrapped pouch. "I've carried this from Gildona's garden. I hope it is still good." He handed the pouch to Mathieu. "To show my gratitude," he offered, "please."

Mathieu's eyes shone bright. "Ollie and Gildona grow the best. Thank you, Last Born." His hand went to his right ear, under his long white hair. "I have something for you as well," he said, and placed a black hummingbird earring in the elf's palm. "When worn with its mate, they will deflect the magic of some minor spells."

Mathieu placed the flute's harness in position. "I will not delay you any longer, Elf." Setting his lips and one hand to the flute, he began to play a tune that sounded like morning birds greeting the sun.

Once again, a crowd gathered.

31 – Ham & Cheese on Bread

Free of the gathering crowd, Chork told the wolves, "We're only a few hours behind!"

Maul and Dirk sensed his excitement. Maul jumped and capered. Dirk twitched his ears.

"Hurry," Chork urged. He sprinted through Three Points and turned north onto Giran Road with the wolves at his side. In this part of town, he drew quite a few stares, but paid them no mind.

Since the road bent east after a short jog north, he thought to gain on his quarry by turning into the woods. A short jog later, he broke free of the trees and entered a small field. Across that, he skirted a small stagnant pond, leaped over a fence, and entered a crop field.

He slashed through the rows of barley, Maul and Dirk in his wake. He heard an angry farmer bellowing his discontent but ignored the man. He continued over another fence, across a greensward, and onto the north road and gained an hour or more on his target.

Maul and Dirk overtook him on the road. They ran with their tongues out and their tails high. Occasionally, one or the other would look back. They thought it was a fun game.

Chork slowed. His side hurt, and his breathing labored. The sprint became a trot, the trot a walk.

Maul and Dirk stopped and stood perfectly still. Maul put his nose high in the air. Dirk stood beside and twitched his ears. They turned their heads, allowing their ears to strain forward. They held their quivering tails high.

Chork squinted and craned his neck. He caught a slight movement far down the road.

"Someone's ahead of us," he told the wolves. "Let's go see who." Hoping it was Bell, and ignoring the stitches in his sides, he sprinted down the road. The wolves did the same.

Nearing the bend, he slowed and left the road. He crept through the brush on the right side, gained a vantage point, and looked.

Two large wagons, each pulled by mules, trundled down the middle of the road. The mule teams strained with the effort to pull the cask-laden wagons over a rough spot in the road.

Maul broke cover first, trotting out onto the road. Dirk followed. Chork watched them for a heartbeat, and then emerged from the bushes.

The wolves had closed half the distance to the wagons when the trailing wagon's driver heard or felt something. The man turned in his seat and saw the wolves. He shouted something to the other driver, stopped his wagon, and threw down the reins. He bent over and rose with something in his hands.

Chork saw the crossbow and started screaming, "NO! NO! Stop Maul! No Dirk!" He doubled his pace as Maul split to the right and Dirk to the left.

The driver pointed his crossbow at Maul.

Chork frantically waved his hands. From deep in his chest, he bellowed, "MAUL. DIRK. NO!"

First Dirk, and then Maul, stopped to glance back at Chork. The elf emphatically drove his palms forward and then down toward the ground. He continued to run toward the wagon.

Dirk sat and twitched his ears. Maul lay down.

The driver hesitated and then lowered his crossbow.

Chork drew up beside Maul and put his hand on the dog's head. He gestured for Dirk to join them. When both wolves lay in front of him, the elf again signaled with his palms, asking the wolves to stay. For the benefit of the drivers, he ordered, "Sit and stay!"

The lead wagon's driver climbed down and stood beside his colleague. Both held crossbows at the ready.

"Please," Chork said, "they will listen to me." A glance at the barrels on the wagon brought a smile to his face. Stenciled on each was a sigil that Chork recognized.

"You work for Sa'Mael 'al Jusur of Boerne!"

"Who are you?" asked the driver from the lead wagon, raising his bow.

"Chork, friend to Sa'Mael. This is Maul and that is Dirk. They have never met Sa'Mael." He pulled the coin from his pocket and offered it for inspection. "He gave me this!"

The lead driver examined the coin and showed it to his partner. With a smile, he returned it to Chork and said, "I am Eloy. My brother Ruben."

Shorter but wider than Chork, Eloy's barrel-shaped torso was all muscle. His arms and wrists were thick from years of driving large wagons pulled by 20 stubborn mules. Short black hair, pomaded or oiled straight back, topped a square head from which black eyes always twinkled with merriment. A thin, black mustache ended at the corners of his thin lips, perpetually set in an infectious smile. His clothes, despite his profession, were neat, clean, and perfectly tailored.

His young brother, Ruben, was almost a twin. A little pudginess was apparent in the arms and belly. He favored an odd-looking hat with a short brim, jammed onto his head to cover his bald spot. His smile and joy of life made Eloy look depressed.

He took their offered hands, and then pointed to the casks. Their heads boasted the crescent moon and date palm stencil. "Wine from the Wurmi vineyards?" he asked.

"Warm Red," answered Eloy, "the best grapes in all of Brehm."

Chork whistled. "Worth a fortune, I'll wager."

"Don't get any ideas," warned Ruben, grinning.

Chork laughed. It felt good to laugh, so he laughed some more. Eloy and Ruben joined him.

A perplexing look on the elf's face ended the merriment. He voiced his thought. "You two have come all the way from Boerne alone?"

Eloy shook his head and explained.

After buying the wine from the Wurmi vineyards, Rabb Sa'Mael had sent them right back out with these 2 wagons, 2 second-drivers, and 12 guards to deliver their load to Giran Castle. On the way, they withstood an attack by brigands. Unfortunately, they lost a driver, six mules, and three guards doing so. A week later, the same bandits attacked again. "This time," said Eloy, "it was all or nothing. The fighting was brutal and desperate." He glanced at Ruben and put a hand on the man's shoulder. "Ruben saved my life."

The short, stout driver paused to collect himself, and continued. The battle ended when the last two brigands ran off. Only four of their party remained standing. Himself, Ruben, and two guards. That night, the guards ran off, taking one of the mules to pack for them.

Eloy shook his head and spat.

"Over breakfast, Ruben and I discussed what to do," he went on. "We both had the same mind. We had a job to finish. And, well, here we are. Now answer me a question or two."

Chork nodded, "Sure!"

"How come you to know Rabb Sa'Mael?"

Chork told his tale. He began with stumbling upon the cherry wood caravan and rushed through the part about slaying the basilisk. He spoke in detail about the dinner he shared with the guards, mentioning each one by name and recalling their jibes and jests. He ended with the announcement of Little Herve as the new chief guard.

"A good choice that," said Eloy, "Herve has a calm head and the respect of the other drivers and guards."

Ruben nodded.

"What brings you so far north so quickly?" Eloy asked.

"Five men, one with broken teeth. Have you seen them?"

"No," answered Eloy. He looked at Ruben, who shook his head.

"They must be ahead of you. And not far." Chork turned to go but hesitated. He looked ahead to the road. *Bell is just a few hours away,* he thought. *Yet, these two could use my help.* He recalled the two children building a snowman.

Eloy sensed Chork's uncertainty. He looked toward the setting sun. "It grows dark soon. We were just about to stop for the night. We would welcome your company around our supper fire."

"Honestly, Chork," Ruben ventured. "If you spent the night, guarding the wagons," he hung his head, "Eloy and I could get a full night's sleep for the first time in days." He looked at Chork with tired and troubled eyes. "It pains me to ask this much of you, but ...we can pay you."

Chork looked at Maul and Dirk. "They ask for our help," the elf said to his wolves.

Maul yipped and nudged Chork with his nose. Dirk twitched his ears.

When his stomach rumbled loud enough for all to hear, Chork laughed, patting his stomach and then the wolves. "Seems the vote is taken. Three to none. Supper will pay enough for a night's watch."

The two drivers moved the wagons to a small patch of grass up the road. They unhitched their teams, tied their mules to a tether line, and fed them.

By then, Chork had sent Maul and Dirk to hunt their supper, while he gathered firewood.

Soon, the fire blazed, and a large ham on a spit sputtered and crackled.

Eloy produced a large loaf of dark bread and a small wheel of cheese. Rather than carve trenchers, or break off chunks of the loaf, he sliced it with a long knife. He did the same with the cheese and ham. He piled slices of ham and cheese between two slices of the bread and handed one to Chork.

Chork looked at the layers of food and hesitated. He supposed he was to eat the top slice of bread first, then follow it with the cheese, meat, and the remaining slice of bread.

Ruben chuckled. "Just take a bite. All at one time." He bit into his to demonstrate.

Chork did so. "By the bow, that is good! Easy to hold! The bread sops up the ham grease. What do you call it?"

"Cheese and ham on dark bread," replied Eloy. Ruben chuckled.

Chork laughed. "You should call it something special. Inns could sell this by the wagonload." He wolfed down the sandwich, and gratefully accepted another from Eloy.

"In Boerne, the inns DO sell these by the wagonloads," stated Ruben. "Sa'Mael came up with the idea. He claims it's less messy but much faster."

Eloy blew some air out between his lips. "Truthfully? He got the idea from his brother who said it was the latest specialty from Donham."

As conversations over a fire and a meal are wont to do, this one turned this way and that, back and forth, with laughter and a tear or three. It came to an end when Eloy pointed to the wine barrels and the reason for their delivery.

War threatened both realms, Wurm and Goole. Between each other and from within. The old dispute over ownership of Wurm's West Vineyards had been reignited. Wurmi and Goolie armies massed along the border.

Internally, the assassination of the sitting Rais jeopardized the years-long peace between Wurm's farmers, the Himari, and its nomadic tribes, the Fili. In Goole, the Blue Monk, a new prophet, incited violent and bloody clashes against the theocratic reign of the Vicar, Defender of the One and the Path. One tiny spark would set all southern Brehm aflame and draw Boerne and Rabb Sa'Mael into the conflagration.

As a result, trade flourished. The buying and selling of weapons and armor offered massive profits for Rabb Sa'Mael. In fact, Eloy explained, he would trade their current consignment of Wurm Warm Red, widely regarded as the best wine in the Eight Realms, for dwarf armor, much prized by anyone who faced a foe's blade.

Eloy stopped talking and pointed to the wolves returning from their hunt. He and Ruben bade Chork goodnight and covered themselves in their bedrolls. Within five heartbeats, both snored.

Chork asked the wolves to sit downwind of the mules. They were unhappy but complied. He alternately dozed and walked the camp.

His stroll took him to the north of the camp. He looked up the road. Bell is not far, he thought. If I ran now, I could overtake Bell tomorrow, or the day after. Before he reaches Giran. That would give me a day, maybe two, to plan and ambush them.

The elf looked at the two drivers. If he left now, he would probably never see them again.

They would wake in the morning, shrug their shoulders, and move on. Over a mug or a cup, they would complain to other drivers and lumpers about the supposed elf-friend who left them asleep on the road. It would just be another story told by men about elves. No one would care. The story would fade with time.

What could happen to them? thought Chork. This close to Giran they should safely make their way without incident. No one is coming along to slit their throats while they sleep.

But then Chork had a frightening thought. *Bell murdered a sleeping Edmod!* What would Bell or someone like him do if he came across these two sleeping, while two large wagons of valuable wine sat nearby?

You gave your word! Chork sighed. He would never forgive himself if he abandoned them. He checked the mules, and then took his seat by the fire.

* * *

As the sun shot its first rays of the new day over the treetops, the two drivers awoke. They stretched their arms, scratched their heads, and smiled.

"Thank you, Chork," said Eloy. He went to feed the mules.

"Yes, thank you and your wolves," echoed Ruben. He walked to a large barrel of water hanging from the side of his wagon and washed his hands and face. When he returned, he said, "That's the first full night's sleep I had in eight days. Feels good."

Chork smiled and said, "Happy to have helped. I'll be on my way. Oh, and thank you for the excellent supper."

"You can't leave without breakfast," complained Ruben. "I fear it is more of the same, and the ham is now cold. But, you must eat before you go."

Chork licked his lips in anticipation, and readily agreed. He saw Eloy leave the mules and walk over to the water barrel. The elf joined him there.

"I know you are anxious to leave," said Eloy, "but I have an idea. You won't run far or fast with little or no sleep. Why not

200

sleep on my wagon while I travel up the road. You can get some rest, while getting closer to Giran. When you are rested, you can move on." Turning to the barrel, Eloy removed his shirt and splashed water over his head and torso. Dripping water, he faced the elf. "What do you think?"

Chork immediately noticed the amulet Eloy wore on a short chain under his now unbuttoned shirt. It was a carved black hummingbird in flight set on a silver background. The elf pointed to it and said, "Interesting."

"Just like your brooch. Bought it in Wurm from an old woman who carved it from an odd looking coin. Funny thing is, I wanted a wolf head." He fingered the medal. "But, she insisted I take this instead. Told me it would bring me luck." Eloy shrugged. "I guess it has."

"Did she have a tattoo on her palm?"

Eloy raised an eyebrow. "I don't remember seeing one. Why?"

Chork shook his head. "No matter." He yawned. "I like your idea. What about the wolves?"

"I can make room for them as well. Or, they can run free if they don't spook the mules."

They ate quickly and broke their camp.

Chork scrambled up the cask ramp onto Eloy's wagon. The wolves followed.

When the wagon began to move, Maul and Dirk became skittish. Chork calmed them by scratching their heads and softly reassuring they were safe. The wolves finally settled and the three began to nod off.

Toward noon, a loud crash awoke the elf. Some men had felled a tree near a large beer wain with a broken axle, blocking traffic in both directions.

Eloy and Ruben and a trade caravan moving in the other direction had stopped to help the bereft driver. Men scurried about rigging ropes and stripping the bark from the hewn tree.

Chork asked the wolves to stay, climbed from the wagon, and helped shape the new axle. While working, he struck up a conversation with a guard from the trade caravan. They chatted for a few minutes, and then Chork asked the guard if he had seen a man with broken teeth accompanied by four other men.

"I did see a man with broken teeth," said the mercenary. "But there were more than four others. He was with a pack of those Green Monks."

"Green Monks?"

"Yeah, you know the ones. They wear green robes and hoods. They say they pray to Mother Earth for the good of us all."

The man stopped working again. He took a good long look at Chork, and said, "Does 'Broken-teeth' owe you money?"

"Something like that."

The mercenary nodded. "Yeah, I once chased a man for 'something like that'." He grinned at the memory. "In my younger days." He shook his head. "You won't get close to him while he's with those monks. Best to wait 'til they get to Giran. 'Broken-teeth' will leave them the minute he sees a common room."

"Thanks."

"Hey, if you need help in Giran, I have a good friend. He doesn't come cheap, but he's discrete and good," the man lowered his voice, "at something like that."

Chork grinned. "Thanks, but this is personal."

"I understand."

Chork walked away to speak with Eloy and Ruben. He told them that he no longer needed to reach Giran as quickly as he originally thought. "If you'll have me," he told them, "we can continue our arrangement until then."

The drivers, ecstatic with Chork's decision, slapped the elf on the back, almost knocking him to the ground.

Ruben growled, "Let's finish this repair job and get on our way."

32 - The Hunted

The Green Monks and their guards crossed into Giran over the Pink Bridge, so named for the color of its granite stone. They crossed in silence. They, their footfalls, their gear, their clothing, all made no sound. It was as if a bubble of silence enclosed them. This bubble pushed its way through the crowds and infected all those it touched.

Though he played no part in creating the silence, Gary Bell derived great pleasure from being a part of it. He perceived the crowd's looks of fear and loathing as admiration and jealousy. Occasionally menacing a child or woman with his broken teeth, he strutted just behind and to the left of the Green Abbot.

At the instant the Abbot reached the city side of the bridge, he turned to Bell. "Your services are no longer required." He extended a bag of coin to Bell.

Bell, whose mouth hung open in disbelief, made no movement to receive the bag.

The Abbott dropped the purse at Bell's feet and walked off. The other five monks followed, in single file.

Bell's eyes followed their progress up the congested street, made easy by the silent bubble. His mouth still agape, he felt a jab at his back.

"You gonna pick that up?"

Bell tossed a quick sneer over his shoulder at Tim Barclay. He looked down at the purse. "Ignorant m-monk." He spat through the hole in his teeth, retrieved the purse, and added, "S-stupid religion, too."

Opening the purse, he let out a whistle. When the monks offered a coin per day per man, he hadn't thought to ask what weight of coin. He had expected copper or, at best, silver. He grinned broadly, baring every one of his broken teeth.

"I tol' ya boys," he beamed, "w-we'd do good here in Giran." He pulled out a handful of gold coins and let them drop one by one back into the bag. "C'mon, fellas," he gestured with his arm, "w-we need ta' find a c-cozy lil' inn."

Bell looked at the three streets that began at this crossroads. He disregarded the middle one taken by the monks. Taking a coin from the purse, he flipped it into the air and caught it. Without looking at the result, he said, "This w-way, gents," and led them down the street on the right.

Bell hesitated at the first inn they reached. After a quick glance, he announced, "Never p-pick the first, it's too p-pricey. It c-caters to them that can afford not to w-walk down the road." At the next, he said loudly, "Never p-pick the second, lads, it's always too crowded w-with them that can't afford the first."

At the third inn, he made a show of inspecting the exterior. "Hmmm," he mused. "W-whadya think, Tim?" Bell figured that if the beer was sour and the maids unfriendly, he could always blame Tim for selecting it.

"I thought the other two looked just fine," Barclay complained. "I'm thirsty, hungry, an' tired of walking." The other three men voiced their agreement, spoiling Bell's scheme.

Bell glared at Barclay. He led the four men into The Ram & Cowherd Inn.

Locals, most nursing pre-supper beers, half-filled the common room. In the corner, a travel-stained bard plucked a few discordant notes on a battered stringed instrument.

Bell picked a table in the middle of the room and called for a barmaid. When a heavy, dark-haired matron approached, he turned to his cronies and whispered loud enough for the woman to hear, "Never p-pick the first, she's too much w-woman." The men laughed.

The barmaid gave Bell a false smile, curtsied, and turned away. She signaled a younger, light-haired woman to the table.

"Never p-pick the second, she's too inexperienced." Bell screwed his face into a frightful leer, so his friends understood his ungentlemanly meaning.

The young barmaid signaled to a heavy-set man behind the bar. He walked over to Bell's table and asked, "What will it be, gents?"

"Once again, Bell," Barclay blurted through a guffaw, "I thought the other two looked just fine."

The others broke out into a roar of laughter. Jim Neal slapped Barclay on the back. The brothers, Mark and Martin Robins, pointed at Bell and shook their heads.

Bell snarled and gripped his dagger.

"Now, now," interjected the barman, "let's have none of that in here. Geordie and Hugh are right there with their cudgels. You'll find yourself in the street with naught but your heads full of lumps and your bellies empty."

Bell forced a chuckle and turned to the man. "You're right, sir. This is the place for m-merrymaking. A round of beers for me an' my c-companions. Bog's beer, if you have it." He put a gold coin on the table. "K-keep our mugs full 'til this runs out." He placed another coin on top the first.

Soon, dust-covered travelers looking for a drink, a meal, and a room, replaced the locals, who left for their home-cooked suppers. Kitchen maids scurried about, delivering plates of fowl and trenchers of stew.

Two young barmaids, obviously sisters, arrived to handle the growing crowd. Between orders, they spent their time ogling the Robins's, who returned their attentions.

The young barmaid, who had signaled the barman earlier and had now ended her work day, sat on Barclay's lap. The dark-haired woman always filled Neal's mug first, which he acknowledged by pinching her cheek – gentle ones to the face, at first, more meaningful ones lower as the evening wore on.

Bell tried to entice every maid who came near but failed miserably. They ignored his lewd remarks and avoided his roving hands. Growing desperate, he turned his attention to the lovely lass seated at the next table with an older man and woman. When her father surreptitiously revealed a long, well-used dagger, Bell threw up his hands in mock innocence and turned away. Tossing another gold piece on the table, he ordered a bottle of wine.

By the time four merchant guards replaced the family of three, Bell was deep in his cups. He listened to the mercenaries' boasts about their individual exploits – bar fights won, bandits repelled, an ogre driven off – and attempted to interject himself into their conversation.

"Child's play!" Bell hooted. The large quantity of beer he had consumed had cured his stutter but enhanced his affliction with rudeness and bad judgment.

"You've done better?" asked the largest of the guards. The man had a shaven head, bent nose, and cruel beady black eyes.

Bell began his boastful tale of raw courage and martial prowess by describing the elf who, one sunny day, dared to enter the peaceful hamlet of Little Creek. His recollection of the image of soiled clothes, matted-filthy hair, dung-encrusted boots, and blazing, evil green eyes drew a favorable response from the mercenaries.

The pointy-eared vermin, obviously suffering from the Curse, was armed for all-out war. He shouldered a wicked looking bow and a quiver of black-fletched arrows with barbed points coated with a green sticky goo, obviously poison. Two single-edged blades, nicked from countless battles, hung at his sides. The handles of daggers and knives protruded from boots, tunic, belt, and pack.

Worst were the two massive dire wolves that slowly plodded alongside the elf. Larger than full grown horses, they were. With heads bigger than an ox's rump. Their slavering beet-red tongues lolled between fangs the size of belt-knives. Bulging, blood-red eyes looked at each Little Creek inhabitant as the next meal. Their claws, honed finer than a butcher's filet blade, still carried traces of their last meal.

Bell's exaggerations and lies had begun to draw a small crowd of maids and customers. Eavesdroppers from other tables silenced their companions and leaned closer.

Neal removed his hand from the barmaid's rump and listened, at first, wondering what Bell was saying that so enthralled the mercenaries. With a quizzical look on his face, he opened his mouth to interrupt. Barclay grabbed Neal's arm and violently shook his head.

Noticing his audience had swelled, Bell raised his voice and continued.

Leaving the wolves outside as guards, the elf stormed into the cobbler's shop. There was a loud crash and then a blood-curdling shriek. The elf emerged with new boots and sat right there in the street trying them on.

The cobbler crawled out the door and cried one word before he collapsed. "Thief."

The elf just laughed.

Then Little Creek's mayor, the kindly and generous Avery Kobs, confronted the elf. But, the elf just laughed all the harder and pushed Avery to the ground and kicked him.

"That's when I unsheathed my sword," said Bell. He stood and drew his blade to demonstrate. He now had the attention of everyone in The Ram & Cowherd. He took a quick pull on his wine and continued in a loud voice.

The elf, cowardly cur that he was, had no stomach to fight a true and armed Giran man. He ordered his wolves to attack.

As the nearest beast leaped for Bell's throat, Bell swung a mighty blow and lopped off its head. He would have succumbed to the second wolf but for his friend, Tim Barclay. A truer friend no man could have. Tim deflected the second wolf's leap with a club. Whereupon, Bell ended the wolf's life with a well-placed lunge of his sword.

Bell had imitated his two killing blows for the crowd, who shouted their delight, some with fists raised, others with mugs held high.

A woman at a nearby table asked, "What of the elf?"

Bell replied that the elf used several magic spells to hide his flight into the hills surrounding Little Creek. Bell said he organized a search party which failed to find the elf.

"But!" he shouted. "He returned that night with comrades. They slew the mayor in his bed while he slept an' torched the public barn, tryin' to burn Little Creek to the ground."

Bell plopped back into his seat. Feigning grief, he reached for his glass, but found it empty. A barmaid rushed in with another bottle. He thanked her, drained the glass, and signaled her for another.

"We drove them off," he whispered. "Me an' Tim led the charge that broke their will. We been huntin' 'im down since."

"A good story," said the beady-eyed mercenary. "Tell me, if the elf never drew an arrow, how did you know the heads were barbed and coated with poison?"

"Yeah," his companion, a bearded Girani, said. "And, why was a man the mayor in Little Creek?" Some in the crowd demanded Bell answer.

"You never killed no dire wolf by slicing off its head with that piece of dull iron," said another, pointing to Bell's sword. This one a dark-skinned, barrel chested brute.

Bell looked up from his wine glass. "You callin' me a liar?"

"Yeah, we all are," beady-eyed said.

Their eyes locked.

Complete silence fell over The Ram and Cowherd.

Before anyone could act, Bell and the mercenary had each other's throat.

Barclay jumped to Bell's aid. To help his comrade, the Girani mercenary intercepted him. Both tables were overturned, mugs crashing to the floor, as all nine men began to scuffle.

The barman signaled to his doormen. With cudgels raised, Geordie and Hugh pushed through the crowd, who became irritated, and pushed back. Within seconds, the normally peaceful Ram & Cowherd was now host to a massive brawl.

Hours later, Bell slept soundly on a straw mat in his cell. Barclay, Neal, and the Robins brothers snored nearby. In the next cell, the beady-eyed mercenary glared at Bell. "It was a good story, but you're still a liar," he growled and passed out.

33 – The Starling's Song

Chork sat next to Eloy on the wagon as they crossed the Pink Bridge into Giran. Maul and Dirk sat beside Ruben in the other wagon. *Odd*, the Last Born thought, *Maul is sitting to Ruben's right, and Dirk to his left, opposite of how they sit and walk with me.*

This late in the evening, few people used the bridge across the Rose River, which originated in the Aril Mountains and fed into the Mud River just a few miles downstream. Those who did use the bridge were challenged by three members of the Brigade of Thorns.

The Thorns showed no interest in Chork or the dogs. They wrapped their attention around the casks of wine, whistling and offering to taste the goods. An officer silenced their remarks by clearing her throat. She then looked up at Eloy.

"Wurmi wine for the castle buttery," Eloy called.

"And you, Master Elf," asked the officer, her skepticism apparent, "are you a driver as well?"

"Our guard," replied Eloy. To which, the woman raised an eyebrow.

"A messenger as well," added Chork. "From Mage Timo Koira, the Master Breeder, to Mage Paul Keyes at the Starling's Song."

"We hired him on in Three Points," Eloy started to explain.

However, the Thorns officer turned her head and began to walk away. She waved them across the bridge.

At the crossroads, Eloy stopped his wagon and turned to Chork. "Our paths part here, my friend," he said, offering his hand. "The Song lies that way." He pointed to the left. "Ruben and I go to the castle." He pointed straight ahead. From his jacket, he took a small pouch. "Your pay."

"No, I couldn't," protested Chork. "You let me ride when I was tired. You fed me and taught me much about mules, wagons, and ..."

Eloy chuckled, "I deducted for the food. The ride and lessons were free." Eloy put the pouch in Chork's hand.

"Thank you, my friend." Chork grasped Eloy's right forearm. "May the wind give distance and accuracy to your arrow." He jumped down and walked toward the other wagon.

Ruben met him half way and shoved another small purse into Chork's hand.

"Eloy paid me," argued Chork, thrusting the pouch back at Ruben.

"Not enough, I'll wager," Ruben joked. "Now, don't argue with me. Just take it. You'll need it in this city."

"Thank you. For everything."

"Meh," said Ruben. "If you have time, look for us at The Ram & Cowherd Inn on the East Bank. The first round is on me."

Ruben clambered back up into his wagon seat. "Now get out of the way before we run you down."

Chork watched as his two friends slowly rolled away. Maul sat at his left and Dirk stood on his right. Chork frowned but said nothing to the wolves.

Eloy had told the Last Born that the Starling's Song belonged to Osila Byd and her daughter, Saylaso. The driver had said Mistress Byd ran a very clean and respected inn. Her food was some of the best in the city and her portions were very generous. Unlike some inns in Giran, she paid no heed to race or religion, opening her doors to anyone who behaved.

"Let's go," Chork said after Eloy and Ruben passed from sight.

* * *

The Song's common room, quiet at his hour, had large windows facing the river. Neat rows of drawings and paintings lined two of the other three walls. All were portraits – many of the same woman – but others of men, women, and children of all ages. A toddler's interpretation of her mother held an honored spot on the wall above the bar.

With his wolves in tow, Chork strode across the room to stand at the bar in front of a young lass who was absorbed with charcoal and parchment. She obviously had created the portraits. When Chork leaned to see who she was drawing, his head cast a shadow on the corner of the paper.

"Back off," said the girl, "you're blocking my light." She pointed to the tables, "If you want a drink or a meal, choose a table."

"I'd like a room for me and my friends," said the Last Born.

The lass looked up. Maybe two years younger than Chork, she had a slender nose separating large black eyes, and long, wiry black curls pulled back from the unmarked skin of her face. Her full lips curled into a slight smile, which brought an inner glow to her eyes. She looked beyond the elf into the room. "Where are your friends?"

"Here, beside me, on the floor." Chork pointed to Maul and Dirk who lay at his feet, yawning.

From behind the bar, an unseen woman said, "We don't welcome drunks, sir. Try an inn on the East Side."

The girl leaned over the counter and saw the wolves. Her eyes opened wide. "Not drunks, mom. Wolves! The biggest wolves I ever saw."

Osila Byd stood up. The inn's owner was a taller, heavier, and older version of her daughter. "Wolves? Dogs are kept in the kennel out back. A copper a day. But, wolves?"

"Mom," Saylaso interrupted, "I don't think these wolves will fit in the kennels." She had come around the bar to sit on the floor. She had begun to sketch Maul. When she motioned for the wolf to raise his head, he complied.

It was Osila's turn to come out from behind the bar. When she saw Maul and Dirk, she caught her breath, and reached for her daughter. "Those ARE big wolves! At least that one is." She pointed at Maul.

"Bred and trained by Mage Timo Koira," declared Chork.

"May I pet them?" asked Saylaso.

Chork nodded and said, "Palm up, and slowly."

"I know," Saylaso said in a sassy voice. She reached out with both hands and caressed the wolves' chins. "What are their names?" She scratched behind their ears.

"The big one is Maul. This is Dirk."

"Dirk!" Saylaso laughed. She placed both hands around Dirk's head and hugged him.

Dirk twitched his ears. The twitching fur of his ears tickled Saylaso's cheeks. She laughed. The more she laughed the more the ears twitched.

Osila began to laugh too. Chork joined in. "You should get her a dog," Chork said to Osila.

"I've considered it."

Suddenly, Chork remembered Timo's note. He pulled the crumpled paper from his pocket and handed it to Osila. "Before I left him, Mage Timo gave me this."

Tell the girl's mother that a suitable friend will arrive on the summer's last full moon.

Osila read the note. When she saw the hummingbird signature, she threw a quick glance at a man with his head on a table in the back of the room. "Why?"

Chork shrugged.

"You can have the side room," said the innkeeper, again looking at the note. "It has a private entrance and is large enough for you and your friends. It costs extra. One gold coin per day." She stuffed the note into her bodice. "How long will you stay?"

"As long as I need to complete my business." He withdrew five gold coins from his purse. Two were Roses, the coin of Giran. Three, slightly heavier, were Wurmi, stamped with the crescent and palm.

"Your friends look hungry." Osila remarked, scooping the coins from the counter.

"I'll feed them!" exclaimed Saylaso. Osila looked to Chork, who nodded.

"Give them those leftover joints of mutton," directed Osila, again looking at and receiving a nod from Chork. "Ask Retta to fix one last supper plate for our new guest."

"C'mon, Dirk, let's eat! You too Maul!" The three passed through a doorway, laughing and yipping.

"I'm Osila Byd, the Song's owner." She waved her hand at the kitchen door. "The young one is my daughter, Saylaso." From beneath the bar, she retrieved a bottle of wine and two wooden goblets. She led Chork to the nearest table, sat, and poured the wine. "Not Warm Red, but passable."

The elf joined her at the table. "My mother named me Lye Tella'estela Hummien'dulin, but I prefer Chork." He sipped the wine. To his young, inexperienced palate, the wine tasted like any other.

"I'm not good with elvish, so I prefer Chork as well. What brings an elf with two large wolves to Giran?"

"I'm looking for someone," replied the Last Born. "Actually, two someones. Mage Timo bid me give this to Mage Paul Keyes at the Starling's Song." As he produced the block of wood, he felt a slight tingle.

Osila stole a furtive glance at the man at the back table, who now snored. Ignoring the wooden cube, she asked, "And the second someone.

"A man with broken-teeth, named Gary Bell."

"I don't know this Gary Bell. I haven't seen a man with broken teeth. Why do you search for him?"

"It's my own business."

"Usually, when a man says it is business, he means murder." She got up from the table. "I'll not be a party to killing. I'll return your gold. You can seek shelter at an inn down the road."

"Wait," pleaded Chork. "The man murdered a Blue Bolt in Kent and killed my dogs. He would have killed me had my legs been slower." He withdrew his rumpled Blue Bolt jacket from his pack. "I am a Monck Blue Bolt on Lord Monck's authority." *It is a small white lie,* he thought.

"So, it's justice you seek." Osila said. "If what you say is true, then you must go to the Brigade. Deliver the man to the Queen's Justice."

"It would be the word of a man against an elf," Chork spat. "There's no Queen's Justice in that."

Osila shook her head. "You're wrong."

Chork raised his eyebrows. "As you say. What of Mage Keyes? Is he here?"

The snoring man raised his head. "How is dear Timo? Probably running with his pack no doubt."

Chork turned to face the man. He saw the bright blue eyes first. They dominated what would otherwise be a nondescript face except for the colored tears tattooed on his cheeks.

"I am who you seek. Paul Keyes, at your service."

The man pulled back his cowl to reveal a bald, shiny head. He had a whisper of a grey-brown mustache and goatee, surrounding thin white lips, covering perfect white teeth. His cheeks and nose were red from drink.

"Landlady Byd," said the mage, joining them at their table. "Please," he put his two hands together as if in prayer, "bring me a bottle of my usual." At a look from Osila, the mage quickly added, "No, no, I promise. There will be no violence at the Song." He turned to the elf, "Do I speak true, Lye Tella'estela Hummien'dulin?" He showed Chork the black hummingbird tattoo on his palm.

Just then, Nettie, the barmaid, appeared with a trencher of lamb stew. She set it before the elf and told Osila she would be leaving. Osila thanked her and asked about Saylaso. "In the kitchen, drawing those wolves while they gnaw on the joints," answered Nettie.

"Ah," said Paul, "Mistress Byd wishes to close the common room for the night. Finish your plate quickly. I have my own room out back. We will talk there."

* * *

The mage walked directly across a small courtyard to an oak log building. The door, made of hand-rubbed maple without a knob or handle, bore the same image as on the mage's palm.

The mage waved his hand, palm out, in a circle at the door. A short thrum sounded. The door sprang open, revealing an orderly workshop and living space.

A large window on the left looked out on the river. To either side, hung shelves of matching sets of wood-carved tableware – plates, cups, mugs, and bowls.

To the right sat the living space. A straw filled mattress occupied the corner with a small oak table, piled with neatly arranged books, scrolls, and a reading lantern. A carved-oak table with three matching chairs, a cedar chest of drawers, a cedar cupboard, and a walnut privacy screen filled the living area.

Between the workshop and the living space, a large fireplace stood. It provided warmth and the ability, not only to cook, but also to heat water to bend wood. In front of the fireplace stood two chairs carved of the same polished maple as the door.

"I like working with wood," said Paul. He pointed to the oak table. "Sit and eat." The mage removed his cloak to reveal a plain grey tunic and pants. He hung the cloak on a wooden peg by the door and waved his hand again to close the door.

Chork walked over to the chairs and looked them over. He hesitated before sitting. The chairs looked very hard and uncomfortable.

"Sit," insisted the mage. "They are much more comfortable than they look."

Chork sat down and immediately jumped back up. "T–the chair moved under me!" He looked at the seat of the chair. He expected to see something different from the same flat, hard-looking surface he had first noticed.

The mage chuckled. "Please, sit. The chair will not harm you."

Chork sat again. He realized that the chair seat, back, and arms were rearranging themselves to conform to his body. When the movement stopped, the chair was possibly the most comfortable he had ever sat in.

He laughed. "A magical chair!"

"No," contradicted the mage. "Magical wood shaped into a chair. Much like that magical wood is shaped into a door." Mage Keyes pointed and moved toward the door. There came a light knock. The mage waved his hand and the door opened.

"Your wine," said Osila. "I assumed you have two cups in there."

The mage laughed. "Thank you, Mistress Osila." He closed the door and fetched two polished wooden cups. Sitting opposite Chork in the other chair, he poured the red wine and offered one to the elf.

Chork examined the cup carefully.

Mage Keyes chuckled again, "No. That's normal wood."

"Normal wood, magical wood," Chork snorted. "Magical wood shaped into a chair produces a magical chair."

"Magic can be found most anywhere," said the mage. "Wood and stone, as well as mages and elves." He extended his tattooed palm and whispered a few words. The elf heard a soft hum. "You possess several objects which contain magic," Paul said, extending his hand. "One which is for me?"

Chork pulled the wooden block from his pocket. "It tingles when I touch it."

"You sense the magic within, just as you felt the chair move beneath you."

"But, I can't perform magic," Chork said.

"All elves have magic," assured Paul. "Have you tried to cast a spell?"

Chork nodded, his face flushing with the lie.

Paul pursed his lips. "Then you have experienced the Test of Bowls?"

"No," Chork admitted.

"Until you do, those baubles you wear are nothing more than just that – baubles."

34 – Friends & Foes Together

Her Majesty Terilyn Rose, Eldest Female of the House of Rose, Holder of the Alliance, Defender of the Pass, Queen of Giran, was sovereign to more than three million people scattered from the Thumb River in the north to the Sun's Anvil in the south, and from the Mud River in the east to the Aril Mountains in the west. Her palace, named the Style, cut from a single, solid spire of pink granite, stood 200 paces high in the center of a circular keep of overlapping walls called the Petals.

Surrounding the Petals sprawled an inner city known as Dorothea, so named in honor of the Queen's ancestor, who had formed the First Alliance. Dorothea lay behind the thick, outwardly-curved outer wall called the Sepal, constructed of massive green granite blocks.

The Rose and Mud Rivers, respectively, flowed along the southern and eastern legs of the Sepal. Between the Sepal and the rivers lay the outer city, satirically called Parfum by Giran nobles because of its everyday odors of cooking food, perspiring workers, and plodding livestock.

To deliver their priceless cargo of Wurm Warm Red, Eloy and Ruben had passed through Parfum to the Sepal's Gate of Bouquets. From there, they had wended their way through Dorothea to the Petal's Buttery Postern. Because of the late hour of their arrival, they had left their wagons under guard outside the Buttery.

This morning, the brothers, after a good night's sleep in beds and an even better breakfast, directed the unloading of the wine into the keep's cellars.

"On a clear day," said Eloy, looking up at the Style, "using a magical stone called the 'Iris,' the Queen can see all of Giran."

Ruben followed Eloy's gaze upward. "You think she's up there now looking down at us?"

Queen Terilyn was not looking down, nor was she in the Style. She was making her way to the Hall of Guests. She had just instructed her chamberlain, Sean Burchell, to organize a caravan to supply Lavanham, a budding fiefdom along the Thumb River.

As Chamberlain Burchell hurried across the bailey, he spied Eloy and Ruben. "Just in time," he said, "the Queen plans a feast the night after next. I'm afraid much of this," he indicated the wine, "will disappear that night." He took Eloy's proffered hand and clapped Ruben on the back.

"We'll be happy to fetch more," offered Eloy. "We can be on our way as soon as we load the dwarf armor."

"Ah, yes, well," muttered Burchell. "It hasn't arrived yet."

"When will it get here?" asked Ruben.

"A week, maybe two. No more than three." The chamberlain pressed his lips together and shrugged. "With the rumors of war to the south, the dwarves say they are hard pressed to fulfill the many orders."

Eloy shook his head. He expressed his dismay with waiting for three weeks in Giran without pay. After all, what would he say to Sa'Mael? The driver suggested the chamberlain invite the brothers to wait in the castle as guests of the Queen while paying them for their lost time.

"Of course," said Burchell. "I will make the arrangements just as soon as ..." He paused and thought a moment. "Maybe, I can do better than that and solve two problems with one caravan."

Burchell explained his need for at least two large supply wagons for Lavanham. The trip, up and back, would take four weeks at the most. A squad of Thorns and Lady Lavan's recruits would furnish escort. The Crown would provide provisions, and "pay, oh, say a Rose per day per wagon."

Eloy looked at Ruben. Ruben scratched his chin stubble.

"By the time you return," urged Burchell, "your armor will likely have arrived. If not, which I seriously doubt, then you find yourselves as guests here."

"A month up and one back. Make it two gold coins per day per wagon," Eloy said. Ruben nodded his head.

"A Rose and a Bud. You can leave the Queen's wagons and return on horseback," the chamberlain countered.

"Two Roses," Ruben insisted. "You'll have to pay twice that to find someone else and cover your costs while we sit here, drinking your wine and eating your food."

Now, it was Burchell's turn to scratch his short black beard. He knew Ruben was right. Getting the brothers at such a price would save the Crown money. "You drive a hard bargain. You'll leave this afternoon."

* * *

Across the bailey in the dungeon, an over-weight jailer banged on a tin bowl with a wooden spoon. The noise was enough to wake the dead and the nine hungover brawlers in adjoining cells.

Holding his head in his hands, Bell shouted, "W-when're you goin' to let us out?"

"After breakfast," replied the jailer. He shoved a bowl of brown oats into Bell's hands. "Why the Queen insists on feedin' the likes of you is more'n I unnerstan'." After serving all nine, he growled, "Eat up, gents. If'n one spoonful is on the floor or in the pots, you'll spend another night with us."

Bell hunkered down in the front corner of the cell, spooning oats into his mouth. Beady-eyed sat down next to him in the other cell and pulled a tooth from his mouth.

"Good fight!" he claimed. "Got my tooth knocked out."

"I tried to knock 'em all out," Bell chortled.

"Whatcha gonna do when we get out?"

"Get me a drink. W-why? You w-wanna get another tooth knocked out?" Bell finished his oats and set the bowl aside.

"I was thinkin' we'd talk a bit." Beady-eyed glanced at Bell. "By the by, name's Odom Rogue. Friends just call me Rogue." He slid his hand through the bars.

Bell ignored the proffered hand. "Talk about w-what?"

"A job." Rogue slurped the last of his oats. "A bleedin' good'un. Good pay. Usually a silver Bud a day for little work."

"Doing w-what?"

"Walkin' aside some wagons. A bonus when we get where we're goin'."

"All right, gents? Well nourished, are we?" The jailer returned with a large ring of keys. He counted and checked the bowls. He threw cursory looks at the cell floors and into the chamber pots. Fiddling with the key ring, he said, "Our Queen's hospitality is over." He found the two keys he needed and placed his hands on his wide hips.

"Now, gents," he looked at each one in turn. "If'n I see you in here again. Well, that's the work gang for three days. Chamberlain Burchell is buildin' a new privy for the castle Thorns. It's honest work, gents, from sun-up to sun-down. Luggin' and layin' stone. The pay is three meals and a straw mat, right here with me."

The jailer opened the cell doors. "Now out with you. An' don't forget to bow to the Style to thank the Queen for puttin' up with your drunkin' backsides."

Outside his cell door, Bell quickly conferred with his comrades, telling them about Rogue's offer. Barclay said he would follow Bell.

However, Neal and the Robins brothers declined. They preferred what Giran, specifically the Ram & Cowherd, offered.

223

Previously, the three had discussed their distrust of Bell and Barclay and determined to abandon the two ex-Blue Bolts at the first opportunity. They demanded their remaining shares of the Green Monks' gold.

Silently, Bell cursed the moment he stacked the gold coins on a table for all of them to see. He grudgingly paid the three off, mumbling about their lack of camaraderie and stupidity.

Bell then faced Rogue. "Gary Bell," he said and extended his hand, "this here is Tim Barclay. W-when and w-where're these w-wagons goin'?"

"Today, north," answered The Rogue with a gap-toothed smile. "Along some of the quietest roads in Giran. To a place called Lavanham."

"W-who's in charge?"

"A dark-haired gent in service to Lady Lavan. But, you'll be takin' yer orders from me."

35 – Dishwater and Integrity

At mid-morning, Saylaso, with Maul and Dirk, appeared in Chork's doorway. "You better get downstairs for breakfast. Mage Paul has already gobbled up all the bacon."

The Last Born roused himself. He had slept late because he went to bed late. Chork and Paul had talked into the wee hours of the night. Chork had done most of the talking, recounting his entire life story until he had arrived at the Starling's Song.

The old mage had sat and listened, asking odd questions for clarification. He had shown interest in hearing about his friends: Timo, Gildona, and Mathieu. He had frowned when Chork said Mathieu received the pouch of Gildona's tobacco.

Chork smiled at Saylaso and then looked again. Maul stood to Saylaso's right, Dirk to the left. *They do it for a reason, he thought. How can I get them to tell me what it is?*

Saylaso rubbed the toe of her right boot along the doorframe. "Mother has given me two errands in the city. Could I take Dirk and Maul with me? She said to ask you. I'll be careful," the young girl pleaded. "And the errands aren't that far away. We'll be back quickly."

Chork grudgingly nodded his assent. He caught the wolves' attention and signaled to them with hand gestures.

"Will you teach me how to do that?" asked Saylaso.

Chork smiled, "Yes, but not now. Go run your errands. I hold you responsible for the safety of our friends." He turned to the wolves, repeated the gestures, and said to them, "I hold you two responsible for the safety of our new friend."

* * *

Breakfast at The Starling's Song was a popular meal. Patrons occupied nearly every table in the common room. Most eschewed conversation for the fare on their plates and in their bowls.

Mage Paul sat at his table, licking his fingers. "Ah, the young elf! Sit, Chork Two-Wolves, and dig in."

As Chork sat across from the mage, Osila placed a large plate in front of him. "The greedy mage has eaten all the bacon. We're cooking more. Start with this." Off she went to serve other tables.

Chork looked down at the plate. "What's this?" He saw yellow fluffy curds speckled with red, orange, and black crumbs.

"Are you serious?" asked the mage.

Chork pushed at the curds with a spoon.

"Ready your palate for a treat, Chork. Those are hen's eggs, mixed with cow's milk, sharp cheese, hot red peppers, and black olives. Try a spoonful."

Chork hesitated but did as the mage had suggested. A look of delight crossed the elf's face. Within seconds, he cleaned his plate, and looked around for more.

Paul laughed. "Mistress Byd, another plate of eggs for my guest! And me! And more bacon, if you please."

The two ate their fill.

Paul sat back. "Told you Mistress Byd served a tasty and filling breakfast, didn't I?"

Chork sighed and patted his stomach.

Paul laughed. "Don't get too comfortable. We've work to do."

"Work?"

The mage stood up. "C'mon, we'll help with the dishes."

"Dishes! I'm no kitchen scullion."

"Neither am I," replied the mage. "But I do choose to be helpful. I make it part of who I am. Besides, breakfast dishes take less effort than dinner dishes."

A short hour later found Chork bent over a tub of hot soapy water. He had continually rolled up his sleeves. Though why he bothered now, he could not say. His cuffs were wet, and twice in the soapy water, he had mistaken them for the dish rag.

"I suspect," said Paul, "you believe your pursuit of Bell and his comrades is a righteous cause."

"I do." Chork declared. "I suspect you do not and plan to tell me so." He sighed. "I don't wish to sound ungrateful for any help you can give me. Not for avenging my friends." He fumbled for words. "That is, I would be thankful for that help, but I meant for helping me to realize my dream of knighthood."

The mage pulled the last plate from the rinse tub and placed it on a stack. "We're finished here. Follow me."

On his way out of the kitchen, Paul grabbed two large red apples from a bowl on a table. He took a bite of one, held it up for all to see, and asked the cook, "Jeff Lambert's orchards?"

The cook smiled and nodded. "You're getting much better, Mage."

"Thank you," he responded. The bald mage tossed the other apple to Chork. "I know just the spot to enjoy these."

* * *

"Here we are," said the mage. He sat facing the river with his back against a half-buried boulder. Munching on the apple, he patted a spot next to him.

The two enjoyed their apples and the quiet of the river for a time. Then, Paul stood up and walked a short distance away. Bending down, he dug a small hole in the ground. He took apple seeds from his mouth, placed them in the hole, and covered them.

With a nod of approval, he reclaimed his seat against the large rock. He withdrew another apple from within his billowing white shirt.

Chork, astonished, stuttered, "H–how d–did you? Now that is more impressive than the magic wood!"

Paul shook his head. "You saw what I wanted you to see. The apple in my right hand. You neglected what my left hand was doing."

Chork laughed. "So, it wasn't magic at all."

Paul smiled. "Misdirection," he said. He became serious. "Some of us think your pursuit of vengeance is misdirected."

"Yes, Gildona told me." Chork said. "So, you believe I will return my race to its former glory?"

"Perhaps," Paul said. "But I wasn't referring to the Prophecy."

"I made a promise at my friends' gravesites. I will see Bell dead."

"I, for one, believe you must complete the task you have set for yourself. To keep your oath to your friends. I believe it to be a matter of integrity. Something you must learn if you are to fulfill your dream of knighthood."

Chork smiled. Finally, he thought, someone who believes as I do.

"Don't look so smug," Paul abraded him. "You have much to learn and little enough time to learn it. Especially so since you must relearn what you have already forgotten!"

Chork began a protest, but Paul cut him off. "When have you last practiced with sword and bow? Do you think yourself a master of each? Where is the hard work and humility Pogi taught you?"

Chork's cheeks turned as red as a new rose. He said feebly and with little conviction, "I practiced when I could. Since Little Creek, it's difficult to find the time." He felt the lies dry on his tongue. Their taste was bitter and made him wince.

Paul raised his eyebrows. His first instinct was to scold this young elf. Yet, he sensed another lecture would do more harm than good. After Mathieu's outburst and ultimatum, the Last Born now needed a gentler hand.

"It's good that you find the lies distasteful, Chork Two-Wolves." The mage gave the elf a fatherly smile and placed his hand on the elf's shoulder. "You should know though that the more you tell a lie, the more palatable it becomes. Even small lies."

"I'm sorry," Chork breathed.

"I accept your apology." Paul nodded, realizing the elf was sincere. "Sir Gunter Taafe. You have heard of him?" When Chork nodded eagerly, Paul continued, "I heard this great knight say: 'Honesty is the truth we give others. Integrity is the truth we give ourselves.'"

"I tried to read Sir Gunter's treatise." Chork made a wry face. "But, it was long and difficult."

"Think of it this way. Honesty is what we say. Integrity is what we do."

Chork considered this a moment. "That's easy. If we always speak the truth, we will always act truthfully."

"Sort of," Paul smiled again. "Integrity requires consistency. No matter how different a situation is, we must say and do the same thing. Earlier, I asked if you thought your pursuit of Bell was a righteous cause."

"I still believe it is."

Paul nodded. "I do too. But, I must warn you of a disastrous trap. Those who wrap themselves in the robe of self-righteousness often believe that they may do whatever they wish, no matter how contradictory to their stated code. They justify their actions by claiming the righteousness of their cause."

Chork puzzled on this. He tried to think of everything he had done since he began chasing Bell. He remembered Little Creek, setting fire to the shearing barn. Had anyone died in that fire? He didn't know. He did know that he had endangered the entire town. Innocent, as well as guilty. Innocent children and women. Those same people, who, the next day, ran Bell and his comrades from the village.

Paul merely pursed his lips and listened while the Last Born related his thoughts to the mage. He nodded and asked, "Have you thought about what you will do when you catch Bell?"

"Practically every night," Chork replied. "Not only what I'll do. I've even rehearsed what I'll say." Chork paused. "But, now, I'm not sure."

"I'll leave you to think about it." Paul stood. "Think about practicing, too." He took two steps and stopped. "You can't think on an empty stomach." He withdrew another apple from his shirt and tossed it to Chork. "Magic is almost as useful as misdirection."

* * *

The Last Born had much to think on, not the least of which was Paul's insinuation that Chork abandoned his oath multiple times, the least of which was by not practicing daily. His worst offense was his attack at Little Creek.

If the town had caught fire ... Chork's heart stopped. I would be no better than those who burned Kent. A murderer.

And what of Bell, he wondered. He had dreamt of using Pogi's sword to run the vile traitor through. Barclay too. Now, he wasn't so sure that was the right thing to do. But, taking Bell back to face Lord Monck's justice would be an arduous task. One that required ...

A movement from the right interrupted his thoughts. It was Saylaso and the wolves. Again, Dirk stood to the girl's left, and Maul to her right.

"Why do they do that?" the elf asked. "Stand on opposite sides with you and others."

"You really don't know?" Saylaso sounded surprised.

"No, I don't."

"You're right-handed. I'm left-handed."

Chork's eyebrows climbed up his forehead while his lower jaw traveled the other way. *Another lesson in humility,* he thought.

Saylaso laughed. Chork joined in.

"Do you have time to teach me some hand signals?" Saylaso asked in between chuckles.

"Sure," the elf answered with a smile, "and then I have to practice." He clapped his hands to get the wolves' attention and waved them over to help with Saylaso's lesson.

36 – The Hunted Escapes

Returning to his room at the Starling's Song, Chork retrieved his sword and bow. He found a small yard behind the inn next to the kennels, removed his jacket and shirt, and began working through the stances and forms Pogi had taught him. At first, he fumbled about, almost tripping himself on a two-handed crossover slice, and even dropped his sword when he attempted a simple parry and lunge.

A small crowd gathered. Passersby joined some of the inn's maids and scullions and a few of the inn's other guests. They made disappointing noises when he stumbled, and a few walked away. However, as Chork became more fluid, the crowd oohed and aahed, applauding once for a sly riposte after sliding his feet in a complete circle.

Maul and Dirk, who lay with their heads between their paws, garnered attention as well. Soon, Saylaso appeared, at first to watch and then to sell mugs of beer and fresh-baked meat pies.

A tall man, named Jerome, with a thin blade on a leather loop approached and offered to spar, saying the two of them seemed evenly matched. Chork eagerly agreed and sized up the man as he removed his hat and tunic. They danced this way and that, kicking up dust and delighting the crowd. Chork won as many times as he lost. When they tired, the man retrieved his hat and found it contained a handful of coins, which he offered to share with the elf. The Last Born declined and asked only that the man return the next day at the same time. Of course, the man agreed, which drew a loud cheer from the crowd.

Drying himself off with his shirt, Chork picked up his short bow and quiver. He had Saylaso draw a fist-sized circle on a sturdy oak plank leaning against Mage Paul's workshop. The elf stepped off 20 paces and emptied his quiver of un-banded arrows, hitting inside the circle with each arrow. He then measured another 20 paces further and scored the same. These feats drew wild applause and several challenges which Chork readily accepted for the next day.

With his practice complete, to Saylaso's embarrassment and the delight of the women in the crowd, Chork stripped to his small clothes and jumped into the river to swim. This garnered him hoots and hollers and a severe scolding from Osila, who marched him sopping wet into the inn's bathhouse where she secured his promise to not "do that ever again, especially in front of my daughter."

* * *

As Chork began his practice, Eloy evaluated his companions for the journey to Lavanham. They stood in two contrasting groups. The first, six Thorns standing in a straight line, looked young and inexperienced. Laden with red-lacquered helmets and breastplates, crossbows, quivers, swords, and packs, they looked anxious to leave. An overly serious, short round captain led them. The second group, eight men of varying ages and cleanliness, ogled the line of Thorns. The men looked like a pack of wolves selecting their dinner from a flock of sheep. Their weapons varied as did their attire – swords, cudgels, war axes, short bows. One large man with beady eyes carried a poleaxe twice his size. Two wrapped themselves in stained brown cloaks with deep cowls. One sported a shirt of steel mail. Another a vest of boiled leather.

This second group, Eloy thought, would be more reliable in a fight, if they didn't abandon their responsibility first. However, he realized, they could just as likely club him in his sleep and steal his wagon. The driver shook his head and looked at Ruben, who rolled his eyes skyward.

Eloy's response was a murmured epithet, which interrupted Spotty Herold's study of the young Thorn with red hair. Named so because of his freckles, the swamper asked what bothered his driver. Eloy, in turn, asked Herold if he had ever handled a team with so many mules.

"Nah, but how difficult can it be?" sassed the young driver. He went back to staring at the red-haired Thorn.

Eloy swore again. He knew the young man would soon have a chance to find out. Driving a nine-ton wagon with 18 mules and two horses was quite different than prancing along in a shay with a pony or two. He was about to say so when he noticed Chamberlain Burchell walking across the bailey with a man dressed in white – boots, pants, tunic, and cloak. Their conversation, though not heated, was spirited.

The chamberlain introduced the man as Master Lesar 'ib Arari, Lady Lavan's retainer. Arari would be their guide to the northern fiefdom. His word would be considered as that of the noble Lady's own, and her authority came directly from the Queen.

Arari, half Eloy's age and twice Spotty Herold's, curtly bowed his head barely a knuckle's length. His raven-black hair, cut short and combed and pomaded like Eloy's, stayed in place. Clean shaven with a square jaw, his thin lips were set in a constant smirk, as if he knew something others did not. His dark eyes glistened, but not with merriment. To Eloy, they revealed an inner intensity that waited for release.

The man-in-white shook hands with the Thorns captain and inspected her troop. At the last, he curtly nodded, shorter than his first bow. Then, he moved to the beady eyed man with the poleaxe. They spoke for a minute and the latter called over two other men.

Probably, new conscripts, thought Eloy. He bolted upright as his eyes widened with recognition. "Wait here," he said to Spotty

Herold. Eloy jumped from his seat and ran to Ruben's wagon. Climbing up, he said to Ruben's second, "Go visit Herold. I want to talk to Ruben alone."

When the swamper was out of earshot, Ruben asked, "Do you think it's him?"

"How many fellows with broken teeth live in Giran?" Eloy whispered.

"A few, I suppose."

Eloy blew air through his lips.

"Yeah, it's too coincidental."

"We've got to get word to Chork."

"How?"

"I don't know. I'll think of something."

Eloy climbed down and said, "Chamberlain, we're short one sack of carrots for the horses. May I ..."

"Be quick about it." Burchell waved his hand in a shooing motion. He faced Arari and made a quick comment, followed by a snort.

This time, Arari didn't even nod. He mounted a white horse and gestured for the troop to do the same.

A short time later, Eloy emerged from the storehouse with a sack of carrots slung over his shoulder. He quickly mounted his wagon and tossed the sack behind him.

"We already have ..." Herold began to say.

"Shut up, Herold," Eloy growled. "Ready!" he shouted.

As Arari led the caravan toward the Postern Gate, Eloy nodded once to Ruben, who replied with a smile and a wink.

37 – Treachery

The Last Born devoured his supper, a trencher of venison stew with red peppers, carrots, and turnips, and washed it down with a pitcher of cow's milk. Wiping his mouth on his sleeve, he leaned back in his chair. The intense practice and filling meal made him feel good. Whole. Centered.

He wanted to thank Mage Paul, but the hummingbird wizard was nowhere to be found. Osila said he had left mid-afternoon without a word.

The Song's common room began to fill. Guests, local merchants, a four-some of Thorns worked steadily at their trenchers while listening to a familiar-looking, shaggy man with a lute. Chork found the scene peaceful and comfortable. He would have liked to stay, but he had a murderer to find.

Leaving Maul and Dirk in Saylaso's care, he slipped out the inn's side door and headed downriver, stopping at the inns and taverns along the way.

At each place, the elf ordered a beer and struck up a conversation with a maid or bartender. He told them he owed his friend some money. None recognized the name 'Gary Bell,' or had seen a man with broken teeth, though two offered to take Chork's money and give it to Bell when they did. Chork politely refused this favor.

He passed the Pink Bridge on his right and continued downriver. The third inn, The Ram & Cowherd, brought a smile to his face. Maybe, he would find Eloy and Ruben instead of Bell among the locals who packed the inn for their last mug of the evening.

Chork wanted to get to the bar, but a crew of stone workers stood three-deep there. Pushing through would likely anger them.

So, the elf took a just-vacated table near the door. When a dark-haired barmaid finally approached, he asked for a cup of wine, her most expensive.

She smiled and nodded. "Herve may have to open a new bottle."

Chork returned the smile and dropped two gold coins on the table. "Would you ask Herve to stop by when he can?"

"He's rather busy. Is there something I can do?"

"I'm looking for some friends. Two wagons drivers. Eloy and Ruben."

The maid nodded. "I know those two. Real gentlemen." Looking around, she frowned. "They're not here right now and I haven't seen them since before the new year."

"I'm also looking for a man with broken teeth, Gary Bell. He's with four others."

Her frown deepened. She shook her head. The maid snapped, "Lemme get your wine."

He watched as the maid worked her way through the stonecutters. Her conversation with Herve was short, highlighted by pointing to the elf.

Herve took a long look. He turned back to the barmaid and shooed her away to tend to the now dwindling crowd. Having retrieved a bottle and cup from the back counter, Herve sat down at Chork's table. He poured the wine but held onto the cup. "The man with broken teeth," he asked, "you really his friend?"

"No."

Herve nodded. "You know most people here have no use for elves." He pushed the wine toward Chork. "Me? I find them to be honest and reasonable people. Did he kill your kith or kin?"

"He didn't kill an elf. He killed two dogs."

"Not wolves?" Herve spat on his own floor. "Yeah, I figured he lied. Yours?"

Chork nodded. He reached for the cup of wine.

Herve pulled the cup back. "You plan on doing something about it here in the Ram?"

Chork shook his head.

Herve pushed the cup toward Chork. "Good. Because if you did," Herve said, "you'd change my opinion of elves."

"He's here, then?" Chork sipped the wine.

"No. He was here the other day. With some lads. Some I liked. Some I didn't. They figure in your plans as well?"

Chork shook his head again.

"Bell left here the other night escorted by Thorns. I suggest you go talk to them." He recorked the wine and stood up. "Finish your cup and be on your way."

Making her rounds among the room, Mary, the barmaid, stopped at the table in the far corner, where Neal and the Robins brothers had their heads together trading bawdy japes.

"Hey, Rosebud," said Neal, looking up, "we thought you forgot us." He smiled broadly and slid a silver coin from the stack next to his hand. "Bring us another round and join us."

"Jim," Mary whispered, "see that elf by the door?"

Neal leaned back in his chair and looked. His eyes opened wide and he sat up straight. The brothers' faces went white.

"What does he want?" Neal asked.

"He's looking for your friend," replied Mary, "the mean one."

"You didn't tell him we're here, didja?"

"No." Mary sounded hurt. "But Herve might. Look, he's goin' over now."

They watched anxiously, waiting for Herve to point in their direction. When the barman got up to leave, without pointing, Neal let out a long breath. He grimaced. His dark eyes bounced back and forth. He looked at Mary with a sly grin. "That elf means to kill me."

"What? Why?"

"I'll explain it later," Neal cut her off. "Right now, you got to help us get him before he gets us."

"Jim, no, I ..."

"Listen, Rosebud," Jim put his hands around her waist, "all we want you to do is tell him that the man he's looking for is in Jubert's stable." He pointed in the direction of the stable which sat across the road from the inn. "You got to do nothin' else. Just walk away. Say nothin' else."

"B–but ..."

"You won't be hurtin' 'im, darlin'. You dun want him to hurt me, do ya?"

38 – A Message Undelivered

Saylaso squinted at the charcoal shading on Maul's back. "Is it the evening light that makes it look too dark? Or, did I use too much?" she asked aloud, tilting her head this way and that.

"It's looks about right."

Saylaso looked up from her charcoal sketch. She saw a young lad, maybe two years her senior, comparing her sketch to her subject.

"Very good," said the lad. Though lanky, he wore a pleasant smile on a pleasant face. Long lashes fluttered over his large brown eyes. His nose, slightly bent to the right, scrunched up, as he commented, "Though I do think Dirk's tail is longer."

Saylaso dropped her charcoal and stood. Maul and Dirk also stood and joined Saylaso. Dirk on her left. Maul on her right.

"How do you know his name?" she demanded in a firm voice.

"The man who gave me my errand told me their names."

"What man?"

"Eloy, a wagon driver. He also gave me a gold coin and told me if I delivered his message to the owner of the wolves at the Starling's Song, I would get another from their owner."

"What's the message?"

"It's not for you," the boy declared. "Where's their owner?"

Saylaso pursed her lips and thought for a moment. She remembered her mother's admonishment that one could catch flies with honey not vinegar.

"I'm Saylaso Byd." She extended her charcoal covered hand. "He left the wolves in my care."

"Gabriel Fass. My friends call me Gabe." The lad took Saylaso's hand and held it for a moment as he gazed into her eyes. When he realized what he was doing, he withdrew his hand and scratched his nose.

Saylaso giggled. "You got charcoal on your nose."

"Oh, um, sorry." He wiped his shirtsleeve across his face. He merely smeared the charcoal across his cheek and onto his sleeve.

Saylaso giggled again. "Here," she said, dunking a cloth into the rain barrel next to her.

"Thank you."

"Since the owner entrusted the dogs to my care," Saylaso ventured, "you could entrust the message to me as well."

"I don't know," he hesitated. "Maybe I should just wait for him to return."

"Only if you let me sketch you." With eyes locked to her feet, she clasped her hands in front of her and turned her body to the right and quickly back to the right.

"Deal." Gabriel spat into his hand and extended it so Saylaso, who now scrunched her nose.

"Um, sorry again." He wiped his hand with the wet cloth.

"Go sit over there," Saylaso pointed. She signaled for Maul and Dirk to join him. She also made the gesture for friend.

"Try not to look so frightened," she told him, as she picked up her parchment and charcoal.

39 – Dig Two Graves

Chork sipped the red wine and winced. Its bitter aftertaste sat on his tongue. He tried to scrape it off with his two front teeth, but that transferred the vileness to his lips. Wrinkling his nose, he pushed the cup aside.

Mary appeared and picked up the glass. "The man with broken teeth is in the stable across the road," she whispered. In a swirl of skirt, she left.

A salty metallic tang replaced the bitterness in his mouth. It took the Last Born a moment to realize the shock of Mary's words had caused him to bite his tongue, drawing blood. His right leg began to bounce with apprehension. His eyes stared at the table but focused on the past. He saw Edmod's bloody shirt. Kent in flames. Pogi's cloven head. Marigold's smashed face. Aelmar's crumpled torso. Gimlet and Slick, their lifeless bodies hacked to pieces.

He vomited onto the table and rushed from the tavern, chased by the screams and bellows of Mary and Herve.

Outside The Ram & Cowherd, Chork gulped huge mouthfuls of air. The odors of venison stew, stale beer, and bad wine caused him to vomit a second time. His eyes teared. He now stood in the middle of the street, gagging, coughing, his legs and arms trembling.

Fighting for control, Chork looked up and down the street. He watched people swerve to avoid him. He overheard several cautions, and the occasional whispered curse. He had to get off the street. *Find an alley!* his mind roared. Frantically, he looked left, right, then straight ahead.

A sign above an open gate read 'Jubert & Sons – Shelter for our 4-footed friends'. Another sign listed the daily prices. 'Horses & Mules – 2 cop. Others – Ask.'

Suddenly, his tremors stopped. He drew himself to his full height. He felt the hilts of his weapons, reassuring himself his sword was at his side, his dirk was in its chest sheath, and his dagger at his back.

The elf looked up and down the street. He saw no Thorns. A few stumbling drunken merchants worked their way downriver. A donkey drawn cart lumbered toward the crossroads.

Jubert & Sons' open gate called to Chork.

A tiny voice in the back of his head urged him to return to the Song. Get Maul and Dirk, it said. Get the bow and the red-banded arrows. Another voice implored him to seek out the Thorns. He quashed both voices with an angry grunt.

The brief glow of pipe embers, the waft of smoke, and the smell of tobacco alerted him to the guard sitting in darkness near the gate. With a short spear balanced against his knee, the man played cat's cradle with a much worn cord. He was oblivious to the elf and would remain so, if Chork did not attempt to enter through the gate.

The small voice warned him again. Find some Thorns. Tell them your story. Let them take Bell. See the Queen's Justice. No! Get Maul and Dirk! Your bow. Your quiver!

He ignored the advice and looked for another way into the stables.

* * *

From the roof of a line of box stables Martin Robins watched the elf. He smiled and whispered, "The fool's doin' exactly what Neal said he would. This'll be easy." He shot a quick glance at where he thought his brother hid, behind a large wooden crate

243

between the stables and the barn. He gave his brother a thumb's up, not knowing that his brother couldn't see him and wouldn't be watching anyway.

Their plan was simple. The elf would crawl through the fence and creep between the two lines of stables to get to the barn. When the pointy-eared, blight-stricken killer reached the end of the stables, Martin would snare him with a noose.

To accomplish this, Martin had tied a hangman's knot in the middle of the rope. Then, he coiled the rope once around the roof's extended keyboard. Holding both ends of the rope, Martin would roll off the roof. One line would tighten the noose around the elf, and the other would, with Martin as a counterbalance, hoist the elf into the air.

Mark would jump out from behind the crate and bash the elf with a cudgel, rendering him unconscious. Then, the brothers and Neal, who was hiding in the barn, would deal with their pursuer as they saw fit.

* * *

Chork examined the fence surrounding the stable's grounds. It was designed to keep four-legged animals in but not two-legged sneaks out. He crawled through and waited, listening and peering into the moonless night.

A clang caused him to crouch lower and grab the hilt of his dirk. Off near where the gate guard sat, there came a curse. The man had allowed his spear to slide onto the ground. He reached down, picked it up, and stood.

Chork, remaining still and barely breathing, heard the guard pace back and forth across the open gate, once, twice. The man returned to his seat with a grunt. This time, the spear lay firmly trapped by elbows across his lap as he toyed with the string.

The elf expected Bell to be in the barn, comfortable in a straw bed, unseen behind wooden walls. However, he knew Bell and his comrades could be anywhere in the stables. They could even be waiting for him. With that in mind, Chork crept away from the fence.

The smells of a stable assaulted his nose from all sides. Two lines of box stalls lay ahead. Some looked to be occupied. The path between them led directly to the wide open barn door.

Chork hesitated. *Maybe,* he thought, *it would have been better to enter the stables from the river side.* This would have put him behind the barn. He looked to the right beyond the stalls, thinking he could slip around them and approach the barn from its side. However, he saw several cages of dogs sitting next to dog carts. Though the beasts slept, his passage would surely wake them. Yapping dogs would let everyone know someone was where they shouldn't be.

Going left around that line of stalls was not an option. First, it would put him within direct site of the guard. Second, he would still be approaching the barn door head on.

Martin looked down on the elf and knew what he was thinking. Yep, you shoulda come in from the back. Nope, you can't walk past the dogs. That's right. Get as close as you can to the stalls and walk right into my noose!

Chork did exactly that. He eased alongside the box stalls, hugging their doors and walls so tightly, his shoulder slid along the wood. At the wall's end, he stopped and peeked around its corner.

The barn lay not 15 paces away. In its wide doorway, a man bent over a lit oil lantern.

When Martin saw the elf's protruding head, he dropped his noose and rolled off the roof.

At the last minute, whether it was the sound of the rope falling or Martin's roll off the roof, the Last Born looked up. One step in any of three directions would have foiled the brothers' plan. However, Chork squatted, thinking the noose would not drop low enough to snare him. He was wrong.

The noose fell around Chork's neck. Martin's weight tightened the rope and hoisted Chork a pace into the air.

Chork gurgled, grasping for breath, his hands clawing furiously at the rope. Luckily, Martin's momentum acted like a pendulum, swinging the Little Creek man into the elf. The force of the collision prevented Chork's neck from snapping and brought the elf to his senses. He drew his dirk and plunged it into Martin's heart.

Martin let go of the rope. Both then fell to the ground. Martin dying. Chork choking.

"N-no-o-o-o!" wailed Mark, as he burst from behind the crate.

"W-a-a-a-h-h-h!" yelled Neal, as he charged from the barn, kicking the lantern into a bale of hay.

Chork struggled to loosen the rope with one hand and to draw his sword with the other. Instead, he tangled himself hopelessly in the two strands of rope.

Standing over Chork, Mark swung his cudgel, catching the elf above his left ear, driving Chork to the ground and near unconsciousness.

"Hit 'im again!" cried Neal.

His head on the ground, Chork looked in Neal's direction. Behind the approaching man, he saw red and orange tongues of flame licking at the barn's front wall. He heard other people shouting, someone beating a metal pot, and boots slapping the ground. Unable to lift or turn his head, he strained to move his left eye further left and upward. To brace himself for the next blow, he needed to see it coming.

What he saw though, through blurred vision, was a red rose blooming from the center of Mark Robins's chest.

That makes no sense. How could a rose grow from a man's chest? He asked himself, before losing consciousness.

40 – An Audience Goes Bad

For the first time in half a week, the mid-day sun glared through the windows. However, it wasn't the sun that woke Chork. It was the pain – not the burning pain of his rope-rubbed-raw neck, or the stabbing agony of his right ankle. It wasn't even the pounding ache in his head, which felt as if an ironmonger beat on the inside of the elf's skull with a large hammer.

No, the pain came from his right hand. A throbbing pain coupled with the bites of countless stinging insects.

Chork tried to move the hand and failed. It was pinned beneath something heavy and furry. He raised his head and saw Maul.

The dog had laid his large head on Chork's hand, stopping blood circulation. For how long, Chork couldn't guess. The hand was purple and puffy, like a too-ripe grape about to burst.

With his left hand, Chork signaled Maul to back off.

Maul lifted his head, licked Chork's hand, and padded across the room near Dirk who lay on a chest, his ears twitching as fast as butterfly wings.

"I thought I would never see you again, my friends," Chork rasped. His throat hurt with the effort.

"Hey now!" said Mage Paul, his head poking through the doorway. He turned away and said, "He's awake. Go tell Chamberlain Burchell.

"Where am I?" asked the Last Born.

The mage raised his hand and took a seat beside the bed, "Let me get comfortable." He pulled a yellow apple from his pocket, and said, "Henri Jaune's orchard." With his belt knife, he sliced the apple in two and offered a half to Chork. The elf declined. "More for me then." The bald mage took a large bite. "By my count, you made nine mistakes."

"I'm aware of what I did wrong." Chork closed his eyes and nestled into his pillow. "How long have I been sleeping?"

"Three days, as a guest of the Queen," relied the mage. "The head wound," he pointed with the apple, "was the worst you suffered. Your ankle was sprained and is healing with my help." Again he pointed with the fruit and then took another bite. "You neck will be scarred for a few weeks at most. I left that to remind you of your folly."

"And those who attacked me?"

"Mostly dead."

"I think I got the one who tried to hang me. What happened to the other two?"

"You killed Martin Robins. The stable guard speared his brother, Mark. The Thorns captured James Neal after a brief chase through the fire. He's a guest of the Queen, but his room has no windows."

"Bell wasn't there," Chork complained.

"No."

A man appeared at the doorway. He gave Chork a brief glance and turned to Mage Paul. "Can he walk?"

"With my help," the mage answered.

"Then dress him and bring him to Court. I'll inform Her Majesty." The man left.

Chork shot a puzzled glance at the mage.

"Lord Chamberlain Sean Burchell. It seems you have an immediate audience with the Queen."

* * *

As Chork and Paul crossed the Bailey from the Guest House to the Style, another man joined them. Matching Paul, four tear-drop tattoos colored white, blue, green, and red graced each of his cheeks. Of average height but powerfully built under his white tunic, he had a shaved head, dark eyes, an aquiline nose, and thin lips. "Is this the one you told me about?" he asked his fellow mage.

"Yes, Friend Justin," nodded Paul. He left Chork to stand as best he could and pulled Justin away from the elf's earshot. They spoke in hushed tones. Then, Justin nodded and hurried into the Style.

"Who was that?" asked Chork.

"Mage Justin DuPriest, the Queen's counselor. Now, your ally." Paul took Chork's arm and walked the elf to the Style's gates. "Some words of caution, Elfling. Do not speak unless questioned. Answer truthfully and do not volunteer anything." He pulled Chork's arm so that the elf faced him directly. "Remember Pogi's teachings. You are a knight-in-training before the Sovereign of the Land in which you stand. Behave as such."

The instant Chork entered the Throne Room he felt like a tiny bug caught in a gigantic rose bush. Green thorny stems with an occasional leafy branch had been carved into each wall, all growing toward the ceiling 200 paces overhead. Behind the Throne itself rose a large carved stalk culminating in a massive, fully bloomed red rose directly above the throne.

Upon that throne sat the most beautiful woman Chork had ever seen. He was instantly smitten and felt an exhilaration that befuddled him. As a young elf, he had never considered the other gender in such a manner.

A few years older than he, Queen Terilyn had long yellow gold hair and pale perfect skin. Her lips were painted as red as the rose above, her cheeks a few shades lighter. From across the room, the color of her eyes was unrecognizable, but Chork assumed they had to be green, the same hue as a new sprout. Her silken pink gown was adorned with gold threads that resembled the vines and blooms of tiny tea roses. The gold crown that nestled in her soft hair bore one red-mithril rose bud, symbolizing that Giran had yet to fully bloom as a nation but intended to do so.

Queen Terilyn addressed a woman with wavy black hair who knelt before the throne with head slightly bowed. Though nearly 100 paces away, the acoustics enabled Chork to distinguish each word.

"We formally welcome you, Lady Cuadrilla Lavan of Lavanham, to the Rose Court of Giran. To all rights and responsibilities as titled noblewoman from our northern border. To attend us as obligated with the full protection of the Rose Throne."

The kneeling woman bowed her head lower and said, "I pledge fealty and service to the Rose Crown of Giran, to sustain and maintain the laws and customs of Giran, fitting my knowledge and ability. Thus swear I, Cuadrilla Lavan of Lavanham."

Queen Terilyn raised her hand in a gentle motion and directed, "Then rise, Lady Cuadrilla, and take your place among the Court's peers and friends."

As Lady Cuadrilla rose and moved off to the right to join the other nobles, a polite applause, somewhat tentative and muted, escorted her to her station.

The Lord Chamberlain Sean Burchell then stepped forward and announced, "Your Majesty, the Elf, Lye Tella'estela Hummien'dulin." He turned to face Chork and Paul and waved them forward. "You may approach the throne."

More than 100 pairs of eyes watched as the elf and mage strode toward the Queen's dais. Subdued gasps and whispers followed them.

With Paul's help, Chork limped along the polished granite floor. His eyes never left the Queen. Three paces before the first step, both took a knee (Chork with difficulty), bowed their heads, and remained that way while the Chamberlain summoned James

Neal, Daisy Wilmer, and Claude Jubert. Neal, his manacles removed, was accompanied by two Thorns.

Terilyn bid them rise and examined each in turn. Her gaze lingered on the elf for a time, interrupted by a whisper from Mage Justin. The Queen nodded. Looking at Chork, she said, "Mage Keyes, you've been too long absent from our Court."

"Alas, Your Majesty, my responsibilities have required me elsewhere."

"We see and understand." She nodded her head toward Chork. "Perhaps soon your obligations will allow you to do otherwise."

"I will make certain of it, Your Majesty."

"Good." Terilyn addressed the Chamberlain. "You may begin."

"Your Majesty," said Chamberlain Burchell, "This is Daisy Wilmer, newly selected mayor of Little Creek." He nodded toward the woman to step forward and speak.

Daisy Wilmer didn't want to be here. But, she accepted her duty as mayor to represent Little Creek. Her friends and neighbors, especially those who were merchants, had insisted she demand redress for their losses. Daisy knew, she and everyone in Little Creek would have to answer for idly casting a blind eye to Kobs' crimes and usurpation of the Queen's authority.

"Your Majesty," Daisy bowed from the waist. Her throaty aged voice cracked. She cleared her throat and declared, "This elf tried to burn Little Creek to the ground. He set fire to a shearing barn while we slept and murdered several of your good subjects. We seek justice."

Terilyn smoothed her gown. "Mage Justin informs us that a man preceded your selection as mayor. How was this possible given the laws and customs of Giran? He also informs us that the good people of Little Creek first killed the elf's dogs without reason and would have done the same to this elf had they laid hands upon him."

"Your Majesty, we ...," Daisy hesitated.

"And you, Master Neal," continued the Queen, "we understand you were a part of this. Yet, you lay a claim of murder against this elf."

"I do, Ma'am," blurted Neal, whereupon one of the Thorns poked him in the ribs. "That is, Your Highness." Another poke and a quick whisper yielded the correct address, "Your Majesty." To the Thorn, he whispered back, "She's not my queen."

Neal was quick to explain out loud. "Majesty, I'm not Girani. None of us were or are. Those of us that are still alive, that is." He pointed toward Chork. "Ones this elf hasn't murdered." A poke from his other side drove him to one knee.

"Enough!" ordered the Queen. "Let this man speak!"

"See, Majesty, we thought we were still in Monck." Neal then wove a tale about joining Avery Kobs, who supposedly had Lord Monck's blessing and authority to secure border hamlets and villages. "This town had no mayor, no one in charge. Just an old dotty woman who could barely see and hear. So, Kobs took charge with our help. Me and the Robins's and a few others."

A few laughs broke out from the Court. The Chamberlain's glare silenced those.

"This elf comes into town and steals some boots from the cobbler. When Master Kobs calls him on it, the elf sets his dogs on him. We just came to his defense. Then, that night, the elf sets fire to the town. Murders Kobs and some others while they slept. We chased him here and he kills Martin and Mark. Woulda kilt me if I hadn't run."

All eyes, including the Queen's and Chork's, returned to Daisy Wilmer.

"Well, Your Majesty," Daisy stated, "a little of that is close to the truth."

Laughter broke out again, but quieted as she told the truth from Kobs taking over the town with a gang of toughs to the women and men forcing the usurpers out.

"Where are your three companions?" the Queen asked Neal.

"A bear mauled Jordy on the road," lied Neal. "The other two?" He shrugged. "They talked about taking a job out of town with a fella we met at the Ram. I ain't seen them since."

"And you, Master Jubert," continued the Queen, "you also have a claim against this elf?"

Claude Jubert had lost his stables and family home in the fire started during the fight between the elf and those he pursued. Also, two customers had lost animals and demanded compensation. Claude's wife argued that since the elf had precipitated the fight, the elf should be held accountable. Though not sure, Claude decided agreement with his wife was the wise thing to do.

"Yes, Your Majesty," Jubert stepped forward and said in a brash tone, "The elf snuck into my place and attacked him," he pointed to Neal, "and the two dead ones. During the fight, they set fire to my stables and home. Two horses and a mule were lost." Surprised by his boldness, the man bowed low and then took a knee.

A wave of anger rolled through the Court.

"My Queen," interrupted Paul, "if I may?"

"No, you may not, Mage Keyes," snapped the Queen. "We would hear his own explanation. In his own words. Your injuries do not prevent you from speaking, do they, Lye Tella'estela Hummien'dulin?"

"N–no, Y–your Majesty," stammered Chork. "I, I ..." The Last Born faltered and hung his head. He took a deep breath and blurted, "I have never seen such beauty as yours. My heart is ..."

A huge gasp arose from the Court. The sound of drawn swords and daggers echoed throughout the Great Hall. Angry protests were voiced.

Paul rolled his eyes and shook his head.

James Neal thought he saw his opportunity and seized it. His guards were caught flat-footed. From the Thorn on the right, Neal yanked her dirk from its sheath and lunged at the elf, screaming, "Murderer!"

Simultaneously, two spells hit Neal. One from Mage Justin, the other from Mage Paul. Neal collapsed to the floor, dead, as a deep thrum reverberated through the Hall.

41 – Banished

Neal's body, charred beyond recognition, had been removed. Several ladies, who had fainted from the sight, had been carried on litters to recover in private chambers. At the insistence of Dame Michelle Lynne, Knight-General of the Brigade of Thorns, extra guards now stood at the dais stairs between the Throne and the remaining Court attendees.

Mages Justin and Paul conferred with Chamberlain Burchell. Paul said very little and finally nodded in agreement. He glared at Chork and said, "Your mouth has placed you in a precarious position, Elfling."

"But, I didn't mean to offend," Chork began.

"You are not talking to some bar maid. I advise you to tread lightly."

Chork shook his head and muttered.

Queen Terilyn returned to the Throne, gazed upon the Court, and declared, "We will continue. Lye Tella'estela Hummien'dulin, we understand you have some training as a Knight of the Lilies. We hope that instruction extends to the proper behavior in Court."

"Yes, Your Majesty." Chork took a knee. "I humbly ask that the Queen and the Court accept my apology."

The young Queen admitted to herself that she found the elf attractive. Holding back a smile, she commanded, "Rise and describe for us the path that brought you here."

Searching for where to begin, Chork stood and glanced at Mage Paul.

The old mage nodded and mouthed one word, Edmod.

With a tear in his eye, Chork began his narrative with his discovery of Edmod's lifeless body. He spoke of Kent's destruction in hushed tones. The Last Born noted the sobs from a few ladies and lords when he told of Fat Nat's murder. Bypassing his discovery of Emig's abandonment and his time with Sa'Mael, he told his version of what had happened in Little Creek. The anguish over his dogs' deaths revealed his anger and desire for vengeance. He didn't notice the alarm in Mage Paul's expression or the grim set of the Queen's lips. He admitted to setting fire to the shearing barn and to killing the guard with a poison tipped arrow. He admitted to killing Kobs and his two henchmen. The Last Born ignored the angry, muted protests of the Girani Court and launched into his description of the fight at Jubert's stables. Finally, he revealed his desire to continue searching for Bell and Barclay, to bring them to justice at the point of his sword.

Spent, but oddly relieved, Chork again took a knee. "Your Majesty, I accept what justice befalls me."

Mages Paul and Justin, Dame Michelle, and Chamberlain Burchell spoke at the same time, trying to catch the Queen's ear. Members of the Court shouted, some asking for mercy for one so wronged, others for retribution for the death and destruction of Girani subjects and property.

The Queen silenced all with an angry gesture. She wanted time to think. Like the Court, she was of two minds. As a Blue Bolt of Monck, he wielded the authority and responsibility of Lord Monck to pursue the murderers. So too, the elf had earned the Crown's gratitude for removing the usurpers from Little Creek, though he warranted punishment for his manner of doing so. As for his actions at Jubert's stables, this Lye Tella'estela. What was the common translation? Our Last Hope? What does that mean? It didn't matter. Besides, she preferred Chork. It danced off her tongue. This Chork had sought his own justice and endangered the outer city with fire by precipitating the fight at the stable. Yet, he had not started the fire and had been drawn into that fight by the now dead Neal. However, the elf had started the fire in Little Creek. He had damaged Girani property and had slain Girani citizens.

And then, she admitted, there were her own feelings. She was strangely attracted to this elf. His long dark hair. His blazing green eyes. His pale, unmarked skin. His broad shoulders. She found herself aroused by his mere presence.

If only she could retire to her chambers away from the Court's eyes and ears, she knew she could puzzle this out in time. But that would signal weakness to the Alliance, the nobles who supported her claim to the Rose Throne. Moreover, as the youngest Queen to have ruled Giran, her strength and resolve were constantly in question. If she showed that lack of resolve, she could lose the throne.

The Court grew restless. A few mumbled their desire for justice. Others, for leniency.

The Queen knew a decision had to be made, here and now.

As the Queen hesitated, Mage Justin glanced toward Paul, who nodded his confirmation. The Girani Counselor looked toward the Chamberlain and Dame and received slight nods of agreement from both. With a prearranged furtive gesture, Mage Justin signaled the conspirators' suggestion to the Queen.

"Lye Tella'estela Hummien'dulin, rise and heed the ruling of the Rose Throne," commanded the Queen. "We find your quest for justice for your fellow countrymen noble ..." Her stern look silenced murmurs of agreement. "... yet the manner of seeking it unacceptable to the laws and customs of Giran." Another look prevented any further comments. "On one hand, the Throne owes you a debt of gratitude. On the other, the murder of its subjects and the willful destruction of their property demand the harshest of penalties."

Queen Terilyn, taking a deep breath, smoothed her gown, and surveyed the court. "Therefore, we order that within two days you depart forever from Giran. If you do not comply with this command or should be later found in our realm, you incur the penalty of death to be lawfully executed by any ladyship." She stood, signaled to Chamberlain Burchell that Court had ended. Striding from the Main Hall with tears in her eyes, she ordered Dame Michelle to attend her.

As the Hall emptied, Mage Justin and the Chamberlain joined Paul at the foot of the dais stairs.

"Thank you, my friends," Paul said to the two Girani. "Had the mood of the court swayed her either way, the Queen could have ended the Prophecy. Banished, the elfling has no choice but to follow my advice."

"For a moment," replied Mage Justin, "I feared that as well. Her Majesty did appear as if ..." He shook his head, denying what he was about to say. He turned to Chork and asked, "Are you fit to travel, Elf?"

"He has no choice," advised Chamberlain Burchell with finality.

42 – A Late Message

Back at the Song, Chork lay in bed and stared at the ceiling. Banished!

He was ashamed. He was angry with himself. He got out of bed and, favoring his ankle, started to pace the room. Yet, before he could form another thought, there was a soft rap at his door.

"Mom said you should eat," Saylaso said. She set the tray on the table near the window.

"Saylaso," Chork began, "I don't know what ..."

"There's nothing to say! You're leaving us!" With sadness but defiance for her feeling of loss, she whispered, "So, eat your meal. I'll feed Maul and Dirk." Her lower lip quivered. "Probably for the last time." Holding back her tears, she stepped into the hall. "He's in there," she said.

Chork's eyebrows arched as a tall, skinny boy entered the room. "Who are you?"

"Gabriel Fass. My friends call me Gabe," he smiled and extended a hand. "I have a message for you if you have the gold coin Eloy promised me."

"Eloy?" The elf gestured around the room. "If you can find my purse, I'll give you two."

Gabe walked directly to the chest of drawers and opened the top drawer. He tossed Chork's purse onto the bed.

"How did you know?"

"I watched Saylaso put it there when they first brought you in." He held out his hand. "Two gold, you said."

Chork paid the boy and asked, "What's Eloy's message?"

"Word for word," Gabe recited, "Carrying supplies to Lavanham. Broken-teeth escorts."

Chork furrowed his eyebrows. "Where's Lavanham?"

"Dunno. Never heard of it."

"Eloy say anything else?"

"Nope."

"Fass, you said?" When Gabe nodded, Chork said, "I knew a Fass, Gerbert Fass."

"That's my great uncle. He owns the Smiling Ox Inn in Kent. You ever been to Kent?"

Speechless, Chork stared at the boy. The elf licked his lips and finally whispered, "No."

"Odd, I thought Laso said you had."

"Laso?"

"Saylaso, she told me her friends call her Laso. So you must not be her friend."

Chork grunted to himself, "Not anymore."

"I ain't never seen an elf up close before." Gabe took another step closer. "Do those pointy ears hurt? "

"No, but if you continue to harass my patient," boomed Mage Paul from the doorway, "yours will, as well as another, lower part of your body!"

"Sorry, Mage Keyes." Gabe bowed his head. "I was just leaving." He sidestepped around the tattooed mage and hurried out the door.

Mage Paul turned to Chork. "What was that all about?"

"He delivered a message from a friend."

"Oh?"

"Where is Lavanham?"

The mage frowned. "Lavanham? Never heard of it. You sure you don't mean Lavan? Lavan sits on the Thumb River, Giran's northern border." He informed, "It's home to those who oppose Terilyn's claim to the throne. Why do you ask?"

"It's where Bell went."

"I see. That was your friend's message?"

Chork ignored the question and sat down before the food tray. "Will my ankle heal before I have to leave? Or will I have to limp out of Giran?"

Paul set a vial next to the food tray. It contained an orange liquid. "You need to sleep well tonight and through tomorrow. This," he pointed to the vial, "will help you do so. We will leave after breakfast the next morning." He turned to go, but stopped and said, "Two Thorns sit outside both doors to ensure your healing slumber will not be disturbed."

43 – Wisdom & Leave-taking

Chork looked for the third time to make sure he hadn't forgotten anything. Not that Osila and Saylaso hadn't laid out every single item he could possibly need -- his freshly washed, pressed, and folded Blue Bolt jacket and a spare shirt, his music box, the hummingbird jewelry, flint and steel, a few spare bowstrings, his weapons, his bedroll, a filled waterskin, some dried meat and fruit in waxed paper. Most of this went into a new canvas pack which would ride high on his back.

Off to the side lay a charcoal drawing of Osila and Saylaso standing before the Starling's Song. They had smiles on their faces and waved. Neatly printed in the corner were the Elven words, *Rina lye,* 'Remember us.'

Tears leaked from the corners of his eyes. No, I haven't forgotten anything. Nor anyone. Ever! I don't want to leave. But leave, I must. Then, he had a happy thought. When I am knighted, the Queen will have to accept my return. I will make you all proud.

Maul and Dirk sat in the hallway, eager to be back on the road. Their tails wagged. Their tongues lolled.

"Well," grunted Chork with another last wistful look, "let's go."

He joined Paul at a corner table in the common room.

"Drink this, it will improve your stamina." Mage Paul slid a white colored vial across the table. "How's the ankle?"

"I won't be able to run if you're in hurry," said Chork. He downed the potion and made a disgusting face.

"I'll set an easy pace. Out of the city ..." the mage stopped.

"And then north," Chork finished the mage's sentence.

"Not along the North Giran Road, you're not."

"I'll find a way."

Paul shook his head as Osila Byd served two huge plates of ham and eggs. "No bacon?" he complained.

"Be happy with that," the Song's mistress snapped. "There're no seconds either." She placed a hand on Chork's shoulder and whispered, "May the gods guide and protect you, Elf-friend."

Saylaso said her goodbyes to Maul and Dirk with hugs and kisses. She approached the Chork and handed him a sketch pad.

"But you already gave me ..."

She placed her skilled fingers across his lips. "Hush. This may bring joy to your heart when you most need it." She was crying as she ran away.

Chork flipped through the pad's pages. He saw sketches of himself, his wolves, Saylaso and her mother at work in the Song's Common Room, the streets and buildings of Giran, among many others. Chork looked at his plate and pushed it away.

"No appetite?" asked Mage Keyes.

The elf shook his head. "Saying goodbye to friends does not whet my appetite."

"Yes, well, you'll have plenty of time to rue that thought." The mage slid the plate in front of him and gobbled down the second breakfast. "You should never pass up a meal, Elfling. Especially when traveling."

Though the sun was warm, Paul wore a large floppy brown hat, a voluminous brown cloak, thigh-high brown leather boots, and brown leather gloves. Over his left shoulder, he slung a small brown pack, which, he said, "is a lot bigger than it looks." In his right hand, he carried a long staff made of the same wood as his door and chair. His only weapon was a short sword with an elaborate mithril handle in a shabby brown sheath.

Chork wore the clothes bought for him by Saylaso. A white shirt, an unbuttoned forest-green jacket that fell to just below his waist, brown pants tucked into his Little Creek boots, and his elven cloak. He had belted Pogi's single-edge, black mithril sword on the left, his belt knife on the right. His dirk hilt peeked from under his coat on his left breast. The handle of a dagger poked from the top of each boot, and one was partially hidden in the small of his back. He carried his bow and quiver over his right shoulder.

"You have more blades than Mistress Byd's kitchen!" laughed the mage.

"You can never have enough blades, Mage. Especially when traveling."

"More useful are quick wit and the ability to truly see," snapped the mage. "With wit, you can avoid and evade, barter and bargain, distract and dissuade, interest or irritate, befriend or ignore."

"And what can you do with the ability to truly see?"

"Know when to do which."

Chork shook his head. "You speak of wisdom. Wisdom comes with age."

"Does it really?" The mage took a large yellow apple from within his cloak and bit into it. "Arlie Marx's orchards. What if I told you wisdom comes from believing?"

"Believing what?"

"Believing what is true and acting on that belief to make you suffer less and enjoy more."

"How do you know what is true?"

"You know it here." Paul pointed to his head. "Or, you know it here." He pointed to his heart.

"Ah, but what if your heart and mind each tell you something different?"

"As when telling the truth may hurt someone's feelings?" The mage smiled as Chork nodded. "Our wisdom enables us to balance virtues when they conflict."

"So, wisdom is good judgment?" The elf paused for Paul's nod. After it came, Chork added, "Which comes with age."

Paul sighed and shook his head. He frowned and pursed his lips. "Then tell me, Elfling," he harrumphed, "how old must you become before you are wise?"

It was Chork's turn to frown as he tried to divine an answer.

"Must all elves reach that age?" Paul prodded.

Chork's eyes narrowed and flit back and forth looking for a reply. Slowly, they opened wide and turned to the mage in astonishment.

Paul laughed, "Realization sometimes strikes like a thunderclap." He faced the elf. "Making reasoned decisions that are both good for ourselves and for others does not require wrinkles. Knowing when to act and how to act does not demand grey hair." He pointed to his heart and head again. "As long as I hold what is true here and here," he paused, "and believe in it." He emphasized each following word with a shake of his index finger. "I see what is truly important, set my priorities, and act accordingly."

With that, the mage started off with long, quick strides, leaving Chork to limp after him.

* * *

The elf and the mage approached the Queen's Bridge, a massive wide avenue spanning the Mud River. This granite structure served as Giran's main thoroughfare to Brehm, and as Brehm's main doorway into the Giran economy.

Large lumber wains, stone and marble laden drays, merchant's fourgons loaded with every manner of goods from pins to armor,

266

noble-bearing coaches and carriages, farmer's wagons, and vendor pushcarts rolled across the bridge, coming and going. On the outer edges of the span, people from every realm flowed like the melting snows of spring rushing down mountain streams.

In such a mass of humanity, Chork expected his departure from Giran to be as insignificant as his entry. However, he was the only elf. Moreover, he was the only elf accompanied by two large wolves and a shouting mage.

"Captain!" called Paul. By some spell or conjure, his shout rose above the din of traffic. Not only did the Thorns' Captain turn to face the mage and elf, so did everyone within a half mile.

Fingers pointed, tongues wagged, brows furrowed. Fear and anger took root. The steady mass of people stopped to see what transpired.

"Here now," yelled the Captain, "those beasts should be caged, or at the least, leashed!" Her tone and gesture seemed to include Chork with Maul and Dirk.

"It's a little late for that, Captain," replied the mage. He took a piece of parchment from within his cloak and handed it to the woman. He then pointed to Chork.

"Well, then," roared the Thorn officer, "be on your way and be quick about it. Can't have these busy people standing around gawking at wolves and curse-carrying elves." She signaled for a squad. "Escort Mage Keyes and," she paused searching for the right words, "his companions safely across the bridge."

Surrounded by a protective bubble of Thorns, Chork, his wolves, and Mage Paul crossed the Queen's Bridge. As they passed, people stopped to stare, whisper, and point.

Once across the Bridge, Paul pulled Chork to the side of the road. "This is where we must part," said the mage. "This road leads north along the river, parallel to the road on the Giran side. Stay on it until you meet a bridge or an elf. Both will lead you east to Cenedril. To learn elven magic, you must take the Test of Bowls. This is imperative."

"Does the road on this side of the river lead to Lavanham?" Chork asked.

"To The Palm and thence west to the Lavan Ferry. Since Lavan lies in Giran, you cannot go there. Or, maybe you can. The House of Lavan is not overly fond of the House of Rose. Along this road," he pointed to the road they were on, "until you reach the Thumb River, you cannot cross back into Giran. There are no bridges or fords along this road that cross the Mud. You could swim, but the river is treacherous, until well past Cenedril at The Palm."

Paul removed a ring from his finger. "Take this. Wear it always. Once you pass the Test, it will offer some small measure of protection against spells that would destroy your integrity – the ability to tell yourself the truth when others bid you lie."

The Last Born examined the ring before he placed it on his finger. It was the mage's signet ring – a carved black mithril hummingbird in flight upon a thin silver mithril band. Chork had seen Paul use it to seal notes and letters. Though it looked two sizes too big, it fit perfectly on his right ring finger.

"Thank you. Thank you for everything." Chork placed his hand on Paul's forearm.

"Yes, well," the mage placed his free hand on Chork's. "Don't forget. Cenedril. The Test of Bowls. You must acquire the ability to use magic to survive whichever path you choose." Paul stepped away but after a few strides, called back. "Catch!" He tossed a bright red apple at the elf. "From Francoise Leone's orchard."

44 – The Road North

Chork stood at the crossroads as Paul walked through the crowd. The elf was truly sad to see the mage go. At the same time, he was also relieved that Paul would not force a direct march to Cenedril and thus delay Chork's progress to Lavanham. The elf believed his pursuit urgent, in heart and mind, not only for retribution, but because he believed Bell would harm Eloy and Ruben.

The Last Born realized that people were staring at him. He could see a few gathering their anger. He heard the epithets – curse, blight, plague, and poison. Soon their courage would grow as well. He thought it best to be on his way. He turned north toward Cenedril.

Maul and Dirk capered alongside, happy to be out of the city. They ran ahead and then back. They circled him, inviting the elf to run with them.

Chork complied and set off at a slow jog, testing his just-healed ankle. He had no pain, no discomfort, thanks to Paul's potions. Laughing, he sprinted, also happy to be out of the city.

The three companions ran well into the afternoon. The wolves made a game of it. First Maul racing ahead, then Dirk. Occasionally, they let the elf take the lead, but not for long.

Thinking he had come far enough along the road to attempt a hidden river crossing, Chork veered left and plunged into brush, around trees, and over fallen trunks. He burst through a berry patch and immediately dug in his heels and grabbed a handful of thorns and blackberries. He looked down at the riverbank, 10 paces below. If not for his hold on the berry bush, he would have plunged down onto the sharp rocks and an old rotting trunk, its one remaining branch pointing up toward the elf's chest.

Maul and Dirk padded up beside him. Maul tightened his jaw on Chork's right sleeve and pulled back. Dirk wedged himself between Chork and the cliff edge, gently pushing the elf backward.

"Thanks, friends," signaled Chork, wide-eyed and breathing heavy. "Ow!" he cried and let go of the thorny branch. His hand dripped with blood and berry juice.

The elf removed the spare shirt from his pack, ripped off a sleeve, and wrapped his hand. He sat down on the edge of the cliff to think.

The mid-afternoon sun gleamed off the brownish water of the Mud River. The current rushed dirt, leaves, branches, and even uprooted trees to the southern swamp. Swimming or rafting would likely end with the three of them drowned.

Paul had been right. The Mud River was indeed treacherous.

Chork sighed. He leaned back and stared at the sky. He would follow the river further north until he found a way to cross.

"I have no choice, really," said Chork to his friends.

Maul nudged his shoulder.

"Yes, go hunt, and bring me something, if you please," Chork gestured.

The elf reached into an inner jacket pocket, withdrew the bright red apple Paul had given him, and shined its skin on his sleeve as the old mage always did. He took a big bite, noting its tart but delicious flavor, and smiled as he chewed.

He recalled Paul's parting advice, "You must acquire the ability to use magic to survive whichever path you choose."

Whichever path I choose. He grunted. I've already chosen one. To avenge those left dead and homeless in Kent. To rescue my new friends from a murderer. My path lies with duty and obligation. As does any knight's.

Though he believed his mind was made, Chork did not feel comfortable with his decision. Some little bit of doubt sat complaining in his stomach like a bite of an over-tart apple. He threw the red apple into the river.

"Bah!" he snapped aloud. What would the hummingbird mages have me do? As Pogi's squire, it is my duty to avenge her murder. As a Blue Bolt, it is my obligation to hunt down the Killers of Kent. As brother to Gimlet and Slick, I must, I must ... But, he could not complete the thought as tears filled his eyes and loss tore at his heart.

He shook his head, fighting to overcome his grief. How? How do I do meet these obligations? By killing? But Timo said never take another life unless I have no other choice. And yet, what choice do I have?

If I capture Bell, where do I take him for justice? To Kent? That's a far march with a prisoner, and it offers too many opportunities for escape or worse. To Giran? To face the Queen's justice? If I could get there alive!

The image of Terilyn Rose, the Queen of Giran lingered in his mind's eye. Her soft curls, her large green eyes. Her rosebud lips. His heart warmed and skipped a beat. He truly had never looked upon a female in this way. To be drawn to one of the other sex. *Why her? Why now?* So too, he felt her interest in him.

But, in reply, rather than confirm her feelings, she banished me. Banished me for the fire in Little Creek and my righteous vengeance against those who murdered. Those who murdered family, friends. Women and children. Dogs and brothers. She would never side with me.

Truly, Bell deserves death. Barclay and the Robins brothers do as well, for the parts they've played. And the Peaches? Yes, everyone. To the last man. A tall order for one such as I. A mere shoot. No, not even yet a shoot. Still a sprout. One who has not yet passed the Test. A half-trained squire who has no magic, no plan.

A plan! I must devise a plan!

"Don't forget. Cenedril. The Test of Bowls." Paul's words echoed again and again.

I don't need magic to best Bell with sword or bow. Moreover, the longer I delay, the greater threat to Eloy and Ruben. Also, I am not ensured that Cenedril will receive me, let alone offer me the Test of Bowls. And, if I do take the test, and fail, what then?

No, my path lies north and across the river. Find my friends and secure their safety. Since Bell accompanies them, I can capture and take him to Cenedril for justice. Such a feat may persuade the Cenedril elves to accept me! It would be easier then to request the Test of Bowls.

Chork thought this last point clever. *I could kill two birds with one arrow.* His plan devised, he relaxed and waited to see what his friends brought him for supper.

45 - The Fog

The dawn of his sixth day north, Chork awoke in the shelter of a copse halfway between the road and forest. At least, he thought it was dawn.

A dense fog had soaked into his clothes and bedroll. The moisture-filled air stilled the sounds from the river and surrounding forest, creating an eerie silence. Trees more than three paces away were not visible, and more importantly, neither was the river or the direction in which it lay.

While eating the last of his dried meat and fruit, the elf checked his bow and quiver. The beeswax on strings and bows would hold up well enough; but, his rosewood arrows had absorbed some water. To reach their target accurately, they required he make an adjustment for their heavier weight. Luckily, the natural oils in the goose-feather fletching withstood the dampness.

Maul and Dirk danced their readiness to depart. Their limited visibility posed them no problem. They relied on their senses of smell and hearing. When they trotted off, hopefully, toward the road, the elf followed.

Traveling to the road proved more difficult than the Last Born thought. Incredibly, the fog had grown denser. A cut on his cheek from a branch persuaded him to walk rather than run. A hole in his cloak influenced him to use his bow as a blind man's stick.

Then, it began to rain. A light misty drizzle, refreshing at any other time but today. Today, it carried a chill and simply added to his misery. Worse, it did nothing to dispel the fog.

Chork could no longer hear Maul and Dirk. He heard no birds, no insects, nothing, but his own breathing and the squish of his boots through the mud. If he had stopped and bent down to look more closely at the ground, he would have seen that he no longer walked the road but had veered off toward the river. He would have also seen the tiny threads of water leisurely working their way to the Mud River. They carried the loose dirt and dust away from this gentle slope and thus gave the river its name.

He stopped when he ran into a stand of trees. *Trees in the middle of the road?* he wondered. It struck him that he had left the road. *But how far back? No matter,* he reasoned, *I will just turn around and go back.*

The Last Born shuffled on through ankle-high grass. He noticed a slight rise to the ground and smiled, thinking he would soon reach the road.

A moment later, the grass blades were now tickling at the hem of his cloak. A few steps more, the grass reached his waist. Then, the stalks stood taller than his head and pushed back when he tried to push through.

He stopped.

Fog that grew denser with every step. Grass that walled him in as sure as stone. The elf wondered if some magic was at work.

Suddenly, he heard Maul's howl. It came from ahead and above. Dirk joined in to beckon the elf onward.

He pulled his sword and hacked at the grass, clearing enough room to slip through. Ten hacks with his right arm, ten with his left, again, and again, and yet, once again. His arms tired, but he pressed on.

Unexpectedly, he broke through, and strained to see what lay before him. He ventured a step and another, poked forward with his sword. It buried in mud. A rise? A hillock?

Above his head, Maul howled again.

"I'm coming," the Last Born griped. He began to climb. His boots squished into the mud. The slope increased. He began to slip. Bending forward, he continued.

His right foot slid too far right. His weight shift pushed his left foot too far left. He rocked back on his heels. Waving his arms to keep his balance, he tried another step forward to steady himself. He leaned forward, and his left leg flew out from under him. He fell, face first into the mud, clipping his chin on his knee. Slowly, on his belly, he slid backward down the hill.

Coming to a stop at the bottom, he didn't know whether to curse or laugh. He thought of his bow and checked it. Luckily, he hadn't damaged it. However, he lost his sword.

A quick scuttle up the hill retrieved the blade, buried half its length in the mud. It gave him an idea.

On his hands and knees, using his daggers as anchors, he crawled up the rise. His progress was slow but steady, passed the point where he had slipped, and continued upward.

"I'll be there soon," he called to his wolves.

Maul replied with a whine. Dirk added a bark. Though both comments came from above, they confused the elf because they also came from behind him.

Chork looked up and saw nothing but fog. Using his sword, he stabbed upward. On his second try, the blade stuck.

Now, he did curse. He had climbed up under an overhang. He should have known when he no longer felt the rain beating down on him.

Taking a deep breath, he cautiously moved about two paces to his left. Again, he stabbed upward. Again, the sword stuck. He continued along the ridgeline in this manner until he bumped into a large boulder.

Risking a fall, he clambered on top and stood. His eyes and nose were now above the fog though it too seemed to be climbing the overhang.

Maul and Dirk saw him and ran over to the jutting ledge, wagging their tails. They called to him to join them.

46 – Bad Wolves

In a light drizzle, Chork stood on the edge of the overhang with Maul on this left and Dirk on his right. The Last Born looked back toward the river.

"It looks like a big bowl filling up with fog soup," he told his friends. He couldn't see the boulders he used to climb up out of that bowl. Nor the tall grasses. He could see the tops of some trees. As he watched, the fog began to spill out of the bowl toward him. He shook his head and turned away toward the road, not five paces away.

"How did you get out of there?" he asked them, observing they wore not one speck of mud between them. He had mud in his hair, on his face, on both sides of his cloak. His boots weighed a stone or two more, encrusted as they were.

He wished the clouds would burst open and release a deluge to clean him and dissipate the eerie fog.

The clouds did not oblige. The miserable drizzle continued.

The fog climbing his pants leg, Chork trudged down the road, idly chatting with the wolves to bolster his mood. They sensed his apprehension, stayed close, and occasionally responded with a bark or a whine. The three companions rounded a bend and began up a slight incline.

The wolves stopped, their noses held high, collecting a scent from a breeze Chork did not feel. Dirk growled. Maul bared his teeth and snarled. Both held their ears erect and forward. They broke into run.

"No! Stop!" he called to the wolves. They paid him no heed. At a lope, they crested the hill and disappeared over the other side. Cursing, Chork wondered what could incite them so. Game? Maybe, the spoor of an ogre? He unshouldered his bow and tested the pull of its string. Satisfied, he nocked an arrow and secured a slight draw with his left hand. With his right, he ensured his sword, dirk, and daggers were free and clear. Spurred by odd-sounding growls and shrieks, he raced up the hill.

At the top, with one quick glance, he saw Maul and Dirk running onto an old stone bridge which spanned a whitewater stream. They raced toward three humans and three hairy beasts gathered around a small fire.

At first, Chork was perplexed. Like a lightning bolt from The Only One, it struck him. Gnolls! It had to be. White furry coats. Dark hairy legs. Long snouts with razor-like teeth. Just like his mother had described. Mortal enemy of elf and wolf and ... and human! Why are they together? And not fighting!

Chork had no time to unravel this riddle. Already, Maul and Dirk were across the bridge. Their six targets, already alerted to the wolves' charge, rose to meet the attack, brandishing swords and clubs. One human unlimbered a bow.

Chork did the only thing he could to protect his friends. Within eight racing heartbeats, he shot four plain arrows at the three men. The first arrow hit the closest squarely in its chest, ending that threat. The plain second also flew true but missed when its target bent over to pick up a burning stick from the fire. The third arrow took the bowman in his thigh and drove him to one knee, his bow and arrow dropping to the ground. The fourth arrow missed and shattered on a stone.

Chork recalled Pogi's charge at the Kent bowmen. *Patience,* he admonished himself, took a deep breath, and drew another arrow.

The bowman screamed, "The elves are attacking!" and pointed to the ridge. His remaining comrade looked at Chork, dropped the burning stick, and ran toward the river and the safety of the woods. The bowman shouted obscenities and shook his fist at the coward. He reached for his fallen bow.

With a quick glance, Chork saw Maul and Dirk cross the bridge together. Shoulder to shoulder, they sped toward the three snarling gnolls. The creatures, running to meet the wolves, roared and waved their spiked clubs.

Deciding the bowman posed the greater threat to his friends, Chork recited out loud. "Stand. Nock. Draw. Fix. Aim. Release. Hold."

The bowman had just set his arrow when Chork's red banded missile hit him in the chest. He looked down at it in wonderment, teetered, and toppled to the ground, still holding the bow and arrow.

As Chork set another arrow, Dirk sped past Maul toward the fastest and smallest gnoll. The wolf leaped. The gnoll swung his club and missed. Dirk crashed into the creature, pinning him. With one massive bite, he tore out the slavering gnoll's throat.

His short, spiked club drawn back in a killing blow, the second gnoll raced up alongside Dirk. The beast roared its delight at catching the wolf defenseless. But its victory yell turned into a painful bellow as Maul's massive head slammed into its back. Huge wolf jaws bit through fur and muscle, severed the spinal cord and tore out the beast's soft innards in a massive burst of blood.

The last and largest gnoll, lumbering toward the wolves, hesitated, kicking up dirt and stone in its hasty stop. It eyed the two wolves and mewled. Faster than its charge, it tore off into the direction its human comrade had taken.

Chork loosed two arrows after it. Both missed. He shouted at Dirk and Maul to stay. Maul complied, licking blood and gnoll bits from his muzzle. But Dirk again disregarded the elf's commands. A silver and white blur, he sliced into the trees and brush in pursuit.

Chork and Maul raced to follow.

47 – No Choices

Though exhausted from weaving such large and complicated spells, Marina Qannoubine hurried through the woods. She had sensed that someone, or something, had been caught in the weaving south of the bridge, and she wanted to know who or what. She doubted that the spells' target, a large, repugnant mob of gnolls and men, had slipped by without her notice. However, she worried their advance guard, three men and three gnolls, had already traversed the Crossroads Bridge and had prematurely triggered her spells.

Two days ago, Cenedril's border scouts had first reported this abomination, men in alliance with gnolls, a day's march north of the Little River. Since these two races fought as mortal enemies (indeed the latter enjoyed eating the former), the scouts believed some new sorcery threatened Cenedril.

When the scouts sent news that the mob had doubled in size and was now marching south, Prince Bomelith's advisors urged he attack the growing army as it attempted to cross the Little River. Such a battlefield, they said, would favor their expert archers and certainly defeat the mob with few if any losses. Besides, they reminded, no army had ever broached Cenedril's borders, not even during the Great Wars.

However, Prince Bomelith had decided he would allow the growing horde to enter Cenedril. Once the mob arrived at the bridge's crossroads, he would spring a fatal trap that would accomplish two important things. First, the number of dead gnolls would result in a near extermination of the creatures along the northern borders. This would benefit, not only Cenedril, but its bordering realms – Giran and Seppa. Second and more critical was the certainty of capturing one or more of the human sorcerers to uncover who, how, and why they had formed such an alliance.

To help him plan, build, and spring his trap, the Prince had turned to his cousin, Cenedril's most powerful mage, Marina. She had used power from the river and its neighboring forest to create the fog of death, which now was set to the south and west, and followed the approaching mob at a discrete distance. She was most proud of this nuance of her spell.

Cenedril's Protectors, led by Prince Bomelith, would close the eastern side at the proper time.

As the diminutive elf picked her way carefully but quickly around a bramble patch, Marina heard the squawks of a gnoll and the vile curses of a man. Surely, she believed, the Prince would not attack the advance guard and risk alerting the main body. She grumbled as she added the question of why to her list of who or what.

She heard someone running through the brush to her left. She immediately prepared an ice dagger spell, further taxing her waning magical strength.

With a sudden crash, a large gnoll pounded through a nearby thicket. It saw Marina, shrieked, and veered to the right, directly into a birch trunk. With barely a pause, the creature bounced back two steps and spun completely around. Narrowly avoiding the same trunk, the gnoll dashed off.

A silver blur streaked through the air and slammed into the gnoll. The wolf and the gnoll tumbled through the scrub. The gnoll growled and clawed. The wolf made no sound. He just savaged the gnoll's face and throat.

A wolf! Have wolves attacked the scouts? There had to be a large pack to attack six gnolls and men in the open!

A man, looking over his shoulder, burst through the scrub. He twisted his body in an awkward manner, stumbled, and regained his balance. An arrow protruded from his shoulder blade.

Another, much larger wolf crashed into the man. The force of the hit broke the human's back with a loud crack. The wolf's massive jaws closed on and crushed the defenseless man's skull.

Marina spun around as a twig snapped and a few leaves crunched. She saw a tall elf, dressed in brown and green, and covered head to toe with splotches of dried mud. A leather cord secured his long, dark hair. His green eyes blazed, but his jaw hung slack at the sight of Marina.

The dark-haired elf signaled strangely to the wolves. The large one came to stand to his left. The smaller with twitching ears sat at the right. Their eyes focused on Marina, awaiting the order to attack.

"That's the largest wolf I've ever seen," said Marina, letting her ice spell dissipate. "Is he part dire wolf?"

"Pure-bred." replied Chork. "Were you tracking them?" He pointed to the dead.

"No." Marina pulled back her cowl to reveal an unruly shock of long bright white hair. Her eyes, icy grey, quickly and thoroughly assessed the Last Born. Satisfied with whatever result she obtained, she nodded and said, "They are the advance scouts of a much larger party. Nearly 200 strong." She pointed back toward the road. "They should be along soon. I suggest we move quickly to someplace safer."

"Are you from Cenedril?" asked Chork.

"I am Marina Qannoubine." Four teardrop tattoos, blue, green, red, and white, fell from the outer corner of her left eye down her cheek. Three, red, green, and blue, graced her right cheek. "Cousin to Bomelith Brethilthand, Prince of Cenedril, and Guardian of the Forest of Dawn."

"Chork of Emig." He asked, "May I see your hands?"

"I am not of that race," she laughed, revealing the unmarked palms of both hands. Her laughter had a musical quality to it. Her smile gave her grey eyes a frosty glint. "We should move quickly." She pointed eastward with her staff. "This way will be safest."

"I must continue north," blurted Chork.

"Perhaps later would be a better time. At this moment, only your death lies north." She moved off in the direction she had pointed.

As they hurried along, Marina pointed south. "I spent considerable energy and time to lay the trap south of the bridge. A trap that you almost prematurely sprang." She stopped briefly to pick up several dry twigs, to which she whispered as they ran.

When they emerged from the woods, Chork was stunned. All traces of the dead had vanished. Only the beginnings of the signal fire remained.

Marina threw the sticks onto the small pile, set the tip of her staff to the wood, and recited an enchantment. Her words grew louder as did a deep hum, and when they reached a crescendo, the wood caught fire, sputtered, and died, sending a thin plume of white smoke curling into the air.

"Quickly," Marina said. She began to sprint eastward.

"I must go north," Chork insisted. "I have need. My friends have need of me."

Marina stopped, turned to face Chork, and let out a long breath. "Chork of Emig," she said in a motherly voice. "Go north now and die by gnoll teeth or man's blade. Go west or south and die in the fog. Go east," she paused, "and live to go north later." She stamped her staff onto the ground. "Choose quickly, or I will kill you right here, right now, to further bait our trap."

Chork had no choice but to go east.

Marina led Chork and the wolves to a small hillock covered with blooming wild plum bushes. She concealed herself on the ground behind an especially leafy shrub and ordered Chork and the wolves to do likewise. From their vantage point, they had an excellent view of the flat approach to the bridge and the signal fire which continued to smolder.

Twice, Chork began to speak, only to be silenced by Marina's sharp gesture and glowering stare. Time passed slowly as Chork waited for what and from where he didn't know. Just as his eyes began to close from boredom, faintly from the north, he heard the footfalls of many feet, akin to the sound of an unruly mob on the run. Soon after, as if a counterpoint to the mob's clatter, the rhythmic tromp of boots emerged.

Marina touched his arm and, with a smile on her face, pointed to the north leg of the road.

A horde of gnolls crested the hill and poured down toward the signal fire. Right behind followed a double column of humans dressed like elves.

Maul and Dirk emitted low growls, their hackles rising, their ears laid back. Chork, at Marina's urgent insistence, quieted them.

The van of the gnoll gang reached the signal fire and stopped.

Marina held her breath.

A squat, slavering gnoll, carrying a wickedly shaped, handle-less blade, snorted and kicked at the smoking fire, sending red embers in every direction.

Marina let out her breath and smiled. She pointed to the hill which Chork had crested.

The fog that had troubled Chork, now thicker and grayer, rolled over the rise, gaining speed as it moved downhill.

Another nudge and pointed finger from the elf mage drew Chork's attention to the wooded area where he had chased the fleeing gnoll and human. He saw another bank of fog, this one pulsating with an inner glow. Without Marina's urging, Chork looked to the north road.

The men had broken their ranks and joined the gnolls massed around the signal fire. Their fear and confusion could be heard and felt from the wild plum bushes.

As the fog closed over them, the mist turned red. Wild, chilling screeches rang out. Blood-curdling screams and wails caused the Last Born to cover his ears. Never had he heard anything so baleful.

A few of the more alert men, seeing they were trapped on three sides, had no choice but to sprint eastward toward Chork, hoping to outrun the deathly mist.

A shout rang out from Chork's right, followed by the thrum of bowstrings. Not one man remained standing as the now red fog rolled over their bodies.

Marina stood and raised her staff with both hands above her head. *"Daro!"* she shouted the ancient Elfish word for stop. The tips of her staff crackled with energy. She shouted again. *"Daro si!"*

Slowly, the fog evaporated revealing two men, both writhing in pain from arrows in their legs. What else remained horrified and sickened Chork. Armor and clothing adorned the blanched, white bones of gnolls and men. Their skeletal hands grasped blades and polearms. Their boney legs ended in mud-splattered boots.

Marina called out, "It is safe!"

Elves emerged from the tree line to either side of the Last Born. A tall, silver haired elf, wearing a mithril circlet, barked an order, "Nibin, take your branch and glean of value what you can. Secure those two men and bring them along. Be quick about it."

48 – Cenedril

Chork was moving north again but not along the road toward his desired destination. Instead, he ran with more than 100 other elves along a game trail toward the Enclave of Cenedril. The pace was much quicker than normal for Chork. Weighted with pack, bedroll, and weapons, and still hobbled by his recently healed ankle, he soon began to lag. If not for the help of other elves, who relieved him of most of his burdens, the Last Born would have collapsed.

"How far to Cenedril?' he asked a white-haired youth.

"If we run all night, we'll be home for tomorrow's mid-day meal." When Chork asked if they would run all night, the youth merely shrugged. "The Prince will decide."

A short while later, as the ebbing moon reached its apex, the silver-haired noble called a halt.

Chork placed his back against an elm and slid down the trunk. He had no sooner closed his eyes when he heard Marina say, "Cousin, this is Chork of Emig."

Standing before Chork was the silver-haired elf. Taller than most elves, he had a regal bearing. His long silver hair flowed well past his shoulders. His eyes were of the same color with white flecks that sparkled from a light within. A long aquiline nose sat atop thin ruby red lips which formed a straight line above a square chin. His fingers were long and delicate, as were his pointy ears. He had a single blue teardrop tattooed on his left cheek, a red one on his right.

Marina added. "Rise, Chork of Emig, and meet Bomelith Brethilthand, Prince of Cenedril, and Guardian of the Forest of Dawn."

Chork stood up straight, bowed his head so that his chin almost touched his chest, and said, "Your Royal Highness."

"Well-mannered," said Prince Bomelith, "but he dresses and smells like a Man."

"I have lived among men, Sir, for nearly three years."

"So we've heard, Lye Tella'estela Hummien'dulin, Last Born of Emig." The Prince displayed the palms of his hands. On the left was the black hummingbird. On the right, a white lily.

Chork gasped and, forgetting his etiquette, blurted, "You've been knighted by Sir Gunter! You are one of the two?"

Prince Bomelith smiled. "We have much to discuss when we reach Cenedril, Last Born. Tell us, can you run the night and into the day?"

"I-I, that is, Sir, I cannot."

The Prince smiled once more. "Honesty. Then we will be honest with you. Some of us must run ahead to intercept another infection. We will leave you in Marina's care with, say, a branch." Here, he looked at Marina, who nodded. "Until tomorrow, Lye Tella'estela." He placed his hand on Chork's shoulder before he walked away.

"More gnolls and men fighting together?" Chork asked Marina.

"No, but not your worry," Marina replied. She reached into a dark green bag that hung over her left shoulder and pulled out a tiny clay bottle. "Drink this," she instructed, "it will help you rest and recover your strength. We won't delay here long." She chuckled, shaking her head and mumbled, "The Last Born." She chuckled again.

* * *

Chork walked among the Forest of Dawn, a green, bright, haven for all living things. Birds sang cheerfully to each other.

Tree leaves glistened in the setting sun and swayed in time with the gentle breezes. A carpet of rich dark earth muted his footsteps among a burst of colorful wildflowers and small green plants striving to kiss the sun. His only indication that he had entered Cenedril was that he sensed the presence of many elves.

At first sight, the harmony of Cenedril and the Forest moved Chork to tears. Every structure, no matter its construction – stone, wood, rock, or earth – appeared as a living part of the Forest. None were taller than the tallest tree. None greener than the greenest leaf. None hoarier than the oldest bark. All in harmony with the flowing lines found in the great Forest within which they stood.

This would have been Emig in 200 years had its Mother Tree lived. And I, I would be standing there with these same tears marveling at the beauty and grace of my home.

Yet, something was not right. Something was … absent.

Chork's brows furrowed as he slowly cast about. Everywhere he looked, he saw elves engaged in the everyday tasks of existence. Here, hunters returned with meat for the cookpots. There, fletchers trimmed feathers. Near one tall oak, four elves, maybe twice Chork's age, told stories and laughed, clapped each other's back in camaraderie. A white haired elf sitting on a stump carved a flute while his apprentice studied every tiny cut.

"Which disturbs you most," asked Marina, "the loss of the Mother or the absence of children?"

Chork searched his heart. He keenly felt the lack of the Mother Tree's serenity and communal link. As for the absence of children, his brief 13 years in Emig was devoid of those younger than him. Nevertheless, the sounds of sprouts' play, so often experienced in the towns and cities of men, did not exist here. He likened it to a forest without bird song.

I'm the youngest one here.

He drew his lips inward, his brows deeply creased, his eyes tearing. "Both," he whispered reverently.

"Some fight valiantly against the loss of one or the other or, even, both," Marina said. "A few despair." Marina sighed heavily. "These often disappear into the Forest, never returning. At first, the number was small." She shook her head with worry and sadness.

The white-haired mage looked sideways at Chork. "My cousin and I pray that your short visit will stem this tide, if even briefly. All here know the Prophecy." She hung her head, choking back emotion. "The Prince will invite you to attend him as he walks about the Enclave raising spirits and rallying hope. It is much to ask of one so young, I know. Yet, the more you can touch with word or gesture ..." She allowed the thought to trail off, waiting for Chork's reaction.

It was then that the Last Born realized that his fellow elves in Emig had not expected him to do anything remarkable or heroic, right then and there. They merely had looked to him for hope for revenge or for glory. Their last hope, *Lye Tella'estela*.

Chork swallowed the lump in his throat. It was indeed much for so many to ask of one so young. Yet, how could he refuse them? He could plead his excuse about the safety of his friends. The prince would surely understand that. He looked at Marina's hopeful face and recalled two lines of the Prophecy.

In a soft voice, he recited them:

'Then comes the Last Born,

On midsummer's morn, to mend what was torn.'

Marina whispered, "We hope."

Chork's mood softened. *How can I refuse this? If a few hours will give comfort to my kith, how can I say no?* One last icy pang of worry about his friends stung his mind. But the stab melted away.

"You may tell your cousin I would be honored to accompany him."

Marina smiled broadly. "He will be pleased and honored."

* * *

As Chork and the Prince strode through Cenedril, they took every opportunity to stop and briefly share a word or two with nearly everyone in Cenedril. It reminded Chork of this first stroll through Kent with Edmod. Chork told the Prince so, who smiled and said he 'would like to meet this man of wisdom and foresight.' This brought tears to Chork's eyes and words of comfort from the prince to Chork's ears as the Last Born unfolded his life story.

"You have chosen a difficult path, Last Born," said the Prince, showing his palm with the lily tattoo. "We, too, once chose that path."

Chork pressed the Prince about his training as a knight.

"It was long before the Day of Doom," said the Prince. "The story is best told after a hearty meal around a pleasant fire. The short of it is that our grandfather, the First Prince of Cenedril, led us to it." The Prince paused to remember. With a nod, he continued, "It was the second-most difficult time of our life, but easily the most rewarding. We are sure you will find it the same on both counts."

"Then, you believe my choice of paths is correct?"

The Prince stopped and turned to face Chork. "Your path is yours to choose and not ours to judge."

Chork nodded, lowering his eyes and head.

"We can say this, Sprout." The Prince placed his hand on Chork's shoulder. "This path you walk today here in Cenedril pleases us. Your presence gives hope to those who need it most, no matter where this path leads you."

289

To verify the Prince's sentiments, the Cenedril Elves welcomed Chork with smiles and gifts for his impending quest. They bestowed such a variety and number of items upon the Last Born that the Prince had to call for help to carry the load. Several young elves, pressed into service, scrambled back and forth carrying the items, ranging from belt knives to helms, from shirts to winter cloaks, from flints to quivers.

Maul and Dirk, who quietly ambled along, obediently accepted pats to their heads and haunches, scratches to chins and ears, and light strokes along their flanks. Maul especially drew much attention because of his size. They also were showered with gifts – spiked collars, curry combs, salted meat, brushes for fur and teeth, shears for removing fur clots, coat rakes, and shedding blades.

Chork quipped that he would need two wagons to carry everything with him on his journey. This made the Prince chuckle, but Chork immediately felt depressed. His jape reminded him of Eloy and Ruben and the need to push on. He said so.

"You have delayed here far longer than intended," Prince Bomelith said, aware of Chork's anxiety. "Your concern for your friends is admirable and must be answered. We suggest you take the Test of Bowls immediately and depart thereafter, if you survive."

49 – The Test of Bowls

All elves have magic. Some more. Some less. Since their magic is elemental, the spells they cast are rooted in one of the four elements – earth, fire, water, and wind.

Normally, an elf possesses one elemental magic. Occasionally, he or she may present the ability of two elements. Rarely does an elf exhibit control of three elements. Before the Mother Trees withered and died, no elf wielded the magic of all four.

Though elves are born with the magic, their abilities do not become available until their 13th birthday. On that day, each elf participates in a ritual called 'Coming to The Only One.' The elves believe their maternal Supreme Being will formally accept the supplicant as a true member of the Elven race and unlock the magic within each, only when the elf successfully completes the Test of Bowls.

During this 'test,' the elf merely places his or her hands in any or all of four wooden bowls carved from various parts of a Mother Tree. If attuned to the element represented by the bowl, the elf fills the vessel with that element. The more he or she fills the bowl, the stronger his or her magic.

"By the Leaf," said Marina, "we've not done this in years!"

"This likely will be the last time," Prince Bomelith sighed.

"I'm quite familiar with being the last for just about everything," responded Chork.

"But, Last Born," Marina stopped and raised a finger, "you are the first to do it at your age."

"A dubious achievement," quipped the Prince.

The three elves, Chork in the middle, continued toward the testing table.

All Cenedril watched them. Most stood around in a large circle. Others climbed atop roofs, boulders, and into tress for a better vantage. Cries of encouragement sprang up, at first sporadically and then with increased frequency and volume.

The oldest Cenedril Elf, Dhory Gysseghymn, nodded as they approached the table. She raised his hand for silence and asked, "Who comes to The Only One?"

"I do," answered Chork.

"Why do you come?"

"I, Lye Tella'estela Hummien'dulin, called Chork the Last Born, seek acceptance as a true elf."

"Who attests you are of age?"

"We do," replied Mage Marina and Prince Bomelith, as one.

"Approach, Lye Tella'estela Hummien'dulin, called Chork the Last Born." Elder Dhory waved Chork forward. She placed her right hand on Chork's forehead, and her left over Chork's heart. "I sense you are of age. You may fill the bowls of your choosing." The old elf stepped aside.

The Last Born took one tentative step forward. His heart beat rapidly. Perspiration dampened his brow and his palms. He wiped his hands on his thighs, once, twice, and a third time. He took another step and looked down at the Bowl of Water, the first to his right. He remembered Prince Bomelith's voiced concern, "You may be too old to survive the test."

Inside and out, the polished wood gleamed. Cut from a sturdy branch low on the Mother, it was dark with a strong grain. On its side, one water drop, carved delicately, faced him.

He closed his eyes and placed his hands in the bowl. Immediately, a thrum filled the air.

With his eyes still closed, Chork felt a raging river, a mile across, break a dam within him. In his mind's eye, he saw clear, icy water pour through the breach, race through a valley, and join a lake of unfathomable size.

The crowd roared its approval as the bowl begin to fill. Their roars turned to shouts of wonderment as water crested the bowl's rim and overflowed onto the table. Amazement gave way to concern as water soaked the ground beneath the table.

Chork opened his eyes. He stood in a growing puddle of water and mud. Alarmed, he yanked his hands from the bowl. He shook violently.

The water stopped. The bowl was once again empty. The thrum gone.

The Cenedril Elves cheered and hollered. Mage Marina shook her head in astonishment. Prince Bomelith laughed.

Chork looked at the Bowl of Wind, immediately left of the Bowl of Water. He plunged his hands into the vessel, woven from thin upper branches. This time, a thin hum hissed but a second.

When a gentle spring breeze touched his face, he smiled. He felt the wind stir. He saw twigs bend. He heard leaves flapping. As he looked down into the bowl, he saw a swirling airstream nearly reach the bowl's edge. It rose no further.

Without hesitation, the Last Born pulled his hands from the bowl and thrust them into the Bowl of Earth. The wood of this basin, cut from the roots of the Mother, carried a damp musty smell. The sound was a low, mournful dirge.

Chork immediately felt dirt surround his fingers. He spread his hands to tamp the earth around a root, alive with warmth and a pulse. Surprised, he peered into the bowl. It was half-full of rich black soil.

The last bowl, the Bowl of Fire, was heart wood. Its polished sheen glowed with an inner fire.

As his hands neared the bowl's rim, the Last Born felt a flame lick his palm. He jerked back in response and heard a moan from the crowd. Slowly, he extended one hand and then the second. Flames rose from the bowl. They pulled at him. He fought, briefly, and then succumbed.

Raging, searing fire engulfed him, pulling him along a tunnel. He heard a distant roar. The fire burned hotter and brighter. Wafted by the flames, he zipped through the tunnel of rock. Another roar pierced the air.

Rock melted. Air burned. Yet, now, he felt no pain.

He entered a large cave. A conflagration of red-yellow tongues licked at him. A raging inferno surrounded him.

He came face to face with the largest red dragon the elf ever had imagined. The beast opened its house-sized maw to let loose another firestorm.

Chork whimpered one word. "No."

Caught by surprise, the dragon choked back its fire. It roared in pain. A deafening rumble arose. It sounded as if hundreds of boulders rolled down a mountainside.

The dragon's chest exploded.

The instant the Last Born placed his second hand in the Bowl of Fire, flames had poured from the basin. They had darted across the table, igniting the other bowls. The table burned, flames running down its legs onto the ground. The soil, itself, then burst into flame. Huge tongues of red-yellow fire exploded from the bowl, igniting the air around the Last Born and catching Elder Dhory.

It was chaos. Astonished and frightened elves beat at the flames that began to spread. Marina and Prince Bomelith sprinted toward Chork.

Elder Dhory's robe began to smolder. She had heard Chork's whimper and reached for the young elf. However, as Chork fainted and fell to the ground, he pulled his hands from the bowl.

The flames vanished, leaving a charred mess.

50 – Courage

The next morning, Marina found Chork sitting on the edge of a small fountain. Clear water poured from an underground spring that fed an arm-sized wooden trough. The water spilled from the trough into a large wooden cup. When full, the cup became heavier than its counterbalance and so poured the water into the stone basin. Many found this spot very soothing.

The mage chose a place beside the Last Born. She placed her hands in his. Neither spoke for a time.

Finally, Marina said, "I was so frightened after I took the Test, I hid for a week. My mother's mother found me in the forest. She took my hands like this." Marina grasped Chork's fingers. "She said, 'Time to grow up, Marina. Time to learn.'"

Chork nodded. "How do I learn? How do I control it?"

"If you stay, I can teach you."

"How long?"

"As long as it takes."

Chork pulled his hands from Marina and stood up. His frustration spilled out just like the water in the cup. "You know I can't stay. I fear I am already too late to save my friends."

"I know that you must leave today, but listen, Shoot." She stood beside him. "You cannot conjure an element. That is, you cannot make fire, or wind, or water, or earth out of nothing. You can, however, summon the element you choose as long as it is present around you."

She turned Chork to face the fountain.

"You summon the element by picturing the image you saw when your hands were in the bowl. Use its energy to complete the spell." She pointed. "Try it with the fountain. Stop the water in the trough."

Chork recalled the icy water flowing into the lake. He felt a slight surge of force and directed it toward the water in the trough. A stuttering hum ensued. The water slowed but continued to flow. He pushed again, harder. The water slowed to a trickle and then gushed forth as if released.

"Very good," said Marina. "All it takes is practice. Add it to your daily training routine. Practice your magic as you would your bow or sword. The more practice, the more magical ability."

Chork gave Marina a warm smile. "Thank you." He gently grasped her shoulders and drew her to him. He kissed her forehead.

"Yes, well, you're welcome," she said breathlessly and red-faced. She patted him on his chest and took her leave, walking quickly down the corridor.

* * *

Chork returned to his room to find Prince Bomelith with Maul and Dirk. The Prince had strung Chork's bow and was testing its draw and examining its upper limb.

"Elf-made by a master. Better craftsmanship than we have seen, but not better than ours. There is a flaw here," said the Prince. He drew the bow twice as far as Chork ever did. The bow snapped. "It would have failed you sooner rather than later." He dropped the broken bow to the floor.

"Master Pengon of Emig made that," Chork lamented.

"Yes, we recognize his hand. We can do better." Prince Bomelith removed a cloth from the top of Chork's bed to reveal a staff of layered wood curved like the crescent moon. "More power with less effort." The Prince demonstrated how to string the bow, bending it backward and hooking the string to its tips. Strung, the bow looked like the snake wending its way over a fallen tree trunk with head and tail on the ground and belly on the trunk. "The arrow flies faster with greater force to its target." He handed it to Chork.

Chork marveled at the craftsmanship and the layered construction. He drew the bow and grinned. The Prince handed him an arrow and pointed to the opposite wall, made of smooth stone. Chork nocked the arrow, drew as far as he could, and shot. Half of the shaft drove into the wall.

"I cannot thank you enough." Chork laughed.

"Here," said the Prince waving his hand at the gear on Chork's bed, "you'll find everything you need for your journey north. We selected some of the more practical items that were given as presents."

Chork recognized the leather belt with pockets and a few others. Beside them lay a set of mithril daggers in the same colors and design of Pogi's blade. Their pommels were a carved hummingbird at rest.

"You are most generous, my Prince." He bowed his head to his chest. Those last two words, 'my prince', startled Chork. They indicated his fealty for the first time to an elven noble.

Prince Bomelith understood this and said so. "When you passed the Test of Bowls, you were bonded to Cenedril and not to Emig. Can you not feel the bond?"

Chork searched his heart and mind. He immediately felt his bonds with Maul and Dirk. He even imagined he could still feel his bonds with Gimlet and Slick, though those bonds had been subdued by death. It took a little while, for you often cannot identify as specific the one thing that you have carried your entire life, even when it had been replaced with a weight like the original. But, there it was! The bond with Cenedril, with the elves of Cenedril, with the Prince as liege lord.

Chork set the bow down and turned to face Prince Bomelith with a serious face. "I'm afraid of what lies ahead."

"We all are, Last Born. It is our nature to fear that we do not know."

"B-but the fear makes me feel like a ... like a coward."

"Do not mistake fear for lack of courage. Courage enables us to do what is right despite fear. Some face difficulty and turn away. Some face difficulty and persist. Those are the courageous ones. Ones who," Prince Bomelith lifted one eyebrow and began again. "One who provides hope to those who fear the unknown." He laid his hand on Chork's shoulder. "It is we who are grateful to you, Lye Tella'estela Hummien'dulin. Your courage yesterday inspired our subjects to hope ... to be courageous themselves."

The Prince removed the silver mithril bracer from his left forearm. It bore a black mithril hummingbird in flight carved into its face. "To show our gratitude, we give you this. Its magic will help your arrows fly true and protect you from minor earth spells." He secured the clasp on Chork's arm. "We will leave you to prepare for your journey."

* * *

The Cenedril Elves, led by Prince Bomelith, escorted Chork to the Little River. This smaller tributary to the Mud River marked the northern boundary of the Forest of Dawn and Cenedril. The Prince advised Chork to follow the river west to the Mud. "Where," he said, "you may cross the Mud into Giran and locate your friends."

"And after?" Chork asked. "May I bring Bell and the others here to face justice?"

"They must answer to those who they have wronged to face true justice."

Chork frowned.

"We would advise a more fruitful path," Prince Bomelith said, as if he were issuing an order to one of his subjects. He placed the fingertips of his right hand on Chork's forehead and charged the Last Born, "Seek out Billy Tipton, the Last Born of Cenedril. Our sister's daughter studies at the Tower of Learning in Northbridge. A long journey, perhaps out of your way," here the Prince showed his lily tattoo, "but one that will be most beneficial."

"Indeed," said Marina, "she can help you to learn the use of your magic as well as I could."

"She will also deliver our personal recommendation to Sir Gunter," the Prince removed his fingers and added, "and answer any questions you have about the Prophecy."

Through the bond with his new liege, Chork accepted this charge, imprinting its completion upon his mind.

With Maul on his left and Dirk on his right, Chork watched the Cenedril Elves disappear into the Forest of Dawn. "First," he said, "let's go find Eloy and Ruben."

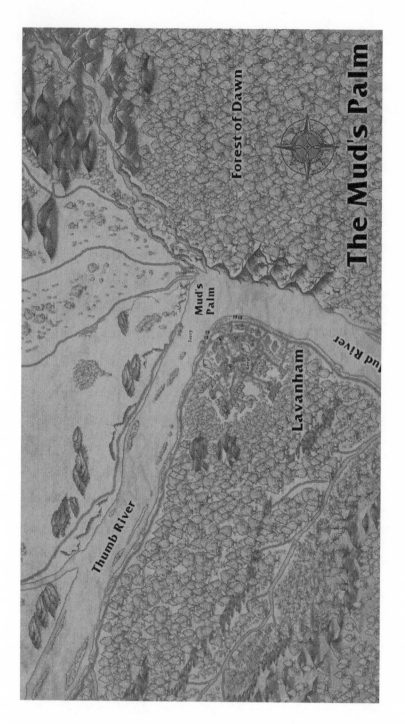

The Mud's Palm

Forest of Dawn

Mud's Palm

Thumb River

Lavanham

Mud River

51 – The Mud's Palm

A soft, warm drizzle began before sunrise and persisted throughout the overcast morning. Early afternoon, the sun finally burned away the thin grey clouds and forced the morning's moisture back up into towering black thunderheads. Several hours later, the heavy clouds burst with a relentless driving downpour. By the time the sun, on its downward slide, lightly touched the treetops, the last raindrop had fallen. Backlit wispy grey clouds hung in the sky, creating pools of bright light and grey shadows.

The Last Born grunted as he climbed the goat path to the top of the cliff. His clothes and gear, thoroughly soaked from the rain, weighed heavily on him. He dropped his pack and bedroll on the ground as Maul and Dirk stepped up beside him. The three companions looked down.

Immediately below, five streams joined to form the Mud River. The elves called this the Mud's Palm.

They named four of the tributaries after each of the fingers, Prime, Rude, Ring, and Little, north to south. These began in the Wind and Fire Mountains to the north and east, respectively. Narrow, make-shift bridges made of logs and stones stretched across each stream which ran clear as spring water.

The widest river, the Thumb arose from the west in the Aril Mountains. Its waters were black and crossed by a small, rope-pulled, ferry barge.

At the bend formed by the Thumb and Mud sat a hamlet. A few outlying farms surrounded an incomplete keep, a few wooden buildings, more thatched huts, and a river dock.

In the dimming light, Chork strained to examine the hamlet for signs of life. He puzzled at the tall poles driven into the ground at regular intervals throughout the village. Atop each pole sat a red-brown melon. Near the ferry, he saw two large wagons, very similar to those driven by Eloy and Ruben.

A flurry of activity grabbed Chork's attention. Figures, some oddly garbed in brown fur, ran from the stone tower and took up positions behind and around the smaller structures.

Maul and Dirk growled low in their throats. They shortened their noses, held their heads and tails high, and bared their teeth.

Chork was about to order them to quiet, when he realized why they reacted as they did. He spun back to the town just as a ray of sunlight crossed its streets. He saw clearly now.

"Gnolls!" he snarled. "Gnolls and men working together as they did on the road to Cenedril." He withdrew a waxed envelope from inside his jacket, selected a string, and strung his new bow. "It's an ambush," he said to his wolves. He looked down the Mud Road and saw no one. "But for whom? Can't be for us."

At that moment, the last shaft of sunlight slid across the road alongside the Thumb River. It briefly reflected off a piece of metal. The glint caught the elf's eye.

Charging down the road came two gilded coaches, drawn by six horses each. At least two itchoaks of outriders escorted the wagons. The metal shimmer came from one of four knights who wore highly polished black armor. The group obviously intended to reach the town before nightfall.

"We have to warn them!" Chork gauged the distance. He did not have the time to intercept the approaching party. Shouting and waving his arms this far away would do no good. He looked at Maul and Dirk and shook his head. Wolf howls would be ignored or spur the carriages faster.

A fire arrow, he thought. A fire arrow signals danger!

The Last Born drew an arrow and cupped it in his hands. Strain as he might with the image of the dragon in his mind, no thrum sounded, no fire came.

Of course! As Marina said, I cannot create an element that is not present.

He had a sudden thought. He gathered a few wet twigs and tufts of grass. A high-pitched whine stuttered and quit. In his mind, he pictured the lake and willed the water out of the twigs and grass. A quick glance told him he had little time. Striking flint to steel produced a spark. The spark a flame.

Now, cupping his arrowhead, he envisioned the dragon.

The tip grew red hot, then white.

Taking careful aim, he launched the arrow across the river into the nearest thatched hut.

Because of its dampness, the roof smoldered. A thin wisp of smoke wafted into the air and dissipated.

With the dying flame of the spent twigs and grass, the Last Born repeated his actions and shot another fire arrow. The instant it landed, the thatch caught. Within seconds, the entire roof was ablaze.

Chork looked at the group on the Thumb Road. They had stopped. A discussion appeared to take place with two of the knights pointing toward the cliff where Chork watched and hoped. The group moved out slowly toward the town.

The elf grinned.

Movement in the hamlet below wiped the grin from his face.

With shouts and a wave of hands, a man ordered several of his comrades to put out the fire. Summoning two others, the obvious leader of the ambush directed their attention to the overhang where Chork stood. With his sword, he mapped their path to the ferry and across the fingers. Six gnolls joined them on the way.

The elf considered his next course of action. He could wait here on the cliff and pick off anyone who approached from the path. He could also attempt to aid the approaching force by shooting down into the town. But in the dying light, such archery would require skill far better than Chork possessed and many more arrows than he carried. He immediately discounted launching fire arrows as that would likely destroy the town in an inferno like Kent.

That frightened him and recalled memories he didn't want to face. *Not now!*

He then looked again at the two wagons in the town. They could belong to Eloy and Ruben. *Are they part of the ambush? If so, why? If not, where are they? Decide!* he screamed at himself. *I need to join the fight. There! On the outskirts and in the town with those about to be ambushed.*

The Last Born shouldered his bow, scooped up his pack, and started down the cliff toward the Little River and its makeshift bridge. When Maul and Dirk reached the bridge before Chork, he shouted for them to wait. The elf glanced at the ferry.

The men and gnolls rapidly pulled across the Thumb. Luckily, the distance between the Thumb and Prime Rivers was the widest. This gave Chork the time to cross the Little River and reach the bridge across the Ring.

Chork increased his pace. He wanted to meet his attackers on land, not on a single-log bridge, where Maul and Dirk would be useless. Every second he delayed could mean the difference in survival for Eloy and Ruben and those in the coaches.

Fortunately, his impending adversaries felt likewise, thinking strength of numbers on land would overwhelm the lone elf. They slowed, waiting for the elf to come to them.

The Last Born raced across the Rude Bridge as his foes crossed the Prime Bridge. Pogi's words rang in his memory.

"Speed, Elfling, speed," the Dame counseled. "You'll not overcome everyone with strength, but you can with speed. Do not hesitate."

When his feet touched land, he signaled to the wolves. Maul veered left, Dirk, right. At 50 paces, Chork unshouldered his bow and let three arrows fly in rapid succession.

Two gnolls went down, impaled through their chests. A third gnoll twisted its body to avoid the same fate. The gnoll behind though did not. It took the arrow in its shoulder and tumbled to the ground.

The two men, who ran behind the gnolls, stopped, their eyes and mouths agape.

The three remaining gnolls roared in fury. Their tongues protruding, their eyes blood red, they shook with rage and charged the elf. It was their undoing.

Dirk, always the faster, tore into the gnoll on the right. The wolf's razor-like teeth nearly severed the creature's leg. Dirk spun in mid-air and drove his muzzle into the gnoll's stomach.

An arrow from the elf's bow felled the center gnoll.

Maul took the last gnoll head-on. Avoiding the beast's axe-swing, the wolf slammed headfirst into the monster's chest. Ribs cracked, their shards stabbing into heart and lungs. The gnoll died before hitting the ground.

While this happened, the Last Born sprinted forward. He shouldered his bow and unsheathed his new daggers. Three paces from the waiting men, Chork launched his body forward in a tumble. Passing a hand's height over the supine gnoll, he raked his daggers over the beast's throat and belly. Behind the men, he rolled to his feet and whirled around in a crouch.

Both men turned to confront the elf. The smaller hefted a long iron sword, rusty and pitted. He smirked at the elf's shorter daggers. The other twirled his war hammer and sneered.

Chork stood erect and smiled. He twirled his daggers, mimicking their menacing moves, holding their attention.

The two men narrowed their eyes and bit at their bottom lips. Each clearly waited for a signal from the other.

"Not even a full-growed elf," remarked the man with the hammer.

Before the other could reply, Maul and Dirk, who had silently crept behind the men, lunged from their slinking crouch, taking huge bites from upper thighs and rumps.

Chork leaped forward and drove his daggers into the men's bellies. He twisted the blades and pulled them across, spilling innards onto the ground.

"Quickly," said the Last Born, as he wiped his daggers on the dead men's jackets. He turned and ran for the ferry. Maul and Dirk followed.

52 – Justice or Revenge?

By the time Chork reached the barge, the battle across the river had already begun. Clanging metal, shouts, and growls filled the air. The two coaches had stopped nearly opposite the ferry landing. The soldiers, now on foot, defended the coaches' occupants from an onslaught. The knights on horseback tried to break the gnolls by charging into their line, hacking this way and that with swords and maces. Ambushers countered this attack with long, barbed pikes.

The battle raged back and forth. The outcome looked uncertain.

"We can tip the scales," the elf yelled to his wolves. Halfway across the Thumb, he encountered the river's growing current. His progress slowed, as the moving water tugged at the small barge.

The tide of battle quickly changed when a green bolt of light struck one of the knights. The armored defender collapsed in a puff of smoke and cinders. The ambushers roared with renewed enthusiasm and doubled their efforts.

Chork quickly glanced about looking for some way to speed his crossing. An idea struck him. "Hold on," he signaled the wolves. He let go of the pull rope. With his mithril sword, he cut the two ropes that tethered the barge to the trees back across the Thumb.

The barge lurched as the current grabbed it. Chork fell to his knees. Maul and Dirk lay flat and whined.

Slowly at first, then with gaining speed, the barge swung pendulum-like across the Thumb. When its momentum began to wane, Chork sliced through the north line. Pushed by the current, the barge completed its swing and crashed against the shore on the lower end of the village.

Bow in hand, the Last Born leaped onto land. He pointed to the gnolls around the coaches and made a fist. Maul and Dirk eagerly joined the battle there.

Methodically, the elf used his bow as he walked toward the battle near the ferry. His first targets were the crossbowmen that had killed another of the knights. Next, he eliminated the bowman behind the town well. Still unnoticed, he picked off one, two, three pike men.

That got the attention of a small group of men waiting to press any advantage the gnolls made toward the coaches. They pointed at him, yelled a challenge, and started toward him. They wielded swords, cudgels, daggers, and hand axes.

It was then that Chork allowed himself to see Kent. Not as it was after its destruction. He saw it as if he had been there to help prevent its death. The flames from the thatched roof he had set alight now spread to the Smiling Ox Inn. The knights who fought from horseback were Pogi and Aelmar. The soldiers who protected the carriages were Marigold, Aldrik, and the Kent Archers.

Amid this battle in his mind, Pogi's advice again echoed. "When in close quarters, do not forsake the bow too quickly. An arrow loosed from arm's length will kill as surely as one from 20 paces."

With an outward calmness that belied his pounding raging heart, the Last Born sprinted toward the toughs loosing arrows so rapidly he was a blur. When he closed to within four paces, Chork fell to his knees and slid through the mud, firing one last arrow up into the chin of the man leaning over the elf.

Still sliding, in one motion, he shouldered his bow, drew his single-edged sword, and sliced the legs out from two more. With the silver mithril bracer on his left forearm, he deflected an axe blow. Gaining his feet, he whirled in a complete circle. His blade's wide arc took the head of the man with the axe.

The blade of a short sword cut through the elf's tunic and sliced fingernail deep across his right side. By a whisker, a knobbed mace missed his skull but ripped out a handful of his long hair.

Dodging the swipe of a dagger, Chork coiled and jumped to his right. He faced two men, both taller and larger. One held a sword and dagger. The other readied his pace-long mace, still adorned with the elf's hair. They both grinned, knowing they had the advantages of weight, reach, and strength.

The Last Born extended his hand, palm out, as if telling his foes to wait. In his mind, he pictured the dragon. A deep-rooted thrum began.

The men looked at each other and laughed. They moved in for the kill.

Like dragon's breath, bright red flame shot from the elf's palm. It hit the swordsman in the chest, setting him ablaze. While the man with the mace stared in amazement, Chork stepped forward and sliced open his throat.

The Last Born quickly looked around. Alarmed, he saw that the coach defenders had not fared as well as he had.

Four surviving soldiers readied their blades. They, with one remaining knight and the coaches' attendants, formed a loose circle about two men and two women, who had obviously left the safety of the coaches to join the battle. Lords and Ladies, they wielded gem-encrusted swords and daggers, more useful for court show than for hacking at gnolls and thugs.

The ambushers gathered their numbers for a final assault. Only a handful of gnolls remained. Twice as many mercenaries stood beside the sorcerer, who had cast the green spells. He began to conjure another.

Maul and Dirk appeared at Chork's sides. Their snouts and fur were covered in blood, some, their own. Their eyes blazed with hatred for the gnolls. With his wet nose, Dirk urged Chork to join the fight. Maul licked at a cut on his paw.

Chork breathed heavily. He laid his hand along his side and felt his blood slowly oozing from the wound. He looked skyward, asking The Only One for strength. Chork's eyes fell on one of the long poles he had noted earlier. He looked atop it and saw Eloy's head.

The elf's heart thumped audibly in his chest. His stomach lurched, forcing bile into his throat. The elf fell to his knees, retching and sobbing. He cursed himself for his delay in Cenedril. He railed at The Only One for Her lack of patience.

Maul butted the elf, knocking him flat. The dog placed his nose a finger's width away from the elf's nose and howled. Maul then spun around and, with Dirk, raced toward the gnolls.

A raging anger filled the hole in Chork's heart. Images of Eloy and Ruben laughing and sharing their meals roiled in his mind. A piercing war cry escaped his lungs, so loud, the combatants stopped and stared at the elf.

Slowly, quivering with fury, the Last Born stood and drew his bow. He took careful aim and shot with his last arrow.

As if time slowed, men and gnolls watched the shaft head directly for the sorcerer's chest. At the last possible moment, the man grabbed the arm of the thug standing beside him and pulled the poor man into the arrow's path.

Immediately everyone turned to Chork.

"Foolish, Elfling!" cried the sorcerer. All eyes swung back to the man. "Do you know who I am?" He stepped forward.

With a glower, the elf shook his head from side to side.

"I am Lesar 'ib Arari, brother to Nav and Clianore, Servants and Pillow Confidantes from birth of the Arch-Sorceress Cuadrilla Ode N'Jaa, liege only to the Great Emperor Himself."

Chork shrugged. He reached for another arrow. His quiver was empty.

Arari took another step forward, curling his wrist one last time to finish his spell. "Do you know what I am?"

The elf answered this. "You are the killer of friends and the innocent."

The coach defenders voiced their agreement. The ambushers grumbled with irritation.

Chork took a step toward the sorcerer. "You are the dodder vine that chokes saplings and steals life." He drew his sword and stepped closer. His voice rose in anger. "You must be burned from the orchard so that the tree bears fruit." He raised his left hand.

Before the Last Born could envision the dragon, Arari threw his spell.

Chork reflexively shielded his eyes with his left forearm. A useless gesture, he thought. Pogi's words, "Don't hesitate" flooded his brain. An apt sentiment for my grave marker.

The bracer absorbed the spell with a flash.

Heeding Pogi's advice, the elf leaped forward and ran Arari through. Nose to nose, Chork held the sorcerer's eyes with his, and watched as Arari's life faded.

A voice to the left cried out, "You!"

Chork turned his head and saw Gary Bell, a cudgel in one hand, a long dagger in the other. Rage surged through the elf. In his mind, he saw a wall of water racing toward a lake. He pulled his sword from the sorcerer's lifeless body and faced Bell.

A bubble of water, the size of a man's torso, sprang from the elf and hit Bell, knocking him to the ground. As the sound of rushing water ebbed, the cudgel and dagger clattered away.

Bell's grunt unleashed the coach defenders from their astonishment. They set upon the remaining ambushers and slew all but two gnolls, who tried to run. Maul and Dirk disposed of them after a brief chase.

Chork stood over Bell. "You have much to answer for." The elf's desire for revenge burned hotly. Images of Edmod, the Kent Archers, Slick and Gimlet, Eloy and Ruben, and even the unseen barmaid in Dale flashed through the Last Born's mind.

"Do it!" shouted Bell. "Do it now!"

Though Bell outweighed the elf by at least four stones, Chork grasped the man's tunic and pulled him to his feet. A glint on Bell's chest caught the Last Born's eye. It was the hummingbird pendant once worn by Eloy.

"Did you take this before or after he died?" He snatched the pendant, snapping the cord from around Bell's neck.

Bell saw the bright red blood at Chork's side. He licked his lips, considering. The man knew he was finished and had to decide. Dead here now by the elf's hand. Dead at the hands of the coach defenders. Dead when hung back in Giran. Dead, dead, dead. He snorted through his broken teeth and decided to take the elf with him.

"I took it after I skewered him and his brother while they slept!" Bell said defiantly, hoping to incite the elf even more and gain an even wider edge.

Chork's self-control wavered. Truly, he thought, of all who died tonight, this man deserves it most. None here would say otherwise. His hand tightened on his sword.

The Last Born recalled something Timo had said: "Without self-control, we are no better than reckless criminals, charging through life for our next gratification."

"No, Master Bell," whispered Chork, as he sheathed his sword. "You shall face the justice you deserve." He shoved the man toward the nearest soldier. "Bind him, hand and feet."

Bell used the elf's shove to disguise the drawing of a hidden belt knife. He spun around and lurched at Chork, driving the knife into the Last Born's wound.

Whether it was a ray of moonlight, or the dying flames of the burning hut, the resulting gleam of metal caused Chork to react. He laid his hand on Bell's face and unleashed the dragon.

Epilogue

Nav 'ib Arari was the first to feel it, a sharp stab of pain to his heart that drove him to the ground. At the sound of a clatter, he turned to see his sister, Clianore, writhing on the floor a few paces away. To his horror, his mistress, the powerful Arch-Sorceress Cuadrilla Ode N'Jaa, liege only to the Great Emperor Himself, dropped to one knee, clutching her chest.

"Lesar is dead," N'Jaa pronounced. "Dead." With effort, she rose to her feet and unleashed a spell across the room. A green bolt of light struck a bedside table, which disintegrated into blackened particles floating in the air.

N'Jaa wailed as the agony of her loss spread throughout her body. Another bolt shot from her left hand through the open window briefly bathing the Bailey of Style's Keep with a green hue.

There came a frantic, insistent pounding at the door, punctuated by a desperate cry, "Lady Lavan, are you all right, Lady Lavan!"

* * *

Back in Lavanham, Tim Barclay had just watched Gary Bell's death. It wasn't pretty – toasted like a deer steak left on the spit overnight. Barclay knew if he stayed any longer, he would probably be the next to roast, courtesy of that pointy-eared, blighted, no-account elf. Barclay wished he possessed the ability for magic. He would zap that bastard here and now.

Then, the elf collapsed.

An unvoiced cheer on his lips, Barclay practically leaped from behind the torso-sized carved stone. Realizing what he had done, the ex-Blue Bolt slithered back behind the stone. He saw that the elf was still alive and that several people attended to him.

Best to get away from here as quick as I can, thought Barclay. He had been hiding among the construction stone for the village keep which provided a dark and secure place to hide. By luck, he had seen the elf make land near the net-maker's house. As a Kent Blue Bolt, he had seen the elf train with Dame Pogi. That's when Barclay decided to skip this battle. He tried to find Bell to convince him to leave Lavanham as well. However, as usual, Bell was in the thick of things. Barclay decided "to hell with Bell." He liked the ring of that and said it out loud again, "to hell with Bell."

Barclay had watched as Arari, the sorcerer who thought he was lord and master over all, died. Killed by the elf. Barclay had watched as the mighty Bell who could lie, connive, incite, and murder (especially if the murdered was asleep) better than most, died. Killed by the elf.

But, Barclay, the clever and cunning, did not die!

Not for long, if he continued to dawdle. He slipped out the half-framed rear door of the Keep and eased into the woods. Around some brush, past some elms, and through a stand of birch, he came to a tended field. Slithering through the planted rows, he passed the farmhouse and entered another wooded area. By a large boulder, he stopped and wondered where he was going. He was without horse, without bedroll and gear, without a ranged weapon to hunt game, but he was not without hope.

"South" he decided aloud, "that sorcerer worked for a Ladyship. She'll pay good money to know who killed her dark-haired bauble." He returned to the farmhouse to see what he could salvage.

Afterword

Thank you for reading The Last Born.

I do hope that you enjoyed it and that you'll spend a few moments to provide a review
on Amazon or Goodreads or wherever you purchased the book.

Reviews will raise the visibility of my work
and provide valuable feedback on what my readers enjoy
and do not enjoy
about The Last Elf Series.

For bonus content, including a glossary, maps and origin stories, future special offers,
and updates on upcoming books in The Last Elf Series,
visit my website, johnfedorka.com.

While there, sign up for my bi-monthly newsletter and blog posts,
or contact me with your questions and comments.

79962499R10196

Made in the USA
Middletown, DE
13 July 2018